It's Killing Jerry

• A COMEDY THRILLER •

Sharn Hutton

It's Killing Jerry © Copyright 2016 by Sharn Hutton.

All rights reserved. No part of this book may be used or reproduced in any manner whatsoever without written permission except in the case of brief quotations embodied in critical articles or reviews.

This book is a work of fiction. Names, characters, businesses, organisations, places, events and incidents either are the product of the author's imagination or are used fictitiously. Any resemblance to actual persons, living or dead, events, or locales is entirely coincidental.

For information contact www.sharnhutton.com.

Book and cover design by Sharn Hutton.

ISBN-13: 978-1539731849

First Edition: November 2016.

10 9 8 7 6 5 4 3 2

persevere

per|se|vere [pəːsɪˈvɪə] VERB

continue in a course of action even in the face of difficulty or with little or no indication of success

To Kathryn, I hope that you enjoy it!

love Jason x :)

PROLOGUE

THE IMAGE OF A CRISP-UNIFORMED police officer filled the TV screen. Bathed in sunshine, his features were rounded and friendly, but said more hopeful puppy than hardnosed detective. He ducked his head, cleared his throat and gazed down the lens.

"My name is Detective Dinwiddy," he began, speaking slowly and carefully, "and I am investigating the disappearance and suspected murder of one Jeremy Brian Adler, a British man."

Three pairs of eyes widened on the sofa and snapped to the screen.

"Do you have any suspects, Detective?" barked a voice out of shot.

"Well, I am still conducting my investigation." He nodded deliberately to someone beside the camera, then back to the lens. "But there are certainly some individuals I would like to interview." Dinwiddy held up a photo and the camera zoomed in.

The line of people on the sofa recognised it as Jerry's passport photo, but only two jaws descended in a gape. The newscast had arrived out of the blue and with such authority: a nugget of truth beamed over the airwaves and into their living room, a living room that hadn't seen much honesty for a while.

In the short-lived hush that followed, Isabell's heart beat so hard she wondered if the people to either side could hear the pounding in her chest. Jerry being dead changed everything. It meant she didn't have to pretend

.

ONE

FOUR MONTHS EARLIER

JEREMY DEAR, CAN YOU COME OVER ON SUNDAY TO CONNECT MY NEW COMPUTER TO THE DANGLE—DADDY DOESN'T UNDERSTAND IT. THANK YOU. THIS IS YOUR MOTHER.

Jerry lounged against the kitchen counter, new green jogging bottoms pinching up a roll of flab at his midriff. He surveyed the text and tapped reply.

NO NEED TO TELL ME WHO YOU ARE MUM. TO THE DANGLE EH? ARE YOU INTO SOMETHING KINKY? NO WONDER DAD'S A BIT FLUMMOXED

He tapped send and smirked. Jerry's mother was not a woman to be trifled with and wilful misinterpretation of her words was guaranteed to get her hackles up. Jerry knew she'd be forced to restrain herself as she was looking for a favour. Almost immediately it beeped in reply.

DON'T BE SO PUERILE JEREMY. YOU KNOW PERFECTLY WELL WHAT I MEAN. WHAT TIME SHALL I EXPECT YOU? MUMMY.

Of course, Jerry's attendance was never really in question, so he angled for lunch in his reply. Decent food had been in short supply since Rachel had returned from the hospital with their first child in tow a couple of months ago. One of Mum's Sunday roasts would go down a treat.

Jerry slid the phone into his back pocket, put his hands on his hips and pursed his lips. "Jeh-remy!" he called out in impersonation, "Don't mock my dangle! Daddy doesn't understand it!" He minced over to the table, right arm held tightly cocked to his chest, fingers bent over. "Jeh-remy, really!"

He let his eyes trail across the spread of unopened brown envelopes on the table and settled instead on the paper, flicking it open from the back. The Blues were dicing with relegation.

"Nearly ready?" Rachel appeared in the kitchen doorway, crumpled T-shirt hanging limp over faded grey jeans.
"Hmm?" Jerry turned another page, looking for news on the Gunners.

"The bottles, Jerry. Is the steriliser running?"

"Steriliser?" He looked over his shoulder at her, tapping at his bottom lip with a stiff forefinger. "Was I meant to...?"

"Yes, you were meant to. Of course you were meant to. When I say: it's time for a feed, could you put the bottles on? What else could that possibly mean?"

"Oh. Um. I thought maybe put the bottles on the counter, ready, you know?"

"No."

"Well, ready to the put the milk in."

Rachel looked up and down the kitchen work surface with exaggerated sweeps of her head. "So where are they then, these bottles that you've put on the counter, ready?"

"Um." Jerry turned, perched on the table's edge and pushed back a floppy mouse brown curl from his eyes. "Hey, well, I had to get changed, of course, ready for the gym. Leaner, meaner, fitter husband and all that and then there was the, er, message. Very important one actually. One's expertise is required." He wobbled his head in feigned pride, but Rachel didn't want to hear it. She raised her palm to stop his flow and let out a warbling laugh that rattled a little too high. "Don't tell me any more. You haven't done it. Why am I surprised? Why should I be surprised? I'm not surprised. You never fucking do anything." She started sorting through the waiting crockery at the sink, dismantling bottles and tossing them into the bowl. "I'll do it, shall I? Yeah, why not?"

She cranked the hot tap on full and shoved through the clutter to reach for the detergent. A displaced dirty coffee cup slid from the counter to the floor, where it chinked off its handle and rolled to rest in a puddle of grey milky liquid. Rachel closed her eyes for a beat then plunged on with the bottle washing, banging each soapy piece down on the drainer as she went. "I'm amazed you can even get yourself to the gym." She turned to look him up and down. "Although of course, you haven't yet, have you?" She gave the bottles a hasty wipe over with a muslin cloth and wedged them into the steriliser. "Don't wear yourself out, don't know what I'd do without you."

Jerry snorted out a laugh, but a quick glance revealed Rachel not to be smiling. She stared down at her feet and scraped a stray lock of chestnut hair behind her ear. "Look, Jerry, do you think you could cover the night feed tonight?" Her tone was short and tired. Jerry rubbed at his neck. "Um, well I'd like to help, but she doesn't seem to like it when I do it."

"You'll get the hang of it."

Jerry sucked his lips against his teeth. "There'll be all that crying and you'll end up awake anyway. I think she needs her mother, Rach."

"She cries anyway."

Jerry blew out his lips in a fleshy rattle, "Yeah, but I have to go to work in the morning. I'll be dead on my feet."

"Unlike me." Their eyes locked for a moment and Jerry was the first to turn away, suddenly interested in the newspaper again. He heard Rachel trudge from the room and up the stairs. The steriliser hissed.

"Jeh-remy! Look at Daddy's dongle!" He cocked his hand back to his chest and gave a little head wobble. "Ah, mm, yes," he sighed and looked over his shoulder to where his wife no longer stood. He really ought to be a bit more helpful. Wouldn't hurt him to make up just one bottle.

With that in mind he drifted over to the steriliser, which gurgled and clicked, still busy with its business. He could get a bottle ready, wiggle his way back into Rachel's good books. The trouble with all this domestic stuff was that it was all just so dull. It was an endless cycle of thankless tasks where there was never any progress, only the maintenance of equilibrium. Life at the office felt much the same. Every day he worked on PR programs to sell the sizzle of his client's newest sausage, only for it to be replaced a few months down the line with something tastier. He was a cog in a churning machine and it was all just so dull, dull, dull.

Jerry pulled his phone from his pocket and pressed it to his ear. "Remi here." He spoke in a hushed tone, pretending to answer a non-existent call. "A mission? I'm listening, Aqua. Yes, I can put together a hydro bomb. I'm on it." He squinted out into the hallway, checking for spies and, seeing none, made his way to the furthest wall cabinet, next to the kitchen window. Snapping open the door, he scanned its contents: marmalade; Super Noodles; SMA. "Ah, there you are, the secret formula."

Jerry carefully manoeuvred the tin of milk powder with both hands from cupboard shelf to countertop. He pulled at the neckline of his sweatshirt and spoke into the collar. "I am 'go' for formula. Commencing opening sequence." Jerry cracked his knuckles, spread his feet apart and flexed at the knee. Very slowly he clicked up the rim of the lid and ran his thumb around the circumference to free it. Once it was loose, he cautiously lifted the lid and placed it beside the tin on the counter.

"Clear, clear, lid clear," he informed the fantasy Spy Master.

A quick scan of the instructions on the side of the tin revealed the necessity for boiled water and accurate measurement using the doll-size plastic scoop Jerry had discovered inside. He laid his palm against the kettle and snatched it away again to tuck into his armpit, belatedly remembering the cup of tea he'd just drunk. He bit at his lip and eyed the steaming steriliser suspiciously. He wasn't taking any chances with that.

"Aqua, radiation levels are increasing, switching to thermo tongs."

The cooking tongs hanging behind the hob would do nicely.

"Agent Remi on point," Jerry breathed, pinching off the steriliser lid and tossing it into the sink. A great cloud of steam mushroomed into his face and up to the ceiling.

He found the tongs were remarkably agile, considering their culinary heritage, and picked out a bottle with ease. Jerry filled it with water from the kettle and scooped in the requisite amount of powder. The top and teat proved somewhat more difficult to capture with the tongs and spent a brief time on the floor. Jerry checked the hallway for spies once more. "Five second rule," he mumbled, scooping them up and giving them a blow, before screwing them into place. Returning to the tongs, he clamped the bottle and transported it to the kitchen table, where he stood it in central isolation.

"Aqua, mission complete, Remi out," Jerry informed his collar, "Don't know what all the fuss is about."

He surveyed the kitchen counter and decided that the clutter should wait for Rachel. After all, she'd need to make up the rest of the bottles and she was bound to spill a bit too, wasn't she? No sense cleaning up twice.

Jerry snatched up his gym bag and bounded out into the hall. "I'm off, Rach, see you later. Milk's done."

"Oh, oh thanks, Jerry," Rachel called, from out of sight. She actually sounded really pleased: a rare response to Jerry's activities. Amazing what a little imagination could achieve. It was rather a shame that a few minutes later, whilst Jerry bounced happily along the High Street toward the gym, Rachel would discover his parting gift to be much less pleasing. Returning to the kitchen, mewing baby clutched to her chest, she would find the lidless, steam-free steriliser, open formula tin and scattered powder. "Lovely," she'd say with a sigh, "Just lovely."

TWO

Adam consumed the sweet scent of new leather and pinched soft nubuck between finger and thumb. Eyes closed, he sank into the chair and pictured it in his near-empty apartment. Vacant space by the living room window could be handsomely occupied by this Eames lounger. Minimalism just wasn't him anymore: he was filling up.

He'd allowed work to seep out of the courtroom and pollute the rest of his life. Staking its claim on early evenings and eventually weekends, it had absorbed him, until nothing remained. The only release had been time spent at Solomon's Gym, burning off stress that came hand in hand with his salary, not at home, never at home. Home reflected his personal life and was to be avoided. Bleak in its rich emptiness, his kitchen was all stainless steel and granite, but he never cooked. Plastic-wrapped instruction manuals lay undigested in the bellies of professional appliances. Cooking was so elaborate, especially when it was just for one. He'd had no reason to bother when there were so many talented chefs a taxi ride away.

Adam spun the chair with boyish enthusiasm. He made a full turn, the colours and shapes of the shop rushing past in a blur, then walked the chair around a second time, stopping to face out into the elegant showroom. Sofas and lighting, dining tables and crockery: snippets of the home he craved. A dozen room sets: lost in this cavernous space, but still each one held promise.

Adam raked through his dark mop of hair, grown long since it didn't matter, and considered his options. He could buy anything here. He could fill his home with furniture, shag pile to chandelier. He could build the vision of his dream, but the most important element would not be found amongst this shop's displays of linen and glass.

His bright eyes scoured for inspiration and away to the left came to rest upon an unexpected pair of floral pumps, flopped over the end of a sofa he could see only from the back. Their owner was lost behind its cushions. Soles being uppermost, whoever they were, they must have been face down. Adam smiled; there was company in his fantasy today.

He rose from the chair and picked his way across the floor, toward the vast windows that spanned the front of the shop. Bedroom sets spread out before him: cherries and stripes; daisies and leaves. With no idea what to choose, he pushed his hands deep into jean pockets and ambled on. A fashionable futon or an opulent four-poster?

Bedroom paraphernalia gave way to sofas and chic table lamps, slotted together in a sociable jigsaw. Adam wandered amongst them: considering; imagining.

Up ahead, sun streamed in from the street to creep across the deep pile of an ochre rug and up a velvet sofa's plum upholstery to where the woman lay—the wearer of the floral shoes. As he rounded a bank of tall shelves, she came into full view. Golden rays lit the waves of brunette hair that fell across her forehead. Frozen in their warmth she lay still, aside from the gentle rise and fall of her chest in the even rhythm of sleep. Adam recognised her at once. Grace.

Hope edged past surprise. What was she doing here? Had she intended for them meet? How could she have known where he was? Adam tried to shake off his reaction. It was ridiculous for her to affect him like that after all this time. He'd moved on, forgiven himself, hadn't he? But now she was here and unwelcome emotion clawed its way through.

Adam rubbed his chest and leant heavily against a bookcase to absorb the impossible vision: sheer pink cotton fell across long slender legs and just short of the floral pumps he'd seen from the other side of the room—anonymous then. The soft wool pashmina that draped across her shoulders enveloped her in a blanket-like embrace. The image transposed so easily into Adam's vision of home, he accepted it too readily, lingering over her 'til stars sparkled at the periphery of his vision and reminded him to breathe. She was still beautiful. Her eyelids fluttered. She was also waking up.

With consciousness came the obvious realisation of where she was and, fighting off the cushions, she scrambled upright. Adam watched, mute and immobile, as she checked the immediate area and, not spotting him stuck limpet-like to the bookcase nor anyone else, assumed a more dignified position with a mortified smile. On her feet and then sauntering away from him into the depths of the store, she paused to examine items here and there and was soon lost in her appreciation of the fine things around her. The thin cotton of her dress clung and billowed in turn as she walked, giving Adam tantalising glimpses of the form beneath. Her pale skin glowed. Engrossed as she was in her own world and utterly detached from his, Adam felt a rising need to be noticed.

He broke his cover to pursue her at a distance, pausing to watch as she caressed the sparkling crystal set out for an imaginary banquet in an opulent dining room charade. She pulled out a chair and sat, admiring the scene.

It had been years. Five at least since she'd got tired of waiting. 'Marry the damn job,' she'd said before she left, so he had. Twenty-four-seven: consumed by the system, the caveats and back doors. Clients fought for a spot on his schedule: the man who lived and breathed manipulation of the law. There was no time for loneliness. Until enough was enough.

Five years could change a person. That silky brunette hair seemed the same, but the line of her jaw? A crack of doubt crept into Adam's hope.

Moving closer, he examined the tight smile that broke across her lips and the violet shadows smudged beneath her eyes. Her expression: inscrutable. Her features: not entirely familiar. Perplexed and fascinated, Adam drew closer, longing to reach out to her and to take her hand in his.

He was just ten feet away when she leapt to her feet, scraped back the chair and abandoned it askew. She strode toward him, though her eyes were fixed on a spot far behind. Silenced by surprise, Adam stumbled away from the suddenly shrinking distance between them. He saw her clearer then: cheekbones too high; no mole on her cheek and his improbable hope was crushed. It wasn't her, it wasn't his Gracie. Bewildered and ignored, he caught a fleeting breath of the stranger's scent as she strode past without looking back. All too soon she was out of the door and taken by the crowd.

Adam felt the loss in his chest.

THREE

Spink craned his neck for a better view of the new junior as she rushed through the central office, arms piled high with fat manila files. "Gemma!" he bellowed and she juddered to a halt, satisfyingly startled, three files sliding from the top of her stack to spew their contents onto the floor. He watched them fall from the comfort of his private office. "Dying of thirst here, Gemma," he said.

She turned her whole body to face him, clamping the top of the remaining stack with her chin. Shame those files were blocking his view of her figure.

"Sorry, Mr Spink. Would you like some tea?"

So subservient, just how it should be. "One sugar this time and pick up that mess." He turned away, a smile creeping across thin lips, then checked his reflection in the computer monitor on his desk.

Donald Spink was in his early forties, but could have passed for a decade older. His hair greyed at the temples to match unruly eyebrows, and his diet of cigars and single malt had yellowed his eyes and drawn a thousand tiny thread veins across a bulbous nose. At a mere five foot five, he believed he more than compensated for his short stature with a powerful aura and superior wit and that as Sales Director at Locksley PR he was sure that no-one could doubt his success.

Adjusting the angle of the screen, he watched Gemma's skirt ride up her thigh as she wrestled her load safely to the floor to pick up the escaped files. Another figure joined her there. That prat Jerry Adler was helping her. What was the point of beating junior staff into submission if middle management were going to scrabble about on the floor after them? Spink's fingernails drummed the desk and his lips pursed. "Adler. Get in here, would you?"

Adler's reflection rolled its eyes and Spink's jaw tightened. He turned to glare at him directly as he sauntered in through the doorway, wearing that stupid grin.
"Morning, Spink."
"I assume that if you've got time to chat up the office girl you've finished the PC City bid?" Spink raised a questioning eyebrow.
"Hey, I only got that last night. Haven't had a chance yet," Adler said, examining his scuffed brogues. He was thrown, Spink observed happily. "Then you don't have time."

Adler rolled back around the door frame and out into the department, pushing an errant lock of mouse brown hair back from his eye and trundling away through the hum of clacking keyboards and telephone conversations. Hands in pockets, he eventually wheeled out of sight into his own side office.

Spink narrowed his eyes then pulled a folder across his desk to scan through the staff reviews inside. Gemma wouldn't be getting a pay rise. She was still on her trial period and as such he could get away with skipping over her. The rest of the staff was only getting twenty-five per cent and a few heads would have to be lost by the end of the year too. Spink wanted the low salary kids to work extra hard so he could cut a high earner or two from his budget and boost his own commission.

Nicotine-stained fingers tapped at his keyboard and the screen flicked from the accounts package over to William Hill. He laid five hundred pounds on Lucky Lass to win in the 2:30. She felt like a winner.

A skim through the runners in the 4 o'clock offered no inspiration so he logged out of his account and tabbed back to the office software. Pushing the keyboard away, he swivelled his chair to face the opposite side of his U-shaped desk. From here he could look out into the office beyond. Gemma scuttled up the central walkway that spanned its length, clutching laden crockery. Either side, the staff of Locksley PR busied themselves with the business of the day. Pale smart office furniture nestled in convivial groups upon the dark checkerboard carpet tile. Iconic Warhol sang from the walls.

Spink watched Gemma's perky breasts jiggle beneath her thin grey sweater and licked his lips. Her eyes were cast down. Embarrassed and compliant, she came into his office and set a cup of tea and a plate of unrequested chocolate digestives onto the desk in front of him. Spink gazed down her top as she leant forward and when she stepped back and met his eyes he gave her a smile of appreciation. "Thank you, Gemma. That's wonderful." One hand crept to his crotch.

"You're welcome," she mumbled, wide-eyed, and hurried away to her filing. Eventually Spink's gaze fell away from her receding behind and back to the bonus biscuits that waited on his desk. He snatched one up, dunked it into his tea and consumed it with gusto.

FOUR

Jerry's lungs burned, but he battled on. Side by side at Solomon's Gym in the village, he and Adam occupied the first two of a bank of twelve running machines that lined up parallel to the windows. Adam's feet struck the whirring treadmill to the rhythm of the music gushing overhead. Jerry fought for enough oxygen to fuel one foot in front of the other.

From this first floor vantage point, he could see shopkeepers pulling down their shutters across the street and locking up for the night. Even though Solomon's windows didn't open, he was sure he could pick up the aroma of fried chicken rising from the shop below. His stomach growled.

Adam pounded on, chatting away with hardly a bead of sweat on his brow. To Jerry, he didn't look like someone who'd been chained to a desk for the last six years. He was all lean muscle and bouncing hair.

"Screw Dinky. He's a worm," Adam was saying.

"Dinky, yeah, I'd forgotten you called him that."

"School nicknames get a lot worse. If he hadn't made such a fuss about it, it wouldn't have stuck." He paused for reflection. "I may have helped it to stick. I don't remember, it was a long time ago." Adam grinned.

"Yeah, right," Jerry puffed out, stabbing at the treadmill controls to slow it to more of a manageable pace and then rolling to a stop. "Easy for you to say, anyway—the worm's not your boss." He staggered off the machine and bent to lean heavily on his thighs. Sweat dripped from his forehead to the thin blue carpet. Adam stepped off his own machine and stood by Jerry's side.

"Be your own master, Jerry. Those bastards at BSL owned me for too long."

"Yeah, must have been really shit being a top defence lawyer, earning bucketfuls of cash every time you walked into a room." Jerry slumped against the exercise bike behind him. "I don't understand why you're giving it up, you loony."

Adam cocked a scathing eyebrow and Jerry climbed onto the bike without enthusiasm.

"Four years at uni, Jerry; three more as a subservient dogsbody; another ten climbing the stinking ladder, just to get there—just to get to BSL. All that time and effort." Adam shook his head, straddled his own bike and stood on the pedals. He pumped his feet to the relentless beat.

Jerry could see: Adam had sold his soul to BSL. His talent for getting off villains had earned him an invincible reputation and pay cheques that convinced him what he was doing was right. Of course he was in demand. Eighteen-hour days hadn't been unusual and with the money pouring in it was crazy to stop, wasn't it? Six years went by in a flash. Until McGinty: the nasty piece of work that tipped the balance. Now Adam was out for good.

Leaning on the handlebars, Jerry rested his forehead on his arm, chest heaving only slightly less. "Pathetic." Adam jabbed without turning around. "Get your legs moving." Jerry groaned and forced the pedals around without lifting his head. "I'm not sure if this is a good way to rekindle our friendship. You ignore me for years, completely disappearing out of my life. Then pop up all Buzz Lightyear and try to give me a heart attack." Adam turned and scowled. "Buzz Lightyear?"

"Yeah, you know: saving the universe from evil; all biceps and bounce. It's exhausting, even before you drag me to the gym."

Adam snorted and went back to pedalling.

Jerry knew he was not a natural where exercise was concerned, but since passing the landmark of forty, his own mortality was bothering him. Telling Adam he wanted to get fit for the sake of his new wife and even newer baby had seemed like a good idea at the time.

They'd bumped into each other in the locker room after at least five years of not seeing one another. Lost in the excitement of seeing his old school pal, Jerry had admitted he was struggling to train. He was unaware that Adam had just left the job that 'sucked the life from him' and now had endless spare time in which to berate him for his flabby gut, jelly arse and bingo wings. A mistake. He should have remembered Adam was like a dog with a bone. Perhaps if he kept pedalling slowly he'd leave him alone for a bit.

"Free weights now, lard arse. Quick, there are two free spots."

Oh good.

The gym was packed. The six 'til eight slot was always jammed with office workers squeezing in a flurry of activity before an evening slumped on the sofa. Solomon's was a popular place. Situated on a smart run of local shops in the village, it occupied the first floor above Michael's Deli, a barber shop and the ubiquitous Finger Lickin' Chicken. Locals had made a fuss about the chain opening up there, saying that it spoilt local character, but fellow shopkeepers were glad to see it. Mr Solomon appreciated the symbiotic relationship between their businesses: exercise made you hungry and fast food made you fat.

Adam threw his towel down next to the mirror and motioned for Jerry to join him.

Jerry hated the free weights or, more specifically, Jerry hated the posers gathered in front of the mirrors using the free weights. Two free spots meant six others occupied by musclebound narcissists, flexing and grunting, posing for their peers and ogling their neighbours.

Adam held out two 10kg dumbbells for Jerry to take, then swiped a couple of 20's for himself.

"Nnnngh. Nnngh. Yeah." The beefcake in a tight cut-off leotard next to Jerry strained at his weights. Jerry swallowed back a little bile and turned his back on the mirror. "Think I'll sit on the bench."

"Healthy body, healthy mind, Jerry."

"Don't let me stop you. I know you want to get match fit for saving the world and everything."

"There's nothing wrong with wanting to make the world a better place. God knows, I didn't improve it keeping so much toxic waste out of prison." Adam switched to work on his left arm.

"What I'm going to do, I don't know, but for now, I'm all yours." Adam stretched his arms wide to Jerry and gave him the benefit of his winning smile. Jerry shook his head, took up a weight and started a set.

"Hey, what you need is a little imagination. You don't have to run around knocking yourself out. Take me, for example. Boring job, spend my days pumping up the hype for people to buy shite they don't really need and my evenings trying to avoid dirty nappies."

"You're not selling it to me, Jerry."

"I'm not finished. I may lead a humdrum life but, with a bit of imagination, I can turn it into something exciting. Earlier on, for instance, making up a baby bottle to keep the love of my life happy. Boring stuff? But no!" He wagged a finger at Adam's increasingly incredulous expression, "Not if you put a bit of imagination into it. Plastic bottle? No. Bomb case grade titanium canister. Milk formula? No. Hydro bomb primer."

"What?"

"Never mind. The point is that I am no longer Jerry: career-stunted, shit beleaguered new father, I am Remi: sports-car-driving secret agent sex god. You see? It's all about what you make it."

"But it's not real."

"Doesn't matter. Perception governs experience, Adam. You're all dissatisfied and lost. No need! Imagine yourself happy!"

Adam's face scrunched. "Nah, I need a change. I can't just pretend that the last six years didn't happen. There are consequences, Jerry. I have to make amends."

"Live out your dreams in your imagination—you can achieve anything!"

"Still not real." Adam shook his head and turned back to the mirror, checking the angle of his arm.

"Look, OK, you've got me. You can't pretend to go to work and earn pretend money because obviously the pretend food at the pretend supermarket isn't all that filling. But it's something to keep you going. Remi lives it up in my imagination: goes on adventures; total babe magnet; lives the life." Jerry's cheeks were starting to burn.

"And what's he doing now?" Adam enquired with creeping sarcasm.

"Acapulco. On a mission for MI5."

"And you think I'm a loony."

"Look, it's just a little light relief, OK? Something else to think about through a nappy change or a dull meeting. Remi gets to do all the stuff that I don't. It's all the excitement I get these days." Jerry plonked his weights down onto the rack. "I'm going for a shower."

Adam's eyebrows dropped back into their normal position. "OK. Enough for today eh? Let's go."

Jerry scooped up his water bottle and strode for the exit. The thought of a post workout pint had given him an extra surge of energy and he pushed open the door grinning at Adam over his shoulder.

"To infinity!" he said, punching the air. Adam rolled his eyes and flicked Jerry with his towel.

"Bugger off, Jerry," he said.

FIVE

Jerry's tatty Fiat bucked to a halt at the curb. He was outside the house he shared with Rachel and their new baby, known currently only as 'Peanut'. It was a mid-terrace Victorian nestled on a pleasant residential road. An oblong of walled concrete with a rotting wooden gate set it back four feet from the pavement.

The layout was standard Victorian fare: a small lounge off the narrow entrance hall at the front; the kitchen and dining room knocked together at the back. A small lobby beyond gave access to the garden and a downstairs bathroom. A steep staircase led to two reasonable sized bedrooms and a tiny third. Jerry's boy's toys had recently been relegated to the tiny third when Peanut arrived and commandeered the Man Cave.

Rachel had done her best to decorate in various tones of white and grey. Homemade cushions and curtains gave the place a homely feel. The furniture, though pretty new, was showing the strain of a baby in the house. Mysterious stains adorned the sofa while towers of paper teetered on the coffee table. Painted bookcases groaned under volumes of parenting manuals and abandoned half-drunk cups of tea.

It was pushing eight-thirty by the time Jerry scraped the garden gate across the path and made his way to the flaking blue front door. He crept in, clicking the door closed behind him. The hallway radiator was draped with a platoon of babygros, preparing to take on the next onslaught of milk vomit. Jerry sidestepped the pile of mail on the mat and slunk into the kitchen. "Sorry I'm a bit late, Rach, met Adam at the gym."

Rachel rolled her eyes. Sitting at the scrubbed pine table with their baby cradled in her arms, she wore her usual uniform of baggy T-shirt and leggings, chestnut hair pulled back into a stubby bunch at the nape of her neck. Looking down at the infant through tired eyes, she pulled the milk-soaked muslin from her shoulder and shifted Peanut to the other side. "Pass me a fresh one, would you?" Rachel waved toward the pile of muslin cloths on the crammed kitchen counter. The clean bottles and formula tin from earlier jostled for space with last night's dishes and folded laundry.

Jerry passed one over and the feed continued. Podgy hands pushed the bottle away and piercing cries filled the air.
"How's the Peanut?" Jerry asked.

"Cranky." Then to Peanut, "You're hungry, right? Well here it is: Milky, milky." Peanut grabbed the bottle, sucked furiously for a few seconds then sicked the whole lot back up and down the front of her Micky Mouse vest. Rachel closed her eyes and sighed. "God, I need a break. Can you take over for a bit?" Jerry shuffled from foot to foot and his mobile rang. "Ah," he said with a feigned seriousness, "I'd better answer that."

The heavily accented voice of his Spanish ex-wife rushed down the line, "Oh my God, Jerry. I need you to coming here!" Isabell. Not the comfortable distraction he'd hoped for. "Hey, I'm a bit busy right now, Isabell." Rachel snapped to attention at the name, narrowing her eyes at Jerry. He gave her a weak smile in return and retreated to the hallway.

"No. No too busy for me. Is emergency!" Isabell shrilled into his ear.
"What is it then?"
"Oh my God. I am having the nightmare. You have to coming here. I cannot doing this on my own."
"Yes. All right, but what is it, Isabell?" Jerry sank to the bottom step of the stairs.
"You come. Good. Ten minutes, Jerry." She hung up.
"Shit." Jerry scrubbed at his hair and glanced back into the kitchen. Rachel stood fuming in the doorway. "Don't you dare," she hissed through clenched teeth.
"I didn't say I would—she assumed. You know how she is. Look, better to get it over with, eh? Won't be long." Rachel

glowered as he side-stepped over to the door. "I'll do the night shift," he blurted. She didn't look impressed, but Jerry had slammed the door shut behind himself before she'd had a chance to respond.

SIX

"In, come in." Isabell grabbed Jerry's upper arm and yanked him into the hallway. "What is it, Isabell? What's the matter?" He peeled her grasp from his sleeve and Isabell snatched her hand away before tossing it over her head and spinning around to flounce off, long black hair flying out behind her. "Is big problem, Jerry. I can no go on this way."

Jerry slunk to the lounge doorway and peered in, mumbling swear words under his breath. Beyond the frame Isabell navigated the enormous sofa: a taupe island in an ocean of deep pile ivory carpet. She moaned. "So many things. I am a woman alone." She shook her hair out with manicured fingers and patted at the curls. "Is too much to expect." Rounding the back of the sofa again, she lifted her eyes to Jerry and batted copious false eyelashes at him. Jerry gawked. "Erm, what exactly is it that I'm doing here?" Isabell snatched a wodge of paper from the console table and shook it at him.

"Shoes!"

"Shoes? Yes, right, shoes." God forbid he got dirt on the carpet. Jerry kicked off his tatty brogues and shuffled into the room. Isabell strode over to meet him and thrust the papers into his chest. "Is what I have to deal with!"

Jerry leaned away from the smog of perfume and examined the credit card statement now in his hands. With grim curiosity he followed the alarming rise of the balance over seven pages, but was finally compelled to shake himself loose from the horror when fines for non-payment and exceeding the credit limit bumped the total into five figures. Jerry squeezed his eyes shut and rubbed at his face. When he opened them again the bill was still there and it still had his name in the top corner. He felt around for the sofa, slid down the arm onto the seat and let out a wobbly laugh. "Isabell, this is quite something."

"Is nothing good for me. I have no clothes. I have no social life. How can I survive?" She flopped down next to Jerry and clutched her hands to her face.

"Isabell, I can't pay this, I'll never pay this off."

"You must free space for me, make payment, big payment."

The unopened brown envelopes on Jerry's kitchen table skittered across his mind's eye. "It's not a good month." It was never a good month.

"Then increase limit. One more thousand should do it."

That wobbly laugh again. "You were supposed to be paying it off. This isn't what we agreed."

"All is different now." Isabell squeezed at herself with folded arms. "I am alone."

"Still alone, yes."

"You have new wife and now baby." Her bottom lip pulsed in a forced wobble. "I am alone."

"Ah, I see. This is make Jerry suffer for getting on with his life, isn't it?"

Isabell scowled.

"Hey, we're divorced now. You've got to sort out your own finances." He pulled down the corners of his mouth in what he hoped looked like determination.

"You are wrong."

"No." Jerry tilted his head with confidence.

"Yes. You give to me the money to pay mortgage and alimony. You pay credit card. Is no my finances, is your finances."

"Um."

"You no pay, you go to court. Besides, Jerry, if you no do this for me I will take to baby wife and show." Isabell snatched the bill from Jerry's damp hands and swiped him with it. "How do you like that?"

Jerry did not like that at all. "Give it to me." He made a grasp for the bill, but Isabell was too fast. The last thing he needed was Rachel finding out about all the money Isabell got every month. This was the kind of documentation that could really get a man in trouble.

"No." Isabell raised a perfectly shaped eyebrow. "You will have to prise it from my cold dead fingers."

"Ugh." Jerry flopped back to the sofa, exasperated. "Does everything have to be so dramatic?"

"No. Just make space on card."

"No."

Isabell abruptly stood, stuffed the bill into her back pocket and produced her phone. "I am telephoning Rachel." She tapped at the screen with scarlet fingertips. Jerry leapt to his feet. "No!"

"She will be very interest, yes?"

"Stop it!" Jerry snatched at the phone and actually caught it. "Ha, ha!" Isabell grabbed at him with both hands and they seesawed back and forth, fighting for possession. Isabell grinned and kicked him in the shin. "Ow! I'm not letting go!" Isabell kicked him again, then pulled Jerry off balance so he flung out his hands to save himself and dropped the phone onto the floor. By the time he'd righted himself Isabell was stroking it in her palm.

"Oh, Jerry, make payment, hmm?"

Bloody Isabell. Everything was always a battle. He'd have to concede the phone round. Tactics, he needed tactics. He let out a long exaggerated sigh. "OK. You win. OK. I'll call them."

"Good, Jerry. You know it is the right thing." Isabell softened her stance a little.

"I need to call the number on the bill," said Jerry, thinking how he needed to get the bill and run away.

"Yes, is at the top." Isabell moved to tug the bill from her pocket and Jerry stretched out his hand to take it. There must have been something in his eyes: a glimmer of hope or a wrinkle of satisfaction. Whatever it was, it stopped Isabell short. "You are going to call them, yes?"

"Oh yes."

"And make bigger limit?"

"That's right." He wiggled his fingers to beckon the document of destruction to him. He really didn't want this getting into the wrong hands.

"I will call number for you."

"No, no, no need." Jerry shuffled toward her on his knees, but Isabell was already tapping at the screen.

"I'll ring from home. If you could just give me…"

"With Rachel?" Isabell tapped at the screen again, negotiating the automated call system.

"From the office then."

"Have call for you. No problem." She tapped at the screen some more. "Here, now you." She thrust the phone to his ear. An operator asked for the first and fourth digit of his security code. He turned his back to Isabell and cupped his mouth to reveal the numbers. Damn, he should have got that wrong on purpose. It would have been the perfect out. Address? Yes, another chance. "*10* Grove Gardens."

"15, Jerry." Isabell called out.

"Oh, yes, silly me. 15, of course I meant 15." Jerry ground his back teeth together. Isabell walked around to look into his face. "Two thousand more, Jerry."

"What? Be quiet, I can't hear what she's saying." Jerry flapped an ineffectual hand at her.

"That's right, yes. A credit limit increase, yes."

"Two thousand, Jerry."

"One thousand," he said emphatically, with a scowl directed at Isabell. "Yes, that's right."

Isabell pouted briefly, but her mouth crept up at the corners.

"Yes, yes, to the bill address, yes. No, you have a nice day. Yes. Bye, bye." Isabell snatched back her phone. "Thank you, Jerry. Now, as you are here, garden gate is broken."

Jerry looked down at his empty palm. "Gate?"

"Yes, gate." She pulled him to his feet and drove him to the front door. "Is best to go from side. Shoes." Jerry scrunched his feet down into them and popped the backs up with his finger.

"I have left tools." She opened the front door and Jerry stepped through. "I'll just have a look then, shall I? At the gate?" In a matter of seconds he'd gone from his knees in the lounge to literally out in the cold.

"Yes. To the side." She simulated walking with her fingers.

"Right then." Jerry backed off the doorstep and Isabell closed the door.

SEVEN

Rachel clung to the wooden banister to stretch across the squeaky step. She wasn't going to risk disturbing Peanut, not now when she was so close to a few precious minutes of peace.

The kitchen door thudded shut too loud behind her and Rachel froze, listening and holding her breath.

"No, no, no," she pleaded, looking to the ceiling. Remembered shrieks of pain or hunger or plain old bad temper scratched at the back of Rachel's eyes, waiting for their echo. They pulled up short the muscles in her chest and plugged her throat.

"No more, please." She pressed her forehead against the door and waited. Ten seconds passed without event. Twenty. Thirty. She dared to breathe and moved away.

The kettle clicked and popped the water at its base and Rachel settled her bones at the kitchen table. Envelopes fanned in a toppled stack, all addressed to Jerry and unopened. Rachel slid the uppermost toward her and worried at its corner. Something from the council. Why didn't Jerry open them?

She tugged at her waistband and lamented the flesh still clinging to her stomach though the baby was long out. When would it ever go? The kettle rattled on, bubbles tapping at the sides. She stretched out both arms across the table top and lowered her cheek to the cool smooth pine, just to close her eyes for a moment and then she'd make some tea.

The train was longer than she'd realised. A narrow corridor that stretched on into infinity and curved away to places unseen. It rocked in a gentle rhythm that matched her stride.

Clickerty-clack, clickerty-clack.

She strode on, relaxed in its warmth and curious to see where the corridor led. A buffet car perhaps? She felt in her pocket for change, and found instead a handle, smooth and curved. She pulled it free. A long surprising blade glinted in the fluorescent light and a breeze whipped at her hair. It was hers, she'd always known it. Too long and sharp to negotiate back into her pocket, she let the knife hang limply by her side.

The train lurched sideways, clickerty-CLACK and she had to raise her other hand to steady herself. Her palm pressed into the grubby wall, sticky fibres squelching up between her fingers. Rachel snatched her hand away, revolted.

Clickerty-CLACK, it rocked hard again, but Rachel kept her feet, moving faster now, breaking into a run to find the end. Cold air rushed down the corridor toward her. Missing windows left great yawning holes, thick darkness outside.

Clickerty-CLACK. There at the end, a door, at last. She grabbed the handle and yanked it up. The door fell away and she found herself so very high that sweat prickled on the soles of her feet and the palms of her hands.

Clickerty-CLACK. A lurch too big to hold on and she was lost, falling, the knife gripped firm in her right hand. A noise too loud and her face pressed hard against the ground.

"Rach? You asleep?"

She lifted her head, clammy flesh peeling from the table top.

"Anything to eat? I'm starved."

Jerry. Sleep hung heavily at Rachel's shoulders and she blinked away its mist. Her hands were balled into fists that ached with tension. She uncurled stiff fingers and rubbed at nail marks pressed into her palms. The knife.

"Something in the fridge," she managed and Jerry turned his back on her to dig noisily through its shelves.

"What time is it?"

"Just gone midnight."

So late. What was she doing here? Her back complained as she tried to sit up. "You've just got in?"

"Well, duh."

He'd been with Isabell all this time. "Why have you been so long?"

"Well you know Isabell." Jerry shifted from foot to foot and ran his fingers through his hair. He pulled a selection of things from the fridge to construct a sandwich. Rachel knew Isabell much more than she wanted to.

"So what did she want?"

"Nothing a handyman couldn't have fixed," Jerry mumbled through a mouthful of cheese.

"Well that's what you are, Jerry, hmm? A handy man."

Jerry shrugged, but kept his back to Rachel. "Her gate got whipped back by the wind and came unhinged."

"How appropriate."

Jerry snorted at that.

"And this puts her life in peril, does it?"

"Hey, I never said that, but you know how she is." Jerry took a brief look over his shoulder at Rachel. She couldn't summon up a scowl and just gazed back with empty eyes.

"Looks like I might be in more danger," he said just loud enough for her to hear.

"Mmm."

Bloody woman. Was Jerry not aware of all the things that needed fixing around their own house? She felt her heart beat harder in her chest and with it came the energy of exasperation. The balance here was off.

"Since when do you do DIY? Lots of life-endangering inadequacies here to fix, you know." She rose from the table and paced the room to point things out.

"The piece of skirting by the door that continually falls over and snags at your socks; the plumbing that hammers throughout the house every bloody time you use the tap; the holes in the wall where the cookbook shelf used to be; the sodding flap in the vinyl that catches on the back door every time you open it and the draught excluder that's still in the damn pack." Rachel waved the box at him with a flourish.

Jerry took a large bite from his sandwich, gaze fixed on her the whole time.

"Ugh. Why do I bother?" She squeezed closed her eyes and leaned back on the kitchen counter. She and Jerry side by side but disconnected, neither looking at the other. She drew in a breath to bolster her: there was something that had to be said.

"The thing is, Jerry, I'm struggling here. Everything's so... unstable. Peanut, well, I never know where I am with her." Her throat clenched and she had to pause, not wanting to cry.

"I've got no control of anything anymore. When I was working, it was different. There were goals to achieve, you know?"

"Oh sure," Jerry interrupted, "You knew where you were. How to achieve results."

"Right."

"Get that commission."

"Well no, not really that. I didn't earn commission. I mean, I was someone. A real person." Rachel stared down at the floor through a forming film of tears.

"Now I just feel like I'm fading away."

Jerry munched beside her. "Go back to work then. Get a job."

Rachel shook her head. "I'm so tired, Jerry. I couldn't do it."

It was all she could do to get through the day. The relentless baby timetable ruled her life and there was something more, an elusive element that made it so much worse: hours of crying after feeds that Rachel couldn't find a way to stop. It ground her down, the first whimper taking her straight back to the end of hours spent trying to sooth, rocking and cooing, gnashing her teeth.

She looked around the room to find a way to escape the subject and settled on the letter stack.

"Jerry, why haven't you opened those?"

Jerry rubbed at the back of his head and turned away, back to the second half of his sandwich.

"Is there a problem with money? You said it would be OK for me to stop working."

"Hey, no problem."

Rachel made her way back to the table and scooped up a handful of envelopes. "This is a problem, isn't it?"

"It's OK." Jerry didn't turn around.

"We're not OK, are we? God, I could kill you sometimes!" She slapped at the table.

"At least let me bump up the life insurance first, then you can pay off some debts."

"So there are debts?"

Jerry rubbed at his face then pushed his shoulders back to stand taller. "No, course not," he said, and then that laugh, too high and too long.

"Oh, Jerry, you didn't? You haven't?" Her suspicions were true. "We're in the shit, aren't we?"

"No, no, honestly, it's fine." Jerry bustled to the table, a sudden light in his eyes. He scooped the letters from the table and stuffed them into his work bag.

"I'll deal with them tomorrow. I promise."

EIGHT

Jerry peered in through the misty kitchen window and clapped his arms around his body, trying to warm up. Rachel worked at tidying the kitchen, adding abandoned cups and plates to the gaggle of crockery crowded at the sink, waiting for attention. Baby bottles steamed in the sterilizer and Peanut slept in her Moses basket in the centre of the dining table.

Jerry had to make up for last night. Rachel had reeled off an oppressive list for a DIY phobic like him and he could see that if he was going to get anywhere near the edge of the hook, he was going to have to tick some things off.

She'd whirled around the house all morning: a dangerous mixture of raging hormones and sleep deprivation, so Jerry had decided on a job outside, just to get out from under the cloud of seething indignation.

He eyed the kitchen window mournfully. It had been replaced by Rachel's father, Bob, the day before, having rotted in the corner to wind-whistling effect. Replacing a window was way beyond Jerry's abilities, but Bob was a very hands-on kind of guy. He'd encouraged Jerry to observe so he could do it himself next time. Jerry knew this was a waste of time so he observed the footie from his favourite bar stool at the Dog and Duck instead and met Adam later at the gym to ease his conscience.

Jerry ran his fingers down the smooth frame, pretending to appraise the work. Rachel stood at the sink on the other side of the window. She caught his eye.

"What are you doing?" she mouthed, eyebrows raised. She plopped a couple of cups into the soapy water.

"Thought I might give it a lick of paint," Jerry shouted, "Finish the job off for good old Bob." He couldn't resist a little dig. Rachel pushed the window open a crack. "It's uPVC, Jerry. Don't touch it."

So it was. Jerry's brain scrabbled for a comeback. He scanned around the window. The render surrounding the frame had been touched up, but the pebble dashing was not as dense at the window's edge as it was on the rest of the wall.

"The pebble dash is a bit gappy, maybe I'll patch it up?" It was a statement with the tone of a question.

"Maybe." Rachel narrowed her eyes at him and Jerry took this as approval.

"I'll do that then. Finish it off for good old Bob."

Rachel sighed and closed the window.

How hard could it be? He'd show Bob that he knew a thing or two. A bag of leftover pea shingle sat by the back door to his left and several blobs of render remained splattered onto the patio slabs at his feet. Jerry gave one a tentative poke with his toe and found that it was still pliable. When Rachel wasn't looking, he dove into the kitchen, swiped a teaspoon from the cutlery drawer and returned to scoop a glob from the ground.

Using a combination of fingers and spoon he pressed about five inches of render onto the stone-free surface. Easy. Bob would be impressed. He grabbed a handful of shingle from the bag and poked the first stone into the bed he'd made.

It immediately fell out. He tried again, this time giving it an extra hard push.

It fell off, taking the render with it in an orange peel curl. Rachel caught his eye and he gave her an enthusiastic thumbs up. He scooped another glob and decided to go for a more aggressive approach. He spooned and pressed render into all the gaps that surrounded the window. No quick task. The render was drying out and, in places, was not co-operating. He'd seen professionals do this. They heaved great buckets of stones at the wall—no wonder some of them stuck. All at once, in one big hit, that was the key.

Jerry took a handful of stones and chucked them at the wall with all his strength. They clattered on the glass, ricocheting off in a multitude of directions, but mostly back in his face. "Argh!" Jerry put his hands up too late and ducked beneath the window sill. Peanut choked out a shocked whimper from her basket, then revved up for a full on fit.

"For the love of God, Jerry!" Rachel yelled from the kitchen. He peered over the sill just in time to see her scoop Peanut up and storm off to the front room.

Right. Jerry took up a new position, at an angle to the window. He scooped and then hurled another handful. A couple stuck, but the vast majority bounced off. Jerry adopted a machine gun action, scoop and hurl, scoop and hurl, scoop and hurl. Multiple sharp pointy stones ricocheted into his face and body, but he ploughed on, eyes screwed up tight.

When the bag seemed to be empty, Jerry gingerly opened one eye. He stood ankle deep in a sea of shingle. The occasional gap had been filled by a stone. The glass was pitted in numerous places. Jerry bit at his lip.

He sank to his knees and pushed at the pile with his hands, encouraging them back into the bag. Those at the bottom had mingled with the odd dollop of render and stuck together. Of course. Jerry reached for his teaspoon and scraped together the remaining render on the floor, mixing it with a good measure of stones. He scooped a handful, rolled it into a sausage shape and squelched it into place with his hands. It stayed. He worked his way around the frame and stepped back to admire his work. It had a certain rustic charm, in a knobbly uneven kind of way, but there were definitely stones now.

Drawn by the silence, a curious Rachel appeared at the back door, a placated Peanut in her arms. She eyed Jerry's handiwork with a furrowed brow. Sensing disapproval, he wasted no time passing the buck.

"Hey, Bob really has used a very poor quality render here, Rach. Got absolutely no strength to it. I think you should tell him that you're not happy with the materials."

Rachel stepped forward to examine the window more closely. Sunlight glinted off the pits in the glass. Random stones protruded from Jerry's misshapen sausage like sweet corn in a turd. She turned impassive eyes to Jerry, who stood hands on hips, shaking his head and tutting.

"Yes, he really has done a shit job, hasn't he?" she said, deadpan. "I'll call him, shall I? Ask him to come over and fix it." Jerry's eyes widened and his jaw flapped.

"Ah, well, we don't want to seem ungrateful though, do we? Good old Bob."

Rachel looked at him for a long moment, eyebrows raised and Jerry managed a weak smile. "Just perfect," she grumbled and turned on her heel to go back inside, stumbling over the flap in the vinyl as she went.

NINE

Jerry fiddled with his pen and thought about the weekend. Isabell had run rings around him, again. This latest game was getting on for blackmail. He had to sort her out, somehow. Rachel didn't exactly suspect, but she was catching on. He could see it in her squinting eyes, her hesitations to reply. She knew. She didn't know what she knew, but she knew.

Jerry leaned back in his office chair. The ceiling tiles, stained yellow from a leak, hung ominously bowed above his head. Remi wouldn't stand for this, he thought. Remi would have got that statement, he'd have sorted it out like 'that'. He mentally clicked his fingers.

"Agent Red, this is Aqua," said the phone call in his head. "We need you to retrieve a Top Secret file from your arch enemy, Kitty Princesa. She's hosting a fundraiser at her Acapulco mansion. Your mission is to gain access to her private study and steal the document. The British government is relying on you."

Yeah, that's a good one. Jerry settled back in his chair to picture the scene.

Princesa's mansion stood at the top of a particularly jagged cliff face. Its buttressed walls were a good twenty feet high and armed security flanked the gate, checking invitations and searching through cars. Remi wasn't going in through the front door tonight though. Scoping out the mansion from the safety of his yacht earlier in the day, he'd spotted a service stairway carved into the craggy cliff. A crumbling jetty at its foot was the perfect place to moor his mini jet boat. Remi scaled the steps two at the time, designer tux moving easily with his athletic frame.

The concrete foundations and plinth on which the mansion stood loomed grey and foreboding above his head. With every stair climbed, sounds of the party filtered down a little louder.

A metal gate, seven feet tall and barbed with razor wire, stood lone sentry at the top of the stairs. A keypad and a heavy padlock held it shut. Remi had no code or key. He examined the gate, running his fingers around its edges, deducing that the gate hung from two pin hinges just visible through a millimetre's gap. Remi took two Semtex pads from the Agent pack strapped to his chest and slid them in the gap just below the hinges themselves, connected detonation wires from his watch and stepped back down the steps, as far away as the wires would allow. Music fell down from above, chatter gliding with it on the wind and Remi listened for the beat. The explosion synchronised with the music exactly, blowing the back gate off its hinges. It swung wide on its pointless lock and Remi stalked inside.

You'd never get away with it in real life, obviously, but Jerry wasn't worried about that. In his fantasy world he could get away with anything. In this fantasy world Kitty Princesa was Remi's Isabell: an ex-partner who continued to interfere in his life. Kitty had been Remi's partner at MI5, until she went bad and stole millions from the British coffers. Destroying the gate was enormously satisfying after his hour and a half spent freezing in Isabell's garden. He had to get his kicks where he could find them.

Beyond Princesa's broken gate the path stepped back behind a fat concrete wall and widened to a long curved courtyard. To his left the natural cliff face climbed steeply up, domesticated by decorative ferns and succulents, to the right a series of louvered shutters, stretched in a protective arc toward a pair of tall glass doors. Fine voile flapped with the breeze, flashing glimpses of the partygoers within: bejewelled women in fine long gowns and tuxedoed men all looking like each other.

So this was how Princesa spent the money she'd stolen from the British Government.

Remi peered in through the dipped shutters. The first room was a storeroom of some kind, the second, a gym. The next looked more promising. Its own door to the courtyard was unlocked and Remi slipped in, still undisturbed.

An enormous expanse of glass curved around the outer perimeter in place of a wall. Beyond it a flat terrace reached out, seemingly into air. The view of Acapulco Bay was both breathtakingly beautiful and alarmingly high.

Remi tore his eyes away to scour the room. Princesa's long 70's styled desk stood in its centre and Remi wasted no time rifling through the drawers. The final drawer, lock picked in seconds, gave up the secret file that Remi sought. He flicked through its pages: plans for a new superweapon that Princesa intended to use against the government. "Now this is the kind of document that could really get a girl in trouble," he mused aloud.

"Oh, I don't think so, Agent Red."

The voice, thick with malice, came from behind him and Remi spun around to see his old adversary, Kitty Princesa, her Mediterranean good looks marred by unnatural golden teeth, glinting in her withering smile. She cradled a hairless Sphynx kitten in her arms and stroked its wrinkly head.

"I'll take that if you don't mind, *mi amigo*," she said and two tuxedo-clad henchmen followed her into the room, sneering and flexing their fists.

"You'll have to prise it from my cold dead fingers," Remi crowed and leapt into a sprint, toward a thin opening in the glass wall. Out on the terrace, he slid to a halt just shy of the platform edge. Beyond its unguarded rim lay a five-hundred metre drop to certain death in water topped with moonlit foam, whipped up by jagged rocks beneath.

Princesa swished out after him, scarlet evening gown clinging to her voluptuous figure, skirts skimming the concrete.

"Where are you going, mi amigo? It is a little late for a swim, no?"

Laughter rumbled through the henchmen, but Remi wasn't beaten yet. He tucked the secret file into his waistband and pulled off his jacket to reveal a body harness. Reaching behind his neck, he pulled a wad of folded silk from the slim pack on his back, gave Princesa a wink then tossed his fabric bundle into the air. The updraft from the sea snapped it open into a parabola.

"So long, Kitty," Remi said and stepped over the edge to disappear from view.

"¡No! ¡Vuelve aquí, cabrón," the henchmen above his head shouted and ran to the rim.

Remi barrel-rolled the paraglider to glimpse his pursuers gaping mouths then dropped into the darkness as they reached for their weapons.

He'd got what he'd come for. It was time to get back to his boat.

TEN

Rachel stifled a yawn, the dull red glow of the nightlight pooling at her feet. Peanut gripped the bottle with mittened hands and guzzled milk, while out in the hallway Grandma Ray's clock marked time. Tick. Tock. Tick. Tock. The slow metallic *thunk* echoed in its wooden coffin. She tried to match her breathing to its beat, but the rhythm was too slow, too unnatural and made her feel, even more, like she was drowning.

Peanut coughed out a mouthful of milk and whimpered and Rachel's spirits dropped farther still: another feed that was to be punctuated with despair. Her infant gasped and, tiny body rigid, let out a cry. Helpless, Rachel pulled her close, rocking and patting, turning her this way and then that, trying to find relief.

Nothing she did made any difference. Peanut yelled out, high pitched protests that clenched Rachel's jaw and wrenched her guts. Shrill screams that lasted seconds? Minutes? Rachel closed her eyes and rocked and after a while, spent black and helpless, the writhing calmed. Rachel knew she'd done nothing to help. Time had passed and that was all. Peanut relaxed and grasped the bottle once again when it was offered. Rachel drew the thin cotton of her dressing gown up at the neck and hunkered down.

The nightlight threw long shadows: the bars of the cot reaching fuzzy fingers full stretch to the ceiling, confining the ever present Bilbo Bunny in their prison. Gay curtains turned grey in the night's half-light. The nursery, so jolly by day, became her dungeon in the gloom. Rachel's bleary eyes starred blindly into the red-tinged darkness and her thoughts wandered back to the hospital, back to the maternity ward.

She hadn't expected it to be so busy: endless visitors flocking in to meet the latest additions to their families. Peculiar to be surrounded by strangers when you felt so fragile and overwrought. Of course, Rachel's parents had visited and Jerry too. The most vivid memory though, was of the hours just after their baby had been delivered. She'd been so tired. Every muscle ached, exhausted and elated. Her heart swelled with love for their precious child. She'd looked at Jerry through softer eyes then. Up until the phone call came: Isabell with her latest drama. Jerry shouldn't have gone, shouldn't have given in. He should have seen it for the game move it was, but he didn't or couldn't. Isabell laid on the guilt and he had buckled under the pressure.

Looking around the maternity ward that afternoon, Peanut clasped to her breast, she'd felt the emptiness of the chair next to her bed in the hollow of her chest. Other cooing new fathers fussed around their clever wives and embraced their babies with tenderness and joy, while she had sat alone.

A lump formed in Rachel's throat as she looked down at Peanut in the grim nursery, reliving the sadness. Tick. Tock. Tick. Tock. The clock beat on, consistent and unending. This was how it was. Take each breath as it came. It was always worse at night.

The bottle drained, Rachel patted Peanut's back in vain hope. Her stomach growled, but nothing came. Fidgeting in discomfort she cried out again: shrill cries that set Rachel's teeth on edge; escalating sobs that rolled silent tears down her mother's cheeks too. "There, there, little bubba, don't cry, don't cry." She rocked back and forth in the chair and the minutes passed, clutched chest to chest.

ELEVEN

The treadmill hummed to life. Adam punched up a steady six miles per hour and flicked on his music. Guitar riffs filled his head and the gym faded away.

Between three and four was a quiet time at Solomon's: office workers were still chained to their desks and ladies that lunched had had their children thrust back upon them at the end of the school day.

With the place to himself, he zoned out for a 5K run. So much time spent at the gym in the middle of the day was an indulgence his old life would never have allowed. He'd have had his nose buried in the file of yet another degenerate, ferreting out the clink in the law to build his case upon.

Adam took a deep breath—it was good to be his own man again. Bottom line, bad people needed to be punished not helped. He couldn't condone that professional obligation anymore. He'd switched sides. He was a good guy now.

He bumped the speedo up to eight mph and settled into his stride. He'd been used to lying accountants with their fraudulent business practices. Drug and firearms traffickers had been commonplace too. All selfish and vile. His expectations of the human condition had become so depressingly low that he'd accepted their crimes as commonplace. They'd held little significance in his own life. He'd swept them into the system and out through the loopholes.

McGinty had been an eye-opener though—the wakeup call that Adam had needed. Their meeting had been at Wakefield Prison. McGinty was being held on remand until his court date came up in eight weeks' time. Having negotiated security with practised ease, Adam had swept through the echoing corridors, buoyed by his usual confidence. He'd had no inkling then that this would be his last day at BSL.

The stench of institutional floor cleaner mingled with filthy mop and assaulted his nostrils. Exposed brick walls, daubed brilliant white, were lit by overhead fluorescent strips. The air hung in stagnant pools, swirled into eddies as Adam swept by.

The conference room was filthy grey with no furniture save for a table and four plastic chairs, which squatted in the centre of the scratched linoleum floor. A two-way mirror stretched four feet along the wall opposite the door: a dark substitute for windows. McGinty was already slouched at the table when Adam came in. His back to the door, he wore a grey marl jogging suit and cuffs.

"Mr McGinty." Adam reach out a professional hand to his client.

"Fox." McGinty's hands remained in his lap.

Adam sat down unperturbed and retrieved the relevant file from his satchel.

"Errol James McGinty, date of birth 20th May 1981, place of residence 215 Hill View, Camden."

No response.

"That you?" Adam pressed.

"There'll never be another," McGinty growled across the table.

"Why don't you tell me why we're here?"

"If you don't know then you're one useless piece of shit lawyer. What am I paying you for?"

Adam looked up at McGinty from his paperwork.

"Mr McGinty, my purpose is to represent you in this prosecution from the Crown. I am well aware that you have been detained in this facility following your involvement in an aggravated burglary. If I am to do this well I must have all the facts, and I do mean all the facts. Surprises in court don't make for acquittal."

McGinty lounged back in his plastic chair, appraising Adam through clear blue eyes, held lazily hooded. His long black hair brushed back from a receding hairline into a tight ponytail. Pallid skin stretched tight over high cheekbones. Only of average weight and build, he had a greater presence than his size should have allowed. Malevolence oozed from every pore. "It was a slow day. Thought I'd make myself a little entertainment."

Adam rolled his hand, encouraging McGinty to continue.

He jutted his chin out. "I was behind her at the till. Needed some smokes and the stupid bitch took forever to dig out her purse. That's why I noticed her, noticed the rocks on her fingers. She walked so slow with that piece of shit dog that I caught her up."

Adam wrote notes. McGinty was clearly a thug. Before even hearing the rest of the story he knew that there would be no clever twist in his tale. He preferred fraud cases. At least then he knew he was dealing with a certain level of intelligence in his client. Adam supposed that he'd been called in on this case because McGinty wanted to minimise his sentence. Adam wondered how he could afford him.

"So I followed her home. I knew it wouldn't be far, not dragging around a piece of shit dog like that." McGinty grinned at his own cleverness. Adam said nothing, unimpressed. He remembered Tigger, his own dog from childhood: he'd become slow and doddery during the last year before he died. Adam had helped him up and down the steps to their front door. Tigger had been a faithful friend.

"She got the door open and I just barrelled in after her and slammed it shut. She was a stubborn old bitch though. Even when I waved my Glock under her nose she still wouldn't play ball. I had to shoot that piece of shit dog before she'd pay attention."

Adam's eyebrows twitched up and he raised his eyes to McGinty's. He was getting excited by his own story, little globules of white spit gathering in the corners of his mouth. Adam's jaw clenched and McGinty watched the muscles in his face tick.

"You a dog person, Foxy?" McGinty drawled, amused.
"No." Adam's eyes returned to his notes. A thug that was cruel to animals too—something that Adam couldn't abide. Professionalism told him to keep his personal opinions to himself and he tried to control his breathing.
"Continue."

"Had to drag her upstairs with my Glock in her ear. So damn stubborn. Everyone knows old ladies keep cash in the house and with rocks like that on her fingers I was betting there'd be plenty more tucked away in a jewel box up there."

Why did old ladies insist on wearing their jewellery out to the shops? Adam's grandmother was one for wearing big rings. Her favourite had a yellow topaz the size of a fat grape. As the years passed its fit had loosened and it twirled around her finger. He marvelled that she'd never lost it. If indeed, she still had it. He hadn't seen her for a few years now. When his parents had decided to retire to northern France, Grandma had gone too. His whole family gone, just like that. Leaving Adam behind had become a bit of a theme. First his parents and Grandma, then Gracie, his childhood sweetheart. Eventually she'd found someone to pay her more attention than his determination to do well at the firm allowed.

"Wouldn't tell me where to look though, goddamn bitch," McGinty continued, "Had to turn the place upside down. I cracked at her skull with the butt of my gun when I got bored of looking."

McGinty leaned in. From across the small table, Adam could feel his foul breath on his face. "She took a lot of persuading." Tiny spots swam in Adam's eyes and he let out the breath he'd been holding. A muscle flickered under his eye and McGinty smirked.

"Tying her to the bed was a kick. Started making a lot of noise then. Crying and squawking. Had to smack her to quiet her down."

The stench of McGinty's breath clawed at Adam's throat and he felt the mental 'click'. He'd come to this meeting to look for a way to set McGinty free, but why would anyone want to do that? This man was a monster. The unpalatable truth was that he was *another* monster, the latest in a long line.

Nausea rose with the bile in Adam's gut and he squirmed in his seat.

The clients he'd dealt with over the last few years at BSL had all been driven by their lust for money, all morals abandoned in their unyielding pursuit of it. Gun runners and drug dealers had brawled amongst themselves for the biggest slice of pie. Murders and assaults hadn't been unusual, but their human suffering was just par for the course: they were complicit, expendable pawns in their own loathsome game. McGinty's victim had no such involvement. She was an innocent pensioner in the wrong place at the wrong time and McGinty had got off on torturing her.

Adam knew then that he could not defend him, nor anyone else like him, ever again. He levelled his eyes to McGinty. "Did you get what you were looking for?"

"Fuck, man, I already had it by then. She was banging on about the police. No bitch telling tales on me. I gave it to her good, just to make sure."

Adam swallowed back the acid in his mouth. "Mr McGinty, I'm afraid I must call our meeting to a close." Adam stood. "My office will contact you in due course." He stuffed the papers into his satchel.

"What? Where the hell are you going? I haven't finished."

"I am unable to represent you," Adam croaked, heading for the door, but McGinty got to his feet too and blocked his path.

"You need to hear the rest of my story. About how I gave it to her…"

Adam stumbled over this glimmer of hope and paused to respond. "What? What did you give her?"

McGinty grinned, enjoying the effect he was having. "The gift of silence, man. I cut out her wagging tongue. No bitch telling tales on me." He sliced through the air with an imaginary knife.

The uppercut to McGinty's jaw sent him sprawling to the floor. It was hard to say who was the most surprised.

"You wanted to know, man!" McGinty spat onto the lino with a laugh.

Adam's blood raged around his body and buzzed in his ears. His fist was still clenched and ready when the two prison guards burst in. One pulled Adam aside, the other thrust McGinty back into his chair.

"Interview terminated," Adam's voice quavered, shaking with adrenaline. He smoothed the guards away and darted for the door. He fled the building and got out through security in record time.

As he puked in the car park the revelation washed through him. All this time he'd ignored his clients' behaviour. They'd belonged in another world, detached from his own. Gradually time had changed that, of course it had. Their realms had meshed when Adam became the magician who set them free. More and more his life revolved around The Evil and The Lawless, his own success: funded by their crimes.

It had taken McGinty to bring it home, to make Adam see how they terrorised decent people in his world too; to see how he'd kept them on the streets; to see how he was partially to blame.

Led by his own greed, he'd worked for the scourge of society for a fat bank balance. His chest constricted with the shame. Now that he'd seen it there could be no going back. The decision was made: it was over.

In the gym, Adam picked up the pace on the treadmill. He ran from his misplaced loyalty and ran from his past. Striding out, his muscles pumped and his head rang. The adrenaline fuelled his determination to be a better man, to make a difference. Somehow. He'd find a way to defend the weak—to hell with the scumbags and their money. A sob escaped from his throat that broke the spell. He stabbed the treadmill to a halt and staggered down from it, gasping for air and swiping away tears.

A belt of shame squeezed taut around his chest and Adam tried to rub away the pain. A slug of water eased the tightness of his throat, but a guilty conscience needed something more. Alcohol would take away the sting. He'd blot out the memories just like he had that terrible day and every day since.

TWELVE

Jerry bowed his head into the wind and picked up the pace. Crisp autumn leaves skittered across Soho Square and rattled over the pavement at his feet. *Must not be late, must not be late.* Jerry rammed his one free hand into the Crombie pocket and hunched his shoulders against the cold. His portfolio cradled the visuals for that morning's vital meeting.

He rolled the opening lines of his presentation around his mind. Brian Cripps could be a miserable bastard, if he could start the ball rolling with a joke that might lighten the atmosphere. Spink was meeting him there. He'd schmooze off after for lunch with the client, while Jerry got on with some actual work.

He hung a left into Carlisle Street, wind tugging at his coat.

Although nothing official had been said back at the office, the cloud of redundancy loomed overhead. Two people from Accounts had already gone. The company was slimming down for the economic squeeze. Dial Diagnostics was a major client. If they lost them it would be bad news all round. Just to up the ante a little more, the team at Dial were twitchy right now: a high profile merger had put their stock price on the fritz and they were keen to soothe the shareholders.

Spink liked to show his face to make the client feel loved, but it was actually Jerry who handled the account and would be making the pitch today. The directive they'd worked to had come straight from Dial's board, so Cripps would already be unhappy about being side-lined.

Jerry gnawed at a fingernail and scaled the grey stone steps to the main entrance. The heavy glass door swished aside and Jerry beheld the line of people in reception with dismay.

The receptionist was using her best telephone voice to direct each visitor with regal aplomb and Jerry suspected the effort weighed greatly on her. Corkscrew curls of Afro-Caribbean hair jiggled around a peachy plump face. She was about thirty-five and eight months pregnant if she was a day.

"Take the lift to the second floor, Miss Masters will meet you in the lobby," she simpered, then answered a silently ringing phone and looked out into empty air. "Dial Diagnostics. How may I assist? One moment. Yes?" The next person in line advised her of their business.

Jerry bit at his lip and checked his watch: five to. He was cutting it pretty fine. He shuffled up a place, staring at the receptionist, willing her to see him and pluck him out early. She stayed focused only on the person in front of her, but wiggled in her seat. Two more visitors sent on their way and she was jiggling about quite a lot now, corkscrew curls bouncing at her ears.

The coat's collar prickled at Jerry's neck and he sweltered under its woolly weight. He pulled at his scarf and swallowed hard, throat parched. Another visitor stepped away from the desk and took a seat on the leather banquette by the door. Along they shuffled. Jerry flapped his arms and rubbed at his hair and after an eternity, reached the desk.

"Jerry Adler to see Brian Cripps." The receptionist looked relieved to have reached the final visitor in her queue. Checking the desk diary, she directed him to the elevator and prepared to stand. The big glass front door swished open and a motorbike courier barrelled in.

"Oh hell," she breathed.

Jerry looked back at her and she pleaded into his eyes, "If I don't get to the toilet soon." She went rigid and made an 'o' with her mouth, eyebrows raised. She looked as if it might already be too late. "Any chance you could cover for me, just for a minute?"

"Er." Jerry had to get to his meeting. She jiggled desperately on the spot. What could he do? "Just for a minute. Be fast." Jerry bit at his lip, watching her speed-waddle away.

She punched a code into the keypad protected door and disappeared. Jerry stood stock still. Had that just happened? He checked his watch. Nine o'clock dead. Shit.

The courier cleared his throat and held out a slip of paper. "You covering then, mate?"

Jerry leant his portfolio against the wall and took faltering steps toward him. He signed the slip and took the packet. The courier left and Jerry drifted behind the desk looking for somewhere to put it.

One didn't often get to see behind the tall desk counters in swanky receptions like this. A surprising number of things hid beneath the smoked glass counter top at a lower desk level: a silver-framed photo of the waddling receptionist as a bride with her groom; a fluorescent pink fluffy gnome; a miniscule spider plant; a cold cup of tea in a huge mug that said 'Tea for Two' on the side; a keyboard and two flat screen monitors. One was a standard PC, the other appeared to be the switchboard. 'Incoming call', 'Line 5' and 'Conference Room 2' all flashed in red boxes. Jerry put on the headset to see if he could hear anything. Yep, definitely ringing. Wouldn't be answering that.

The glass door swished and another suit swept up to the counter.

"Marcus Barnes," the suit barked.
Jerry looked blank.

"Marcus Barnes," he growled again.

"Oh no, hey, there's been some confusion…" Jerry smiled, trying to explain.

"I'm late. Which meeting room am I in?" growled the suit, eyebrows knitting together.

"That's the thing, you see, I don't know."

The suit was turning puce.

"Do I know you?" he seethed.

"No. No. Just cover, temporary cover."

They stared at each other for a long moment. Beads of sweat rolled down Jerry's back and his scalp prickled. The internal door clicked open and the flustered receptionist waddled through at speed, recognition and fear etched onto her face.

"Mr Barnes. Good morning," she cooed.

"Who's this idiot?" Marcus Barnes demanded.

"No-one. Nobody. Conference Room 2, sir." She pushed Jerry out of her seat and scowled at him.

Barnes stomped into the lift. As the doors slid shut Jerry gathered up his portfolio.

"You're welcome," he muttered.

The receptionist huffed and put on her headset.

In the confusion Jerry's mind had gone blank. "Where am I going again?" he asked.

The receptionist sighed and shook her head. "Conference Room 2," she said.

THIRTEEN

Jerry squatted in the centre of the low white leather sofa with his knees approaching his ears. For the second time that day he was trying not to panic and busied himself twiddling thumbs and sucking at teeth. Spink lounged nonchalantly in the matching armchair to his right, apparently untroubled. Together they waited for John Locksley to return. Jerry examined the room's décor with great feigned interest to avoid any troubling eye contact.

He noted that Locksley's office was clean, bright and about four times the size of his own dreary hole. Floor-to-ceiling windows overlooked a leaf-strewn stretch of lawn, allowing in the last of the day's autumn sunshine. Heavy framed photos lined up on the bank of cupboards behind his desk: an old print of a teenage boy embracing a trophy; Locksley and his wife smiling into the camera while the sun set on a tropical beach; a black Labrador content by an open fire.

"Now you've fucking done it," Spink growled, "I'm not taking the shit for this; you're on your own."

Jerry sighed and rubbed at his forehead.

John Locksley was the CEO of Locksley PR. He'd kept his business afloat this past quarter century by taking decisive action and speaking his mind. Jerry knew that today would be no exception and gnawed at a fingernail in response to his rising nerves.

Locksley appeared in the doorway looking serious, and strode in. At a sturdy six feet, he was in good shape, considering his sixty years, with a thick head of steel grey hair that swept back from his brow. He made for one of the black leather chairs on the visitor's side of his desk, spun it to face Jerry and Spink and sat down, palms on thighs.

"Gentlemen, we are not having a day to be proud of."

Jerry winced. Spink leaned back, nodding sagely.

"I just came off the phone with Marcus Barnes and he's pissed off. He thinks that Locksley PR is not taking their account seriously enough. He thinks that I'm sending out amateurs to work on the most important deal of his life. I'm not doing that, am I?" He leaned forward, looking in turn at Spink and then Jerry.

Jerry shook his head in silent denial, but Spink didn't waste any time laying blame.

"I don't know what Adler was thinking, turning up late and being obnoxious to Barnes. If I'd known about the theme on the stakeholder communications I'd have vetoed them before the meeting."

"I was tailoring for Cripps." Jerry blurted, "I know he likes sailing. I thought a few nautical terms might get him going." *Thanks a lot, Spink.*

"Up the creek without a paddle?" sniped Spink, eyebrows raised, "Sinking without trace?"

"A little humour to lighten the tone."

"You're dead in the water," Spink rumbled on.

Locksley raised his hand to silence them. "Jerry, I can see where you were aiming, but it just didn't come off. They're too highly strung right now. Spink, what was your input?"

Bugger all, thought Jerry.

"I'm all over Dial, sir. I let Adler carry the ball this time and he dropped it."

What? Spink was such a snake. He had no idea what the pitch was about, had done bugger all work and just stepped in at the last moment to lap up the credit. Not that there was an awful lot of that.

Locksley looked back and forth between them, clearly registering the animosity. "We're facing a difficult economic time. I'm handing out redundancies and you two are bitching over one of our biggest accounts. You're screwing it up and not for the first time." He looked over to the window and breathed in resolve. "The business will suffer if things don't change. One of you will have to go."

The ball of nerves in Jerry's gut vaporised to leave a vacuum. He threw a panicked sidelong glance to Spink, whose smug expression had disappeared, at least.

"Jerry, I can see you've got heart and potential, but you've got to work on your empathy and do it fast. This is a people business, Jerry. You've got to get a hold of it." He shook an outstretched fist in enthusiastic demonstration.

"And you, Donald, well I'm not sure what's going on with you. You're distracted. I don't feel like you're on the ball anymore." He waved a derisory hand in an arc that fell back to his thigh before looking once more from man to man.

"You've both got your strengths, don't get me wrong. I like you both, really I do, but you're fighting over the same turf and I can't see it working out long term." Locksley shrugged out an apology.

"I'll give you both a fair crack. Donald, you'll have to go back to the floor so you two can fight it out on a level playing field. Three months should do it. Three months and I will be looking at your clients." He wagged a concluding finger, "Whoever brings me the best portfolio will take Sales Director and I'm sorry, but the other is out."

Jerry and Spink stared at each other wide-eyed.

"Holy shit," Jerry gasped. This was either a massive opportunity or a fucking disaster.

"Don't get excited, Adler," Spink growled, composing himself. "I'm not going anywhere," and with that he stood and stepped out in front to shake Locksley's hand. "I won't let you down, sir."

Jerry unfolded himself from the sofa and crowded up behind Spink to urge him out of the way. He too shook the now standing Locksley's hand, but couldn't find the arrogant confidence that Spink seemed to have in such abundance. He thrashed about his head for something suitably impressive and business-like to say and, "I'll get all my ducks in the pond, sir," was all he could manage.

Spink snorted with delight.

FOURTEEN

Stuck at the other end of the building, Jerry's office wasn't feeling the benefit of the autumn sun. He kicked at the ancient squat heater and it stuttered into life.

His desk was shoved up into the corner of a small dowdy room, in the original Georgian building that fronted the office space. Grey northern light seeped in through sash windows which were barred into eighteen tiny panes, chopping up the unsavoury view of the car park into bite-sized chunks. Their old frames rattled in the wind and Jerry rubbed cold hands together.

Precarious piles of files and loose paper teetered on his desk. This was no way for the next Sales Director to organise himself. Jerry resolved to tidy up. He selected a pile at random and worked his way through it. His nerves jangled and his head ached. What a surreal day.

The meeting with Dial had been a nightmare. Now he understood why Brian Cripps was such a miserable bastard, with Marcus Barnes as his boss. The pair of them plus Spink's off topic ramblings had sent the whole thing down the Swanny. Jerry had never sweated so much in half an hour as he had in Conference Room 2.

And now this job bombshell. Jerry had known the company was under pressure, but to be put into competition with Spink, well it was unexpected and more than a little bit scary.

An hour later, Jerry had put away all his filing, created an 'action' pile and a worrisome stack of personal bills. Rifling through his work bag, looking for today's cheese and pickle, he'd found a wad of unopened envelopes and thought better of continuing to ignore them. It turned out that only a handful had been the junk mail he'd hoped for, the majority being ever more pressing unpaid bills.
He gritted his teeth and opened the bank statement.
As usual, Isabell's monthly maintenance payment cut his salary in half. The nursery furniture had made a substantial dent in what was left and, if history was anything to go by, they'd be in the red by the end of the week with payday still a fortnight off. Jerry scrunched up his eyes and rubbed at his hair. He was living to regret the 'quickie' divorce settlement he'd reached with Isabell.

He should call her and tell her it was too much, that he was getting a solicitor this time. He could handle the hysterics and the late night phone calls and the overdramatised 'suicide notes' posted through his door. Hmm, well solicitors were very expensive and he wasn't feeling all that flush and he needed to be a home for Peanut and, well he didn't like all that confrontation business. OK?

He was scanning through the third page of the credit card statement when his phone rang.

"Hi, Jerry, Phyllis in Accounts. Your expenses have come back unsigned. You coded them against client accounts that aren't yours."

"I don't think so." Jerry frowned into the receiver.

"Well I'm looking at the system now. PC City, Parker & Co and Dial Diagnostics are all allocated to someone else," Phyllis whined.

Jerry tapped at his keyboard and brought up the accounts. The account hander details had been changed to Spink.

"I'll come back to you." He hung up and tabbed through the client list. Spink had gone through the system, claiming any account that he'd visited even once as his own.

Jerry stabbed out his extension number on the internal phone.

"Speak."

"Spink, you can't just troll though the system stealing my accounts," Jerry wailed into the handset.

"Your accounts? No, no, Adler. I've just been doing a little housekeeping, updating the system. I've had a little chat with

MY clients this afternoon, just so they know who to call. I'll keep them happy now." The menace in his voice was unmistakable.

Jerry hung up, shocked by how fast things had degenerated. While he'd been farting about and tidying up, Spink had been pilfering his best customers. Jerry pulled out his card file and punched in the first of many numbers. He needed to get busy before Spink stole the lot.

FIFTEEN

Remi sprang from the sweltering helicopter. Its blades still beating overhead whipped the air into a thick dusty soup. He slipped through the open limo door and settled into his air conditioned haven from the choking desert heat.

Stretching out, he rolled his head, pulled the pack from the door pocket and scanned through its contents. His mission ID was Charles Bamford-Irons, eccentric billionaire, playboy and philanthropist. Remi smiled: Aqua had set it up, just like he'd asked.

Knowing his destination was a mere ten minutes transfer, he was keen to get into character. He stripped away the sweaty black T-shirt and combats, relishing the icy air on his naked skin, before dressing in the sharp charcoal suit laid out on the seat. The limo pulled out into four lanes of traffic and Remi looked out though tinted glass at his surroundings. The gargantuan forms of hotels and casinos that had excited the skyline from the chopper, now seemed looming and oppressive, were his task equally as tall. Remi felt the throb of adrenalin and snapped his attention back to the pack.

The envelope contained a passport featuring one of Remi's more suave headshots, a driving licence, Platinum and Gold cards, fifty thousand dollars in cash, a wad of business cards and an earpiece, which he slid into his ear. A small thin screen unfolded from the ceiling in front of his face and performed an identity scan. Aqua spoke in his ear, "Briefing commencing in five, four, three, two…"

Passport photos and intelligence snap shots flashed up on the screen. "Maximus Pink has been located attending the 'Crusaders of Justice' consortium at the Bellagio, Las Vegas. Already well-established as an underground faction of high level weapons dealers and terrorists, the COJ have decide to branch out. They've set their sights on a new goal: to hold the world's superpowers to ransom and redistribute gold reserves into their own back pockets.

"They intend to achieve this via a syndicate of third world governments." Images on the screen scrolled and changed. "The COJ have corrupt government officials contracted to feed the majority of funds straight back into the consortium to ensure continued inclusion. This front is essential to gain the financial support of philanthropic investors beyond the group's core membership.

"The plans you stole from Kitty Princesa have allowed us to block major resources, but if investors continue to be taken in by their deceptions, it's only a matter of time before they circumnavigate our blockades. Your mission is to gain the consortium's confidence as a backer and infiltrate their circle. Obtain any information you can on the fund management and membership. Good luck, Agent Red. This message will erase in five, four, ..." Remi tossed the earpiece to the floor where it fizzed for a moment, then lay inert.

The screen folded itself away and Remi looked out onto The Strip, its neon taking on new life in the creeping twilight. The pavements were alive with people, all on diversions from their run of the mill. Remi felt their excitement and it compounded his own. Tangling with Kitty Princesa had been a breeze. He'd researched Maximus Pink already and he knew his weaknesses. Pink was fiercely competitive. Perhaps it was his less than average height that made him want to more than measure up. Or maybe looking old beyond his years, ravaged by tussles with other villains and a life of excess, he wanted power to be what attracted others to him. He had to be the richest; the bravest; the smartest. His competitive nature was a flaw that Remi could exploit.

If only Jerry could work out how to exploit Spink's flaws.

The limo turned in ahead of the famous fountains and pulled under the Bellagio's ornate entrance canopy. Straightening his clothes, Remi absorbed the identity of Charles Bamford-Irons and pocketed his wallet.

One nonchalant hand in his jacket pocket, he strode, straight-backed, across the polished marble of the foyer. Head held aloft, his confident demeanour drew the attention of interested eyes behind reception. They followed his progress to an empty stretch of counter, away from the gaggle of weekend gamblers and holidaymakers, and a young smart suited receptionist scurried to the spot he had chosen to greet him. She smoothed her hair.

"Good afternoon, sir. Welcome to the Bellagio. How may I assist you today?"

Remi raised his eyes to hers. "Charles Bamford-Irons checking in." He smiled with a twitch to one eyebrow. She fluffed at the keyboard and blushed, staring hard at the screen. Remi guessed she was scanning his profile: Charles Bamford-Irons would be listed as a primo high roller who warranted special attention.

"Our pleasure to welcome you again, Mr Bamford-Irons. We are delighted to offer you our Presidential Suite for the duration of your stay. Your secretary has called ahead to check you in. If I could just have your passport, please, sir." Remi plucked it from his pocket and placed it in her hand. Their fingers touched for a moment and she blushed a deeper shade of pink.

"Here is your key card, sir. Please also accept our Noir Loyalty and Club Privé cards with the Managers compliments. These cards will afford you access to privileges reserved only for our most treasured guests."

"Oh?" Remi raised a quizzical eyebrow. She gazed back at him.

"Yes. Our spa therapists are at your disposal. We can make dinner reservations or perhaps you would like some show tickets? Of course you are also welcome at Club Privé—our most exclusive private gaming rooms."

Remi drew his cards and passport across the cool counter and tucked them into his top pocket.

"I'll be sure to remember that, thank you." With a smile he turned to the patient bell hop, now clutching his Louis Vuitton. "Lead the way."

~

Remi strode through the welcoming doors of Club Privé the very image of a billionaire playboy. Debonair in bespoke Armani and expensive cologne, diamonds glittered at his cuffs. Comfortable with the art deco splendour of warm wood and sparkling glass, he tasted the oxygen-rich air and felt his confidence grow. He'd have to be careful not to relax too much.

The small group of men inside this room were the elite staying at the hotel. A couple were rich businessmen, a handful of celebrities, others from titled families, but most important of all, members of the COJ. Remi had had no doubt that the top brass would be here tonight and his confidence was rewarded. Right away he recognised Maximus Pink from the briefing and other faces fell into place as he scanned the room.

The club hostess swept across the oriental carpet in Chanel and Louboutins to greet him.
"Mr Bamford-Irons, good evening. What is your pleasure?"
There was an opening at Pink's table. "Blackjack. Let's start there."
"Of course." She guided him to the seat he'd already picked out for himself.
"A bottle of Krug, 1990 if you've got it," Remi said, surveying his fellow players.

At the other end of the table a fat man in a grey lounge suit pressed himself against the cushioned table edge, eager for the next hand: unlikely to be part of the consortium. Beside him a swarthy man, probably mid-thirties, uncomfortable in a tuxedo, worried at his collar: a henchman. Next along was his target, Maximus Pink. The long scar that ran through his eyebrow and on to his cheekbone marked him out from the crowd. His hair greyed at the temples to match unruly eyebrows and his diet of cigars and single malt had yellowed his eyes and drawn a thousand tiny thread veins across a bulbous nose. His tuxedo was crisp and well cut. He spun an emerald pinkie ring with the adjacent finger and starred at Remi quite unselfconsciously. Remi had interrupted their game and pressed Pink's first button by ordering expensive champagne. Another knowledgeable and rich man at the table would need to be enlightened as to who the alpha was.

"Good evening, gentlemen, may I join you?" Remi wore his most congenial smile.

Pink appeared content to have been asked and nodded. "Please." He eyed the bottle, placed between them in a cooler. "Celebrating already?"

"It's been a wonderful day."

Pink pursed his lips and returned his attention to the game.

The players pushed their chips out onto the table and the dealer placed two cards before each man, flipping over a jack and leaving another face down in front of himself. Fat man took another card and bust. Henchman watched, detached. Pink took another card and bust. He didn't look all that bothered about losing five hundred dollars. Remi turned over his cards. Seventeen. His five-thousand-dollar bet loomed large on the table and he felt the eyes of the other players on him.

"Hit."

The dealer laid the four of hearts next to his hand and flipped his own remaining card to reveal a six. Twenty-one for Remi and sixteen for the dealer. Pink exhaled. Now Remi had shown him Bamford-Irons was a risk taker and a potential threat.

The next hand and, not to be outdone, Pink matched Remi's five-thousand-dollar bet. This time he won and Remi lost. He twiddled the ring. "Bad luck."

"No problem, I've had a superb day. Won't you join me in a glass of Krug? I hate to drink alone."

Pink accepted the drink and the two men chinked glasses.

"I come every year. It's my vice." Remi went on, "Everything I win goes to my charities. Makes the gambling OK in my book." He snorted a laugh into the flute.

Pink watched him with scepticism. "Oh yes? What did you win last year?"

"Just shy of a million. It would have been more, but I was just learning Baccarat and couldn't get the hang of it." He grinned at Pink. "Men like us, well we don't need the winnings, do we? The payoff is in the exhilaration of the game and a bloody good holiday. I'm giving it to the street kids in Mumbai this year. Poor little buggers."

Pink twisted his seat to face Remi full on. His head tilted in thought. "You like to think of yourself as a philanthropist?" Pink was probing.

Remi chuckled. "Well that's a big word for a small deed. I like to share things out a little." He pushed ten thousand dollars into his betting circle ready for the next hand. Pink watched it slide and turned back to the game. "You and I are similar creatures," he said.

Pink was taking the bait.

"I'll leave my winnings in play," Remi told the dealer. They played the hand, both Pink and Remi won. They grinned at each other, Pink sizing up his competition.

"So how are we similar?" Remi leaned in. "You looking out for the street kids too?"

"Not specifically, but I am in Vegas to be part of a group of like-minded men—all looking to help our third world brothers and sisters."

"Oh?" Remi nodded with enthusiasm and Pink indicated to the dealer that he too would let his winnings stay in play. A pair of jacks for Remi: another win. Pink's nineteen beat the dealer too.

"The superpowers have held too much of the world's wealth for too long." Pink's nostrils flared. "My colleagues and I want them to see the error of their ways. We must convince them to be more even handed."

Another hand, the winnings added to the pot. Remi had around thirty thousand dollars in play, Pink a little less. Henchman was pulling at his collar. Fat man removed his winnings, if any, each time and stacked them with precision. The bet was always the same. He was breaking even.

"How would you go about convincing these superpowers?" Remi asked, looking at the next pair of cards placed before him. A five and a six. "Hit." A queen. Pink checked his cards, a natural Blackjack. The cards were running in their favour.

"It's no easy task. A political minefield, as you can imagine. Our consortium seeks the thing that is most important to them and threatens to deprive them of it if they don't do what we want."
"Sounds like terrorism."
Pink bristled. "More like disciplining a naughty child. They must behave themselves or get their treats taken away." He looked down, his eyes almost closed for a moment. When he spoke again his voice was hushed. "Our members have the power to redirect oil away from its intended destination. Convoluting the route has huge implications farther down the line in our favour, but the cost to us is enormous."
Remi nodded, "How exciting, a truly proactive approach. Straight to the heart of the matter."

Both men nodded to the dealer that their chips remained in play. An ace and a nine for Remi. A king and a seven for Pink. Pink paused in deliberation then decided not to risk another card. The dealer revealed nineteen, beating Pink's hand. Henchman went rigid, flicking only his eyes to Pink, whose jaw clenched as his chips were swept away, regret of his cowardice evident in his expression.

"Oh bad luck," said Remi, resisting a smile.

Pink declined to make another bet, but Remi's chips remained in play: seventy-five thousand teetering in his betting circle. All eyes at the table were on him. He accepted two cards. Just him and the dealer now.

"Charles Bamford-Irons." Remi smiled, extending his hand to Pink. Pink took it, dragging a smile past the disappointment of his loss. "I like a man prepared to make a stand," Remi went on. "I'd like to help out your consortium. Have another drink." Remi topped him up. He didn't want to lose him now, not yet.

"Maximus Pink."

Remi turned over his cards, a six and a four. "Hit." An ace. The dealer held two jacks. Another win. Pink looked from the cards to Remi and back to the cards. "Lady Luck is with you," he coughed out.

"Lucky for me we met. It's destiny, Pink, destiny." Remi ramped up his enthusiasm to contagious levels and a sparkle developed in Pink's eye. Who could resist Charles Bamford-Irons?

"You know, the orphans have already done quite well today—a big win at Caesars earlier. What do you say we put tonight's winnings toward your cause instead?" Remi bobbed up and down with excitement, playing his part.

"That would be an excellent start."

"An excellent start, yes." Remi gave Pink an exuberant slap on the back, slopping a little Krug onto his trousers.

The dealer laid another pair of cards. Remi didn't look at them and turned instead to Pink. "If we're going to take this forward I'll need details. See some reports, bank accounts, that sort of thing. I'm a generous man, but no fool."

"Of course. All our investors are kept up to date."

Remi surveyed his cards and paused to think.

The room held its breath.

"Eighteen, I'll stand." Remi looked to the dealer who revealed their cards. A four and a five. They took a hit. Another five. They had to take another. An eight and bust.

"Ha!" Remi jumped up and hugged Pink, who was so shocked he didn't even try to move away.

"You are my lucky charm!" he cried. "Let's do it. I'll make a transfer tonight." The dealer stacked his winnings—a hundred and seventy thousand now on the table.

Pink turned and beckoned to a man standing sentry by the door, clutching a briefcase. He came over, stood by Pink's side and without instruction held the case level at waist height.

Pink clicked the combination locks and pushed open the lid. He drew from inside the uppermost of a pile of identical plain brown envelopes, which he passed to Remi. "Details of the members of our group, our philanthropic goals and bank account details. For our investors' eyes only. I must request your discretion."

"Absolutely." Remi tucked the envelope into his inside jacket pocket and passed over a business card in response. Pink took it with both hands and then put it into the briefcase. The sentry snapped it shut and returned to his post.

"One last hand to seal the deal." Remi motioned to the dealer to continue. "Two hundred and fifty thousand would be a fitting gift to start our relationship, wouldn't you say, Pink?" Pink nodded, greedy eyes on the chips.

The dealer laid the cards, first a queen and then a king. The dealer was showing a ten.

The room leaned in as the dealer peeled off the final card. An ace.

"Blackjack, dealer wins." In one deft sweep the chips were gone and silence descended.

Remi swallowed hard and rubbed at his chest. Pink slumped in his seat. The room leaned away, murmuring.

"Well, what a blow." Remi rubbed some more at his chest. "All that excitement and I've let you down."

Pink pursed his lips and shrugged, disappointed but resigned. "What can you do?"

Remi leaned back, puffing and rubbing, a pained look on his face.

"Are you all right? Shall I call someone?" Pink could see his newest investor dropping dead from a heart attack. Henchman was on his feet.

"I'm fine, just heartburn, I—I'm fine." He made to stand, but winced and dropped back to the seat.

"Water, here." Pink beckoned to the hostess.

"I have something for it in my room. I'll be fine in a minute. I just need the pills." Remi wobbled to his feet. "Shan't be long. You won't know I'm gone." Remi managed a weak smile and made his way to the door, hunched and puffing. An attendant pulled it open for him and he staggered to the lift, waving away offers of assistance.

When the doors slid open on the ground floor Remi scanned the foyer before striding out across the cool marble toward the exit. Back straight and head held aloft, he rested one nonchalant hand in his trouser pocket and winked at the receptionist, who giggled and blushed anew.

Under the Bellagio's canopy, he slid into the back of his waiting limo, patted the envelope in his pocket and caught the driver's eye in the mirror. "Take me to the airport and don't hang about, I want to get back to my yacht."

SIXTEEN

"Your mum called."

"Oh?"

"Yeah. Said she was wondering why Peanut and I hadn't gone round on Sunday too. You know when you went round. And had lunch. A lovely Sunday roast."

"Oh."

"Yeah. Said she couldn't understand it. I said, obviously, Jerry's very busy at the moment. Obviously, it slipped Jerry's mind that I was available, with our infant, stuck at home, badly in need of a break."

"Uh huh."

"Yeah. Why would you say that was, exactly, Jerry?"

Jerry pulled his lips in and bit them together for a moment. "Hey, well, you know, I was just popping round to help out with the computer. I did try to tell you about it, Rach, but you seemed kind of tired."

"Did I?"

"Yeah. Well you know mothers: always trying to feed their kids." He squeaked out a laugh, "I was just going to pop round for a bit, fix the computer and come home."

"Mm."

"And then she produced this plate of food and it seemed a bit rude not to eat it."

"Rude. Uh-huh."

Rachel struggled to manhandle the lawnmower over to the left. If she could get it to go under the bottom shelf there'd be room for the sun loungers to squeeze in down the side. The shed was too small, stuffed with all those things they'd kept just in case. Evaporated pots of paint, bits of curtain fittings and neglected tools skulked on shelves, just out of reach. An enormous chest of drawers, evicted from the kitchen last year, took up far too much space under the tiny plastic window, its contents a mystery. No-one ever dared to open the drawers for fear of poisonous arachnids, or other such unlikely creatures, waiting within. No-one wanted to risk such an encounter in the name of DIY.

Jerry shuffled from side to side behind her in the doorway and pointed past her to the floor. "You'll have to move those boxes or it'll never go."

"I tell you what, why don't you do it?" Rachel backed out of the tiny space and pushed Jerry in. He was becoming a bit too good at giving out instructions. He concertinaed down to reach around the old mower, pulled out the box and swivelled back to place it on top of the drawers next to her. Rat poison. She picked it up, sniffed it and put it thoughtfully back down.

"Your mum said you left some paperwork there."

"Did I?" said Jerry before adding, "Crap," under his breath.

"Said she was really surprised we could afford to give Isabell so much on a direct debit. Monthly, Isabell's direct debit, isn't it, Jerry?"

"Mm."

"Yeah, thought so."

Jerry wiggled the lawnmower into position. "Pass me a lounger then, would you?" he said, looking sheepishly up into Rachel's pissed-off face. Rachel grabbed a folded lounger from just outside the door and clattered it through the frame. Jerry took it and they both held on for a moment, Rachel waiting for him to meet her eyes.

"It's just until she gets on her feet." Jerry looked down to the gap by the mower and Rachel let go.

"What about our feet, Jerry? Your mum said the account was overdrawn."

"Was it? Oh, maybe just a little. Just waiting on a cheque. Nothing to worry about." Jerry's bobbed unnecessarily up and down as he forced the lounger in.

She could see he didn't want to look at her, undoubtedly hiding something.

"Do you still love her, Jerry?"

"What? No, God no."

"I don't understand why you keep trying to protect her. It's over with her, isn't it? You've got us now, me and Peanut."

Jerry straightened up and pulled her into him, smoothing her head against his chest. "Hey, don't be silly, Rach. Isabell's history. It's just going to take me a while to get her off my back, that's all."

Cheek pressed against Jerry's cotton work shirt, Rachel was aware that she could no longer see his face. "She's just so demanding and it's like you'll do whatever she says, like she's got some hold over you." Jerry's sleeve was getting in her mouth.

"She hasn't. It's just Isabell, you know how she is. It's better to put a stop to her drama before it takes hold." Jerry stroked randomly at Rachel's hair, pushing it into her eyes.

She pulled back, away from him. "Look I don't mind if we have to save up for stuff, money isn't everything, but I don't want to be taken for a fool. If you're still carrying on with her, Jerry, I'll lose it. I will. You can't do that to me." Her voice wavered, betraying the emotion she was trying to control. If Jerry was seeing Isabell behind her back it would tip her over the edge. The daily battle with Peanut was only bearable if they were a team beneath it all.

"I'm not!" Jerry stared down into her eyes, widening his own. "Cross my heart." He made great sweeps across his chest to emphasize it. "Now give me the other lounger."

She passed it to him, a little more carefully this time, and he turned away to try to jiggle it into place. Garden shears rattled on their hook. Blades, pristine from lack of use, glinted high above Jerry's oblivious back. Rachel reached up to touch the steel, to keep the shears from jumping off their hook and remembered her dream. Remembered how she'd felt ownership of that surprising glinting knife, like it was a part of her, lain dormant.

"I'm not going to find out about anything else, am I, Jerry? Nothing else that you're not telling me?" Jerry turned to her and crossed his chest again. "And hope to die," he said, childish grin spreading across his face and irritating Rachel further.

He gave her arm a squeeze and pushed past, stooping slightly to get out through the low doorway and hurried up the garden.

Rachel pressed a finger to her lips and watched him scurry into the house. He wasn't telling the truth, of course. He was shifty, avoiding her eyes and running away when she brought up the subject of Isabell. Isabell, the bloody bane of her life. Curvaceous, vivacious, sexy Isabell, who had nothing to spend her money on but expensive clothes and manicures, but still managed to take vast sums from their family every month. No demands on her time, but trips to the hair dresser and applying that pout. No screaming infant to wear her down. Isabell, who Jerry couldn't seem to let go.

Rachel pushed the conjured images of them together out of her imagination. 'No proof, Rachel. No proof,' she told herself, but her gut still twisted enough to close her eyes.

And who could blame him? Look at the state of her. Most of the time she was spattered with baby vomit, wearing knackered old leggings with the knees stretched out. Her hair was a mess and there was rarely any time, nor inclination for that matter, to apply make-up. And she was tired, so tired. And miserable. Fuck, it was no wonder Jerry was off with another woman.

She pushed the shed door closed and snapped on the padlock. "Good," she said out loud. "I'm glad we've managed to get them in. I'm pretty sure we've seen the last of the good weather." She looked up to the grey sky and shivered a little. "The telly said there's a storm on the way."

SEVENTEEN

Jerry ran frantic eyes over the screen: Spink had plundered his account base, stolen the best for himself and Jerry couldn't do a thing about it. Only members of the board had that kind of access and Spink knew it.

Jerry was going to have to win some new customers, a lot of new customers.

He flailed around his throbbing brain for inspiration. What about beefing up the spend on what was left? For a starter, that was good. He'd have to make house calls. He scanned the screen for a good prospect. Abbott & Gunn could be worth some investment: he'd heard they were developing a new range of consumables and new ranges always got a big hit of PR. He pulled their file from his cabinet and leafed through the contact history.

Jerry rubbed his cold hands together then pulled a tissue from the box on his desk to dab at his running nose. His contact picked up on the second ring.

"Jerry, it's been a while. How are things?"

He was happy to speak to him. Thank God. "Great, Simon, really great." Jerry cranked up the enthusiasm. "We've been running some exciting new schemes. I'd love to come over and talk to you about them."

"Jerry (*BEEP You have a call waiting*) crazy busy right now. Why don't you give me a (*BEEP You have a call waiting*) OK?"

Jerry strained to fill in the gaps. "Sorry, Simon, I didn't quite catch that."

"(*BEEP You have a call waiting*)." Jerry's fists clenched with frustration. "But, listen, I'm here until five if you swing by today."

"Great. Perfect. I'll see you later (*BEEP...*)" Jerry hung up, relieved and his phone rang immediately.

"Adler."

"Jerry. I need you to coming to the house." Isabell.

"What now? Cat flap stuck? Light bulb popped?"

"No be silly, Jerry, you know I hate cats. Is very important. You will no want to delay."

"I really can't right now, Isabell, I'm working. I'll call later, OK?"

"OK. No forget." She hung up.

Yeah, right. He'd call right after he'd made these other two hundred phone calls. He checked the wall clock: twenty to five. If he got a wiggle on he could catch Simon tonight.

He jabbed the PC power button, grabbed his coat off the back of his chair and swept out of the room, leaving the chair in a spin.

Spink was in reception, signing out. Jerry nodded at him deadpan, playing it unconvincingly cool. His sky-high eyebrows and wobbly head got Spink's full attention and he watched him back out of the door through a distrustful squint. With hindsight, perhaps spinning round and running for it wasn't the smartest thing he could have done. He wasn't even halfway across the car park before Spink was out the door after him, in pursuit of whatever he was obviously hiding.

Jerry jumped into the Fiat and cranked her over.
"Come on, come on."
She didn't bite.
He cranked her over again and rammed his foot to the floor.

She spluttered into life and Jerry bucked out of the car park, just ahead of Spink in his Jaguar.

He pulled out into a clear Elmgate Road and raced down to Hale Avenue.

Spink rolled along behind and Jerry grimaced at his smug face in his rear view mirror. Just one client, he wanted to save a least one decent client.

The Jolly Badger roundabout put a spanner in Spink's works and he got stuck for a good twelve cars while Jerry screamed the Fiat's engine toward the M1.

"Eat my dust, Dinky!" Jerry wiggled in his seat, revelling the growing gap between them: Abbott & Gunn was only ten minutes away.

The red light at Sunbury Way was backed up with a line of eight cars. Jerry drummed on his steering wheel, willing it to change. He watched his mirror for Spink, who came into view, but then made a left before the end of the queue. Spink was cutting the corner, taking a gamble on where Jerry was heading.

"No, no, no!"

Jerry slammed the Fiat into gear and coerced it to the lights and left. Spink pulled out five cars ahead and Jerry gritted his teeth. It was all down to the parking. He scanned the road ahead for spaces.

His phone started to ring and he snatched it up.

"It's just so busy around here, this time of night. You looking for a space?" Spink.

Jerry growled.

"Just by the Spar there's a space. Oh, no, hang on. I'm in it." He disconnected.

Jerry sailed by and Spink gave him the finger. He wheeled into a side road and abandoned his car on the pavement. As he jumped out, his phone rang again.

"Piss off, Spink."

"Why have you no called me, Jerry?" Isabell.

Jerry fumbled his client file and it dropped to the floor. He fell onto it, scrabbling at the loose papers. "Isabell. What is it?"

"I wait, but no call," Isabell huffed into the phone.

"I'm working, Isabell. Not now eh?"

"Always not now. I think you don't care."

"We are divorced."

She sobbed, "You no care. I have all this worry. I need help, Jerry."

Jerry grimaced and rubbed at the back of his neck.

"I'll call later, OK? I have to go now."

"OK."

"OK."

Jerry ran from the Fiat, diced with death across Sunbury Way and barrelled into the reception of Abbott & Gunn.

Spink was shaking hands with Simon.

"Donald's just been telling me about our account getting upgraded," Simon beamed. "Getting looked after by the Sales Director himself. We are honoured."

Spink patted Simon on the back and gave Jerry a benign grin.

"Only the best," Jerry wheezed.

"I've got this covered, Jerry," Spink drawled, "Why don't you call it a day?"

EIGHTEEN

Spink's fake Rolex clicked to a minute after midnight and he laid his hand. A single bead of sweat rolled down his neck and soaked into the fraying collar of his shirt.

"Three eights," he growled. The other two men at the table threw their cards down and leaned back, disappointed.

He'd won.

Spink scooped up the small pile of chips in the centre of the table and deposited them into the empty space in front of him. The tide was turning at last.

He'd rolled into the club three hours ago with five hundred pounds in his pocket and a good feeling in his water. Tonight was an important night. If he could double his money he'd have enough to make the repayment on the club loan. If not, he knew there was a chance his membership could be rescinded. He needed The Cranley: there had been nights when he'd left here ten grand richer and he'd be hard pressed to pull that off after a day at the track. The Cranley was his lifeline, especially now.

The dealer flicked cards around the table and Spink pulled them up at the corner: a pair of threes. So much for the change of luck. He chewed on his unlit Havana and mulled on whether to play the hand.

His fellow players were regulars too: both rich businessmen who could afford to sink a few grand into a night's entertainment. That's why Spink came here. Sure, his shirt had seen better days, but it was Ralph Lauren, and his Rolex wasn't real, but he'd had to hand over the one his wife had given him on their wedding day as part payment on a gambling debt. The Mouse had never noticed the copycat replacement. What difference did it make?

You had to play big to win big and this was the place to do it.

Spink shuffled in his seat and stretched his hands out on the table. His fellow players ran appraising eyes over him and he recognised the comprehension in their faces. Damn.
"Gentlemen, I'm out." He nodded to them in turn and stood. Sweeping up his chips, he stalked away to the French windows at the end of the room and let himself out onto the small balcony.

Flopping down onto a cushioned wicker lounger, he sucked on his newly lit cigar and puffed great clouds of rich fug into the cool night air. Bloody smoking ban. He'd catch his death out here. He hated giving away his 'tells'. Shuffling around and stretching out like that, what was he thinking? He ordered a Glenfiddich and looked down over Pall Mall. At least the drinks could go on his tab.

Spink gripped the Havana in his teeth and caressed the chips, allowing them to machine gun from one hand to the other. He was down three hundred. It was all this bullshit with Adler putting him off his game.

No way Spink was going to lose his job to that tosser. He'd streaked off the blocks and left Adler standing, oblivious to the vast quantity of accounts that he'd pilfered today and not just from him, but from all the members of the team. Plenty more were lined up for takeover in the next couple of months too. Spink's place was pretty secure.

Mango UK had been an epic call though. Spink brushed a speck of lint from his thigh as he thought about that. Mango were huge, but Locksley PR didn't get much of their action at the moment. His serendipitous call to their office had blagged him an intro to the VP of Marketing Worldwide at their UK conference next week. This was going to be the deal to seal all deals. Adler didn't stand a chance.

Spink rubbed his hands together with delight, took a sip of whisky and let his eyes close.

"Donald," said a gentle male voice, "You're having a good evening, I trust?"

Spink's eyes snapped open to take in the patronizing presence of Giles VanDerhorn, the club manager.

"Giles." Spink offered up a sycophantic smile, "So lovely to see you."

Giles nodded and fixed questioning eyes upon him.

"I'm sorry to say my evening has not been quite as good as I'd hoped." He looked down at the unravelling stitches on his well-polished shoes. "Of course, I brought along the sum we discussed, but I'm afraid the cards were against me and I got rather carried away." He chuckled in what he hoped was an endearing manner. "All out of cash now and seems the good lady wife removed my cheque book from my coat when she took it to the cleaners." He patted at his breast pocket to demonstrate. He'd been taken to the cleaners all right.

"I'm very sorry to be so disorganised. Could I drop it in to you next week?" Spink batted his best doe eyes at VanDerhorn. "Off on business tomorrow, but I can get in on Tuesday?" He might be able to scrape it together by then.

"I see. You would like to defer your payment until next week." Giles wasn't fooled, but remained soft spoken and polite. Thank God they didn't like to make a scene here—he just wouldn't be allowed access if he continued to fail to come up with the money: a fate much worse than embarrassment.

"Would you, old boy? That would be ever so helpful. Next week suit you all right?"

Giles nodded. "Of course, Donald. We like to look after our members. Members who support The Cranley are always of value. I'll be sure to find you next week." Giles swept away, smiling and nodding at other members as he passed.

Spink wrung his hands. A thousand pounds by next week—worth it to keep his membership. He mentally riffled through his possessions for something disposable. The Mouse had a few good pieces in her jewellery box.

He wondered where she kept it.

NINETEEN

Adam knocked back the Jack Daniels and savoured the burn in his chest. Gregory sighed. "Come on, Adam. You know you miss it. What are you going to do?" Adam stared into his empty glass and pursed his lips. "Can't push the penny back up." He pulled at the knot of his tie, unbuttoned the stiff collar and waved his empty glass at the waitress. She sashayed to the mahogany bar and set its tender to work, all sounds muted in the rich upholstery and thick brocade drapes of The Cranley's bar. Dappled light from a chandelier fell across marble table tops. Deep maroon velvet buttoned into Adam's high-backed chair. The room cosseted its occupants in an elegant protective bubble. Adam fidgeted and scratched at himself. A muscle ticked under his eye. He'd been fooled by it all before. Now it was just another example of misguided loyalty.

Intimate groups occupied tables in cosy alcoves. Immaculate women hanging on the every word of their stinking rich patrons, burst with artificial laughter at their jokes. Another year and then another. He'd let the real thing slip away. You didn't see many wives at The Cranley. What happened at the club, stayed at the club.

A private gaming room door opened to expel a short harassed man who laid a musty trail of cigar fug behind him as he scuttled for the exit. Adam's nose wrinkled as he observed the man's retreating form with contemptuous recognition: Spink. He'd recognised him at the club before, but had always managed to steer clear.

Adam had been here many times, celebrating victory or partying on a bonus. The Partners at BSL were big on The Cranley. Looking around him now, he couldn't remember why.

The waitress set two heavy tumblers chinking onto the table. She batted her eyelashes at Gregory who winked back. Adam snatched up his drink, took a slug and choked out a wry laugh. "This place says it all."

Gregory raised a quizzical eyebrow.

"Do you think she likes you, Greg? Do you think that she appreciates your inner beauty? She can smell your money, Greg. They all can." He swept a derisive arm around the room. "It's all fake."

"I hear she's double-jointed." Greg's tongue flicked unconsciously around his lips.

"Mercurial and manipulative."

"Fantastic arse."

Adam smiled at that. "You said it." He took another hit of JD.

The smile dropped from Gregory's eyes. "Your clients are already being reassigned." He examined his manicure "If you wait much longer there'll be no going back."

"Of all the things I can't undo." Adam's eyebrow twitched. "Who are you working on, Greg?"

"Alister."

"What's the charge?"

"Murder. You know that."

"Did he do it?"

"You know that too."

"Did he?"

"Client confidentiality, Adam."

"That's a yes. You going to get him off?"

"I'll do my best."

"For the money."

Gregory looked perplexed. "It's my job, Adam."

"Anyone else?"

Greg shuffled in his seat.

"Who else are you taking from my cast-offs?"

Greg looked uncomfortable. "McGinty."

"Fuck me." Adam knocked back the rest of his drink and sprawled back into the chair.

"He's got connections. Where did you think he was getting his money? Do a good job and I could make my name."

Adam's head swam, Greg just didn't get it. He pulled his eyes away from the swirling carpet to focus on the far wall. "You want to ingratiate yourself with a pensioner-mutilating psychopath?" He knew his voice was rising, but he couldn't control it. He felt the eyes of the room swivel toward him. The memory of McGinty taunted him. *I cut out her wagging tongue. No bitch telling tales on me.*

Gregory leaned in and spoke in hushed tones. "I don't want to be his best friend. Business is business. If I can pull a good result out of the bag then I'll get myself a good reputation with the right people. I'll be in demand."

Adam shook his head and looked down at the floor.

"Now that their golden boy has deserted them, they'll need someone new to throw their ill-gotten gains at."

"I was not their golden boy."

"Sure you were. Every A-list scumbag had your number in their speed dial. Someone's got to pick it up. Why not me?"

Yeah why not? Just because Adam's conscience had woken up why would anyone else share his newfound values? He knew he wouldn't talk him round; the money shouted louder.

"Everyone has a right to a defence. Innocent until proven guilty, you know? It's the law of the land, Adam."

It was more than that though, wasn't it? Pick a side and show your colours. Adam's lip curled as he watched Greg preen. He fussed at his hair and ran a finger around his collar—it pinched at that double chin he'd cultivated in fancy restaurants. Frown lines were etched into the pallid skin across his brow. He'd sold his soul. He was a cheap slut in a two-thousand-pound suit.

"Get back on the merry-go-round Adam. They steal from society and we steal it back. I'm Robin fucking Hood."
"You're just another bandit."
"I'm just like you."

Too much. Adam launched himself at Greg, pushing his chair over backward onto the floor, hand grasped around his throat. "I am NOT like you!"
Greg was silenced: stunned and gagged.

Rage popped out the veins on Adam's forehead while he pinned Greg's rigid body to the floor. Pushing out the distance between them, he fought to rein in the seething mass of disgust and anger that gripped him. The old Adam had accepted the money and enjoyed the notoriety, he knew and hated that. Greg was just following the same flawed path.

Shame washed over his scalp and cooled the fever. "Not anymore." He released Greg and clambered to his feet, trying not to look at him, displaying empty hands.
"You've lost it, Fox. Lost it!" Gregory shrieked.
Adam's head hurt and he rubbed at his temples. "We're done," he said. There was nothing more to say to Greg, he just wanted to go home.

TWENTY

The door chime sang behind stained glass for a second time. Jerry strained backward to peer in through the slim crack in the lounge curtains. A light was on and he could just pick up soft music. Rain pitter-pattered on the portico roof.

He drew up his inadequate jacket's collar, scurried over to the window and banged on the glass. "Isabell? Are you in there?"

Behind him the door opened.

"Jerry, *mi querido. Has venido.*" Isabell leant against the door frame, a scarlet Lycra mini dress straining over her voluptuous form to eye-popping effect.

Jerry ignored the visual assault and stepped back under the portico. "Why didn't you open the door? I'm getting soaked out here."

"Poor baby," Isabell purred, taking him by the hand and leading him into the dark hallway. She stripped the wet jacket from his back, stood on the heels of his shoes and propelled him forward, peeling them from his feet. "No shoes on the carpet," she chided softly.

She led him on, into the lounge but, when Jerry saw the scene he snatched back his hand.

Isabell lived in their old marital home: a new build with delusions of Georgian grandeur. She had decorated with an expensive eye. The deep pile rug in the lounge crushed under foot. Tones of cream and gold combined with rich wood and, this evening, flickering candlelight. The scent of patchouli filled the air and soft jazz oozed from the sound system. This was Isabell's formula for seduction.

Jerry swallowed hard and watched her from beneath alarmed eyebrows.

Arranging herself on the sofa, she crossed long legs with slow precision and patted the cushion beside her. Jerry obediently sat down, but squeezed himself against the arm at the opposite end.
"Are you comfortable?" she purred.
"Fine," Jerry mumbled, really not comfortable at all.
"Is important to relax. How is baby? Up all night, I am thinking. We used to be up all night too, Jerry." She stroked at her cheek.
Jerry watched her, wide eyed. "Fine. Fine. It's all fine."

"I get you drink, hmm?" She uncurled from the sofa and brushed against him as she passed. "I get you favourite beer."

Jerry loosened his tie. What the hell? He smeared a sweaty palm on his trouser leg.

She returned and handed Jerry his drink, ensuring their fingers touched. She settled beside him, allowing the scarlet lycra to ride up her thigh so Jerry caught a flash of black lace. "Why don't you come stay with me a while? Take a break?" she purred.

The beer caught in Jerry's throat and he coughed it out. "Sorry, have I drifted into a parallel dimension?" Isabell looked hurt.

"It's just that I could have sworn we got divorced and I married someone else. Oh yeah, and had a baby."

"It no have to *mean* anything. Could just be sex, wild dirty sex." She got up onto her knees, levelling barely contained breasts with Jerry's face. His jaw began to flap. "Hey. Look. Lovely. No. Really. Couldn't. Even if I wanted to. Which I can't. Don't. Of course." He wiggled away from under the dangerous looming bosom and got to his feet. "Look, what's this all about?" He pushed an errant curl of hair back from his eye.

Isabell flopped into the sofa and folded her arms. Her long black hair flipped to partly obscure her petulant face, but Jerry could still see her eyebrows knitting together, eyebrows that said she was thinking. The corners of her mouth turned down and she assumed the expression of a wounded puppy.

"I get so lonely here, Jerry. Please can you no stay with me a little?"

Jerry's brain goggled. "Isabell. You hate me, remember?"

"No. No. I no hate you, Jerry." She bit at her lip.

"Isabell. What's going on?"

"OK. Maybe you help me a little then? Yes?"

Jerry screwed up his face.

"*Mi madre y mi padre.* They are coming, Jerry. Could you get them from the airport? Please?"

That seemed rather simple. "Why can't you do it?"

"Busy, so busy. Getting ready." She plumped a cushion.

Jerry narrowed his eyes to watch Isabell get up and bustle around the room, tidying non-existent mess.

"How did we get from the great meaningless sex to collecting your parents from the airport?" Alarm bells clanged.

Isabell giggled and shrugged.

Jerry's brain clunked and whirred. "Oh my God. You haven't told them, have you? They still think we're married, don't they!"

Isabell grimaced.

"Isabell, why? You've got to tell them"

"No. No. No." She paced around the sofa. "I can no tell them, Jerry."

"Yes. Yes. Yes." Jerry pursued her.

"Jerry, please. I'm begging you. I can no put off their visit any longer. I can no be cut off like Cousin Angelina. I am a good Catholic girl."

Jerry scoffed and Isabell scowled at him.

"I can no get divorce. I bring shame on my family. Mi padre—he will no forgive me. I'll lose my allowance, Jerry, please." She chewed at her immaculate manicure.

"What's done is done, Isabell. You'll have to confess sooner or later."

"No. No. No!" She waved stretched-out hands above her head. "No allowance and I can no pay the mortgage, Jerry. Is your house too. You will have to pay. How will you like that?"

"Oh no. I can't give you any more. You're already getting half my salary. We agreed. You'll just have to sell the house."

Yes, this could be a blessing in disguise. Sell the house. There may even be a nice little bit of equity they could split.

"I can no sell the house, Jerry." She examined her nails and pouted as she spoke. "Loans. I secure them on the house. House price drop and now there is no enough."

Jerry scrubbed at his hair. "Oh Isabell. Why did you need *more* money?" Bang goes the windfall.

She leaned in, wagging a finger at him, "I no do it on purpose!" then stuck out her chin in defiance, "I am a woman. I need things."

"What?"

Isabell brushed him away. "It no matter. What's done is done."

Jerry flopped down onto the sofa and put his head in his hands.

"My parents will only be here for a month," Isabell purred and sidled up to him.

Jerry couldn't bring himself to look at her. A tiny strangled scream escaped his throat.

Isabell leant on his shoulder, her mouth close to his ear. "You could come in late from work some days. Maybe other days go up early to 'bed'." She hung quotation marks in the air. "It would no be so bad. Is nice and quiet. No crying baby. Think of the alternative. Financial ruin, Jerry. Nobody want that."

Could he manage it? There was no way he could afford to cough up any more money. Maybe he could put in an appearance, then lock himself away in the den to 'work' and slip out of the window. Or maybe wait for them to go to bed and then go home. They were old. They probably didn't stay up late. He peeked at Isabell over his fingertips.

"When does their flight land?"

TWENTY-ONE

Jerry's Fiat bucked to the curb and stalled. Well at least he'd made it home. He assessed his house: yellow light spilled around the lounge curtains. With a bit of luck that meant Rach was relaxing on the sofa and Peanut was asleep upstairs.

He scraped the dilapidated gate across the path and let himself in. The lounge was empty and the house eerily quiet. He wandered into the kitchen to find the usual cacophony of bottles, cups and laundry at various levels of cleanliness, poised and abandoned.

Rachel was slumped at the table, her head resting upon outstretched arms. Through audible breaths she mumbled something from the depths of a dream. Jerry bit at his lip; Isabell's plan would not be well received.

He poked her on the shoulder and Rachel pulled open her eyes. "Whuh?" She drew herself up "What time is it?"

"It's nine-thirty."

"What? How? Why didn't you wake me?" She stretched out her back and frowned.

"Just got in."

Rachel didn't look in the mood for Isabell news.

"Had to work late. Busy. So busy." Isabell echoed in his head.

Rachel eyed him impassively. "Nine-thirty. God, Peanut will be awake soon. She stood and padded over to the sink. "And the bottles aren't done. Bloody hell," she sighed and sorted through the mess. "This is a bit late for the office, isn't it? Don't they lock up at eight?"

"Yeah, yeah," he stammered, "We've got this big pitch to work on so we locked up instead." Rachel turned to look at him and Jerry dropped his eyes to the floor and shuffled backward, colliding with a chair. Here goes nothing. "Isabell asked if I could pick up her parents from the airport tomorrow."

Rachel huffed out a snort. "That woman has the cheek of the devil."

"Er yeah."

Rachel turned to glare at him. "Please tell me you said no. That would just be the icing on the cake. The last place you should be is running around after that manipulative bitch."

"Oh, right, yeah." Maybe not then. "Exactly what I said. I'm, we're, way too busy for that." Jerry rested his hands on his hips and leaned back, like a jolly policeman. What now?

Inspiration struck. "Actually, Rach, there's a bit of problem with work." He wasn't going to tell her about this, but it could clear the way for some time spent with the ex-in laws. "Turns out they're making people redundant." Rachel dropped a bottle into the sink.

"I'm not out. Not yet, but I've got to prove myself. Work that bit harder." Jerry was getting into his stride now. Yes, this could work. "I'll have to work a lot of evenings, Late every night, I shouldn't wonder. Just until the redundancies get sorted, then we can all relax a bit." It was true. Mostly true.

Rachel was filling a bowl with soapy water, rinsing out the bottles. She shut off the tap, and the plumbing hammered through the house. She raised her eyebrows at Jerry and gave him her best sarcastic grimace.

The unmistakable cries of a woken Peanut rolled down the stairs and Rachel bowed her head, dejected. "Great." Her voice quavered.

"I will help, Rach, but I have to focus on work right now. You don't want me to lose my job, do you?" Ah, how easily it tripped off his tongue.

"No. Course not." Rachel loaded the steriliser, set it running, then trudged away and up the stairs.

TWENTY-TWO

Dragged up through the sticky syrup of consciousness, sucking pseudopodia of sleep held Rachel immobile. A baby's cry. She willed it away and clung instead to the cocoon that enveloped her reticent form. It had been low at first, but the pitch was rising, kitten-soft mews growing more insistent, more shrill. The bonds of slumber snapped and cracked. Responsibility raised an eyebrow to begin the slow peeling away of her first eyelid and then the other. Her body heavy and weary, she crawled out of bed and shivered into a shabby dressing gown. She'd need the warmth: this would take a while.

Head buzzing with the cries from the nursery, Rachel picked her way through the darkness of the house. Even on sleepy autopilot she could navigate without light. Kitchen, fridge, milk, microwave, yawn, ping. Pulled back up the stairs on a visceral cord.

She scooped Peanut from the cot and laid her in the familiar crook of her arm. Bottle in. Hungry sucks and slurps replaced the cries in an otherwise silent night, but it wasn't so easy. It never was. A minute or so in and Peanut paused to cough. She adjusted the position, let her settle and they were off again. It seemed OK, but then another cough, this time accompanied by a whimper of distress.

Rachel was wide awake now, all vestiges of sleep fallen from her, but the heavy weariness remained. Every three hours the ritual with Peanut began again. Another attempt to get it right. Another failure. She stared blindly into the darkness and monsters rose: her insecurity; her loneliness; her fate.

Jerry slept on: oblivious and uncaring. Rachel gritted her teeth and dislodged a tear from brimming eyes. She could see the series of mistakes she'd made now. How could anyone be so stupid? A pang of regret constricted her chest and she forced in a long deep breath.

People liked to complain about work: the boss and the politics; the internal memo and the petty power struggle. She'd done it herself. At the time it had been so important and consuming. Viewed from the outside now, Rachel could see that it didn't matter at all. At least at work you were your own person: making decisions; conversing with adults; achieving a goal. You had purpose and worth. You were significant. Now she was no-one. Trapped in a life she'd never imagined, with a baby she couldn't care for and a husband who was never home—a husband who was probably having an affair. She was fading away and could do nothing to stop it. All hope had turned to despair.

Grandma Ray's clock ticked out in the hall. She let her eyes lose focus and lost herself in the metallic drum beat, marking her passage through misery.

Isabell, bloody Isabell. It was obvious Jerry had been lying earlier about not helping her and she'd gone through his pockets once he'd fallen asleep. His jacket had offered up little to confirm her suspicions: sweet wrappers and tissue grit didn't make a philanderer. She'd checked his shirt collar for signs of Isabell's make-up and, of course, he wasn't that stupid, but it smelt of her. Something indefinable but familiar all the same. She'd lingered over it, analysing the aroma again and again, but couldn't be sure, that was the trouble. She was so tired. Her hormones were all over the place. There was no proof in the ghost of a smell.

The long black hair she'd found clinging to the back of Jerry's shirt felt like more solid evidence, however. Her own hair: much shorter and brown; Jerry's, shorter still. It had to be Isabell's. Would it be wrong to assume the worst?

Why couldn't Jerry have just blown her off? He'd chosen to marry her, Rachel. He'd chosen to bring a child into their world, encouraged Rachel to give up her career. But he hadn't given up anything at all. Not even his first wife. Always off to do something more pressing. "You know how she is," Jerry would say. Yeah, Rachel knew. Knew only too well.

She ground her teeth. Peanut whimpered and Rachel realised she was holding her too tight. She loosened her grip, but Peanut squirmed and coughed out a cry. Rachel looked down through the gloom at the infant in her arms and steeled herself.

No point fretting nor patting. No good would come from walking around the house, shushing and cooing. Hold her to the left, to the right, on her shoulder, at her waist. It was all the same. Rachel sat back in the nursery chair. If her baby was crying she wasn't choking. She was the best that she could be, until it passed.

Inside her mind Rachel backed away to a place with no sound where she wouldn't hear the anguish nor register the pain. If there was nothing she could do for Peanut then she had to do it for herself. Shut it out, before it destroyed her.

She started to hum and the vibrations filled her head. She focused on the buzz it made behind her teeth and counted the seconds she could make one breath last. The metallic tick and tock of Grandma Ray's clock gave structure. She focused on those sounds and nothing else and rocked side to side in the nursery chair. Side to side until it was over.

TWENTY-THREE

Sporting bright yellow washing up gloves and a peg on his nose, Jerry fumbled at the playsuit poppers without success. Bloody hell, he was going to have to take the gloves off.

He'd bundled Rachel off for a 'nice relaxing bath' and was taking charge of all things baby. So far, Peanut had been her usual insubordinate self, complaining and thrashing about in her Moses basket, and rumbles during the feed now led Jerry to believe that a nappy change was in order. They'd relocated to the nursery on Mission Diaper.

Pop, pop, pop. Peanut kicked her podgy legs free from the babygro and the scale of his assignment became clear. The pneumatic nappy oozed poo at its elasticated frills, out onto Peanut's legs and the inside of her sleep suit. Jerry gingerly peeled back the tapes, flopped the bulging packet forward and gagged. The peg meant breathing through his mouth—it didn't seem so smart now. He took it off and gagged anew as the smell assaulted his nostrils.

"Christ on a bike, Peanut. What has Mummy been feeding you?" Peanut waved her feet then stamped in the open nappy, spattering Jerry's shirt. He froze, cringing and scanned the room for inspiration. A smug Bilbo Bunny spectated from the safety of the cot.

A considerable range of baby equipment lined up on the shelves by the mat. Jerry pulled down a bag of cotton wool balls, grabbed a handful and hurled them into the nappy to prevent further poo stomping. Peanut paused to watch. Jerry grabbed another handful and attempted to wipe her down. The balls broke free and rolled gunk up onto his fingers. He stared at them in horror and then smeared his fingers on the mat. Lifting Peanut by the ankles with his free hand, he jammed the used balls beneath her—at least they couldn't roll away from there. He wasn't getting very far with the clean-up though.

Shifting Peanut to one side and then the other, he manoeuvred the noxious nappy out. Folding it up, he trapped most of the cotton wool inside then dumped it into a bag. Next, he pulled the ravaged babygro away and tossed it to the floor. Baby wipes pushed the poo around on her skin but didn't seem get it off. Curious. Tissues, more wipes: the pile of debris grew. At least Peanut was amused—she'd stopped crying and was watching Jerry flounder.

He managed to slap on a new nappy but, ignorant as to where fresh clothes were kept, he decided to defy convention and wind her up in a blanket from the cot instead. He was just sat relaxing with the baby sausage in his arms when Rachel appeared at the door.

She glanced from Peanut to Jerry, to the mess on the changing table and to the poo-smeared sleep suit flung on the carpet. She looked back at Jerry, frowning. "What are you doing?"

Jerry smiled, pretty pleased with himself. "Nappy change."
"No shit."
"No, plenty of shit. Really incredible."
"Why is she in a blanket?"
"Couldn't find any clothes."
"Did you try the wardrobe?"
Jerry shrugged.

Rachel scooped Peanut up, laid her in the cot, unfurled the bundle and transferred her to the mat. Jerry saw the orange-brown globs which framed a lone squelching cotton wool ball lingering on the blanket.

Rachel scowled at it and then him. She examined Peanut, the sticky brown-orange poop smeared up her back.

"For the love of God, Jerry. You have to clean her. You can't just pull off the nappy and fling on another."

"I did. I did." Up the back—wow, who'd have thought that?

Peanut kicked at the pile of spent wipes and tissues, sending it flopping to the floor. A suspect cotton wool ball rolled under the cot.

"For Christ's sake, Jerry, you can't just leave this stuff lying around. Tidy up after yourself. It's disgusting."

"I tried."

"No. You didn't try, Jerry. You made a half arsed attempt and then left it for me to sort out, just like always. There's crap on the carpet. Crap on the cot blanket. Crap up her back, on the mat. It's everywhere, Jerry." Rachel's voice was becoming thin and shrill. Rigid arms pointed clenched fists at the floor.

"It's just so hard to get off. I couldn't do it," Jerry mumbled.

"You're the adult, Jerry, you have to do it. She can't—it's up to you. Were you just going to leave her like that? Covered in crap? Because you can't DEAL with it?" She was pretty much screeching now.

Jerry examined the seam of the chair with a twitchy finger. The clock marked time in the hallway. He risked a glance at Rachel: she was glaring at him in furious silence.

The clock struck one. Time for Jerry to be off. "I'll just pop down to the kitchen to tidy up a bit then, shall I?" and he was out of his seat and heading down the stairs. Even at the bottom he could still hear Rachel ranting on about being better off on her own.

Downstairs the usual jumble of baby detritus mingled with day to day living. Jerry cleared the breakfast things from the table and dumped them into the sink. He gathered mugs from shelves and poured away half a dozen abandoned cups of tea. He gathered up newspapers and added them to the pile by the back door. Most of the table surface was visible now; only yesterday's post remained, unopened.

He sat down and tore at the envelopes. Phone bill—red. Council Tax direct debit form—urgent reminder. Jerry rubbed at his temples. The final envelope was from Legal & General and contained a confirmation of the change of details to Jerry's life insurance policy. Since the arrival of Peanut, they'd decided to increase their cover to a pay out of five hundred thousand pounds should Jerry shuffle off this mortal coil prematurely. Rachel had remembered to post back the form.

TWENTY-FOUR

"No time like the present," said Adam, stabbing at the treadmill controls to increase his stride to a jog. Jerry slunk onto his machine and set it to a stroll. "I could do without this today. Everyone wants a piece of me," he grumbled. "I was looking forward to some quality time at the Dog and Duck."

Adam reached over and increased the speed of Jerry's machine until he was tripping over himself to keep up and pumping his arms. "It's not that I can't do it," he said, "It's just another thing on the list."

"U-huh." Adam was in his stride. Jerry took his machine down a notch and shot a warning glance at Adam, who smirked and looked away.

"You wouldn't believe Spink," said Jerry. "Since Locksley put us into competition he's become an unscrupulous maniac. He's stolen my five biggest clients and I've spent the last week in serious damage control, talking to everyone I can manage so they don't defect to the little shit when I'm not looking." Jerry puffed along at his moderate pace. "Two hundred K straight off my bottom line already."

"So put in some hours. Get some new deals. Have you got any leads?" Adam was nonchalant.

"Put in some time?" Jerry whined, "Time is what I don't have. Crown Princess Pain-in-the-arse wants me to pretend we're still married to her mum and dad so she doesn't lose her allowance."

"To hell with that. Let her get on with it."

"No allowance, no mortgage payments. Negative equity. Major pain in the arse. Can't afford it," Jerry panted.

"Jeez. She's still got you by the balls, hasn't she?"

Jerry grimaced. "I'll have to go there after work and then sneak out when no-one is looking."

"And what does the mother of your child think about this?"

Jerry snorted. "Yeah, like I'd tell her. You know nothing."

Adam shook his head, eyebrows raised. "Don't you think she'll notice that you're never home?"

"I'll have to work extra to keep up with Spink anyway, I'll just exaggerate. I'm more worried about Princess Pain-in-the-arse than Rach. There was candlelight, Adam. She was offering no-strings sex and making up stuff to get me to stay. I think she might have gone a little la-la."

"She was la-la when I knew her years ago."

Jerry frowned and slowed his treadmill a bit more. That was true.

"So, you're turning absent father to run around after the nutcase. Very paternal."

"Yeah, I'm feeling a bit bad about it. Peanut's hard work. Rach is having a tough time. I guess I'm leaving her in the lurch a bit." Jerry bit at his lip. "It would be reassuring to know someone was looking in on her from time to time." Jerry focused on Adam, but he wouldn't look at him. A silent minute passed, then Adam sighed, "Do you want me to check on her?"

"Really? Would you? That would be great." Brilliant.

Adam shrugged. "Saving the universe, one person at a time."

TWENTY-FIVE

By eleven o'clock Monday morning, Adam had already spent a full three hours at Solomon's. A 10K run, his weights programme, a sauna and a long hot shower had eaten up the time, but he knew he was stretching it out. Truth was: he was bored.

Sitting in the locker room, he fingered the slip of paper in his pocket on which Jerry had scrawled his address. The house was only a couple of miles from the gym, a half hour walk tops. He had nothing better to do and a bit of fresh air wouldn't hurt.

He left Solomon's and kicked his way through the leaves that banked up against garden walls, wriggling his nose down into the scarf coiled at his neck. How had Jerry got him to volunteer for this? He didn't even know his wife. Was she going to want to let him in?

He marvelled at Jerry's ability to get himself into a jam. At school he'd been the same. Why do things the normal way when there was a convoluted 'easy' route that wouldn't work and always caused more trouble in the end?

He smiled to himself. Funny. Jerry was such a screw up, but somehow he'd managed to get married, twice, and have a baby—a course of events that had so far eluded Adam entirely.

Adam was supposed to be the successful one, but here he was, lost in his own life, desperately seeking what Jerry had just stumbled into. Jerry didn't even appreciate what he'd got. What was he thinking pandering to Isabell? Jerry's priorities were obvious. What could be more precious than his wife and newborn child?

Adam rounded the corner of Heath Terrace and started counting off the houses.

Where would he find her, his missing piece? His mind wandered back to the furniture shop and the girl on the sofa. Perhaps she had been it. Perhaps that striking resemblance to Grace had been the sign he'd needed to wake up and make the leap. Perhaps he had let her slip through his fingers and out of his life. His one true love.

Adam mentally kicked himself—he should have gone over to her. He wished that he had now. He could have sat down beside her on that huge sofa and brushed the hair from her sun-kissed face, or maybe just struck up a conversation as she wandered through the store, instead of skulking in the shadows, afraid to be seen. He should have joined her at that dining table.

Then Adam remembered her change of demeanour: how the happiness had fallen from her eyes. He could have taken her in his arms there and then. He could have comforted her. Instead, he'd never see her again.

37, this was it. Adam scraped the uncooperative gate across the path, took a deep breath and rang the bell. When the door opened, he blinked with disbelief. There in the doorway, smiling out at him, it was her: the girl from the shop. Adam stared, open mouthed.

"Can I help you?"

Adam's voice didn't seem to be working. He'd found her. The girl. His girl. What were the chances? He couldn't hold back the dopey grin.

"Are you OK?" Rachel looked as if she might be about to close the door.

Think. Think. Pull yourself together, Adam. "Adam," he blurted. "I'm Adam, Jerry's friend." Jerry's friend. Fuck, shit and bugger.

"Oh, Adam. Right. Jerry said you might be dropping by." She looked him up and down with undisguised scepticism. "Know much about babies, do you?"

Adam just looked at her and smiled.

"Well, you'd better come in."

Of all the shit luck: the one time in his life when he'd found a girl that could be someone to him and she was already Jerry's wife. Great. Adam tried to push the furniture shop scenes from his head as he followed her into the kitchen. No billowing skirt today. She wore leggings and an oversized jumper. The jumper had slipped from her shoulder on one side to reveal soft alabaster skin and the delicate strap of an undergarment.

She flicked on the kettle. "Tea?"

"Sure."

Reaching up, she pulled clean cups from the wall cupboard. Adam admired her long smooth neck and the desire to run his fingers down it welled unbidden. *Stop it. Jerry. Jerry. Jerry.*

"You have any children of your own?" Rachel asked.

"No." Adam felt like a fool. What help could he possibly be? "But I'd like to, one day." He smiled into her eyes and Rachel seemed to fluster. She turned away from him to make the tea.

"I'm guessing you've got experience of tidying up though, right?"

"Oh sure." Adam thought about his bleak apartment. It was very tidy. There was nothing there.

TWENTY-SIX

Sliding into her seat at the table, Rachel patted the chair to her left and Adam jumped to her side.

"So I guess you can see the place is a bit of a state." Rachel smiled, embarrassed. "Peanut just seems to take up all of my time." She stared down into her tea cup, as if the answer might be floating there.

"Peanut?"

"Oh," she laughed a little self-consciously and it made Adam smile. "We haven't been able to decide on a name. She looked like a peanut on the first scan so we started calling her that and I guess it stuck."

"Makes perfect sense." They smiled at each other.

It was too easy, too comfortable. He couldn't let himself relax around her, Adam knew where his easy charm could lead. He pulled himself back and got up from the table. "So, yep. I can tidy. Why don't you go and have a nap?"

"A nap? Do you mean it? Are you sure? That just seems so... decadent."

"No problem. Honestly. I am Jerry's stand in." *Jerry's stand in*, Adam sighed.

"OK. If you're sure?" Rachel scraped out her chair and made for the door. She paused by Adam's side. "Thank you," she breathed and reaching up on tiptoe, brushed her lips against his cheek.

That scent he'd first encountered in the furniture store swept up to him, swirled around his chest and brought every nerve ending to electrified life. Cinnamon and citrus. He closed his eyes and let it linger. When he opened them again, he was alone, Rachel's footsteps on the stairs. He clenched his jaw and commanded his feet not to follow her.

It was ridiculous of course. Jerry's wife, hello. His old best friend, Jerry. Good old Jerry. Best buddy Jerry. Jerry, who he hadn't seen for years until a month ago. Jerry, who was actually lying to Rachel so that he could spend time with his ex-wife. Jerry, who didn't make any time for his own child. Jerry, who didn't know a good thing when he had it. Jerry, who obviously didn't deserve it.

Adam shook his head to quiet the demons. *Stop it. Let's just tidy this up and get out of here.* He zoned out and set his mind on the task at hand. Crockery and cutlery washed, dried and put away. He mopped the floor and wiped down the surfaces. He'd even folded some of the laundry, but had to abandon the task when several items of Rachel's underwear came to the fore. A man has his limits.

He was just getting ready to leave when she appeared holding Peanut. Her cheeks flushed pink and her hair falling in shaggy waves. She looked around the room in disbelief. "Oh my God. Look what you did." She was smiling ear to ear. Adam couldn't help but glow a little inside. He shrugged and pushed his hands down into his pockets to stop himself from pulling her into his arms. "Well, I've got to be going. See you another time." It wasn't safe to stay.

Rachel stepped into the room toward him, but he barrelled past her out into the hall.

"Bye then," she called after him.

He clicked the door shut behind himself and set off up the road at a run.

TWENTY-SEVEN

Jerry read to the end of the final paragraph and flipped his proposal shut with a nod. Never at his best in the word processing package, he'd actually managed to produce an impressive document. Several more hours later than perhaps a more proficient typist but, a good day's work none-the-less. Staccato keystrokes rattled his printer to life and sent the client copy spewing out into in a little grey tray on the edge of his desk.

From the doorway Gemma coughed and stuttered into speech. "Mr Adler, I'm so sorry I couldn't help with your copying earlier. Mr Spink has me flat out."

"Hey, no problem, Gemma, really." Jerry scraped his chair around to face her.

"It's just, um, I could try to help tomorrow…" she tailed off, unconvinced.

She was just a kid. How could he expect her to stand up to Spink when it was tough enough for him? "Listen, thanks for the thought, but I can see you've got your hands full." He eyed the huge stack of files in her arms with a single raised eyebrow. She cracked a shy smile. "OK, well, I'll help if I can," she mumbled and scuttled away.

Jerry wrestled the fat proposal into an envelope and sloped around to Reception to put it in the post. Margi, the receptionist, had her back to him, pumping a great stack of envelopes through the franking machine.

"Can we send this one first class please, Margi?"

She turned to look at him, lost her rhythm and jammed a couple of envelopes in the rollers. "Sure, sure," she sighed, "Just got to get this mail shot out for Donald." Jerry's eyes prickled with tiredness. Mail shot? He scanned the heap of letters on the floor—about eighty or so at a guess. He weighed the solitary envelope in his hand with dismay.

Margi took it from him. "Don't worry, it'll go today." Jerry pressed his lips together in a tight smile of thanks then beat a sullen retreat to his office. Behind the closed door he flopped into his chair and slumped over the desk.

Immediately the phone rang and he clutched the handset to his ear, eyes closed. "Adler."

"No forget, Jerry, flight IB7462 landing eight-ten tonight. Mama is very excite to see you."

Jerry doubted that. Mama was not Jerry's biggest fan, although it was difficult to deduce exactly what she thought. Past communication had consisted of clipped translations via

Isabell's father and a fantastic quantity of tuts, sneers and vigorous arm waving. Jerry sank a little into his mental quagmire. "OK, yes."

"We will have family dinner together or they will wondering why."

Jerry grimaced. And so it began.

"Jerry?"

"Yes, Isabell. Yes."

She hung up.

The window frame rattled and the cold breath of autumn brushed across his knuckles in the already freezing office. Outside a persistent wind whipped around the grey car park and vexed the last limp leaves from defeated trees. He kicked the heater under his desk for old time's sake, pulled out his mobile and rattled off a text:

HI RACH. STILL IN MTG. TAKING CLIENT TO DINNER. DON'T WAIT UP. JX

Ah, texting—the fraudster's friend. Jerry spun the phone on his desk, awaiting the reply. When it beeped he snatched it up and scanned the message for signs of suspicion.

LUCKY YOU. TRY NOT TO WAKE US UP WHEN YOU COME IN. RX.

Lucky you? A touch of testiness there, but not disbelief. Seemed about right. Good, she'd bought it.

TWENTY-EIGHT

Isabell swirled her fingers on the bed's satin quilt and appraised the contents of her walnut armoire. The array of men's charity shop clothes, now laundered, pressed and hung, made a persuasive wardrobe for her 'husband', Jerry. Yes, it would serve her purpose nicely. She closed the doors and swept away to the bathroom to lay out items at the sink.

A daub of shaving foam smeared by the tap would lend a little authenticity. A plastic razor, popped from its pack also took its place in her charade. She slid away the protective cover and overhead halogens glinted on the blades. Isabell ran her fingertip along their biting edge.

A scarlet bead dropped to the cold enamel and Isabell sucked in a slow breath. She let the razor fall from her hand and squeezed out another drop and then another. The woman in the mirror shook out her long black mane, down over an arched back. There was no need to make a drama, but the sting felt sweet. Jerry was coming, coming to rescue her. She allowed herself a little smile then washed the blood away.

The razor landed, clinking, into a glass by the sink, followed by a toothbrush torn from its wrapper. Lastly, his aftershave. Isabell held the new bottle of Paco Rabanne in her hand—an old brand, but Jerry still wore it. He was a creature of habit. She snapped off the lid and returned to the armoire to spritz its contents and breathed in the memories of Marsaskala and their honeymoon. Romantic days spent exploring the hot dry landscape with passionate nights in their freshly made marital bed, exploring each other.

Of course, it couldn't last. Jerry was a pussycat, all fluff and belly rubs. He'd been overwhelmed and eventually cowered from her claws, instead of facing her down like the predator she'd wanted. But his domesticity fell in her favour now: Jerry would do what he was told.

Isabell padded out of the bedroom and made for the kitchen. She would need to be ready by nine to provide her family with an evening meal. Jerry would be on his way to Heathrow by now. Doing what he was told.

On her way down the stairs, Isabell noticed their wedding photo listed at an angle on the hallway wall. She blew its dusty top clean and set it straight. She'd have to have a word with the cleaner about attention to detail, especially now that she'd be so busy, looking after her family.

The kitchen was primed: her ingredients already gathered together in an organised line up. It took no more than a minute to stab the chicken, over and over with the stubby vegetable knife, making holes to ease in slivers of garlic. A quick rub over with herbed butter and the bird was ready for the hot hell of the oven.

Drawing out a long chef's knife from the block, she glimpsed a flash of herself in its surface. Olive skin. Dark hair. She adjusted the hair extension clipped in at the back of her scalp and undid another button at her bosom. If she could persuade Jerry to stay tonight, so much the better.

With long sweeps she carved the peppers into tender strips; and sliced spring onion to the same even dimensions. Both were added to the baby leaf green salad and a dressing whisked up in a jug to be added later.

Red fingernails drummed the granite, impatient for the game to begin. She was ready.

TWENTY-NINE

Jerry squirmed on the metal bench, switching his weight from left to right buttock. The Iberia 7912 still hadn't made an appearance and he was getting restless. Not that he was in any great hurry to see Isabell's parents again, but time was marching on and he didn't want to be too late getting home.

Jerry shared the Arrivals Hall with a sprinkling of other unfortunates, who either leaned against pillars or patrolled the shiny concrete floor with slow sweeping footsteps, their hands pushed deep into their pockets. He'd watched their progress, pacing like fellow caged animals, but was only able to maintain so much interest in other people's boredom. He took a slurp of bitter coffee and considered Remi's progress.

The hilltop retreat just outside of Avignon made a perfect meeting place for the philanthropic investors of the Crusaders of Justice. A picturesque stone built citadel set high in the hills provided lofty solitude for men gathered to contemplate the welfare of the world, men whose investments would bring equality for the persecuted and the poor. Or so they thought. Maximus Pink had chosen the location carefully: a place where his targets would feel the privilege of their existence and be even more compelled to help the third world peoples the COJ purported to assist.

Maximus Pink stood before the enormous limestone fireplace that stretched eight feet across the far wall of the central state room. A fire crackled in its hearth. The evocative click and spit of burning wood enhanced his stage with reminders of comfort and home. Its warm glow back-lit Pink in an angelic halo. He cupped a large glass of cognac in his left palm and swirled it slowly. Remi watched his expression warm with recognition as a balding man in his late fifties crossed the room to greet him. To the unsuspecting, Pink gave a great show of philanthropy, but Remi knew the truth.

Attending the meeting as Charles Bamford-Irons, Remi was taking a chance. His timely exit from the blackjack game at the Bellagio had been the perfect end to his charade, but now he had his work cut out to gain the trust of the group.

Maximus chinked lightly on the cognac glass with his emerald pinkie ring and the room fell silent. "Gentlemen and loyal supporters. Thank you all for taking the time out from your schedules to attend our little gathering, here in the beautiful hills of southern France. Now that our dinner has concluded, I have exciting developments to share with you.

Please, collect a digestif from our hostesses and follow me down to the presentation."

Waitresses in high-buttoned shirts with dove grey ties and waistcoats held loaded trays either side of now open double doors, and the small crowd started its slow transfer to the next location in Maximus Pink's production. His audience looked to be mostly European well-heeled men in sober suits, ages ranging from middle age to long past retirement, men with money to spend.

With the brush of feet on the sumptuous carpet came the return of conversation, rising volume punctuated with good-natured enthusiasm and champagne-fuelled laughter. Remi took his place amongst them: Charles Bamford-Irons in full flow.

"Fabulous meal, wouldn't you say? These fellows really know how to look after you, don't they?" Remi smiled congenially at the businessman strolling casually by his side.

"Oh yes," the man agreed, "They're certainly making us comfortable."

"Now for the sting."

"Yes, time to separate us from our money." He gave an easy laugh, delighted to be part of this fundraising venture. "All in a good cause."

"Indeed."

Remi took a cognac and flowed with the river of men down into the vaults of the ancient building, into a room with no windows for prying eyes. Great curves of ivory painted brick spanned the ceiling in three bounds and beneath the central arch a silent video played out, its images agitated by the rough surface. Starving children, villages washed away by floods and makeshift refugee camps. The contrast to the dinner they had just left was powerful and immediate.

At a small rostrum the presenters waited patiently for their guests to take their seats and as bodies lowered into chairs Remi noticed that Kitty Princesa was amongst them. He ducked down into a seat. If she recognised him it would be a disaster—his cover blown. He had to get what he came for and get out fast.

Remi's mission was to steal a monogrammed flash drive owned by Maximus Pink. Intelligence shots pictured him wearing it on a long fine chain around his neck and Intel suspected that it never left his person. He'd have it with him here tonight, probably be wearing it right now.

"Charles! So glad you could make it!"

Remi looked up surprised and stood, turning his back totally on Kitty, trying to hide his identity from her. "Maximus, how could I miss it?" He reached out and shook his outstretched hand.

"You're feeling well now, I hope?" Pink's eyes pinched into a squint that searched Remi's face.

"No cards tonight. Give the old ticker a rest." Remi offered a shrug and a bashful smile.

"Good. Good." Pink patted him on the shoulder. "I must get backstage. Get my facts and figures uploaded." He pulled from his pocket the flash drive, distinctive crest just visible below his grip.

"Right. See you later."

Remi ducked back down into his seat to watch Maximus disappear behind a screen at the side of the room and emerge again a few minutes later. Lights dimmed and the sound kicked in on the video. Children crying. The COJ were going straight for the heart. Kitty stood at the rostrum with Maximus and another man Remi recognised from intelligence as her brother. They'd never crossed paths and he'd no intention of meeting her family tonight. He flicked a look back to the door they'd come in through and saw that security had followed them into the room. Men wearing wires to their ears now stood at the doors.

Remi suspected the flash drive now lay behind that screen, possibly in the hands of a technician running the presentation from backstage. The path from his seat was clear, but totally exposed.

"Forgotten my glasses," he mumbled to the man on his right. "I'll have to get up a bit closer." A powerful orchestral element climbed in the video soundtrack and with all eyes on the screen, Remi slipped out of his seat. He walked evenly down to the front and dipped at the last moment behind the screen.

A single technician, dressed entirely in black, sat at a sound desk with a laptop off to one side. "No guests are allowed back stage, sir," he said, but did not take his eyes from the screen he was working from. Remi saw the flash drive plugged into its side. "I've an extra presentation to tag on at the end," said Remi, digging in his inside pocket and producing some folded papers. He had the technician's attention now, an expression of annoyance plain on his face. "Last minute changes won't look professional. I'm not a miracle worker, you know."

"Just do the best you can." Remi spread the pages over the laptop, shuffling from one to the next, unplugging the drive under their cover. "Not this one, not this one, damn where's the page? I must have left it in my briefcase. I'll be back in a minute."

The technician raised his eyebrows to stare at Remi with undisguised disdain. "Don't be too long about it or there won't be time to get it online."

Remi slipped the flash drive into his pocket, nodded his head and slipped back out into the room, heart pounding.

He moved smoothly along the room's edge, pulled his phone from his inside pocket and pretended to answer a call, before clutching it to his shoulder. The security men at the door stared at him with emotionless faces and as Remi approached he gave them an apologetic look. "No phones are allowed in the auditorium, sir," growled the smaller of the two.

"Absolutely. Quite understand, but must take this call so I'll just pop into the corridor, if I may?" They stared at each other for a moment, the henchman scanning Remi's face for signs of trouble. He smiled back amiably, but could feel beads of sweat forming on his brow. The henchman stepped to the side to let him through as the presentation abruptly ground to a halt—the video replaced with a black screen and the white words 'file not found'.

Remi leapt through the door and ran. Behind him the technician could be heard shouting out, "The drive! He took the drive!" and hubbub rose from the audience. He flicked a glance over his shoulder; security were in pursuit, heavy muscular bodies pounding along the carpet twenty yards behind.

The slope from the vaults led out into an airy reception where more security flanked the doors so Remi scaled the stairs instead, three steps at a time in great leaps that took him up four flights, before he turned off to race down a corridor. He hoped to have put a little time between him at the heavy security, lumbering their body weight behind him. Time to try some doors. The first—locked. The next, locked too. He ran at the third, blasting it open with his shoulder. The suite had great French doors which opened out onto the magnificent view, but the drop of four floors was likely to hurt. He scanned left and right—to his right a gently slopped roof with rounded clay tiles. Remi stepped up onto the rail of the balcony and leapt, landing like a cat and streaking away along its ridge.

The tiles cracked and clicked beneath his feet, but held firm. To his left the vertiginous drop continued, but to the right a series of balconies took in the magnificent view. Remi side-stepped down the roof and dropped over the edge to land in a crouch on the balcony floor. Thuds and cracks came from the roof far behind him—security were lumbering their way over the tiles. He had to keep moving. Two further balconies stepped out from the magnificent old building below. Remi stepped over the stone balustrade and gripping the fat ledge, lowered himself down to the next level. And then again, and again to the shaded terrace.

Relieved to be back on solid ground, Remi ran at full sprint, leaping over the loungers by the pool and streaking out under a gothic arch to a field of gravel. With a squeeze of the button in his pocket the indicators of his Maserati Granturismo flashed once with a comforting bleep and he slid into its safe haven with a laugh. He punched the engine into life and roared out of the car park in a spray of gravel.

The road ahead wound down through trees and then out into open farm land. The road snaked right and then back to run alongside the perimeter wall of the citadel. Remi glanced up. Security were still on the roof.

THIRTY

The front door flew open as Jerry rolled the Fiat to a halt and Isabell rushed out to the car: all waving arms and flapping hair. "Mama! I've missed you so much!" Isabell's mother, Domitila, heaved herself out of the back seat, great rolls of fat jiggling at her sides. She squeezed Isabell's arms and smeared her face with kisses. "My baby!" Isabell swept away her mother's tears of joy with painted fingertips and Jerry retreated to the back of the car to wrestle suitcases from the Tetris puzzle boot.

Isabell's father, Arlo, joined the Mediterranean scrum. "Papa! Oh, Papa!" More kissing and jostling. Jerry kept a low profile. What was wrong with a nice firm handshake anyway?

They washed into the house on a wave of emotion, leaving Jerry behind the luggage barricade, his shoulders slumped. Ten exhausting minutes later, he'd hauled all six cases to the foot of the stairs and was feeling uneasy about going any farther. This was Isabell's place now and going upstairs felt like crossing a line. Besides, with all action currently focussed in the kitchen, this was an excellent chance to slip into the unoccupied lounge instead.

Listening out all the time, he crept across to the bureau in the corner and picked through the paperwork. Isabell's credit card statement didn't take long to find and he stuffed it into his trouser pocket. Thank God Isabell couldn't use that against him anymore. Getting it out of her clutches almost made this whole charade worthwhile. He gave himself a mental pat on the back for his Remi-like stealth and ambled back out to the hallway, considering his escape.

Hubbub rose from the kitchen and Isabell caught his eye and waved him over. Too late to run, he sidled in and leant just inside the doorway, keeping a safe distance. "Come. Come. Everybody sit," Isabell cooed, wafting people toward the kitchen table, now laden with food. Mama was there like a shot, heaping the best of the chicken onto her plate before Jerry had even been coerced into his chair. Isabell flapped. She poured drinks, fetched napkins, brought salt and olive oil. Eventually she settled into the chair beside Jerry, who gawped at her. Was she wearing an apron? Isabell beamed at him then leant in and kissed him square on the lips. "How was work, darling?"

Jerry thought his eyes might pop out of his head. "Excellent. Yes, excellent," he stuttered. Mama puffed out a sigh and mumbled something to which Arlo grunted in reply. No kissing! That was not part of the arrangement. He gave Isabell a dig under the table. She just smiled.

"We are very busy," he said loud and slow for the benefit of Arlo.

"Uh-huh." Arlo munched on a mouthful of salad.

"I will be working a lot while you are here," he bellowed, "So you might not see much of me."

Isabell was scowling. "But you wanted to be here tonight, to welcome Mama and Papa. Jerry has been so exite about you visit." Isabell cranked up her smile.

"My favourite in-laws," Jerry enunciated.

"Favourite?" Arlo frowned at him.

"Ha, ha." Jerry was still slow and loud. Isabell kicked him.

"Anyway," he rubbed at his shin, "I am very tired and I still have work to do. *Muy* -" he tipped his head to one side, put his hands together underneath, then made little snoring noises.

Arlo and Domitila stared at him.

"*Por el amor de Dios.*" Domitila muttered, shaking her head.

Isabell's smile was looking a bit forced. "Si, you are working so hard. Please, go finish your work. I will making a sandwich for you." Isabell jumped up, pulling Jerry from his seat and on toward the hallway.

Once in the hall, Jerry scanned around for his coat. "Right, I'll be off then."

"Upstairs. Take cases with you."

Jerry choked out a laugh. "I am not going up there."

"Jerry, you can no leave," Isabell hissed. "Is too early. Mama and Papa only just get here. Please, wait until they go to bed. Please, Jerry. You can no just disappear."

"Bloody hell, Isabell." Jerry wrung his hands and looked up the stairs.

She gave him a shove and he stumbled up a step.

"I need to go home."

"One hour. Papa might want to speak to you. Man to man."

"What? Why?"

Isabell pouted and examined her nails.

"Isabell."

"Papa wants a grandchild. He want to know where is his grandchild."

Jerry flapped his arms. "No way, Isabell. I am not having that conversation with him."

"Say you are focus on work to make a good home. Is OK."

"Isabell," Jerry whined and wrung his hands some more.

"Cases, Jerry!" She clapped her hands and Jerry jumped to scuttle up the stairs, first case in his grip. OK, so he'd just get the cases to their room and then plot his escape.

By the time he'd thrown the sixth into the guest room, he was sweating and struggling for breath. He leant against the banister rail, opposite the open door to Isabell's bedroom, and noted its mood-lit opulence with a sigh. He could see she was making good use of all that money he gave her every month. He checked down the stairs and found it devoid of witnesses.

Just a quick look then. Hand over mouth, he crossed the threshold.

All the furniture was different now, but the room still felt familiar. He couldn't resist a peek in the en-suite. He knew that Isabell had had it redone since the split. Nice, very nice. Was that Italian marble? He drummed his fingers on it then noticed the men's toiletries. What was this? Did Isabell have a boyfriend? That put a new perspective on things. At last, a tool he could use. He pictured the scene: Arlo and Domitila pacing the room, Jerry laid out on the sofa 'weeping'. "Isabell, how could you? Another man!" Yeah, that had potential for an easy out. Look at that, he wore Paco Rabanne too. What a coincidence.

Jerry ambled out into the bedroom, listening for signs of anyone else on the first floor. A little peep in the wardrobe. Hmm. As he thought, full of men's clothes. Isabell was in trouble now. He'd run downstairs and pull her parents up here right now to show them the evidence. Ha.

Pretty strong on the old Paco in there. Did he bathe in it? Jerry fingered through the hangers, looking at labels. Nothing designer, a bit of M&S and labels he'd never heard of. Old stuff in here mostly. Didn't seem like an Isabell kind of bloke. Who would wear this stuff?

Jerry flopped down onto the bed and the penny dropped. Isabell had set it up for their charade. Damn, she was good. Jerry gnawed at a fingernail.

Voices drifted up the stairwell, Arlo and Domitila were moving to the lounge for coffee. Released from the confines of the meal, Arlo might fancy a chat. Jerry checked his watch: 9:40. Rachel would be wondering where he was. The idea of defending their choice to not have children yet to Arlo, when he had one waiting at his real home with his real wife did not appeal. Bugger that, Isabell would just have to make something up about him falling asleep. He was out of there.

He crept out onto the landing and tiptoed down the first three steps. The lounge door gaped at the foot of the stairs and voices spilled out into the hallway. Jerry scuttled back up to the bedroom. Clearly, there was a good chance of being spotted trying to go out of the front door. No, he'd have to climb out of the bedroom window. He slid it open and peered out into the gloom.

Below, terracotta pots stood sentry either side of the French doors from the kitchen. Could he jump it and go out the back gate? Possibly, but he didn't know if Isabell was still masquerading as a domestic goddess, tidying up after the meal. He scanned left and right. The flat roof of the garage finished in a small lip to the right. At a stretch, he might be able to reach round with one foot if he stood on the windowsill. Remi wouldn't have thought twice.

Jerry eased himself out onto the sill and tentatively straightened up, grasping at the brickwork. The crisp evening air ruffled his hair. Jerry pushed it back with his hand then shuffled around to face the window. The bedroom looked soft and inviting and a hell of a lot warmer. The hair on his arms stood on end.

Now that he was out here, it seemed somewhat higher. He shuffled to the end of the ledge, gripped the window frame with his right hand and stretched his left across the bricks. With his very fingertip he could feel the corner.

That was good. If he could just reach his foot around to the lip of the roof he could escape. He stretched his left leg out, scraping his battered brogue across the ragged surface. Shirt buttons scratched between his chest and the wall, sending a fine shower of grit raining down to the patio below. As his toe found the ledge a key turned in a lock beneath him. Jerry held his breath. Arlo stepped out through the French doors to the patio and lit a cigarette.

Beads of sweat sprang from Jerry palms and a momentary woozy blackness crept across his vision. He risked a glance down. Arlo had sat on a patio chair facing away from the house for a smoke. This ledge was actually pretty high. Jerry's leg trembled in its unnatural position, his big toe complaining under the pressure.

Arlo grumbled something to himself and Jerry risked another glance. He was rubbing at his arms, feeling the chill. *Go in. Go in. Yes, it's cold. Bugger off. Bugger off all the way back to Spain.* Jerry pressed his face into the wall. His hand was starting to slip on the frame and his right leg cramped.

The cigarette smoke snaked around him and tickled at his nostrils. God, Jerry could do with a fag. He'd given up when Rachel got pregnant and hadn't had one since, but the addiction still nagged. Jerry sucked it in through his nose. Arlo fidgeted in his chair. He was mumbling again.

Jerry heard the chair scrape on the patio, a couple of footsteps then quiet. *Please go in. Please.* The muscles in Jerry's legs were screaming. Then the glorious squeak of a door handle, the moan of a hinge and the tumble of a lock. Jerry risked a glance down—Arlo had gone.

Right. He looked along the wall and assessed the garage roof beyond. He'd need some momentum to get around the corner. If he pushed off hard from the sill to shift his bodyweight to the other foot, with a bit of luck he could hurl himself onto the garage roof.

The patio loomed hard and unwelcoming in his peripheral vision and the wall stretched out ahead. The jump didn't seem quite so doable now that cramp had set in. *Come on, Jerry, in for a penny.* He took a deep breath and launched.

The side of Jerry's face scraped along the wall and his numb toe gave way, slipping from the lip. There was nowhere to go but down.

The potted conifer jabbed its needles into Jerry's plummeting behind before snapping beneath him, shattering the pot. At least it had broken his fall. Locking eyes, albeit briefly, with Isabell as he'd fallen past the kitchen window, Jerry suspected that she'd have preferred it if it hadn't.

THIRTY-ONE

The sun shone down on Heath Terrace and glinted in the glass of Victorian sash windows, thrown open to welcome unseasonably warm autumn air. Adam strolled along the pavement, the tips of his fingers tracing the mortar in a low wall. Soft moss caught beneath his fingernails, its cool velvety texture in contrast to the rough stubble of brick. Heath Terrace wasn't really on his way to the gym, but he'd taken to parking a few streets away and walking the last bit. A warm up, if you like. An opportunity to breathe in a bit of oxygen, before shutting himself away in the stale aired box that was Solomon's. And you never knew who you might meet, of course, out in the real world. Or see. Just for a minute or two.

Number 25. He slowed his pace to a dawdle, the flaking blue front door of number 37 in plain sight ahead. He'd seen her coming out, about this sort of time before. This time last week he'd seen her walking with the pram, head bowed against the wind that day. It was just coincidence they'd walked the same way. Her, toward the church hall and him, the gym. He'd held back, not wanting to allow himself to get too close, but close enough to see her. Close enough to see her chestnut hair swept back in waves from delicate features. Close enough to see her gazelle-like frame slip through a crack in the church hall door and out of sight. Far enough to keep the dream from reality.

Pulled back into the here and now, Adam's pulse quickened to see the blue front door draw open. The hooded canopy of a pram came through first followed by Rachel, squinting into the sun. Adam upped his pace to meet her at the gate. "Rachel! Fancy seeing you here!" he blurted. She looked up into his eyes and Adam snapped them away to his shoes. "Well I do live here," she said.

"Going out?"

"Yes. Actually I'm a bit late. Peanut, well, you know." Rachel rubbed at her face with the palm of her hand and Adam followed its path to her jaw. Lilac shadows stretched down onto her cheeks and made her green eyes shine.

"Keeping you up?"

"Yes, look, I've got to…"

"Right, yes." Adam snapped out of his gaze. "Come on, I'll walk with you."

Rachel set off up the road at a surprising pace, Adam dipping in and out behind her avoiding lampposts.

"So where are you off to?" Adam enquired, trying to sound nonchalant.

"Baby group. Jammy Jingles." Rachel sighed. She tucked her hair behind her ear.

"Ah, lovely. Quality mother and baby time." Adam thought of all the other new mums, all filled with love for their little ones, just like Rachel. It would be a beautiful scene.

Rachel huffed. "Yeah, great. A room full of hormonal nutters waving their babies' hands about singing nonsensical songs. I mean who actually winds bobbins?"

"Er…"

"And do you think that Peanut gives a stuff about what the wheels on the bus are doing? Do you think she even understands? No, of course not. But you have to do the smiling, and the simpering and the lovely sing-song tone of voice because that's what babies like, isn't it?"

Adam gazed at her, mouth flapping. "Doesn't sound like *you* like it much."

"It's a lot of nonsense."

"Then why are you going?"

"Because I have to. The Health Visitor has a desk at the back and I have to check Peanut in, weigh her, that sort of stuff." Rachel sighed again and let her shoulders sag. Adam resisted the enormous temptation to put his arm around her and give her a squeeze. He gave her a nudge with his elbow instead. "Ah come on. It doesn't sound as bad as all that. I'll come in with you if you like."

Rachel stopped walking then and looked up to him, her eyes searching his face for the truth of it. "God, you would as well, wouldn't you? I can barely even get Jerry to make up a bottle and here you are offering to brave hell."

Adam shrugged and looked away, abashed. "I'd do it for you," he mumbled but Rachel had set off again, up the road, talking away.

"I couldn't do it to you. I don't want to scare you off. You might never come and tidy my house again." She shot him a small smile over her shoulder and Adam thought that she could never scare him away. They walked on in silence and reached the door of the church hall in a couple of minutes.

Rachel looked down at her clothes and smoothed them with her hands, as if seeing them for the first time. "Look at the state of me."

Adam looked and saw nothing to worry about. Skinny blue jeans were rolled up to reveal slim ankles and a chunky knit cream jumper hung to mid-thigh. She wore the floral pumps he'd seen in the shop.

"I think you look adorable," Adam said and when he saw her eyebrow twitch, regretted it immediately. "OK, well I've got to get to the gym. Enjoy Hell." He clasped his hands together and marched away, leaving her in a stunned silence.

Solomon's was only another five minutes' walk, but he got there in two, heart pounding and sweaty. He tried not to think about her as he raced up the stairs and into the locker room. He focussed only on his breathing, striding out on the treadmill and put her totally out of his mind concentrating on the free weights and technique, but the man in the mirror looked sad and alone.

THIRTY-TWO

Grandma Ray's clock beat a slow march. Every hypnotic stroke dragging at the eyelids Rachel fought to keep open. Tick. Tock. Tick. Tock. Her head bobbed with the metallic throb: a dishevelled conscript plodding on.

Peanut lay asleep in the crook of her arm. A still full bottle of milk balanced on the worn chintz of the nursery chair arm. All was quiet apart from the clock. They were alone in the house. Alone again.

She looked down into Peanut's peaceful face. It was so tempting not to wake her, to let her sleep on and hope that she didn't wake up at two or three or four. She longed for a reprieve, for just one night of unbroken sleep.

Deep down she knew that without this ten o'clock feed there was no chance of Peanut sleeping through. She had to wake her. Surrender to the ritual. Push in the nutrients and vent the tears. Why so many tears? Why couldn't she get it right? Why was she such a useless mother? Peanut was better off asleep. Maybe better off dead.

Rachel sighed and stared blindly down at the floor. The night light oozed its scarlet glow across the carpet, pooling at her feet. The image of the sharp chef's knife, downstairs in the drawer, dropped uninvited into her mind.

Now that could stop the tears; stop the maddening screaming that punctuated every night and day. Rachel's head buzzed and exhaustion closed her eyes before the tears could rise.

How desperate to even think it.

Peanut stretched a slow arm out above her head and flexed her spine, breaking Rachel's train of thought and the sleepy lull. How gratefully she took the bottle, welcomed it, as if she had no memory of what would inevitably follow. But now it was out of her hands so Rachel accepted the decision made and retreated into the old armchair's hollow.

The nursery glowed hazy red around them, waning into the dark corners where Rachel's demons prowled. Bilbo Bunny stood guard at the edge of the cot. Vigilant and reproachful, he stared Rachel down.

Rachel again. Always Rachel. Where was Jerry? A muscle ticked under her eye and she shifted in her seat.

He'd been the one that liked children so much: the one to home in on a kid with a football for an impromptu game; the one with the comedy voices to send nieces and nephews off into howls of laughter. He'd seemed like such a good prospect as a father, but now that he actually had a child, he was nowhere to be seen. Even when he was there he was bloody useless.

She'd been tricked into this. She'd never have given up her life before if she'd known just how awful it would be. This was all Jerry's fault.

He'd tempted her down a sunny path and buggered off when the weather changed. She didn't recognise this place, this gloomy swamp. A shadow of her former self: undefined and irrelevant, who was she now?

An incompetent mother.

She fought against the guilty weight, but the sticky mud of depression sucked at her weak limbs. Hopeless. Lost. Drowning. Her laughing husband had turned to smoke. There was no substance to cling to, to haul herself out of the mire.

She looked down again at the infant in her lap. Peanut had fallen back to sleep, the teat of the bottle, released from her mouth, hanging ignored in mid-air. She looked so peaceful and the milk in the bottle was only a quarter gone. Rachel pressed her lips together. To let her sleep on almost certainly meant she'd be up again in the night, but it did mean peace now and that release from duty was too good to turn down.

Rachel levered herself out of the chair, laid Peanut as gently as she could in the cot and crept away to her own bedroom. She was so desperately tired. Sleep now and things might feel better later, at two or whenever she got woken.

She shed her clothes to the floor where she stood and flopped down on the edge of the bed to pull a favourite old T-shirt over her head. Teeth, she really ought to clean her teeth. Rachel stared blindly forward for a moment, trying to summon up the energy to go to the bathroom, but then something caught her eye. A tiny paper corner poked out of an improbable place at the top of the chest of drawers in front of her. She reached forward and brushed her fingertips over it to see if it was a trick of the light, but no, the paper bent and flipped back into place. Mystified, Rachel rose to squint at it.

There was a millimetres gap running beneath the top edge of the drawers and the facia below, through which the paper point had escaped. She pinched at it and pulled. Out came an unfamiliar page, clearly part of a credit card statement. Transactions from the month before listed down its length. 'Regal Beauty', 'Karen Millen', 'Phase Eight': luxury shops that Rachel did not buy from. 'Glamour Nails', 'Duchess Spa', the list when on. What the hell was this? Rachel peered in through the tiny gap where this mystery had come from, but it was too dark to see anything else. Perhaps if she poked about with a knife she might be able to dislodge something else.

Fuelled by intrigue, she retrieved a slender chef's knife from the kitchen and returned to jab ineffectively through the gap. She couldn't get hold of anything, but all her probing made the facia move. A drawer. It was a drawer. She pressed in random places hoping to release a lock, but nothing happened. She pulled at the sides and found that it simply slid forward. A secret drawer at the top of the chest. She'd never known it was there. Jerry's secret drawer.

Wide-eyed, she scanned over its contents. Passports, a few scattered cufflinks, a watch and a pile of papers. She scooped them up. It was indeed a credit card statement. Pages and pages, chock full with line after line of luxury purchases. 'Selfridges', 'John Lewis', 'Ocado'—again and again. She flipped through to find a cover page. Jeremy Adler, 15 Grove Gardens, his old address, but the date was recent: last month. The balance was over twelve thousand pounds. Rachel collapsed to the bed. What the hell? She'd never seen anything about this card before. The other papers proved to be more credit card statements, much older, dating back a couple of years, with balances less terrifying, but still into four digits. The beneficiaries listed all had a similar feel: luxurious and feminine.

It came to Rachel in a wash of clarity: Jerry hadn't been weaning Isabell off him, he'd been pandering to her, supporting her, giving her exactly what she wanted. For years! The proof was there to see. While she'd scrimped and saved, Isabell had got exactly what she'd wanted, always had. Fury boiled in Rachel's veins. While she'd been leading the life of a martyr, Isabell was spending their money. Jerry had made a fool of her, made a mockery of her choice to be a stay-at-home mum, an exhausted, depressed stay-at-home mum.

She clenched her jaw and glared at the knife, discarded on her pillow. Where the hell was Jerry anyway?

THIRTY-THREE

Jerry squeaked himself into the final gap on the low leather sofa. Seeing him flap late into Locksley's office, Gemma had squeezed up closer to the other junior to give him somewhere to sit. Spink watched them with disdain. He was sitting in relaxed pole position, on one of the two leather chairs on the visitor's side of Locksley's desk—clearly the early bird. The man himself sat on the other, not wanting a desk to divide him from his team.

Jerry had remembered the sales meeting thirty seconds ago when he'd sauntered out into the main office to find nine empty seats where the sales team should have been. He'd sprinted swearing up the stairs, lobbing the remains of his sandwich out of the window, before blundering into Locksley's packed office.

He gave Gemma a grimace of thanks and, knees approaching his ears, tried to arrange his limbs into a comfortable position. He brushed crumbs from his tie, turned his attention to Locksley and assumed the angelic expression of an attentive student. Spink heaved a sigh of reproach.

Locksley flipped the page of the chart that stood on his desk. "So that concludes individual figures on existing accounts. Now, on to new business." A ripple of relief washed around the room. A couple of the account handlers, who'd brought their lunch into the meeting, ferreted it out from beneath the spare office chairs they'd also been clever enough to roll in with them. Organised, Jerry mused, prickling with inadequacy.

"Right now we're picking up ninety per cent of our new business in response to advertising." Locksley looked down at the note card in his hand. "Fourteen new business enquiries have come in over the last month. Only four have progressed to proposal stages and we are in a competitive bid situation on three. That's just not enough. We need a far more proactive approach if we're going to pick up enough to stave off redundancies."

Mouths stopped chewing. He glanced around the team over the top of his glasses. "We need to look harder and aim higher. We have to set our sights on the big players of the IT world.

"Next week, TEKCOM will be running for five days in the Las Vegas Convention Centre. The biggest manufacturers, developers and systems providers in the world will be exhibiting there.

"It will be attended by blue chip internationals, IT professionals and top brass looking for the latest technology for their companies. This year we will be there too." Locksley spun his chair to face Spink. "Donald, I want you out there flying the flag for Locksley PR. You too, Jerry. It's time to crank our efforts up a gear and play with the big boys."

Jerry's eyes stretched wide. Vegas. Las Vegas. Wow. A bubble of excitement formed in his chest. Just wait till he told Rachel. Oh, no, hang on, that might not go down so well. He'd not been doing much fathering of late. A solo trip to Vegas was unlikely to be met with much enthusiasm.

Still, it wasn't as if he was actually any good at the whole fathering thing was it? Might be best to take the spotlight off that particular shortcoming for a while.

Isabell wasn't going to be best pleased either, but that was tough. Business trips were unavoidable if he was going to 'making the good home'. He grinned to himself. A trip was just what he needed.

"This is a massive networking opportunity." Locksley went on, "Meet as many people as you can. Find out what they're planning, what they're looking for or launching. There will be companies there that we've never even heard of working in unfamiliar markets. Talk to everyone, but most important of all, make friends with Mango."

Locksley turned his attention back to the room at large. "Mango is the single largest information technology company in the world. They have subsidiaries in every country and marketing budgets into the millions. They are respected throughout the industry as precision manufacturers with codes of ethics and fair trade unparalleled by any other organisation, even in broader industries. Get our feet through the door and under the table, gentlemen. What an alliance it would be!" Locksley slapped his hands down onto his thighs with a laugh and Jerry couldn't help but smile along with him.

Spink roared out, "Las Vegas! Yes!" He leaned forward, lifting his flabby behind up from the leather and punched the air. "Why the hell didn't we think of this before?" Tiny flecks of spit showered down, like nickels tumbling from a one-armed bandit.

Jerry was excited, but Spink was positively orgasmic. Jerry flicked his eyes to Gemma who shrank into the sofa to get out of range.

"A brilliant plan! So much opportunity!" Spink's eyes glazed over as he tossed himself back into the chair with a whoop. Jerry gawped at him. Did Spink know something that he didn't? His stomach churned cheese and pickle and he squirmed on the sweaty leather. Shying away from the uncomfortable vista that was Spink, Jerry's eyes fell to the many photographs and framed awards that sat behind Locksley's desk.

He wondered where Locksley was in that sunset photo with his wife. It looked like somewhere he wanted to be, like a location worthy of Remi's adventures. Tropical warmth radiated out from the picture of happiness. Jerry imagined Remi's yacht moored in the bay, just out of shot.

The frame tucked behind held a yellowing certificate: an entrepreneurial award made some fifteen years previously. Locksley had worked his way up, building his business over time and was now captain of an impressive ship.

Jerry considered his personal list of achievements. Captain of the school football team was about as lofty as it got. Even that was only as a sub when Adam had broken his leg. More recent achievements were harder to place. Becoming a parent was more Rachel's accomplishment than his. He'd bumbled along for years, allowing life's events to steer his course.

He wanted the Caribbean holiday and the smiling wife. He wanted professional recognition and achievements to be proud of. Why shouldn't he have it? This exhibition in Vegas could give him the extra clients he needed to get the promotion. This could be his moment.

Imagine not having to steel himself before opening the bank statement every month. A leg up to the next level and he could sort out his finances. A nice big house for his little family (no DIY required) and a ferocious lawyer to see off Isabell, that was the ticket. He was going to get this bloody job and build a career for himself—a proper one. He was going to take control.

THIRTY-FOUR

Adam yanked a couple more meters of bramble from the tangle of shrubbery. It jabbed its thorny protests into his palms, but Adam didn't flinch. He was glad of the distraction.

He was trying to be the good friend: checking up on Rachel and Peanut, just as he'd promised, he told himself, determined to be strong. When he'd arrived, Rachel was rocking Peanut off to sleep. He'd tiptoed into the house under stony-faced instructions of silence and sat quietly at the table, watching her sway the somnolent infant to the rhythm of her improvised lullaby. Adam had been mesmerised by the tenderness. In that beautiful intimate moment he'd felt love manifest in his presence for the first time in more than half a decade, so tantalising and so close. Now he was out in the garden, waiting for the ache to leave his chest. It was safer out here. Just have a bit of a tidy up and catch his breath while Rachel finished up inside.

He yanked out another barbed vine and flicked his eyes toward the kitchen window, unable to resist. Inside, she was leaning her hip against the sink, sleeping baby cradled in her arms. How wonderful to be that baby, Adam mused: secure and adored in Rachel's embrace. The hairs stood up on his arms. Jerry was a fool.

The sun picked out her fine profile and sparkled in tendrils that tumbled to her collarbone. The soft jersey of her shirt slipped down from her shoulder. Without meaning to, he'd edged a little closer.

She turned to walk away and Adam felt a pang of rejection that jolted him to his senses. "Get a grip, Fox," he mumbled, and shaking the sentimental fluff from his head, turned his attention back to the border.

He tugged out a great clump of tangled stems that might have been weeds. More brambles over there. He strode over to tear them from the ground too. A glance over his shoulder. She was there again, at the window, her back to him this time.

She bowed her head forward, freed her hair from its clip and shook out shaggy curls. Adam worried at the neck of his sweatshirt. She drew her hair around to one side, exposing the soft sweep of skin from behind her ear and down, across her shoulder. The bramble slipped from Adam's fingers and, dry mouthed, he moved a little closer still to see her better.

Jerry's wife. Just looking.

So delicate and beautiful. So full of love. Adam let his imagination loose and in that unguarded moment invited in the pain to come. To kiss that neck, that shoulder. To run his finger across her breasts. To kiss her mouth, to find her tongue and she his. He ached to press his body against hers.

Both hands were at her face now so she wasn't holding Peanut anymore. Her shoulders dipped and rose erratically. Odd movements. Unexpected. Adam realised that she was crying and a moment later, stood beside her, wide-eyed. Without thinking, he took her in his arms and she sank against him, dissolving into noisy sobs.

"Hey, hey. What's all this? Don't cry. Shhh." Adam pulled her in a little tighter. Their cheeks pressed together and a salty tear rolled down to his mouth. The taste of her. Adam squeezed his eyes closed for a moment and tried to quiet the adrenalin.

"I can't do this anymore," Rachel blurted out, "I'm exhausted, utterly exhausted. It's the final straw!" She hiccupped into his shoulder then pulled away to snatch a tissue from the box on the table.

"Hey, come on, you'll be OK," Adam soothed. Her words weren't registering. His eyes lingered on her lips, her mouth rubbed red.

"I won't! I can't!" Rachel scrubbed wildly at her hair.

"It's OK. It's OK. What's so bad?" He searched her face for clues.

"Night after night. Day after day. It never stops. On and on. And Jerry's never here. Never!" She flicked her eyes to his. Sharp tortured eyes that seized his attention.

"I can't do it on my own. Peanut cries and cries. I don't know how to do it, can't get it right. How can it be this hard?" She turned away from him and paced around the table, trying to hold back sobs. "He's not telling me the truth. I've found it, he doesn't know yet but I bloody have. He's having an affair with her, isn't he? Tell me! He's having an affair with Isabell, I know it!"

Rachel was suffering, in torment even. He'd had no idea. What was Jerry playing at? Messing about with Isabell and playing house.

As much as he'd have liked it to be that simple, he couldn't let her suffer like this for no reason and shook the devil from his shoulder "No. Really, he's not. Look, Rach, Jerry's got a lot on at work at the moment, hasn't he? You know he's got to put in the hours." He circled the table after her.

"Oh yeah. Jerry's got such a hard life. He's swanning off to Las Vegas, Adam, but I suppose you know that already."

"Las Vegas?" How was Jerry going to find the time to go there?

"Oh yes. It's not enough to not help, to not bother coming home, to give it all away, now he's leaving the country!"

"What?" Adam stopped dead. "I, I had no idea. Vegas?" He rummaged around his brain for a comeback, a logical reason that his time-pressured friend could be going holiday, a reason to remain a loyal friend.

"Treacherous bastard," Rachel sobbed.

Las Vegas? As jollies went, that was pushing the boat out a bit. Pretty unreasonable to swan off whooping it up and leave Adam at home, standing in, without saying a word. What a shyster. Adam met her eyes, still processing Jerry's dishonesty. "What will you do?"

Rachel's head shook. "It's death by a thousand cuts. A late night here, an unpaid bill there, money disappearing. Little things that only a neurotic maniac would make a massive fuss about." She laughed out loud then. "Although now I've an idea where some of it's going." Her expression was wild, torn between fury and destruction. "Sometimes I wish he'd just do something so unbearable that I'd have no choice. Something so destructive that there could be no going back. At least then it would just be over."

Adam understood that sentiment all too well. Without McGinty, his life would be very different indeed. McGinty had lifted the veil on Adam's transformation into a man he despised, an insight that had changed the path of his life forever.

Isabell had Jerry wrapped around her little finger, but it wasn't the affair that Rachel suspected. Jerry was weak-willed and easily manipulated and Rachel might not be admitting it, but she knew it deep down. Him being pushed about by Isabell wasn't enough to finish their relationship, but she'd shown him what was. Infidelity was the unbearable act, too destructive. From that there was no going back.

THIRTY-FIVE

Remi took a sip of cool champagne and settled back in his seat. Excitable chatter bubbled around the table from his fellow diners. This was the category they'd all been waiting for.

"Ladies and gentlemen," the compere boomed over rising music. "Please welcome to the stage, an inspiration to us all, Lord Locksley!"

Remi's table, and indeed the whole room, erupted into enthusiastic applause, some whooping and cheering. The spotlight swung across the stage to find the man himself, smiling in an elegant tuxedo and nodding to the crowd. The compere welcomed him to the podium with an energetic handshake, before stepping back a reverential distance, grinning like the cat who'd got the cream.

Lord Locksley took his place at the podium with confidence, gently set down an engraved crystal trophy and waited for the room to quiet.

"Good evening, everybody. What a marvellous welcome. You are an excitable bunch, aren't you?" A chuckle rippled through the room. "Anyone would think you wanted to know who was going to get this rather prestigious award." He cocked an eyebrow and the crowd rumbled their assent.

Remi grinned along with the rest of the audience. He could be himself tonight, no need to watch his back. With Maximus Pink's precious flash drive now safely in the hands of MI5, he was due some downtime. His face would be far too recognisable to get inside the Crusaders of Justice any time soon and besides, he had other matters to attend to. He cast his eyes around the others sitting at his table. Company directors, senior management and data gurus: they were the loyal backbone of his business, of Remi's life on Civvy Street, away from MI5.

Fluent in seven languages, he'd travelled the world in Her Majesty's service and assimilated inevitable knowledge along the way, knowledge that had helped him to become the president of his own empire. After all, he couldn't chase villains forever.

Lord Locksley picked up the award and weighed it in his hands. "You don't want this," he said. "It's just a chunk of glass. Might even be plastic. You don't want to have come up here to get it. It's worthless. What do you need it for?" He paused, scanning the bemused faces with a cocky grin. "You don't need it. You've already got everything you need: enthusiasm, skill, energy, drive. Everyone in this room is here because they've got something special. Everyone in this room is responsible for building a business admired in their industry. Everyone here is already a winner." A ripple of applause broke out at the back, encouraged by cheers and laughter.

"I suppose you want to know who's the best of the best?" The crowd most definitely did. "Alright then, let's see." The lights on the stage dimmed, purple down-lighters subtly highlighting the spot where Lord Locksley stood. Star cloth sparkled around the room and the screen at the rear of the stage changed from the static logo of the Institute of British Industry to a mostly blank screen, but for the words at the top 'Entrepreneur of the Year'.

"The nominees for 'Entrepreneur of the Year' are," said a disembodied female voice, breathy and deep. "Black Fire—John Timult." Their name appeared on the screen and a table close by erupted into applause. "Thinking Tree—Samantha Rolf." A table further away this time cheered and clapped "And Adler Enterprises—Remi Adler." Remi's team whooped and banged on the table, rattling cutlery and chinking glasses together. Remi smiled and shook his head. Their enthusiasm filled him with pride and his heart purred with anticipation.

The light on Locksley grew more intense and he pulled a golden envelope from his pocket to tear it open at an agonizing crawl. He noted the winner to himself with an appreciative nod. "And the winner is..." he held the audience in his palm, "Remi Adler for Adler Enterprises."

The table exploded in a joyous rush of cheering and hugging and Remi stood as the roving spotlight found him. *Simply the Best* blared from the speakers and thunderous applause filled the room as he made his way to the stage, weaving through people standing at their tables, accepting congratulations and shaking hands.

He stalked up the steps at the front of the stage and over to the podium where he took Lord Locksley's outstretched hand and accepted from him the crystal trophy. Light sparkled in its facets and Remi grasped its weight with joy, turning to face the crowd. His employees were still jumping up and down and whooping. Chandeliers glittered and teary eyes shone. Remi was certain he could never feel happier than he did in that moment.

The phone on Jerry's desk let out a shrill ring and he snatched it up, wrenched from his fantasy.

"Accounts system has crashed," Phyllis whined. "Can't get expenses out until tomorrow. Sorry."

Jerry sighed and rubbed at his forehead. "OK, Phyllis, fine."

The grand setting of his daydream blew away into draughty reality. He huffed and kicked the petulant heater. No awards for him today, instead, the absence of a cheque.

THIRTY-SIX

"Counting down from ten. Keep it going. Ten. Nine."

As he pedalled for all he was worth, Jerry's cheeks flamed beneath a sheen of sweat that rolled sporadically in fat beads to his soggy grey T-shirt. If he could have spoken, he'd have told Adam he was having a heart attack—the single thing he could think of that might make him stop, but breathless and mute, he couldn't escape.

"Nine. Eight. Come on, loser!"

Jerry screwed his face up for the final push.

"Nine. Eight."

They'd just done 'nine' and 'eight'. Jerry glared his objection.

"Seven. Six. Push it, lard arse!"

His thighs burned and his knees wobbled and Adam bullied him on.

"Six, five, four," Adam barked.

Lactic acid numbed Jerry's quadriceps and he pushed at the pedals with ever decreasing impact. Dots danced before his eyes. He closed them, but they didn't go away.

"Five, four."

Was he actually losing consciousness? He could swear that Adam was repeating the numbers.

"Nearly there, fat boy. Last ten."

Right, that was it. Jerry collapsed across the handlebars, gasping for oxygen. The pedals whirled his feet around to a gradual stop. Adam, a mere berating blur.

"All too much eh? Well, what can we expect?" the blur taunted. Jerry opened one eye. Adam was definitely enjoying this.

"Gotta work hard, Jerry. Never mind the office and Dinky. Never mind Isabell and her fantasies and never mind the wife and kid. In the gym your arse is mine." Adam was a teeny bit too enthusiastic.

"You need a job," Jerry wheezed.

"I've got a job, remember? Saving the universe."

Jerry grimaced. "A proper job. One that doesn't involve killing me."

Adam ignored him. "I also do a nice little side line in baby-sitting."

Jerry would have laughed, if he'd had spare breath.

Adam pushed him off the bike and steered him toward the rowing machine. Jerry raised a weak hand and flopped to the floor.

"Time is money, Jerry." Adam tapped his foot.

What was with him today? On their previous Wednesday evening sessions, they'd made slow and reasonable progress around the gym, as befitted a man of Jerry's unfitness. Today he was a madman.

"Are you on something?" Jerry wheezed into his knees. Adam was quiet for a moment, as if considering the possibility. "No. Just helping. Just keeping you going. Old buddy. Old pal." He punched him on the shoulder.

"Ow!"

Jerry crawled over to the bench and Adam followed. He sat and gasped for a bit then slumped back against the wall, waiting for the hammering in his head to subside. After a minute Adam cleared his throat. "So, how is everything? Still in demand?" A whiff of insincerity escaped the tone.

Jerry rolled his head to one side to look at him. He had recovered enough to speak. "Crown Princess Pain-in-the-arse continues to reign, if that's what you mean." He took a slug of water. "But I'm getting away with putting in some late nights at the office so I don't have to spend too much time with 'Mum and Dad'."

"And Rach?" Adam was staring at him from beneath raised eyebrows.

"Yeah, well, she's all right. Doing the mummy thing. I'm no good at it anyway."

"U-huh."

"Spink's taken it to a new level of weird. After all that account stealing bullshit he's gone all quiet. Actually, I haven't told you, the firm's sending us to Vegas." He leant onto his knees and took another drink.

"The firm?"

"Some big industry hoo-hah. Huge business opportunities. I'm going to make Director."

Adam was frowning at him.

"Positive visualisation," Jerry explained.

Adam's eyes narrowed.

"I'm coming back from Vegas the winner. You'll see." Jerry's determination to turn things around had strengthened since the sales meeting. Creaking home from work in the Fiat, Jerry could see that he needed to up his game. Isabell or no Isabell, he ought to be doing better than this by now.

Adam shifted in his seat and leaned forward, elbow to knee, chin resting on his palm. He looked at Jerry with steady eyes. "You're sounding confident."

"I've decided—enough already. I'm forty-two, Adam. I've got a crumbly little house and a bean tin car. Spink thinks I'm his whipping boy and Isabell treats me like her slave. I was in Locksley's office the other day and I took a look around and I thought, yeah, I want this too. I want the Caribbean holidays and the big pay cheques. I want to be the powerful business man. Why shouldn't I be?"

Adam's lips pressed together as he folded his arms across his chest.

"It's my time now, Adam. I'm going on this trip and I'm going to come back top dog." He wasn't sure that he believed that a hundred per cent, but in for a penny. It was time to turn things around.

Adam was staring at him. Processing. "I should come too," he said finally, a gleam in his eye.

"What? No, it's a business trip."

"No problem. I'll tag along. You know what they say: all work and no play makes Jerry a boring bastard." Adam punched him on the arm again.

"Stop that! I'm flying out with Spink. I can't piss about."

"Oh come ON. Vegas, baby! I'll take a different flight. We could have a great time…"

"I dunno. This is important, Adam. I can't cock it up."

"Come on. What would Remi do? Huh?" Adam flashed him his winning smile.

Jerry bit at his lip. Las Vegas was Remi's home turf after all and he didn't know if he'd ever get the chance again. "I suppose it would be a shame not to explore the local culture…"

Adam whacked him on the back. "Atta boy!"

"Well OK, but don't tell Rach: she already thinks I'm going on a jolly."

"Imagine that. Mum's the word." Adam 'zipped' his mouth. "Absolutely no fun to be had in Vegas."

"None at all."

THIRTY-SEVEN

Mama twisted the tissue in her hands. "Poor Maria! Her husband cut down in the prime of life. Poof! One minute he was painting the house then, wham! Broken back, fracture skull." She dabbed at her eyes.

Sitting in the corner of the Cavalli sofa that Isabell liked for herself, Mama had been recounting family stories since mid-afternoon. Papa, who'd heard it all before, had escaped for an evening walk, but Isabell was trapped. She prowled back and forth in front of the empty open fireplace, gripping at her upper arms.

"All the family come to the hospital, but they could no save him. Poor Sal. So sad." She made a hearty blow into the tissue. "Now she has to look after those children all alone." She peered at Isabell over her glasses. "At least she has the children."

Isabell turned her back and stooped to plump a cushion. Not this again. "Mama."

"Hmm. Well, the family have pick her up and taken her to the heart. Sancho has finish the paint. It never look so good! And Alba picks the children up from school while Maria is at work." She paused to peer at Isabell again. "Ibbie, why you no have a job? If you help to make the good home maybe Papa and I can have our grandchildren. Hmm?"

For once, Isabell was thankful to hear the backfiring Fiat bucking up the drive and stalked over to the window. It gave her an excuse to change the topic. "Jerry's home at last." Isabell scowled at her watch: 9:30. It was about time.

Jerry bounded into the house, scraping his gym bag along the two-hundred-pound-a-roll wallpaper before tossing it to the floor at the foot of the stairs. Isabell bit her tongue and scampered over to peck him on the cheek: the dutiful wife.

Jerry slapped her on the arse. "Evening, darling! Had a good day?" Isabell wobbled backward. What the hell did he think he was doing? He pushed past her toward the kitchen. "Chuck that in the wash, would you? Any dinner? I'm starving."

Isabell stood, jaw flapping, for a moment before catching her mother's eye, who was shooing her after her husband. Isabell hoiked up a smile and scuttled into the kitchen.

"What the fuck are you doing?" she hissed.

"Back from a hard day at the office," Jerry bellowed as Mama appeared in the doorway. Isabell felt her presence and switched on the goddess.

"Chicken salad OK?" she simpered. Jerry flopped into a seat at the table and shoved Isabell's flower arrangement backward, away from the middle. He knew it would annoy her.

"Again? Oh all right, if that's all you've got."

He'd pay for that later. The Domestic Goddess routine was all very well, but Isabell only had a few dishes that she could make. With Mama peering over her shoulder all the time it was difficult to pass ready-made stuff off as her own. Jerry was going to ruin things if he carried on like this. She rummaged around in the fridge, cursing under her breath.

"I say to Ibbie, why she no get a job." Mama sat down opposite Jerry at the polished oak table. Isabell seethed behind the fridge door. She couldn't bring herself to look at Jerry's undoubtedly smug expression.

"A job? Yes, that's a marvellous idea, darling."

"Great. I look tomorrow." Isabell cut the comment dead and tossed a selection of salad and a half-eaten chicken carcass onto the pale stone counter. She snatched a knife from the block and hacked at its flesh.

"I've got a business trip coming up, darling, so you can lay off the gourmet menus for a few days." Jerry snorted a laugh at Mama then went on to examine his fingernails. A business trip? A likely story. It was just another excuse not to play ball.

"Really? Oh?" She scowled at Jerry just long enough for him to see, but not Mama. "Where are you going?" Let's see what he can come up with.

"Las Vegas Convention Centre. TEKCOM. It's a huge event. Locksley's trusting me to represent the firm." Jerry buffed his nails on his trousers and gave her a grin.

"Is that right? Well that is news. How long will you be away?" Little shit. He wasn't keeping to his side of the bargain here at all. How could he pretend to be her doting husband if he was out of the country? She spun the knife's point on the work surface, drawing a thin squeal from the stone.

"Oh well, the exhibition is on for five days and I'll need a couple of days either end for travel and recovery."

"Travel and recovery," she echoed through gritted teeth.

"Yeah, so about ten days."

Isabell annihilated the salad and threw a heap onto his plate followed by the hacked chicken. She clonked the plate down onto the table in front of him. Jerry wolfed it down, made a big show of stretching and yawning and after saying how terribly tired he was from all his hard work, sauntered off 'to bed'.

Isabell heard the Fiat backfire on the corner, but Mama didn't seem to notice.

"No worry about it," Mama said at last, "Is just a business trip. He works to make the good home."

"Yes, yes." Isabell wasn't sure how to play it. Was she pleased that her husband worked so hard, or upset that he was going abroad while her parents were visiting? Jerry was irritating her so much it was clouding her judgement.

"You are lucky. He'll be back. Think of your cousin Maria. Her husband will never come home again."

That might not be so bad. Distinctly appealing, in fact.

"You know, Ibbie, life can take you on many different paths. A good choice here…" Mama waved her hand, "A bad choice there… Fate will have its way. Think of Cousin Angelina." Isabell winced, God forbid she got *her* fate.

"She thought she was the modern woman asking for divorce. A bad choice. Where did it get her? Ostracise from family that's where. No-one want to know her. Flouting God's law! Selfish whore!" Mama crossed herself, got up from the table, ambled to the kettle and switched it on, calm again. "Is strange. You think of Maria and Angelina. Both single women now and how different their lives have turn out. The family can no do enough for Maria. Fate. I'm telling you."

Isabell wiped the knife clean and slid it back into the block. Didn't you make your own fate?

THIRTY-EIGHT

A shower of fine plaster dust rained down into Jerry's eyes. He squeezed them closed and shook his head to dislodge the grit.

"Puh! Is this really necessary, Isabell?" he complained, looking down at her petulant pout from the top of the step ladder. She had that look in her eye.

"Is important to change. Old electrics have a lot of danger."

"I really don't think it was that old, Isabell. This place was only built in the eighties."

"Do you want for me to die in a fire?"

Jerry squeezed his lips together.

"Do you want for me to choke on the fumes when the old electric explode?" Isabell spat, swinging her arms in a two-handed demonstration. The step ladder wobbled and Jerry grabbed at the curved bar that ran around the top platform.

"Isabell! The ladder!" She laid an ineffective hand on a waist-height step.

"Pfff."

"Hold it steady, can't you?"

"Such a baby."

"It's the carpet making it unstable. It's too luxurious. Like everything else," he mumbled and turned his head back to the pendant light fitting, taking care not to move any other part of his body for fear of setting off another wobble. He could really do without this. Spending time at Isabell's when her parents weren't even there was well beyond the call of duty.

He looked back to the exposed electrical connections and bit at his lip. "You have turned off the electricity, haven't you?"

"Of course." Isabell waved her hand in encouragement. "Carry on."

Jerry looked back to the wires. Where to start? "Isabell, are you sure you don't want to get an electrician to do this?"

"Jerry, we can no afford tradesman. You know how they are. All suck of the teeth and lies and big bills. Especially for me. They will take advantage of a woman on her own." Isabell flipped her hair and looked up at him with a bat of her eyelashes.

Jerry rolled his eyes. "All alone, yes, let's not forget that." He looked back dubiously to the wires. "Now you're sure that the electricity is off?"

"Si."

"Could you just try the switch to make sure?"

Isabell tutted and flounced over to swipe at it. The bulbs sprang to life with a shocking fierceness centimetres from

Jerry's face and he turned a stony wide-eyed look on her, freezing her in his glare.

"I'll do it, shall I?" he squeaked and Isabell shrugged and looked away, suddenly terribly interested in her hair clip.

Ducking his head down into the cupboard under the stairs, Jerry surveyed the fuse box with its convenient labels. "You've turned off upstairs, dimwit," he called out, carefully changing the switches and reversing out. He didn't hear her reply, but Isabell sneered and backed away from the living room light switch as he approached. Jerry flipped it on and off, on and off. Firmly on and off.

Back on the step ladder, he steeled himself for the poking-in-the-metal-screwdriver part. Isabell was right, a professional electrician was likely to charge a small fortune for what was, in appearance, a simple job and, as it would be him footing the bill, it made sense to at least give it a go. Didn't it?

The driver made contact with the screw without major incident and the removal of wires from their locations was equally drama free. Jerry gave himself a mental pat on the back and even the final cloud of dust that fell into his face when the backing plate came down could not quell the smug feeling of confidence that swelled in his chest. "That's that bit done," he said, laying the old light fitting on the sofa and picking up the new. "This'll be done in no time."

He even managed to summon up a cheery little tuneless whistle, perched up on top of the ladder. Getting the wires back into the fitting took a bit more concentration and he didn't notice that Isabell wasn't holding the ladder anymore, until he heard her banging around in the cupboard. He tried shifting his weight to test the safety of his position, but the ladder's feet seemed to have sunk into the deep pile of the carpet and gained some stability. This job was a doddle. Now just to ease the final wire in with the screwdriver.

In a flash, Jerry's hand was white hot with pain, the muscles in his arm spasming into a rigid rod that pushed his hand into the ceiling and his body off balance. He toppled backwards, stiff as a board, and landed with a muted clap on the lounge floor. His body fizzed with pain.

When Isabell's face came into focus, peering down into his own, his arm was still outstretched and his eyes wide. She looked him over and returned to his immobile face, finally poking his cheek with a sharp fingernail. "Jerry?"

His jaw flapped and she visibly deflated, rolling her eyes to the ceiling and sitting back on her haunches.

"It... you... hurts." Jerry's arm felt cramped and his ribs bruised. He lowered his hand and dropped the screwdriver, revealing an angry red welt on his palm.

"Electrocuted," he managed, "I've been electrocuted!" Jerry's voice squeaked out in a rasp. "But... I..." Isabell twiddled hair around her finger and looked at the carpet.

"Is good is luxurious carpet, hmm? No hurt to land."

"Isabell."

"Is good choice now, hmm?" She rubbed an appreciative palm across its pile.

"Isabell, the electric?"

She got to her feet and backed away. "I don't know."

"Isabell."

"You said it was done."

"No." Jerry struggled up to lean on his elbows.

"You did. You put it there." She pointed to the old fitting on the sofa, "and said it was done. How do I know you not done?" She waved a dismissive hand, before bringing it back to cover her mouth.

"I was on the ladder." Jerry looked to the ladder, now leaning at an angle against the sofa, "With a screwdriver in my hand." He flexed it into a fist and regretted it immediately, the pain refreshing itself with a million pins, jabbing into his muscles and burning inside his flesh. "How, Isabell? How?"

"I switch back on, of course," she mumbled and cocked an arrogant eyebrow, "Dimwit."

THIRTY-NINE

"Yes, absolutely." Spink swung his feet up onto the birch desktop and leaned back in his executive leather chair. "I would be delighted to meet some of the other directors on the Worldwide board. U-huh. Yep. Yes." God, this Drinkwater bloke could waffle on. Yada, yada, yada. "Yes. As it happens I was planning on visiting TEKCOM this year to catch up with some of my more, shall we say, high profile clients," Spink simpered into the phone with a little head wobble. "Of course, I mean you. Ha, ha, ha."

Oh yes, this guy was going to be his meal ticket. Turned out, they both liked golf (well Spink had played a couple of times) and they both loved Elton John, who just happened to be playing in Vegas while TEKCOM was on. And guess who'd managed to procure two tickets at enormous expensesable expense? Spink, that's who. Yup it was like they were brothers: destined to meet. He didn't know it, but Eric Drinkwater was going to save Spink's job.

"Seriously for a moment though, Eric. May I call you Eric? Fabulous chat at the UK Conference last week and I hope you've had a chance to read through the proposal I sent over. Yup. Yup. Great. I'd appreciate a few minutes of your time at TEKCOM, just to pin a few things down, dot some I's. U-huh. Sooner we can get the old rubber stamp on things, sooner we can get to work on your behalf."

Spink prodded his filthy keyboard with nicotine-stained fingers and the William Hill website flicked up on screen. He ran his eyes down the fixtures for the afternoon. "So excited to be working with you. Yup. Just looking at it now actually." Spink glanced at the two-inch-high pile of unread company literature that Mango had sent through about their ethics and procedures. "Fabulous approach. Yep. Couldn't agree more."

Spink supposed he might take it home to read. After hours he didn't have anything better to do. It wasn't as if he had hundreds of friends beating down his door. In a hangover from school days, when he'd often been bullied, he'd worked out ways to keep unwanted attention out of his personal space, but never quite how to invite anyone in. He'd discovered the comfort of gambling in his twenties. It started with a flutter on the Cup Final. The thrill of the win had pumped him full of endorphins that fuelled his later addiction.

Spink typed 'Las Vegas' into the search engine and the screen filled with images of paradise. A million lights set against the pitch black of the desert; fantastical structures and opulent excess, the stuff of his dreams.

"Sure. Me too. Busy, busy. See you Friday? Eleven o'clock. Perfect." Spink kicked his feet off the desk, hung up and swung round to better view the screen.

Around the world in a day: the Eiffel Tower; the Statue of Liberty; the Sphinx; Venice. On and on, wonders to behold, all of them. He scrolled down. Night time panoramas gave way to internal shots of the incredible hotels: gondolas on a canal; a great illuminated wheel of fortune; a forest of one-armed bandits; roulette tables surrounded by beautiful winners.

Now his heart was racing. He could win big! Play well a couple of nights and he might get invited to play with the high rollers. The Cranley would pale into insignificance. Spink drummed his fingers on the desktop, palms itching.

Once the deal was signed with Mango Worldwide there was no way Adler would be able to beat him. He couldn't wait for that moment when Adler realised he'd lost. For every adrenaline-fuelled rush to the winner he knew there was a gut-wrenching crash for the loser. Spink rubbed his thighs and grinned at Adler's impending pain.

It was a bit early for celebrations, but a cuppa would go down nicely. "Gemma!" he bellowed. He wasn't bothered about biscuits, but maybe there'd be a glimpse of something else tasty on the side.

FORTY

Jerry swept across the cool sea of marble, drinking in the glorious air conditioning. A vast bank of video screens stretched behind the reception desk. They washed the foyer with hypnotic light and video, extolling the rewards of giving in to temptation. They battled an army of slot machines across the foyer for Jerry's attention. Everywhere was loud and bright and buzzing.

Spink barged past, knocking him sideways with a snort, scurrying to be the first to check in. Jerry ignored him. It had been a long trip, made longer by his smug companion.

Spink had developed curious Jekyll and Hyde tendencies during their journey. One moment he'd been a supremely confident self-satisfied tyrant, the next, an excited school boy, devouring the in-flight magazine and tourist information with undisguised glee.

"I'd use this trip to find a new job if I were you, Alder," Spink had said in a darker moment, "Resign. Save us all the embarrassment. You'll never beat me, Adler. I'm already at the finish post and you're not even out of the trap."

Minutes later he was giggling at pictures in the tourist brochure and rubbing his thighs. Jerry had squirmed in his cramped seat for the first hour of the flight, but as Spink demonstrated no intention of explaining himself he'd soon resolved to ignore him. The remainder of the journey had been the better for it.

Wearing a dopey grin, Jerry purposely joined a different line from Spink where, after a fifteen minute shuffling wait, a smart-suited clerk turned her attention to him.

She smoothed her hair. "Good afternoon, sir. Welcome to the MGM Grand. How may I assist you today?"

Jerry raised his eyes to hers. Charles Bamford-Irons smiled with a twitch to one eyebrow. "Er Jerry Adler, checking in."

She rattled at her keyboard and soon sent him on his way, sadly unadorned with privilege cards, but delighted to have officially arrived. Jerry jabbed repeatedly at the lift buttons, but Spink managed to squeeze his girth in through the closing doors before they sealed shut.

When they slid open again both men stepped out into the 4th floor lobby. Side by side they marched down the corridor, Spink giving Jerry's squeaking case withering looks. Jerry, pretending not to notice, stretched his stride, forcing Spink to scuttle at twice his pace to keep up. Jerry pulled ahead, scanning the doors for numbers as he passed. 417, 419, 421. The corridor stretched on ahead, bright and golden. He rounded a corner, Spink at his heel. 435, 437, 439. Here.

Jerry presented the key card and barrelled into his room grinning, leaving a sweating Spink fumbling at the door opposite.

He clicked the door shut behind him and let out a low whistle. The room was just as he had hoped: spacious and elegant, a luxurious bolthole from which he'd shape his destiny. Sleek walnut fitted units ran the length of the room with sharp chrome handles that glinted in the soft light. Here, Jerry was his own man. A loaded champagne bucket perched on the desk, poised for celebration. Jerry grinned. Ah yes, he had arrived.

For everything the room had: wide flat screen TV, rich walnut furniture, sumptuous soft furnishings and a dazzling view of The Strip, it was the notably absent aspects that cleared Jerry's mind for battle. The room was blissfully free from disapproving glares and expectant silences. Not one scrap of baby paraphernalia was to be seen and the bed was utterly free from piles of folded laundry, changing mats and soggy muslins.

He abandoned his case and flopped wholeheartedly onto the king-sized bed. Smooth satin caressed his cheek and he sank into the mound of pillows. Too excited to lie still, after a moment he rolled off, manoeuvred his squeaky companion over to the wardrobe and flung its contents onto hangers. Start as you mean to go on and all that. With one hand in his pocket, he swaggered over to the window.

The voracious Strip sprawled beneath him. Four lanes of traffic pumped in either direction, feeding life and heat and money. Neon signposts bedazzled pedestrians and swept them inside, to consume and be consumed. The sidewalks oozed with fat Americans and soon-to-be-thinner wallets, but there were winners out there too. Las Vegas was the place of dreams. Wide-eyed and glorious, Jerry refocused on his own reflection in the glass: a new hopeful face with sparkling eyes. Remi winked back.

FORTY-ONE

Jerry stretched out in king-sized luxury and flopped away the satin quilt. Cool air flooded over his skin and coaxed him into consciousness. Already at home, he swung out of bed, dug happy toes into the soft pile of the carpet and sauntered to the bathroom. Marble surfaces shone clean and clear, with only Jerry's meagre wash bag occupying space. He showered and dressed in a guilt free, unharassed bubble. No grumbling tick from Grandma Ray's timepiece, nor piercing cries from Peanut. No accumulated junk of infanthood nor DIY ignored. No dishevelled stacks of laundry nor abandoned tea cups. No other living soul.

Straightening his tie, he admired his reflection in the side lit mirror. His complexion was even and clear, dark shadows banished and replaced with a twinkle. Jerry puffed out his chest, hitched up his trousers and smoothed the dark lapels of his jacket. An unruly curl flopped into his eye and Remi raised an eyebrow. Ah well, you couldn't have everything. Jerry scooped up his wallet and hustled out the door.

He strode straight into the lift, catching it just before the doors slid shut. It silently dropped five floors then stopped of its own accord. It did not open. Through the glass doors, frowning would-be passengers stabbed at the exterior buttons. Jerry jabbed at his own and off they went again, this time dropping straight past the foyer to the level below. The doors opened and a wave of babbling tourists flooded in, squashing Jerry against the side. He punched at the button for the foyer again and up they went. This time finally stopping at the right floor, the temperamental lift spewed its jabbering load out into the foyer. Jerry brushed himself down, stuck out his chin and strode off toward the monorail.

At the platform, arms of grey steel and glass stretched out a wide embrace, enclosing passengers in a pocket of neutral space. Not the outrageous excess of the hotel, nor the arid concrete landscape of backstage Las Vegas. It felt like he'd infiltrated the villain's lair, waiting to board the internal shuttle to take him deeper. The sleek bullet of a train eased to the platform and Jerry climbed aboard, along with the minions, ready to be jettisoned out into the desert and on.

He claimed a seat amongst his fellow excited passengers. Some were smart-suited like himself and there for business, others bulged in Bermudas and irreverent T-shirts. The P.A. system babbled unendingly, publicising promotions and pointing out the vast hotels visible through the window. "Let luck be your lady tonight!" crooned the presenter. Yes indeed.

Alighting at the Conference Centre Station, Jerry swept along with the crowd and down a long walkway. The exhibition hall opened up before him, a cavernous space carved into a criss-crossing maze: a tiny city where the streets were paved with thin grey industrial carpet. Jerry strode forward, dwarfed by the enormity of the stands. Some were built double-decker, with meeting rooms on top or balconies. Others sported vast models, mysteriously supported by trade show magic: a glittering spinning globe; a polystyrene mobile phone to send Dom Jolly into raptures; glass and steel; technology and touch screens.

Time to scope out the lair and get the lie of the land.

Jerry pulled out the exhibitors list and ran his eyes over the highlighted names. He made a random turn, looking for a name he recognised. Beautiful women lined the route, holding trays of orange juice and bagels, bacon sandwiches and muffins. Reward for the early birds. Jerry's stomach growled.

He approached the smiling woman with the muffins, who offered him a napkin. "All our representatives are in conversation at the moment, sir but, if you'd like to wait...?"

"No problem, I'll come back. I want to look around anyway."

"Have a nice day." She smiled and before Jerry had moved away she'd broken eye contact and was gazing over his shoulder into thin air, face fixed in a grin.

Jerry nibbled at the muffin and backed away, into the stream of visitors that ebbed along the gutter between the rows of stands. He sauntered on, gnawing as he went.

By midday Jerry reckoned that he'd covered a third of the labyrinth, marvelling at the structures and circling likely candidates for approach on his list, if he could ever find them again. He decided to stop for a bite to eat and, as he sat with a coffee in a seating plaza, Jerry's eyes fell upon the Holy Grail: rising above the artificial skyline of steel and polystyrene, 'Mango'. No gimmicks or gizmos, their name stood proud above all others. Orange letters in a sharp no-nonsense typeface that was recognised the world over to stand for ethical business. A name you could trust.

Jerry's heart beat a little faster. It might take him a few tries before he got to speak to the right person. He needed to get to work on them. No time like the present. He knocked back his coffee and scurried past the stands in the shadow of his prize. The constructions along his way grew with every step. This was blue chip boulevard.

The route twisted this way and that. Then, with a final turn he was confronted with those orange letters, suspended high in the air. He paused to gather himself, then let his eyes trail down to assess the people.

To start with it was hard to distinguish staff from visitors but, once he'd spotted the orange name badges, the well dressed and confident Mango employees became obvious. At least fifteen of them. Ages ranging from late twenties up into the fifties. Rising age meant rising responsibility so Jerry decided to sidestep the younger easy marks and aim high.

A gaggle of grey hair was drinking coffee and laughing to one side. Jerry started toward it, regulating his breathing and holding his game face. Ten feet away and the closest member of the group turned, revealing a bulbous nose and wayward eyebrows.

Jerry stopped dead and their eyes met. The briefest flicker in Spink's expression told him he was too late. He turned back to the group, said something Jerry didn't catch and they all erupted into laughter, the closest member patting Spink heartily on the back.

Jerry's eye twitched and he backed away. Bloody Spink, he had to get there first, didn't he? Jerry twisted round and scuttled back into the labyrinth, the white noise of adrenalin hissing in his ears as he navigated back to the coffee piazza.

No need to panic. There were plenty of other people to see. Jerry pulled the exhibitor list from his pocket but, his eyes slid from the highlighted names and sloshed into the pool of harassed fear in his head. He needed new clients, lots of new clients. If Spink had Mango though, all was already lost.

He tried to shake it off. *Positive attitude, Jerry. Come on.* He sat at a table and unfolded the map, locating his next target, Interchip. He scooped up his papers and headed off down a corridor of towering graphics and other people's conversations.

So determined was Jerry to get there that he found himself on top of it before he'd slowed his pace and had to pull up at its borders like a gangly foal. Already at the foot of three steps which led up onto the stand, his sudden arrival and flustered demeanour caught the attention of the Interchip employees above. They scanned the face he realised too late was a picture of desperation, and undoubtedly made assumptions. Jerry rearranged his features into a smile and stepped up into the fray, palms sweating.

A tightly wrapped woman in smart tailoring popped up out of nowhere and offered him her own smiling mask. Jerry wanted to turn and run.

"Good afternoon, sir. May I help you with an enquiry?" Her teeth glinted in the unnatural fluorescent light.

"Yes. Yes. Absolutely. My name is Jerry Adler. I'm wondering if there is anyone here today from your marketing team?"

The tightly wrapped woman's brow relaxed a little. "I myself am collecting visitor details for our marketing database. Shall I scan your badge and send you an information pack?"

She'd lifted her laser gun and shot the badge on his chest before he could answer. Jerry flinched.

"No. Well OK but, that's not really what I meant." She switched her expression back to questioning and traced the slow roll of a bead of sweat down his cheek with judgmental eyes.

"Actually, the company I represent provide PR to this sector and I'd like to talk about ways we could work together."

"You and I? I don't think that's possible. I don't have that kind of input."

"Well not you then, probably. Someone more senior."

Bristling, she straightened her back with a wobble of her head. Jerry cringed.

"Do you have a card? I could pass it on. To my superior." The plastic smile cranked up a notch.

Jerry fumbled in his pockets and produced a card which she took between pinched fingers. "Have a nice day now."

"Yes absolutely. You too." Jerry's smile got a fake one in response. He turned, stumbled down the steps and scurried away.

Sitting back down at a table he scrubbed at his hair, berating himself. *Horror. Nightmare. Really pathetic. Get it together, Adler. Jesus.* So Spink was at Mango. It didn't mean anything. Possibly. OK, so they looked pretty chummy. Probably already knew someone, maybe from that club he goes to. They were probably all funny handshakes and backstage passes. Oh God.

Would explain why Spink was so painfully confident though, wouldn't it, why he'd acted like a tourist on the plane. He didn't need to win any business here, he'd already got it. Shit and double shit. Spink was going to get the job. Jerry was unemployed. Bloody hell. Rachel. Peanut. He was the worst father ever.

FORTY-TWO

Ensconced on the monorail, Spink stretched his arms out along the back of the seat and sighed. Obviously, Eric Drinkwater recognised a good thing when he saw it and he'd seen it in Donald Spink. Yep, no doubt about it, his vast experience and superior intellect were shining through.

Drinkwater was just another corporate buffoon, of course, on the lookout for real talent to make himself look good. If Drinkwater wanted to pick Spink's brain, well he was welcome. In exchange, all he wanted was an enormous slice of that delicious marketing budget and everyone was happy. It wasn't rocket science.

He was confident Mango Worldwide was in the bag and itched to get on with his celebrations, to get on with the best part of this whole trip. With luck on his side, the gaming tables called.

Spink squeezed at his thighs and switched over to a forward facing seat for a better view of Nirvana. He craned his neck to drink in a blast of the air conditioning, its cool velvet swelling his chest.

This was the place. He belonged here. By day, the revered public relations guru, by night, the high roller he'd always known he could be. He fingered the smooth chrome of the handrail leaving hot prints. The ball of a camera unit looked down on him from the ceiling. He smirked into its lens. At the other end of its optical fibres was probably a fat security guard staring at a monitor somewhere, gorging on donuts. Another nothing, another nobody that he was passing by.

Drinkwater was responsible for a marketing budget in the millions. The Mango Worldwide PR machine worked the trade press and pedestrian papers relentlessly; that spotless reputation forever enlivened and endorsed. It was their most prized possession. Spink was about to sign on the Public Press contract, a contract to take his earnings up into the stratosphere. He rubbed his hands together with glee. Adler was screwed.

After the doors swished open to release a noisy group of trainer-wearing tourists, only a handful of passengers remained. Their absence revealed a slumped Jerry Adler at the far end of the carriage. His dejected demeanour spread a slow smirk across Spink's lips. He couldn't resist the temptation and slithered over to torment him.

"Bad day, Adler?" Spink leaned over him, pulling a face of sarcastic sympathy. "Did you only just realise you won't get Mango? Oh dear, oh dear." Adler stared at his shoes, little flecks of Spink's spit landing on their shine. He was hugging at his chest.

"That deal was done weeks ago. On. The. Ball. Adler." He prodded at his shoulder for emphasis. "Thirty years in the industry and a black book full of gold. Unfair match really." He sniffed and puffed out his chest, then leaned in again, closer this time, his lips brushing Adler's ear as he spoke. "I'll keep my job, Adler, it was always mine and you, you're in the gutter, you arsehole. I'll stay with Locksley long enough to collect my fat commission but, I'm destined for better things. I'm on my way up. Locksley can build his own dreams."

Adler jerked up a cringing shoulder and turned his face away. Spink tasted the delicious nectar of power—a delightful digestif to the devouring of a perky spirit. He pulled back a little to see how pathetic Adler had become: he still looked down at the floor and, although he couldn't see into his eyes, Spink suspected tears were forming there. How easy it was to be the bully. Spink's turn now.

"Don't get all girlie about it, Adler. Let's face it: you never had it in you. No idea how to manage staff for a start. That Gemma strumpet, she likes you, Adler, fuck knows why. If you'd had any sense you'd have had her on the recruitment couch, working to keep her job. She might even have liked it.

Not you, not *Jerry*." He hooked his lip into a sneer. "Running home to the little woman who's turned into a neurotic flabby fat arse, I bet, since the squawker came along." Spink swam with confidence and his mouth moved on its own: words infused with sour breath to slash and stab.

Adler rose from his seat, surprising Spink into a brief silence. He flinched back. After all, Adler was much taller and fitter. A superior wit wouldn't protect him from a punch in the mouth. It was a sudden movement that caught the eye of the other passengers left in the carriage. He felt them watching.

Head bowed, Adler tried to turn away, to get away. He was hiding his pain and Spink wanted to see it. He wouldn't be robbed of this. After all these years, the tormenter, ha! He grabbed Adler's shoulder and spun him back for a better look, making him stagger and fall back onto the seat. He stared up, his jaw clenched shut. There was a determination there not to speak. Was he afraid he'd cry? Spink laughed out loud. "Oh please!" See the big boys aren't so tough. Look at that, a single move and he's on his arse, defeated.

Back on his feet, Adler made it past the second time, but before he could get out of range, Spink took his final shot and shoved him in the small of the back. Adler hadn't expected that. Spink's newfound strength surprised even him: he was delighted to see Adler stumble and fall, a gangly ragdoll that flopped to the floor.

At his feet where he belonged, Spink sneered down his nose at the scrabbling loser. The train was coming to a stop, his stop. Spink snapped his jacket straight and swept away, past the garbage on the floor.

FORTY-THREE

Adam waited. The perfect balance of sharp and casual in Levi's and a crisp shirt, he drummed his fingers on the seat. It had been a long journey, but settled now in the cool marble foyer, he felt his focus sharpening to the task at hand. Showgirls pranced on the giant screen behind the desk, diamante winked from elaborate costumes and feather-fan topped faces smiled out over weighty implants. If he could do it anywhere, this desert of temptation was the place.

After what felt like an eternity he saw him, sloping toward the bank of lifts. Adam waved, the amiable friend, but Jerry's eyes were cast down to the floor. He was blind to the world and lost inside himself, as usual.

Unperturbed, Adam jogged over to his side, cranking up the camaraderie with every stride. "Jerry, you old bastard!" he cried, giving him a hearty slap on the back. Jerry baulked and snapped into the moment. "Oh God, it's you. I'm not going to the gym, so don't even ask." His face was the picture of gloom.

"Cheer up, you miserable fucker! It's Vegas!"

Jerry grimaced. "Woo hoo."

Adam slung an arm around his shoulders and steered him into the lift. "Come on, get changed. It's party time." The corners of Jerry's mouth drooped to the floor. He was going to be hard work.

"I don't feel like it."

"You're coming out with me."

"I am not."

"Are."

"Not."

"Are."

Jerry cracked a tiny smile and threw an exasperated look at Adam. "I have had a SHIT day."

Adam squeezed his shoulders. "Time to blow it off. What floor?"

Accompanying Jerry to his room, he barged in after him, kicking the door shut. "You can't sulk. I've come all this way."

Jerry huffed and thrust his hands deep into his trouser pockets, but Adam knew he'd win his weak will over eventually: he just needed the right hook. "It's time to start living out those dreams, Jerry. What would Remi do?" Jerry snorted out a laugh. He tossed his jacket over a chair and pulled open his tie. "I need a shower," he sighed.

Bingo.

~

Adam knocked back his Jack Daniels and laughed. "Make us rich, Jerry. I'm counting on you!" He flipped the Machiavellian switch between the two paths of behaviour that jostled in his mind. Now he was the best friend: encouraging Jerry to take risks and have a good time. The alternative course twisted and plotted a trap.

Jerry shook the dice in cupped hands, looking unconvinced. "And what am I trying to do again?" He screwed up his face in confusion.

"Whatever you roll this time, you've got to roll the next time too."

Jerry frowned, but there was a boyish twinkle in his eyes: he was having fun. He tossed the dice down the table.

"Eight, the easy way," the dealer said, retrieving them. He placed the puck on eight and took a couple of chips from Jerry's line. Jerry looked like he wanted to stop him, but thought better of it, throwing a questioning look at Adam instead.

"This is good," said Adam, "Roll again. See if you can get another eight."

Jerry sang, "Oooo-kaaay" and bounced the dice off the table's back wall.

"Eight: five and three." The dealer stacked chips and slid them over to Jerry, who grinned and added them to his bank.

"Nice!" he nodded to Adam, with a growing smile. Another roll, another win and Jerry progressed to giggling. It was hard for Adam to stay mad at someone so agreeable. He tossed the dice again. Six. "Come on six!" Jerry called and launched the dice down the table. He was getting the hang of it.

Showing Jerry the ropes was unexpectedly engaging. Adam found playing his part was easy and natural, but it was hard to hold on to the ulterior motive. It felt like preparing to kick a kitten. Sour expectations had been sweetened with friendship and Adam was having a good time, in spite of himself.

Being with Jerry, doing boy's stuff, just having a laugh: now he realised that he'd missed this. Adam had been floating alone and lost for so long, it felt good to bob around with his old school pal.

The waitress brought them a couple more drinks. Jerry took a pull from his Bud and rolled a three and a four. "Seven ends play," stated the dealer, hoovering up chips and stacking them in front of himself.

"Boooooo!" Adam bellowed. "Right, my turn. Watch and learn." Adam arse-bumped Jerry over to the left and took his place at the head of the table.

"All right, Buzz," said Jerry, smoothing himself down, "Chill." Adam covertly gave him the finger and selected a couple of dice from the dealer. They giggled and jostled, Adam's act merging with reality.

They laid bets and launched dice. Adam spun to toss them over his shoulder. The dealer didn't approve, but Adam was racked with juvenile giggles now too. "Vegas, baby!"

Next thing, Jerry was bounding up to a couple of strangers who'd appeared at the edge of their table, watching Adam and Jerry with amused smiles. He gambolled over, ever the irrepressible friendly puppy, and welcomed them to the game. "I'm Jerry and this is my friend Adam," he said, wafting his bottle in Adam's direction.

"Ed and this is Oona," said the man with a smile, gesturing to his female companion. Ed was about five feet ten, in his fifties and thinned right out on top. What was left of his hair was a pale nutty brown. Friendly blue eyes smiled out from crow's feet.

"Come on, join in," Jerry said, "I've got no idea what I'm doing, so you're bound to win."

The man threw a glance to his companion who shrugged with a half-smile and then looked over to Adam.

"Plenty of space for newcomers," Adam confirmed.

"OK, thanks," said Ed.

"Now for Christ's sake, stop flirting, Jerry!" Adam berated with mock indignation, "I've told you before!" More giggling. Their new friends smiled and Jerry ignored him.

"You and your wife here on holiday, Ed?" Oona spluttered into her drink. "Actually we're colleagues, here for the exhibition," she said.

"Ah, gotcha," Jerry nodded and turned to face Adam, pulling a face of mock seriousness, "Continue," he said and waved his hand. Adam played on and found himself on a roll: his numbers coming up, again and again. With every win he and Jerry got a little sillier and before they knew it their new friends were joining in and part of the gang. Their game was too infectious to resist.

Adam made a half-hearted assessment of the new female in their presence. Did she have the potential to lead Jerry astray? She was probably mid-thirties, but it was difficult to tell exactly. She had utterly clear skin and green eyes that watched with the presence of a hunter. Her hair was a choppy ruffle of black that fell across her cheeks in feathers. No: she'd eat Jerry for breakfast, not that he'd get that far.

She launched her dice down the table and produced a six. "Come on, six," she breathed, rolling the dice around her palm like a pro. They booed in unison when she crapped out on the next throw.

"I don't know about anyone else," said Oona, "but I'm starving! Who's up for a burger?"

They staggered together over to Mina's and slid into a snug booth, in the grip of a sudden and ravenous hunger. They all ordered the house burger, which looked delicious on the front of the menu not one of them bothered to read.

"You two must have known each other for a while," said Ed through a mouthful, "You've got a whole routine going on there."

"You hear that, Woody? We're a team," said Adam.

Jerry replied with his best sarcastic eyebrow.

"What do you do?" asked Ed.

"PR," said Jerry. "And law," said Adam.

"Do you work together? If you don't, maybe you should. We're always looking for fresh faces at M.E. You should look me up when all this is over." Ed waved around them, gave an amiable grin and took another bite.

Interesting, thought Adam. "Actually, I am between jobs right now."

"Are you? What happened?" Ed seemed genuinely interested.

"Worked in criminal defence for years. One too many bad apples and I couldn't stomach it anymore. I studied law to make the world a better place, you know?"

"Sounds like M.E. might be just the place for you, Adam."

"M.E.?"

"Yeah, Mango Europe."

Jerry stopped chewing and went all wide-eyed.

"Your kind of energy would be a welcome asset. What about you, Jerry? Where do you fit in?"

Jerry swallowed down his food. "I specialise in PR across the IT industry. I'm here for the exhibition too."

"Great. Just great. I'm so pleased we ran into you two. We should get together another time to talk shop."

"Absolutely. I'd love that. I mean really, that would be brilliant," Jerry stammered over his burger. His grin was so wide it was making Adam's face hurt.

~

"That was AWESOME!" slurred Jerry again. "Mango wants to work with me! Work with us! I am hot stuff, baby!" He fell hiccupping into the lift, followed by Adam who punched buttons for their respective floors. Jerry's came first.

Adam shoved him out into the 4th floor foyer. "Totally awesome," Jerry repeated, "I've fallen on my feet at last."

"That wasn't falling," said Adam with a smile as the doors began to close, "That was flying, with style."

FORTY-FOUR

Ed and Oona strolled down the MGM concourse and out onto The Strip. Their destination was a short hop made long by eight streaming lanes of traffic that separated them from the Monte Carlo Hotel and ultimately their beds. They took the pedestrian overpass, happy in the drowsy glow of alcohol and soon the Monte Carlo was upon them. They traversed its marble foyer in a bubble of contented chatter.

"Oh God, when Jerry crapped out straight off for the second turn running I thought I'd die laughing." Ed rubbed at his eye with the back of his hand, stretching out the happy crow's feet.

"His face. It was classic." Oona shook her head. "They were a find. I like them. They'd be fun to work with, wouldn't they? A real boost to Head Office."

"For sure."

Memories of the evening ebbed and flowed.

"We should ask Jerry to pitch for Europe's PR contract."

Ed nodded in agreement. "Perhaps we'll let him get some sleep first."

Oona rolled her eyes. "U-huh." They stepped into the lift. "I'll call him in the morning."

FORTY-FIVE

Jerry's brain sloshed to the other side of his skull and a wave of nausea gripped his throat. Rolling over had been a bad, bad move.

With slits for eyes, he gradually focussed through the hangover fug. Painful daylight glared around the edge of closed curtains and he squinted at his watch: it was after two. Bugger, he'd missed the whole morning at the exhibition.

His guilty conscience dragged him upright, but his spinning head was having none of that and slithered him back down to the pillow, rubbing at his forehead with a sweaty palm. His stomach snarled and cramped, then launched him out of bed to the bathroom to puke. The dishevelled wreck he eventually saw in the mirror, was distinctly grey around the gills with blushing pink pillowcase creases wobbling down the right side of his face. His hair stuck up in a lopsided Mohican. "Oh God, I'm never drinking again," he moaned.

Groping his wash bag from the empty marble, he shambled into the shower cubicle. Rachel's magic hangover cure would go down a treat right now, but pathetic and alone, he didn't know what to do with himself.

Ugh, the exhibition again. Yesterday's visit had been a disaster and he was none too keen to repeat the experience. Feeling how he did, he wasn't sure he could even make it out of the room.

Wrapped in a towel, he was retracing the trail of crumpled clothing, back to the relative security of the bed, when he stubbed his toe on something unexpected. He was used to that, of course. Sharing a house with Peanut meant all kinds of unexpected things strewn on the floor, on the table, on the bed. But it wasn't a rattle or an agonisingly pointy shape from a puzzle. It was an empty champagne bottle that rolled chinking into the coffee table. That was why he felt so bad. Why the hell had he drunk that? What was there to celebrate?

Jerry's stomach sank farther still. He missed Rachel and Peanut. He even missed the mess that surrounded them, that defined the edges of home. He tossed the bottle upside down into the ice bucket and threw his clothes at the chair. He'd deal with them later. Right now, he just needed to lie down.

FORTY-SIX

Leaning into empty air, Adam willed his feet to leave the ground. He rose into the sky and swelled with the elation of flight. Cruciform, he looked down upon the uneven pavement of Heath Terrace. Warm air ruffled his clothes and hair and he flew with silent ease. A gentle lean steered his course, shifting the invisible tiller to cross houses and view the gardens beyond. It was effortless, as if he were drawn on a preordained path.

But then, without warning nor command, his legs drooped at the hip. Robbed of the streamlined flying position, he lost height but gained speed, and no adjustment that he made corrected the course. He skimmed dangerously close to sharp roof tiles and scrabbled to pull up while twiggy tree tops scratched hot grazes into his palms.

Now desperate to regain control, he saw her up ahead: an exquisite butterfly of finest translucent silk. She beat her wings to an irregular rhythm that brought about a rise and fall of unpredictable grace.

Adam swooped and fought against his terror, managing to slow his descent a few feet behind her. The sun danced over golden threads that laced the surface of her wings and Adam wanted her for himself, more than anything he'd ever known. Full stretch, he strained to touch her, but she bobbed and wove ahead, always just out of reach.

Distracted by the chase, he'd sunk low, out of the sun's range. Colours were muted in the cold grey gloom. Only inches from the ground now, he struggled to climb again, his knee scraping painfully over jagged rock. That's when he noticed that the earth was moving. Thousands of beetles formed a black armoured carpet that weaved and flowed over the land below.

In horror Adam pulled back, managing to rise a few feet, but the butterfly had sunk down to be with him and settled on a hillock not twenty feet ahead. He tried to shout, to warn her, but no sound came. He tipped his position to fly faster, to save her, but instead veered away, off course, out of control again.

The dark beetle flood, irrepressible and all consuming, flowed in every direction. In seconds it would be too late. Adam fought in vain for control: they were going to envelop her and he was too far away to do anything about it.

The snap of a wind change and all around was black. Buzzing wings pulled scrabbling bodies into the air. They battered into his face, scrabbled at his nostrils and crawled into his throat. All at once the air was an oil slick of evil. Adam crashed thrashing to the ground.

And woke up, bathed in sweat.

Adam's suite on the 23rd floor was quiet and empty. In the cool comfort of reality his nightmare glowed in stark contrast, still pin-sharp in consciousness. He took a deep breath and willed his heart to slow.
It's all right, just a dream, he told himself and threw back the clammy sheets to recover for a moment, still in the nightmare's grip. His chest burned with tension, tiny movements sending stabs of pain into his arm. He slowed his breathing and willed his muscles to relax. His body cooled and the physical pain abated, but his mind raced on, conflicted and desperate.

When anxiety nagged him out of bed, he pulled on some shorts and checked his watch: two-thirty in the afternoon. The exhibition would still be running for a few hours yet. He was his own man for a while. He padded across the suite to take a juice from the mini bar, then dragged a dining chair to the window and settled onto it, rubbing at the hollow in the centre of his chest. The Strip's jagged geology stretched out to the horizon, a view that should have been impressive but, its magic was weak without nightfall's neon.

He took a sip from the juice, tipped back his head to rest on the soft padding and closed his eyes. Last night had been a blast but now, now he didn't feel so good about having a good time with Jerry. Then, buoyed by alcohol, he'd been swept away on a wave of camaraderie. Today he felt disloyal and alone.

A vision of her drifted into his mind's eye. His silken butterfly, his Rachel. The pit of Adam's stomach stirred and he squeezed his hands into fists. He wanted her so badly now his lungs ached for the cinnamon citrus rush of her perfume and the swell of her bosom pressed hard against him while she cried. That salty tear: he shuddered at its remembered taste and touched his lips. She'd cried at Jerry's treachery. Her words echoed in his head: *"I wish that he would just do something so unbearable that I'd have no choice, something so destructive that there could be no going back."*

He could make it happen. He could set her free to be with him.

Jerry made her miserable. It was all wrong. Too wrapped up in his deceit to see how she suffered and she was everything: beauty and passion; mother and lover; the essence of life, of good.

McGinty flashed across his synapses, relishing his cruel story, another player for the devil. Adam's heart rate rose. That terrified old lady: humiliated and abused. The acid churned in

Adam's gut. Another flash: his grandmother: still elegant but frail. A beatific smile he hadn't seen in five years or more; and then the house, windows turned to soulless eyes when curtains were torn down and shipped: his childhood home made sad when they abandoned him and moved abroad. He clenched his jaw. It was all so unfair. He had to tip the balance back and make it right.

He had to make it happen.

FORTY-SEVEN

The birds chirruped in the budding trees and a small boy on a tricycle rattled past, tongue poked out in avid concentration. Winter sunshine cast a hopeful glow.

Sitting on the wooden bench, Remi could see across the open parkland to backstage suburbia's erratic fencing and garden sheds. Dog walkers traversed the twisting park paths, swinging plastic bags, while their dogs charged back and forth, chasing balls and each other. Occasional good-spirited tussles sent them rolling through puddles and brought their owners together in a momentary meeting of lives.

At the bottom of the hill crouched a colourful playground, where a huddle of mothers encouraged toddlers up gentle climbing frames and down slides. Their voices carried in a unified jolly murmur and Remi absorbed their contentment, bolstering his jaded soul with the purity of childhood.

It was strange how an afternoon spent freezing his arse off in the park had held no appeal for Jerry until he wasn't able to do it. He may have been holed up in an oasis, but the Nevada desert was too extreme to be comfortable: too hot in the sun and too cold in the air conditioned flow that swept down across his bed. You knew where you were with the temperature in England. The weather was crap and you wrapped yourself up. Here he always seemed to be wearing slightly too much or too little.

Remi had met up with department heads during his morning in the office and now had pressing business to attend to: an afternoon in the park. The fresh snap in the air put an invigorating tingle in his lungs.

Beside him square-toed Mary-Janes swung back and forth, impatient to be moving on. She put her tiny hand in his, soft plump fingers squeezing tight and turned rosy cheeks to face him. "Daddy, can we go to the playground?"

Remi smiled. "OK. It's getting cold just sitting here." He planted her, giggling, onto his shoulders and they set off down the hill. "You warm enough?"
"Yes."
"Want to wear my hat?"
"No."
"Need to pee?"

"Daddy!" She giggled and off they went. Saving the world and running an empire could wait until tomorrow.

FORTY-EIGHT

Spink gazed out through the expanse of glass at the top of Mango's tower, down to the scurrying delegates below. They scuttled from stand to stand, still searching for their crumb. Spink's lay before him on the thick glass table: a letter of intent, confirming that he, Donald Spink, was to handle the new working relationship between Locksley PR and Mango Worldwide.

He'd bloody done it, beaten Adler hands down. Where was that snivelling idiot anyway? He needed to rub it in, make sure that Adler knew he was the better man. He'd vaporised since yesterday's encounter on the train.

Spink tapped his foot, impatient to be on his way. The creeping gap between shoe leather and sole flexing in irritated gasps.

They were in the final throes of the latest Mango corporate video Drinkwater had insisted on showing him 'to get his creative juices flowing'. The only lubrication Spink was interested in, however, waited in green glass behind the hotel bar. A celebration was in order.

Drinkwater flicked off the plasma with a slim silver remote. "So that's it, Donald. That gives you a good idea of where we are."

"Yup, yup. Very interesting, Eric." Spink plastered on an enthusiastic grin. "Can't wait to get started." *Can't wait to crack the whip over the juniors—remind them who's boss.*

"I'll get legal to draw up the contract as soon as I get back and we'll have you over for lunch and to sign on the dotted line when it's ready. How does that sound?" Eric extended his hand for Spink to shake.

"Excellent. Can't wait to blue sky some ideas. Perhaps we can throw a few against the wall over lunch, see what sticks?"

"Sure." Drinkwater turned and headed for the door. As he moved away, a small piece of paper fluttered from him and wove its way down to the floor. Spink bent to pick it up. It was a restaurant receipt, excellent. He stuffed into his pocket before Drinkwater had a chance to notice. As he patted him on the back, they ambled down the stairs together. "Been an excellent exhibition, wouldn't you say?" said Spink.

"More to come. I'll see you in London."

Spink shook his hand one final time then made off through the fluorescent sprawl toward the monorail.

~

Comfortable on his double seat, Spink examined the receipt: dinner for four at Andre's. What luck, he could pretend he'd taken Mango out. The casino had torn a strip off him last night so an extra three hundred and fifty dollars in his expense claim would help to claw some of it back. Even so, he'd better take it easy from now on.

Winning Mango was going to keep him his job in the long run but, short term he'd still got some serious cash flow problems. The Cranley would want their money when he got back and the Mouse's jewellery wasn't safe in the pawn shop. She hadn't noticed it was missing yet and, if he continued not to take her anywhere good enough to wear it, she might never. Still, it was good to have the jewellery held in reserve to get him out of sticky situations just like this.

Disembarking the train he headed to the bar for a scotch or two to steel his nerves. Tonight he had to beat the casino.

FORTY-NINE

The door swung open to reveal a pitiful sight: Jerry, hunched in a hotel bathrobe. He turned, groaned and shuffled away.

"Oh dear." Adam pushed his hands into his pockets and followed Jerry into the room, kicking the door closed. "Jerry, have you been like this all day?"

"Mm."

"You didn't make it to the exhibition?"

"Mm."

Adam strutted around the room, observing the mess that Jerry had made of it. Extracting a fist from his pocket, he stood a tipped glass and straightened its coaster. "Are you like this at home?"

Jerry sighed and gave him a petulant look. Adam had put the mess down to Peanut but, now he could see: Jerry was responsible for that too. He refocused on the task at hand. "Anyway, come on, we're celebrating." There was more than one reason to get Jerry plastered, again.

Jerry scoffed and flopped backwards onto the dishevelled bed. "Yeah, right."

"Yeah, right? It's not every day that Mango Europe pick out their new PR people, now is it?"

Jerry's blank expression grew wider eyed, the dim light of a distant memory creeping through the dark recesses of his brain. "Mango Europe?"

"In. The. Casino." Adam was speaking deliberately slowly. "They're calling you. Remember?"

"Oh! Oh crap!" Jerry leapt up and scrabbled through the heap of clothes on the chair, eventually pulling out his phone. "Two missed calls. No!" He stabbed at the phone and thrust it to his ear, listening to voicemail.

The expression on his face, initially panicked, evolved into horror. He stabbed at the phone to move on to the next message and closed his eyes, listening. Eventually, he tossed it to the bed and slumped down, head in hands.

"So?"

After a deep breath Jerry said, "It's OK. They had full afternoon with an important client. Oona wants me to call her in the morning." He looked up at Adam and laughed with a shake of his head. "Jesus. I thought that was it for a minute."

"Idiot."

"Wanker."

"Get dressed."

Jerry rolled his head back and slouched into himself. "I feel like shit."

"What you need," said Adam, circling the end on the bed, "is the hair of the dog." He laid his hands on Jerry's shoulders then gripped and pulled him up. "You've got Mango in the palm of your hand, Jerry. We need to celebrate. A couple of drinks inside you and you'll be right as rain, you'll see."

Jerry looked doubtful.

"Bathroom. Shower. Clothes." He spun him around and pushed him on his way. Jerry shut the bathroom door behind him, grumbling.

"This room is a shit hole."

"I didn't let the maid in," Jerry called through the wood.

Adam prowled around the bed, replacing pillows and pulling the covers straight, until it was smooth and made. He approached the tangled heap of clothes on the chair and searched through them for Jerry's key card, which he slid into his own back pocket. "Don't take too long. I'm going down to save us a place in the lobby bar." The sound of water gushed on the other side of the door. "Jerry?"

"Yeah. OK."

"Don't go back to bed."

Something mumbled, then, "I'll be there in a minute, God."

Satisfied, Adam turned on his heel and left. The room was good enough.

Down in the lobby, he positioned himself on the banquette facing the lifts, pulled out his phone and called the number he'd researched back in the UK: a licensed brothel outside the Las Vegas borders that followed regulations and would send the girls to you. The financial transactions all happened on your credit card and out of town where it was legal. A loophole he intended to exploit, for himself this time.

"Vegas Nights. What's your pleasure?" A woman's voice oozed down the line.

"I'd like to arrange some company. A surprise for a friend. He's kind of particular. Can you help me?"

"Sure, honey. What's your friend's name?"

"Jerry."

"And what does your friend like?"

"She needs to be small, slim, you know. Dark hair, not too long or wiggy and pale skin. Pretty." Adam thought of Rachel. There was no hope of them even getting close to her, but a passing resemblance might help if Jerry was drunk enough.

"Anything else?"

"Straightforward stuff. It's a treat."

"We have just the girl: Adora. Where are you, honey?"

"I'd like her to meet me at the MGM Grand, by the main entrance at ten-thirty tonight."

"Sure thing. I just need your credit card."

Adam gave her what she needed, took a deep breath and pocketed the phone. The heat of adrenalin burned in his cheeks: he'd set the cogs in motion.

The lobby bar was jumping. Music pumped and the crowd swayed. He squeezed through, ordered a bottle of champagne then spotted a table and staked his claim. Tonight had to be a celebration. He needed Jerry to feel good and get into the vibe.

Girls danced up on the bar in brazen short skirts that flashed their panties, pushing out their breasts and popping their hips. Salivating men gazed up at them. Adam watched impassively and wondered if they were hookers too. It took all sorts, after all who was he to judge, given what he'd just done. He wondered if somewhere there was a malicious pimp that took their money. A pang of regret crept up his back: he'd been on the payroll. He'd proved beyond all reasonable doubt the inculpability of a rich villain, over and over again.

Paying for the hooker didn't feel good but, at least the girls from Vegas Nights worked under the protection of the law, with health screening and regular pay. It was a means to an end, for them and for him.

He checked his watch. He had a little more than two hours to set the scene.

Twenty long minutes later Jerry wobbled up the steps and paused squinting around the bar. Adam waved him over. Sauntering up to the table, Jerry eyed the ice bucket with disdain. "Champagne?" he groaned.

"Celebrating, remember?" Adam sloshed out two foaming flutes. "Cheers!" He chinked with Jerry and stared at his glass with wide expectant eyes. Jerry sighed and took a sip. Adam smiled. "Took your time."

"Couldn't find my key card. Had to get another from reception."

Adam made no comment, but prayed the pilfered card in his pocket had not been cancelled. Adam tipped his drink into his mouth and grabbed the bottle for a refill. Jerry's glass was still full. Adam rolled an encouraging hand at it. "Celebrating…"

Obediently Jerry knocked it back and shuddered.

"Atta boy." Adam filled it to the brim.

A change in music cued the dancing girls' return.

"Why don't you get us some beers?" said Adam, sending Jerry up closer.

He slouched over to the bar and stood, unavoidably, a few feet from one of the girls grinding to the music. Her hands skimmed down her body and Jerry gawped up at her, along with the other enraptured men that clapped along.

Jerry turned to look at Adam, a half-smile creeping across his face. *That's it, Jerry,* thought Adam, settling back in his seat.

When Jerry returned he drank more convincingly from the bottle of Bud he'd chosen for himself.

"I guess it's not so bad in here," he laughed with a juvenile snort and Adam nodded along.

"Look at the blonde on the end." She jiggled to the beat. Jerry guffawed into his beer and took a hearty slug. He was getting into it. Leaning in he said, "M.E. could save my job, Adam. Hooking up with them last night has changed everything. I'd still like to know what Spink's got up his sleeve, though. He's obviously not dealing with Ed and Oona."

"Maybe his cronies aren't in the right department."

"He seemed pretty confident yesterday."

"Dinky's full of shit. Ignore him, you've got it, Jerry." Adam chinked his bottle onto Jerry's. "Another?" He was on his feet before Jerry could answer, and heading into the crush.

"Two bottles of Bud and a Jack on ice," he told the bartender. He'd needed to get away for a moment, to regroup. A shot of Jack would settle him down. Still at the bar, he took a slug and relished the burn that travelled down his gullet. It joined the churning acid in his gut, the only thing inside besides emptiness. It would be worth it. It was cruel and she'd be upset, but it was a kindness: the unbearable act. Then they could be together.

Another slug to ease the constriction in his throat. All he had to do was discover them. Discover Jerry in the arms of another woman and feel compelled to tell Rachel. How could you, Jerry? And that would be it: the event so destructive that it would all just be over.

The music changed and the crowd responded. A hen party squawked and bounced, drunk and sweaty at his side and Adam seized the opportunity, signalling Jerry to join him and bring the champagne.

Jerry bit at his lip sidling through the crowd toward them, but Adam took the champagne from him before he had a chance to protest. "Ladies! Join us for a drink?" Their eyes were drawn by the bottle he proffered and the closest, a bouncy-haired blonde, gave Adam an appreciative smile. "Come on, girls! Champagne!" she crowed and the others crowded around.

"Jerry—get some more glasses," said Adam, turning his back and trapping him next to the bar. He heard him call the barman.

"Out celebrating?" he enquired of the blonde.

"Tia's getting married." She waved at a girl with long dark hair in a shocking pink veil who winked back.

"No kidding. I'm Adam, this is Jerry. We're celebrating too. Jerry here's getting promoted."

By now Jerry had lined up some glasses on the bar. Adam thrust the bottle back into Jerry's hand. "You pour, I'll get some more." He dove behind Jerry, leaving him now in the spotlight. He started pouring and the girls drew in, accepting their glass and bopping to the music.

Adam tapped the beat out on Jerry's shoulder from behind and Jerry's head began to nod along. "Enjoy yourself, you've earned it," he called out and ordered two more bottles. This would be easy. Jerry was so pliable, so compliant. He would follow Adam's lead.

Adam topped up glasses and homed in on the bride to be—she was the least likely to want anything from him beside the champagne. "He's shy," he told her, "See if your friends can bring him out of his shell."

"He doesn't stand a chance." Tia knocked back her drink and putting her glass on the bar, took the dancing up a notch, encouraging her girls to join in. They were happy to dance around Jerry, shimmying up and down, daring each other to go further. Adam kept the drinks flowing. Increasingly drunk and lost in the music, Jerry was a willing pole substitute. He laughed and clapped, wiggled and bopped, utterly oblivious to his mercurial companion.

Adam egged the girls on to try to embarrass him, but in no time he was way beyond that. Adam checked his watch: it was 10:30.

FIFTY

Adora waited outside. A slim built Latina, she arched against the wall, tight pink rhinestoned T-shirt stretched across inflated breasts. A short open denim waistcoat skimmed around the nipples that protruded through her thin cotton shirt. She snapped her gum.

As Adam approached she looked him up and down, a knowing smile tugging at the corner of red lips.

"Adora?"

"Jerry?"

"No."

"I thought it was too good to be true." She touched his chest and ran a long fluorescent fingernail around a shirt button.

He swept her misconception away. "Save it for Jerry. Can you go up to the room and wait? Here's the key. Room 439. I need to get him from the bar."

"Uh-huh." She peered at the offered key card, considering his words and Adam gripped her wrist. "Don't even think about ripping us off."

"All right already." She shook him loose, her voice escalating, "I won't take no crap. Don't think you can treat me bad." She jutted out her chin in defiance and Adam reeled himself in to continue in a whisper.

"I know. Look I'm sorry. I'm just a little nervous for my friend. I want him to like it, OK?" Adam didn't want Jerry to bottle it and run away. "Go gentle."

She smiled, relaxing. "It's OK. I get it. Don't worry. Your friend will have a good time." Snap of the gum.

Adam pulled out a twenty-dollar note and tucked it into the pocket of her waistcoat. "I'm sorry." It wasn't her fault. Was she another pawn in the game, or a player? Adam wasn't sure where the lines were anymore.

"Forgiven," she said and turned to click-clack into the lobby, round bottom wiggling away in spray-on pleather.

All that remained was for Adam to get Jerry to his room. He needed a reason to take him from the bar. What argument could he build to take their party upstairs? Could he send the girls on ahead—send them to a phoney room number? Then they could follow on 'behind'.

Adam strode across the lobby, homing in on Jerry, whirring through his options. Sitting at their table, hot and happy, Jerry was leaning back in his seat, enjoying a moment's recuperation. The girls still crowded at the bar and Adam saw his chance to persuade them, without Jerry hearing.

Adam rehearsed the speech in his head and, lost in the argument, didn't even notice Spink until he was right on top of him. Shoulders slumped and eyes downcast, Spink's drooping mouth did nothing to pull the furrows from his brow. He was undoubtedly a worried man.

Adam pulled up just short of slamming into him and, surprised, Spink looked up, his expression shifting from worry to wide-eyed fear. He recognised Adam from all those years ago. His tormentor had found him.

Adam looked coolly down at the rabbit caught in his headlights. "Well what do you know! Dinky! Fancy seeing you here!"

Spink cowered.

"What's the matter? Not pleased to see me?"

"What are you doing here?"

"Enjoying the sights. Until now."

Adam felt a surge of power, remembered from school days. Then he'd been invincible: badgering Spink into humiliated submission. The smug little shit who thought he knew best and got kicked around the playground on a daily basis. Back at school everything had been so much simpler: my gang or your gang. No confusion. He'd ruled over Spink. Why couldn't Jerry? It was yet another confirmation of the void between them. Jerry could never stand in his shoes, be the man nor the match for Rachel.

Spink squirmed backward, but Adam didn't want to let him off the hook and stepped in closer. Their toes touched and Spink recoiled. Adam stepped in again, this time standing hard on Spink's tatty Oxfords.

"Leave me alone, Fox! I don't need this today!" Spink whined.

Adam looked down at him in silent reproach. The foul reek of stale cigar smoke caught in his nostrils.

"I've lost it all!" Spink was shaking, "You happy?"

Adam raised an unconcerned eyebrow. A gambler, of course. That was what membership at The Cranley was all about for him, wasn't it? Spink had been drawn to his own. Grasping, miserable excuses for human beings, all of them.

That day with Greg: tight-collared and rotten, he'd been nauseated by the comparison and the shame. There'd been no choice but to change, not like them anymore.

Adam's head blurred and flickered. McGinty taunted him. *I cut out her wagging tongue.* He clenched his teeth against frustrated anger, spurting now through tight capillaries to find expression in muscle beyond. He drew in breath to hold it back and watched Spink sink down, unable to escape.

"Leave me alone, Fox!" he squawked, hands rising to protect himself from the onslaught he felt coming, "It's been years, can't you move on?"

Adam tossed back a laugh. "Oh yes. I'm moving on." He'd left all that behind. No point in letting the past take over, not now his future was so close to starting. Adam eased the pressure off Spink's foot, who took his chance and lurched away across the foyer, putting as much distance between himself and Adam as those short legs could manage. Adam let him go: he had more important things to do.

The gaggle of girls were still where he'd left them and Adam marched straight into the centre of their circle. "Girls! Who wants more champagne?" he shouted over the music, over the voices in his head.

The group whooped and cheered, just like he knew they would.

"What do you say to carrying this party on in luxurious private? I've got a suite on the 30th floor and money to burn!" Money. Always money. He leaned over to the bartender and ordered a couple more bottles of champagne, which he awarded to the eager girls.

"Suite 3025. Take up the bubbles. We'll be there in a minute." Adam waved at Jerry who gave him the thumbs up.

Already high on Adam's generosity, the girls bounded unquestioning out of the bar. Another step accomplished, Adam had to focus on the final crucial piece.

He noted with pleasure that Jerry was looking a little disappointed, craning his neck to watch the departing hen party. He slid into the chair beside him.

"Aw, Adam! What did you say to them?"

"They're going up to your room. I suggested a little private party."

"You what! Adam, I can't…"

"Sure you can. They're fun girls. We're just going to have some fun."

"But I…"

"Don't be selfish, Jerry. What about me?"

Jerry pouted at him and narrowed his eyes. "You don't need a wing man."

"I do, Jerry. I need this, please."

Jerry took a long pause. "Get me another drink and I'll think about it."

"Jerry, the girls…"

"One more. Then we can go."

Adam knew that Adora would wait and the girls were heading in the wrong direction anyway. He sighed and conceded. Jerry was allowed a last request. "Bud?"

"Yeah." Jerry grinned. "Get one for take-out too."

FIFTY-ONE

Spink squeezed at his temples with shaking fingers. His run in with Adam Fox had upset him more than felt rational. Just overwrought, he reasoned, the pressure of the last few days taking its toll.

That evening he'd pushed it too far and lost everything in the casino and was dragging his depressed self to the bar to find more whisky and distraction when he'd seen him: Adler, sitting smiling at a table drinking champagne. What the hell did that little shit have to celebrate? Spink's ego had felt the erosion of its foundations and swayed. Was there something that he didn't know?

He'd had to get away, to head for his room, before Adler spotted him, unable to hide his defeat.

Spink clenched his fists. He needed to secure his job more than ever now. Couldn't have Adler whipping the rug out from under him. Not now, not when he was so close.

Spink paced to and fro in the rising glass lift. Fists clenched at the ground, he counted the floors passing. A dull ache spread across his chest: aftermath of the ghastly encounter. Adam Fox, Jesus. A noxious coincidence that was. He hadn't seen him for years, not since school and there he was, popping up when he needed him least.

Spink's flesh crawled with the oppressive memories. He'd been the short kid with the big mouth 'asking for a slap'. He'd always overdone it. He knew it. What he'd lacked in height he'd tried to make up for in volume. Adam Fox had taken it upon himself to silence him. "Still not listening? Let's clean out those ears…" Another flushing, the choking water that left him gasping, that trickled down his back in the classroom after: the marker for the other kids to see.

To hell with Fox. He didn't know why he was letting it get to him so much. Things were different now. It was bad luck bumping into him when he was feeling low, that's all. He was a businessman now, a success. He didn't know what Fox did for a living, but he was still a terrorist as far as Spink could see. He hoped his life was a flop, hoped that the world had seen through his good looks and convenient charm and knocked him on his arse. Spink was the better man now, he was sure of it.

The lift doors slid open on four and, straightening up, Spink made off down the corridor at a lick, toward his room.

Ten paces to go he noticed that the door opposite his was ajar. Adler's door. Spink checked up and down the corridor then crept over, pushing it open to discover a voluptuous Latina hooker. She smouldered on the bed in nothing but black lace knickers and a short skin-tight sparkling top. She spoke through scalding red lips, "Jerry? I've been waiting so long, I thought I'd get comfortable." She stroked at her naked thigh.

Spink laughed out loud. Adler was celebrating, wasn't he? He'd seen him downstairs quaffing champagne and looking quite comfortable. Shame to leave the tart here all alone, especially when she clearly didn't know what Adler looked like.

Spink slid into the room and clicked the door shut behind him. The hooker watched him, adjusting her position for maximum cleavage. Her perfume reached through the air: snaking tendrils of sticky sweet temptation. Why not? He lit a cigar and puffed out a plume of rich smoke. Was this part of Adler's celebration? Well Spink was going to take it from him. "Well, well. This looks like fun."

"Oh yeah, we're going to have some fun. Why don't you come and sit down?" she said, patting the satin quilt.

Spink wasted no time. Hauling at his belt buckle, he dropped his trousers to the carpet, stepped out of them and strode over to the bed, licking his lips, eyes focused on her nipples. She rose to her knees to meet him and Spink shoved his hand into her knickers before she could say another word.

He could do what he wanted: he was Adler and she was just a whore.

The hooker's eyes popped a little, but he saw she knew the ropes and fought fire with fire. She slammed her hand straight to Spink's crotch. Senses numbed by alcohol, he smiled and thrust into her palm.

"So what have we got here?" She felt around but, found nothing worth mentioning. Spink shrugged. Hell, after the day he'd had, not surprising little Spink wasn't up to the job. He wasn't giving up on the hooker though, not one with jugs like that, especially not when Adler was paying.

Spink rested his cigar on the bedside table and dragged his sweaty palm down over her breast, pinching and grasping. "Why don't you help me along?"

Pulling herself out of reach, she whipped his Y's away like the pro she was, pushed him down onto the bed and got to work. Sitting astride him, she pounded and pumped with her hands to bring the flaccid flesh to life.
"Oh yeah, you're getting hard for Adora!" she squealed, writhing with obvious fake enthusiasm.
Insincerity had never been a problem for Spink, who quickly climbed to the peak of excitement without ever achieving much form and it was all over. All over his flabby gut.

"Well, OK. Don't worry about it, we can try again in a minute," said Adora snapping her gum and surreptitiously wiping her hands on the bed.

Spink lay spent, all embers of desire turned to ash. Asphyxiating tiredness crept over him and sucked at his conscious. He didn't want to try again, that was all he could manage tonight.

"You can go."

"I'm paid up for a full hour…"

"I said I don't want you. I'm tired," Spink spat.

"OK." She backed away and pulled on her clothes, "You're the boss."

Spink heaved himself vertical, wiped the folds of his flesh on the quilt and let it flop to the floor. He gave the hooker a minute to get down the corridor then left the mess of Adler's room behind to go to his own smug bed.

FIFTY-TWO

The blue spark fizzed and cracked. It arced across the terminal and searched beyond. It probed and fluttered and groped for purchase.

Dry paper convulsed, drawn to its friction. Surface blackening, it absorbed the energy. Too delicate to sustain its flow, it glowed, then crumbled and passed on the flame.

Yellowing memoranda took the baton and twirled it on. The flames consumed last month's rota, the thank you note and the holiday forms. Declarations of Health and Safety fed the fire in the kitchen no longer feeding people.

Fancy hoardings masked it from the Monte Carlo's clientele: the unused kitchen anticipating refit to bring it up to standard. Inconspicuous and quiescent until the impatient fingers of electricity drummed up some action of their own.

Fire stretched up the wall and licked around the suspended ceiling, into the void. Corpses of long poisoned rats combusted in its path and through the flimsy plasterboard, it found the clutch of paperwork. Orders and invoices, internal requisitions and staff records: all held for reference but, apparently, not important enough to protect. The flames engulfed that locked room and produced a heat so fierce it punched through the air conditioning ventilation shaft running over head and gushed its noxious fumes into the air superhighway that ran a circuit of the hotel.

Down in the kitchen, the sprinklers squatted above the cold steel of unused burners, oblivious to the climbing flames that ignited an inferno in the store room above.

The ventilation shaft made progress easy. Silently it swallowed up grey death. Sweeping unseen above the ceilings, black arms of smoke reached out down sleepy corridors. Their grisly fingers plunged uninvited into vents, bypassing locked doors and gaining entry unknown.

Dark smoke gained weight and sank toward the sleeping.

FIFTY-THREE

Adam pulled Jerry out of the lift into the 4th floor lobby. He'd get him to the room, make a show of going to find the girls, then return and 'catch' him. Adam swallowed down the tension in his throat, grasped Jerry's arm and steered him down the long corridor.

"Are you taking me to bed? I do hope you're not planning to take advantage of me?" Jerry slurred and stumbled a little. Adam gripped tighter at his elbow and propelled him on. He wouldn't see the mocking eyebrow raised for his benefit, refused to register the humour.

He scanned the doors for numbers as they passed. 417, 419, 421. The corridor stretched ahead of them, bright and deserted. Adam pushed on down the tunnel of no return, adrenalin singing in his ears. He had to do it: a harsh act to put things right. Righter of wrongs and defender of the weak: he'd save Rachel from her tormenter and protect her himself. She would fill the emptiness. Be his family. Be his everything.

They rounded a corner. 435, 437, 439. Here.

"Key card?" Adam demanded, not recognising the rasp in his own voice.

Jerry leant against the wall and started a slow ineffective pocket search that poked at Adam's raw impatient nerves until he yanked his hands aside to rummage through one pocket then another. He tore the card from Jerry's jacket and slid it into the metal jaws of the lock.

Intending 'not to notice' the hooker waiting for Jerry there, Adam pushed the door wide open. His eyes scouted around the room, surreptitiously checking that all was as it should be. They found a dishevelled bed, its luxurious quilt knocked partially to the floor, but no Adora to ignore.

Jerry peeled off the wall, ricocheted off the door frame and staggered inside, leaving Adam blinking with disbelief in the corridor. After a moment he strode inside himself to pace the perimeter, checking that she truly was not there.

The poisonous remnants of cigar smoke caught in Adam's constricting throat. He pressed dry lips together and balled his fists. Where the hell was she? His chest tightened and his vison flickered, flashing snippets of memory: the nameless hen party girl running her hands over Jerry's willing chest; McGinty, so self-satisfied behind those hooded eyes; Rachel venting noisy tears; six! Come on six!

Jerry bumbled around the room oblivious, finally attempting to open a beer on the edge of the walnut desk and chipping away veneer.

"For fuck's sake, Jerry!" Adam swung his arm to snatch the bottle away, knocking Jerry on his heels. The satin quilt, already puddled on the floor, enveloped Jerry's feet and sent him twisting backward.

His head cracked against the sharp corner of the bedside table, his face at once wide-eyed and pained.

"Jesus!" Jerry gasped and Adam was on him, wrenching him to his feet by the lapels.

"Nothing's ever fucking easy with you is it, Jerry?" he yelled. Anger boiling in his veins, he yanked Jerry up onto his toes. Too close now to contend with, he threw him away, adrenalin-fuelled muscle launching him into the bank of cupboards that stretched the length of the room. Strong and righteous. Justice personified. The furniture shuddered from the force thrown against it and Jerry groaned with the air knocked from him.

Rage and repulsion filled Adam's head. He saw McGinty's face, *'Yeah I cut her. I cut her good. No bitch telling tales on me.'* Adam roared with the injustice, with the shame of defending the despicable. He would defend those worthy of it! Rachel. He could defend sweet Rachel. Jerry made her life a misery. Jerry was a fool. Why didn't he understand what he had?

His wild eyes found Jerry scrabbling, trying to get to his feet and Adam moved toward him. Lurching dangerously against the desk, Jerry smashed against the champagne glasses set up on the counter, slicing deep gashes into his palms. His shirt back was torn and bloodied where the chrome door handles had gouged at his flesh.

Incredulous at Jerry's ability to make a terrible situation even worse, but too angry to laugh, Adam grabbed at his arm and swung him sideways, away from the glass and the desk, across the room. Jerry took a faltering step, impeded by a low coffee table. It crushed his shins and felled him in a rag doll flop that splintered the inopportune table under his weight.

Adam stood, slack jawed and immobile, his vision snapping between the images in his mind and a painful reality playing out before him: Rachel's shuddering shoulders as she clung to her child, to her sanity; Jerry's search for purchase on the broken fragments of the table, slipping in his own blood—fear evident in his desperate scuffle to get up. McGinty's laugh, *"You wanted to know, man!"*

Jerry managed to get to his feet and stumbled forward, arms wind-milling against gravity. Through the bathroom door he charged with increasing speed, out of control.

Adam saw him then: saw his head connect with the glinting metal of the bath tap; saw him sag to the floor, leaving his left arm flailed across the tub above. His palm, wet with exertion and blood, clung independently to the slick enamel. It squeaked and bumped its way across the surface. Ultimately losing the battle, it fell limp and lifeless to the cold white tiles.

Adam too sank to the floor, his head a tornado of conflicting emotion. He wanted justice and love, not this violence, not death. Jerry was his anchor, his earth.

Adam had flown high in an unscrupulous world of crime and money while Jerry took the earthbound path. He'd been idiotic, chaotic, but he'd achieved what Adam never could.

Adam was alone. More alone in that moment than ever before. Wealth was not the measure of a man's success, he understood that now. He'd understood it, landing that shocking punch on the malevolent McGinty. There was no lasting happiness to be found while the devil held your soul. Jerry had found the Holy Grail: a loving wife, a new-born child. Why didn't he get it?

Adam tore at his hair with both hands, folding his chest down to his knees, he roared in anguish. Eyes screwed tight to block out the world, his chest imploded with misery.

Tears came now. Unfolding his body, he let the spasms run their course. A torrent of uncontrolled sobs rushed from Adam's heart. The flood washed thorough him, taking with it the sticky mire of deceit that had clung to him since his sorry plan's inception.

It left behind it grief. Grief for the life he'd lost: the old Adam gone for good; grief for Rachel—she would never forgive him for this; grief for his friend.

Collapsed in ruins against the broken wardrobe door, he had a clear view of Jerry prone on the bathroom floor, blood pooling beneath his head. His arm lay flopped unnaturally behind his back, his fingers pointing toward the guilty maniac in the next room. What had he done? He couldn't comprehend it.

Loss and desperation dragged a veil through Adam's vision. Unseeing open eyes stared out into oblivion and then the numbness came.

FIFTY-FOUR

It was a new cacophony of sound that brought Adam back. Adrift in the tragedy of his own sorry story, he had lost all sense of time and reality. Now something was happening outside. Barely functioning, he stumbled to the window to see.

The Strip was usually awash with people and banks of neon that lit the dark desert sky. Tonight smoke billowed from the hotel opposite and six fire trucks blocked the road below. Their red flashing lights made an incongruous contribution to the wonderland of colour. Flames licked from the Monte Carlo's 3rd floor windows.

People streamed frightened and disoriented into the street. They fled through the grand arches in their pyjamas and their Prada. Great snakes of police, guiding arms stretched wide, shepherded them away from danger, along the street toward the medic base camp set up two hundred meters away. Some ran, some screamed and cried, others ambled slow and shocked away from their personal horrors. Stretcher-bearing paramedics hurried past them, pushing loaded gurneys toward waiting ambulances.

Adam watched. The magnitude of what he saw danced beyond the glass. His mind was quiet and still: the centre of the tornado. Around him his emotions whirled, fast and invisible, cutting him off. As he stood the blood returned to his tingling limbs. His arteries reopened, recovering from the crushing uncomfortable position he'd held stupefied on the floor. He took a deep breath and turned to face the atrocity of the bathroom: Jerry motionless on the floor.

How long had he lain there? Adam dropped to one knee by his side. Jerry's body lay contorted, his cheek resting in a pool of glutinous scarlet. He reached out a tentative hand to touch the curls of hair slicked to the bathroom floor. Hard and surprising. Adam withdrew, clasping his hands together with steepled fingers.

Adam listened, at first disbelieving, to the sound of tiny shallow breaths. Jerry was breathing. He'd been so sure his friend was dead and that he was to blame. Now he nursed a spring of hope in his chest. It wasn't too late.

"Jerry! Jerry? Can you hear me?" Adam patted his cheek.
No words came.
"Jerry! Jerry! Come on, buddy!"

A soft groan rumbled deep within and Adam pulled Jerry up to clutch him to his chest. He was cold, freezing cold. He pulled the bath sheet from the rail and swaddled him as best he could. He had to find help. Shaking, Adam scooped him up and hurried out of the room.

Jerry's hair brushed against the bedroom door as they jostled through and left a bloody smear on the door frame opposite too as Adam swung around to pull the door closed.

He jabbed at the lift button with his elbow and watched impatiently while the indicator above the doors continued to read 'G'. With the lift stuck or held on the ground floor, Adam's feet itched to be on their way, the weight of Jerry pulling at his shoulders. He strode out for the stairwell, pushing the door open with his back, and focused his mind away from the burn that was rising in his thighs. He'd descended several floors before realising that he had no plan and when he finally made it out into the lobby, the scene was one of mayhem.

Guests and gamblers alike were fearful of the fire raging in the hotel opposite. Afraid that it could spread to touch them too, they were making good their escape, streaming through the lobby and out onto The Strip. Adam was swept along with them.

An anarchic combination of curiosity and panic sucked the people out into the street. Their eyes saw only the burning building and the victims running from it. They had no time for their fellow gawkers, jostling each other and stepping on toes.

Adam found himself amongst them, washed along the river of voyeuristic suffering straight into the back of a police officer.

The officer spun around, easily agitated and over stressed, but his face softened when he saw Adam carrying Jerry, when he realised, erroneously, that he was carrying a victim. Adam was a citizen assisting the injured and the officer moved aside to let them through. A few steps on and a bustling paramedic took Jerry from his arms.

No words were spoken. The silent contract of a medic's responsibility for life assumed, he laid Jerry on the gurney he'd been hauling and turned his back on Adam to check his patient over.

A thousand men's disaster had brought good fortune for just one. Jerry would be safe now. Adam could detach. Sirens and shouting filled his ears and fed the cyclone, giving it momentum, lifting it over him. He backed away. Too many people, too many faces filled with horror. They knew, knew him, knew what he'd done and it burned. Smoked stung his eyes and squeezed his throat. He pushed back against the tide of people, not caring if they yelped or cursed. He had to get away.

FIFTY-FIVE

Hands clamped tight over his ears to keep the noise at bay, Adam pushed through the gawking crowd. Mesmerised by the unfolding scene, their urgent need to escape the hotel had dissolved into paralysed curiosity. Immobile beings that blocked the sidewalk and served no purpose, but to witness. Adam kept his head down and eyes in slits. His head was full, no room for more. Just the pavement—that was all he needed to see, to know that there was still the ground beneath his feet, while his head spun and the tight belt of pain around his chest hunched his shoulders. The sirens pierced his brain in shrill daggers and he sank away, into himself, but still he staggered on. "Watch it, buddy." A man: his face screwed up and angry. Adam looked into his eyes, unable to connect, then lurched away to leave their meaningless encounter behind.

The Strip was full of people, no matter where you went and looking on uptown the crowds continued. Adam couldn't bear to be amongst them: brushing shoulders, inhaling their used breath, shrinking with guilt beneath their stare.

A corner gave an opportunity to turn away and Adam took it. Less people on this route. He felt the empty air around him and it soothed the crush inside his head, but still there were people.

Another corner and a quieter street. He straightened up and slowed his pace. All but deserted: better still. A tramp in a doorway shouted out, "Too loud for ya! Ya crazy fucker, you get away from me!" He swung a paper-wrapped bottle to his lips and took a greedy pull. Adam tried to focus and remembered his hands clutched to his ears. He let them fall and dragged his eyes from the filthy wretch squatting on the floor. Music thumped from the bar a few doors on, but the mass of voices no longer pressed against his senses. The beat felt familiar, like somewhere to lose himself.

Swarthy men in ripped jeans and faded fashion spilled out of the bar onto the street, one unfortunate pushed around between them. A flurry of swinging fists and punishing feet exploded in a noisy drama up ahead as Adam continued to approach. The victim pulled himself out of the scrum and ran, scratching at the floor with his fingernails to gain momentum. In seconds he was sprinting and one of his aggressors pulled a gun from their waistband, loosing off a couple of pot shots that missed and made his comrades laugh. "Yeah, you better run," he crowed.

The door to the bar stood open and Adam turned before the huddle on the pavement and wobbled through its grimy frame, the need for alcohol suddenly all-consuming. The man with the gun watched Adam's progress and raised an eyebrow to his friends. They followed him inside.

FIFTY-SIX

Jerry felt his stomach drop and vibrations that rattled his teeth together. It brought him up from the depths of unconsciousness. A swish he recognised as sliding doors and then the rattling stopped, to be replaced with swift motion and the squeak of rubber on lino. He couldn't move. He couldn't speak. His eyes were closed and his mouth was dry. He couldn't see them, but he knew that they were there: an indefinable presence of humanity that encircled and lifted him, that laid him out.

A man's voice, "Unknown male, approximately forty years old. Significant head trauma to the upper right side, cause unknown. G.C.S. score of 4, resp's 14, pulse 85, BP 200 over 100." And then a woman. "My name is Doctor Delacruz. You are at Canyon Springs Hospital. Can you hear me?"

Jerry tried to speak, but only rattled air in the back of his throat.

"Can you open your eyes?"

He knew he could, but somehow couldn't find the command.

Fingers touched his face and probed his scalp. "Facial blood has come from the cranial injury only." Light flooded into one eye without form or explanation. "Right pupil is blown. Are there any injuries to the rest of the body?"

"Lacerations to both palms, forearms and back." The man again.

"No signs of smoke inhalation. Breath sounds are good bilaterally. Thank you, crew. Nurse Cosenza, intubate and get our John Doe on oxygen. Nurse Neill set up BP, cardio and sat's monitors. Let's get him anesthetised and taken up for a CT. Then call Neurology and let Doctor Applebaum know we've got another one for him."

Jerry felt the movement in the room, heard dragging trolley feet and the pop of plastic packaging. His clothing fell away to be replaced with cold air and sticky pads against his skin.

A needle scratched at the back of his hand and a flood of tingling ice crept up his arm.

"Where did you pick him up?" the woman called out. "The Monte Carlo," came the man's reply, quiet and distant now. "Everybody's coming from the Monte Carlo." The cool wave sloshed over Jerry's shoulder and swept away the world.

FIFTY-SEVEN

The next he knew, Jerry drifted out of a cloud of morphine. He still couldn't move and his eyes were still closed, but he didn't think that he was dead: he could hear people arguing.

Surely in Heaven it was all harps and angel song? And if he'd landed up in the other place, then it really wasn't sufficiently hot to match his preconceptions. Perhaps irritating arguing for an eternity would be hell enough? He just needed Isabell to pitch up to nag him and that would probably swing it.

"Of course I don't have the notes. If I had them then I wouldn't be asking you, now would I? This is shambolic, Nurse Bowman—"

"Brown."

"Nurse Brown, right, that's what I said."

"I think they might be at the desk, Dr Applebaum."

"Well go check, go check."

Jerry's feet dipped down and to the side, as if someone had sat beside him, and in the peace that followed Jerry allowed his mind to drift in the fluffy cotton wool of prescription narcotics. His eyes rolled and brought him back when the doctor started to speak.

"Another. Another. What can we see? U-huh. Yes. Hmmm." He shuffled his position, and leant on Jerry's leg. "Cerebral contusion, but the pia-arachnoid membrane does not appear to be ruptured. No subarachnoid haemorrhage." He took a slow nasal breath. "He'll have to go to theatre. Make ready to transport, Nurse Bowman."

"Brown."

"Brown. Right, that's what I said."

The doctor got up and continued to talk, but his voice was more distant. "Applebaum ... space in theatre ... neurological team ... decompressive craniectomy. Bump it, we're on our way."

That sounded significant, but Jerry hadn't quite caught it all. His brain was too tired and someone was making a right old racket next to his bed. Cables clonked against steel and plastic rustled and cracked. Then he was moving.

The bed squeaked along and came to an abrupt halt, the sound of tumbling containers rattling a few feet away. Doctor Applebaum spoke, closer now.

"For goodness sake, Nurse, we can't have any more patients sustaining injuries whilst actually inside the hospital. The press are already full of it. We're walking the plank here, you know." He paused for a slow breath and continued, more composed. "Oh. No. No. Let's leave the fittings behind and just take what we need, hmm? Steady as she goes. Theatre three."

The ping of a lift door closing and stomach dropping motion. Fingernails drummed on a rail.

"Just two more years, Nurse, and I'm retired. Two more years to keep this rabble afloat and it'll be all golf days and tequila sunsets from then on. No more aching tiredness. No more responsibility. No more accusations. This is the safest bet on our John Doe. A craniectomy will relieve the pressure inside his head, while the brain's swelling over the next few days and, if we put him into a barbiturate induced coma, brain activity will be at a minimum to aid the healing process. There are no guarantees, of course, but it's the best I can come up with."

They rolled out of the lift and continued to trundle for a minute of two, Jerry couldn't judge the time, but they were stationary when he was aware of Applebaum speaking again. "Nurse Bow- -rown. Brown—ha. Prep side room thirteen for our Mr Doe. Nice and quiet, tranquil and unstimulating. Lose the hubbub. Keep the traffic around him down. All these extra people from the Monte Carlo, all these extra germs." He paused for another unnaturally long breath. "Of course, tidy it up in there. Get rid of the cleaning equipment. Mop, bucket, broom: they'll need another home. Maybe the cleaner could actually take them. We do have a cleaner right? Of course. Ha. Seriously though, low stimulation. Keep the station banter for the canteen. Shhh." Jerry imagined his finger at his lips.

Nurse Brown yawned. "Absolutely."

FIFTY-EIGHT

Adam swallowed down the sickly burn and closed his eyes.

"Now, sugar, why don't you come along with me?" She leaned in to be heard above the music and purred into his ear. Adam shrugged away the pink-talonned hand on his shoulder and looked back to his drink.

"I can make it all better, honey," she persisted.

"No, thanks." Adam stared down into his glass, the last of the amber liquid swirling with a twist of his wrist. He knocked it back and signalled to the barman for another.

"Rita can make anything better. Rita got magic power." She pressed herself against Adam's side, looping a leg around him and pressing her breasts against his arm. She smelt of peppermint and sweat. Adam shrugged his shoulder up to dislodge her and turned his head to briefly look her in the eye.

"I said no thanks. There's nothing you can do to help me."

Rita stepped back and brushed herself down. "Well ain't you just the pity party."

"Yeah." Adam took a sip from his new drink.

"Who's this bum you talking to, Rita?" The voice came from behind him and Adam craned his neck around to find the pot shot-happy gunman from the street. He curled his lip at Adam and looked him up and down. He wore black ripped jeans and a grey marl T-shirt bearing a complicated Aztec design. It was dark with sweat in drooping ovals beneath his armpits and down the centre of his chest. His hair was black and shoulder length, swept back in a greasy slick from his forehead. He jutted out his chin when he spoke and Adam saw McGinty in his hooded eyes.

"There's no fucking escape, is there," Adam slurred, rolling his head back round to his drink.

"What did you say? What did he say?" The man thrust his head out toward Adam and waved a pointed finger.

"Nothing. He just drunk is all," Rita replied.

"Well he better start ordering up some business or he be dead." He pushed Adam in the back for emphasis, slopping a little Jack over the top of his glass. Adam felt his heart jump with the adrenalin release and instinctively drew in oxygen to fill his lungs. He pulled his head up to look straight ahead, then round to Rita.

"Oh sure. We just negotiating, ain't we, honey. Don't you worry, Seb." Rita fiddled with the zipper that ran down the front of her short black nylon jacket. She swished her head to flick back a sheet of jet black hair. Her lip beaded with sweat.

"Time is money, Rita. You got your own debt to pay." Seb pinched at Rita's chin and turned away to swagger into the crowd. She crumpled against the bar when he disappeared from view.

"You gotta cut a girl a break. I'm real cheap. I'll even give you an introductory deal. Four hundred. You won't regret it." She slid a flat palm up her high and over denim hot pants.

"Not interested."

When would she get the message? It wasn't a hooker Adam wanted, it was oblivion. He took a hearty mouthful from his glass and Rita leaned over the bar to hail the bartender. He brought her a tall, free glass of water.

Adam let his attention drift in the beat of the music and glazed over. His mind's eye transporting him back to the hotel room and Jerry's desperate scrabble to escape. He felt ashamed about the monster he'd become and searched back to find his motivations. Rachel pressed against his chest and the taste of her tears. The sorrowful empty windows of his childhood home. The note that Gracie'd left the day he'd got home late again: the one that said she wasn't coming back. McGinty: *'Don't you want to know what I gave her?'* One grim brick upon another. The pain welled up and he choked it back with another slug of bourbon.

"You really putting that away. It ain't good for your health, you know. In here, it could be real bad." Rita looked around the room, sizing up its shabby clientele.

"I need it."

"Shit, don't look like it doing you no good." She turned and leant her back against the bar. "Alcohol's a depressant you know? Looks to me like you could do with cheering up."

Adam snorted with a nod.

"There's better things to put a smile on that handsome face…"

"I told you…"

"No. I mean, how about I find you some snow? That'd do it. Ain't no shortage of primo drugs in this town. How about it? We could get you happy in five damn minutes."

Adam had had a line or two of coke on a big night out in the past, but it was by no means a habit. He knew the risks, but he didn't think his one-offs had done him any harm. He wanted to be free of this pain and it was an answer.

"How much?"

Rita's face lit up. "I'll go see my man, Seb. You stay put." She hustled away into the crowd, skipping back to him a few minutes later. Adam didn't care about the cost. The deal was done before she'd even named her price.

"Come out back," she said and led him by the elbow through the roomful of sweaty strangers.

Dark wooden floor and mirrored walls had misled his eye from the bar and he realised now that the room stepped away to the left, opening out into a square of booths with a central space where people leaned against each other and swayed. Rita slid onto an empty bench, pulling Adam in behind her and he shuffled up the sticky PVC, not quite by her side. They took turns at the lines that Rita chopped and she was up before him, laughing and jiggling in her seat.

The fine white powder swept through Adam's head and brushed out the weight that had held him down. The music was better now. He saw the bodies moving on the dance floor and wanted to be amongst them. He slid out of his seat and stood tentatively at the edge, watching, then feeling the beat and starting to move. The mass of people opened up and swallowed him in. He forgot about it all, just absorbed the beat and felt the sweat on his back. He shimmied up behind girls who laughed and seemed to appreciate his slightly bedraggled good looks until thoughts of Rachel burst his bubble and he returned to the booth for another line and then another. He hated his own obsessive mind and wanted to turn it off. He drank and swayed and slurred into strangers' ears, all the while watched by Seb and his unsavoury friends. Rita danced around in his peripheral vision, simultaneously predatory and protective, and when the high of his final line ebbed away, Adam was glad to see her leaning on a pillar close by. The bar was closing and the suddenly empty space around him brought back the loneliness and he didn't want to bear it. Panic crept up through his bones.

"Rita. I need some more. Can you get some more?"

"Sure, honey, but we gonna have to go for a ride. My man has left the building."

"Like Elvis." Adam ran the back of his hand under his nose.

"That's right." She swung a chain-handled bag over her shoulder. "Come on. We'll get a cab."

Adam followed her hot-panted bottom through the dwindling punters and out into the street. He stumbled through his fog and into the back of a cab and came around as Rita hauled him out onto the pavement.

The street was wide and dark, a single round pool of light picking out an entrance. Rita tottered up to the oversized door and Adam slouched in after her. A tatty stairwell stretch up ahead and the stench of piss hung in the air. Rita climbed a couple of steps and turned back to Adam to appraise his condition.

"I don't think you gonna make it. Wait here. I'll be back."

The stairs did look like hell. He could barely stand, let alone climb stairs. He slid down the tiled wall to sit on the bottom step and took in his new dubious surroundings. Graffiti stretched across the metal face of an out-of-order lift and empty beer cans rolled clunking over concrete tiles in the breeze. He was alone again and felt like shit. Who was he trying to kid?

That was when his emotions overwhelmed him. He knew he had to tell her and the phone was in his hand and ringing before he'd had a chance to think better of it.

"Rachel? Rachel, I, it's me, Adam." He rubbed at his forehead and swallowed hard.

"Adam, hi." Her voice in his head brought both elation and terror.

"Look, I just need you to know, I just wanted to tell you myself, it wasn't meant to be this way."

"Sorry?" Rachel's voice was so clear, she could have been right there next to him. His heart beat harder in his chest.

"It wasn't meant to be like this. I, I did it out of love. Fucked up, confused love. A fresh start. A bit of hope, you know? After everything."

"No. What? What do you mean?"

"It was supposed to make it easy, easy for us." Adam's head spun with the effort of conversation and he turned to lean his forehead against the wall, willing it to steady him. "Pathetic." He let out a desperate laugh that sent a spasm across his torso. "I couldn't even stitch him up properly. I'm pathetic."

"What..?"

Adam's chest grew tighter and he rubbed at the centre, trying to push away the pain. "God it hurts." He pulled himself up by the handrail and wobbled across the grubby foyer to turn and perch on a windowsill, somehow hoping that being higher up might ease the cramping behind his ribs. "It's nothing more than I deserve." His breath came out in gasps.

"Adam? Where are you?" Rachel sounded more distant now and it was too hard to hold the phone up to his ear, so he let his hand drop and the phone fell to the floor.

Adam heard footfall on the stairs, two sets of feet and then Seb came into view, a black-denim-wearing copycat by his side. He looked Adam in the eye and raised one eyebrow in a sneer. A belt of daggers gripped tight around Adam's heart and he flinched out from his perch and crumpled at the knee. The pain lit up his brain more brightly than the cocaine had all night.

FIFTY-NINE

Beyond the dirty glass, yellowing Astroturf hugged at a small pool. A couple of leaves floated there, caught in a rainbow slick of suntan oil. Dinwiddy told himself that the leaves weren't his to clear and set about folding his laundry. He folded his tighty whities inward, from the edges on both sides—side seam to centre and then again closing them like a book, repeating the process for every pair before placing them in a neat stack in his underwear drawer. Socks were paired, smoothed flat and rolled, toes first, into woolly swirls that were wedged at the drawer's other end, each providing the pressure for the last to keep the roll in place. Of course, this would mean that as the drawer emptied pressure would be lost and the rolls would unravel, leading, inevitably, to a repeat of the process. Dinwiddy didn't mind. He found reassurance in knowing that everything was as it should be. It would be time well spent. There was little to do with his evenings currently, anyhow.

The beige plastic phone trilled on his nightstand and Dinwiddy sat himself down on the bed beside it to put the receiver to his ear. "Dinwiddy speaking," he said in his southern drawl.

"This is Captain Kabawitz, Robbery and Homicide. I know it's your day off, but can you come in? There's all kinds of hell breaking loose down here. The whole department's swamped. The Monte Carlo's tipped us over." Kabawitz sure sounded tense.

"I'm not in Robbery and Homicide, sir. I've been invested in the Tourist Crimes Division."

"I know that," the captain sighed, "It just so happens that the Gang Crimes Bureau were already flat out working on a long planned bust in Naked City so TCD are pitching in with all the looting over at the Monte Carlo. Your number came up. Congratulations. Check in with Robbery and Homicide. Can you be here in half an hour?"

"Right away, sir. You can count on it." Dinwiddy hung up.

"My, my. Momma will be proud. Calling on me already to get them out of a jam." He lifted his laundry basket from the bed to its position on top of the wobbly pine wardrobe and shrugged out of his dressing gown. He slid its shoulders onto a hanger, tied the cord in a single bow and hooked it onto the back of his bedroom door. Then he buttoned and hung his pyjamas next to it, to air.

Dinwiddy's Las Vegas Metropolitan Police Department uniform was crisp and new. He pulled on the sand-coloured shirt and slacks, fingered the neat embroidery of the badge and admired his proud reflection, sucking in his paunch. Perhaps he'd been a little economical with the measurements he'd provided.

When he'd looked into a transfer, the LVMPD had stood right out. The team exuded military confidence and organisation that Dinwiddy was drawn to. Not one of them was under six feet in their buzz cut and all as fit as fiddles. He needed to build himself up, Momma said so—he cracked open the tin of home baking she'd sent along with him and eased a muffin from its wrapper.

In just under a week he'd settled himself into the Tourist Crimes Division, which more than anything, it seemed, was about shuffling paper and being the butt of their jokes. He didn't mind. They just needed to get to know him. They had a different way of going about things in Alabama: slower, more methodical. It got the job done. Here in Las Vegas everyone was always in such a hurry.

He smoothed a wrinkle from the bed and straightened the picture beside the door: a hasty vase of flowers, faded to a spectrum of blues by the desert sun. He smoothed the bed again and checked the lights were off by switching them on and off just once. His room was as neat as he could make it so he shut the door carefully and went in search of his landlady.

She was working in the kitchen chopping vegetables.

"Mrs Hong. I'm heading into work today. They called me in."

She grunted and carried on chopping, not lifting her head.

"I'll be back at my usual time. Nineteen hundred hours, you can count on it."

Mrs Hong made no comment.

"Well goodbye then." Dinwiddy turned to leave, uncertain if she'd even noticed him. Chief cook and bottle washer, always busy.

Dinwiddy's economy rental started first time. He clicked the indicator stalk up and down, tested all three speeds on the wipers and checked the angles on the air vents. Then he buckled up and flipped down the sun visor to reveal a precise hand-drawn map of the best route from his digs to Area Command. He was pretty sure that he'd learnt it, but liked to refresh his memory all the same and sure enough, twenty minutes later he'd made the journey through wide dusty streets.

The elevator opened on the third floor into a broad buzzing office. It was a mass of six-by-six cubicles. Grey felt panels chopped shoulder-high cells out of open space. Officers buzzed along pathways under fluorescent landing strips. Those that came close swooped around him and on.

He scanned around for name plates. "Excuse me, can you tell me where Captain Kabawitz's office is?" The woman he'd intended to ask didn't slow, didn't see him, didn't respond, just steered around. He tried again, this time stepping side to side to block the path of a man in plain clothes. He was drawn out of his preoccupation and looked Dinwiddy up and down, focussing on his sparkling clean and razor sharp uniform. He was impressed, Dinwiddy could tell. "Far side, to the end, name's on the door, buddy."

"Thank you, sir."

The man snorted and bustled on.

Dinwiddy picked his way along the central aisle, avoiding oncoming traffic and excusing himself. From time to time he peered into the private cells, noticing half-eaten snacks and empty coffee cups, piles of paper and flashing lights on telephones: an unexpected shoddy state. Most of the officers were head down and working, tapping away at their keyboards or on the phone.

The captain's office was in the far corner. Dinwiddy knocked, went straight in, closed the door and stood beside it, waiting to be acknowledged. The captain was on the phone in the midst of a heated conversation.

"I don't care what colour it is. A twisted ankle won't stop you doing admin. Get yourself in here or you're on traffic for a month." He slammed down the phone and noticed Dinwiddy for the first time.

"Who the hell are you? In fact, I don't care who you are. See these files?" He pointed to the pile on his desk. "I need people working on these files today. Take them."

Dinwiddy stumbled forward and scooped them to his chest. "Yes, sir." The pace here sure was a lot quicker than he was used to. He didn't want to disappoint his new captain. Best to just to go with the flow. He stepped backward to his previous spot, eyes front and high, soldier-style.

Kabawitz leant back in his chair and considered him. "What did you say your name was?"

"Detective Dinwiddy, sir."

"Well, Dinwiddy, you've got yourself a nice pile of administration there and a murder call from the MGM. A murder with no body. Ha, sounds like a fat waste of time to me, but you'd better check it out. You can tell us all about it at tomorrow's briefing."

"Yes, sir."

Kabawitz looked him up and down and let the suggestion of a smile creep up. "Find yourself a desk to call home. There should be an empty one out there somewhere."

"Will do, sir."

Kabawitz waved him out.

Turned out the only vacant spot was the one right outside the captain's office. That suited Dinwiddy just fine. .

SIXTY

Dinwiddy followed the manager down the corridor, a zip-up wallet tucked snug under his arm. It was a pack of his own devising and contained everything an investigating officer might need. This investigation was a step up alright and he intended to make his mark.

Diverting himself from the pressure of this first opportunity, he counted his paces along the golden carpet of the corridor, flipping open his file to make a note of the total when they drew to a halt outside the room. Two plump Hispanic women, dressed in the plain grey cotton suits of maids, waited there, wringing their hands. Dinwiddy estimated them to be between forty and forty-five years of age.

"This is Marcie, one of our 4th floor housekeeping staff," said the manager, "She discovered the room this morning."

Marcie, the more flushed of the two women, attempted a shaky smile. She looked nervous as a long-tailed cat in a room full of rocking chairs to Dinwiddy's eye and he smiled at her with a mind to put her at her ease.

"A pleasure to meet you, Ma'am." Dinwiddy said with a nod, poising pen over paper. "Can you tell me what happened?"

Marcie stepped forward, squeezing her hands together. "I was doing my round and reading the roster and saw this room got missed out yesterday so made sure to check it. I noticed the blood on the door right away, though I didn't know what I was looking at then." She shuddered. "It's such a mess and I seen enough of that all right, but not the blood. That's when I called Marjorie." She thumbed over her shoulder to the nodding woman behind.

"Did you touch anything, Ma'am?"

"I know you're not supposed to so I used a towel to open the door and pull it shut after me."

That was the fingerprints on the door blown. Dinwiddy gestured toward it. "Would you mind?"

Marcie obliged and Dinwiddy stepped in, gauging the minimum number of steps he could take into the room and still make a reasonable inspection. He rounded the bed and looked at the furniture, smashed to firewood. Then, craned his neck to look through the wide open door of the bathroom. The floor was a slick of raspberry with smears and shoves that could easily have been down to the effort of shifting a corpse, but there was the nub of it: no body.

Dinwiddy straightened up and turned on the spot, surveying the scene and pinching at his chin. His audience crammed in the doorway with Dinwiddy centre stage.

He retraced his steps, slid a small camera from a pocket in the wallet and looped its cord handle around his wrist. He switched it on, then off, then on again.

"I don't know about you, but my bed doesn't look like that when I get out of it. *Click*. The pillows are bunched and everthang's all mussed up. The sheet's all pulled, but only on this side, closest to the door. Pardon my indelicacy, ladies, but I don't believe it got that way through sleeping." He stooped to sniff at the pillow and slid his eyes over to the ash on the bedside table. There was a spot of blood on the floor. *Click*. *Click*.

"Is smoking permitted in this room, Mr Jackson?"

"No, a non-smoking room was requested by the occupant."

"There's no sign of a butt. Maybe who ever smoked it took it with them. Suggests someone still thinking clearly enough to try to cover their tracks." Dinwiddy let the camera swing from his wrist so he could write a note. His tongue peeped out over his lower lip to help with the concentration. He ran his eyes over the sweep of cupboards, checking their surfaces.

"There's a lot of damage, a lot of blood and the coffee table, well now, that took a real pounding. Suggests a fight now, doesn't it?" He bent down to visually inspect a broken stemmed glass on the desk, searching the rim for the kiss of a femme fatale. *Click*. *Click*.

"Champagne and broken glasses. A bed not ruffled from sleeping and a fight that started in the bedroom and ended with a blood bath. Could be a fight between lovers. A woman's blood on the floor, not the resident's at all. Or perhaps she turned on him, surprised him. Hell hath no fury, you can count on that. Depends whose blood that is on the bathroom floor now, doesn't it? What else do we know about the resident of this room, Mr Jackson?" Dinwiddy turned to peer through the door of the bathroom. *Click. Click. Click.*

Mr Jackson consulted a slip of paper pulled from his pocket. "This was a single occupancy room. The resident's name was Jeremy Adler. A British guy here for the TEKCOM exhibition over at the Centre. A corporate booking by Locksley PR in the UK. He arrived with another Brit a couple of days ago."

"When was the last time anyone saw him?"

"We can check the key card system to see when he came to his room and circulate a photo around the staff, but this is a very large establishment, officer. It would be impossible to remember every guest."

"That would be fine. Thank you. I'll take everything you've got, Mr Jackson, registration, corporate information and that of his colleague. Marcie, I'll need you to come make a statement, if that would be all right?" Dinwiddy's gaze skipped between Mr Jackson and Marcie. Both nodded.

Dinwiddy pulled the mobile from his belt and called the captain. "Sir, I'm calling in from the MGM Grand, investigating the suspected murder, sir."

"And," the captain crackled down the line.

"And I believe there is sufficient evidence here to warrant a full forensic sweep."

"What do you want me to do? Fill out the paperwork for you? Dinwiddy, I'm busy, Call Forensic direct."

"I apologise, sir, I was just seeking your authorisation."

The captain took a beat. "All right, I get it. Shall I patch you through, Detective Dinwiddy?"

"That would be fine, sir."

The line went dead. Dinwiddy stood blinking for a minute then checked the phone display. He'd been accidentally cut off. He redialled.

"Kabawitz."

"Captain, this is Detective Dinwiddy, we seemed to get cut off."

Brrrrr. The line dropped out again.

Perhaps a more direct approach to Forensics would be better. There seemed to be a problem with the captain's line.

"Mr Jackson, I'll need to get on to the DA and organise a forensics team. That might just take me a minute." Mr Jackson stepped aside to let Dinwiddy back out into the corridor. The door opposite had a welt of blood on it too. *Click.*

He tucked the camera back into his wallet and retrieved instead a roll of crime scene tape which he proceeded to apply in a careful cross spanning the bedroom door frame.

"This area will be out of bounds until Forensics have completed their investigation," he said, pulling himself up to full height.

"Of course, officer."

"Access to this floor will also be closed until further notice. I'll be waiting in the fourth floor lobby to guard the crime scene until their arrival. I'd much appreciate it if you could direct them to me when they get here?"

Mr Jackson had a twinkle in his eye. "Of course."

All three had a wide-eyed look about them as they turned to leave.

"One more thing, before you go, Mr Jackson," said Dinwiddy, pointing to the blood-smeared door opposite Jerry's, "Can you tell me whose room this is?"

SIXTY-ONE

Dinwiddy perched on the edge of his chair and sized up the felt wall of his desk pod. Phones rang, keyboards clacked and conversations rattled on but to him, holed up in his soft cell, they all churned together into a creamy comfort of white noise. Dinwiddy was getting organised.

His desk was laid out like the counter in a sweet shop: a pot of drawing pins next to a reel of sticky tape; a fat marker pen by rectangles of card, white for times, pink for people, blue for places; a spool of thick red thread and a nice sharp pair of scissors. All present and correct.

One side of his padded cell was free and clear of furniture and made for a giant pin board. He fixed the victim's passport photo into its centre and squeaked out a name tag on pink. 'Jeremy Brian Adler, 42' got taped beneath. He squealed 'MGM Grand' onto blue and pinned that to the left. Someone was sighing in the neighbouring cubicle, but they didn't have anything to say. He tacked up the bloody selection of photos he'd taken at the crime scene.

The top section was for other characters associated with the victim. So far, all he had was Marcie, the maid and the business associate, Donald Spink. He pinned up their photos and squeaked out more labels. The hotel records showed that both the victim and Spink worked for a PR company back in the UK. Dinwiddy pinned up a card for Locksley PR and carefully wound red thread around pins to link them together.

The bottom section of his giant pin board was for places. So far, the Convention Centre was all he had. He pinned it on, poking out his tongue a little to help with the accuracy.

This was shaping up nicely. Now, the order of events. Key card records said that on Saturday the bedroom door lock was operated electronically at 03:14, 22:42 and again at 23:00. The final time with a new card, issued that evening. He squealed the fat marker over white slips to write 'Door unlocked' and the three times, and added them to the picture map.

Looked to Dinwiddy like the killer had been lying in wait, getting to the room just ahead of the victim. He considered Marcie. She'd said housekeeping missed the room that day. The lock records showed access coming in, but there was no way of knowing about going out, when the door was unlocked manually. If this fella was a businessman, was he actually doing

315

any business and where? What about the day before that? He'd sure got in late. Dinwiddy flipped open his investigation wallet and made a note to ask for key card activity for the entire stay.

The subject was supposed to be at the Conference Centre. Dinwiddy tied a length of red thread to the MGM's pin, ran it over to the Conference Centre and wound a liquorice curl around its thumb tack. He snipped off a couple more threads and connected Marcie to the MGM, Spink to the MGM and Spink to the Conference Centre. There wasn't much to go on.

He needed to find out what the victim had been up to. CCTV from the hotel had already been seized, on which Dinwiddy hoped to find some clues, but didn't the monorail have a CCTV system too? Perhaps he could follow him around through a lens?

The most pressing question, of course, was: where was the body? A substantial amount of blood had been lost by someone in that bathroom and if they weren't dead they'd most certainly need medical attention. Dinwiddy pulled out his list of local medical centres and tapped out the first number.

The lined burred out six rings before it finally picked up. "Sunset Medical. How can I help?" The words were polite, but the tone was tired and unfriendly.

"My name is Detective Dinwiddy of the Las Vegas Metropolitan Police Department. I am currently investigating a disappearance and suspected murder and would like to rule out the presence of the victim at your facility."

"U-huh."

"The victim's name is Jeremy Brian Adler." Dinwiddy heard the tap of a keyboard over the operator's silence.

"We have no-one of that name registered, officer," they said eventually.

"I see. And do you have any John Does?"

"John Does? Admitted on what date?"

"Last night."

"Last night? They won't even be on the system. We're overflowing down here with people from the Monte Carlo. Patients are laying out in the corridors with notes piled up. It's going to take us days to catch up."

"Ma'am, my enquiry is of a most urgent nature."

The operator sighed and gave their pinched response, "I understand that, officer, but we're drowning down here. No-one's got the time to sit at a computer."

"I see. Well now that is most unfortunate."

"Unfortunate, yeah. What can I do?"

They meant it in the rhetorical sense, of course, but Dinwiddy was not so easily put off. "Please make a note of my enquiry and check your system regularly." He gave her his direct line, giving out the digits slowly to make sure there was no mistake.

Dinwiddy got the same story at High County and Canyon Springs and drew a blank entirely on the other two he called. The conference centre, at least was a little more co-operative, and put him on hold while they checked through their visitor badge data.

Dinwiddy sat straight and patient, eyes ahead, but after a couple of minutes they started to wander and he became aware of snickering behind him. A pair of uniforms peered over the top of his cell at the sparse web of information on the opposite wall. Discovered, they snapped up and went about their business. That was when the helpful lady at the Centre came back on the line. "Mr Adler was registered in physical attendance on the first day of the exhibition, but not at all yesterday. Shall I email you over the report on which stands he visited?" Dinwiddy thanked her for her help and considered his timeline. Las Vegas was one heck of a journey from England. Why travel all that way if the victim'd figured on playing hooky? It didn't make sense. Maybe the monorail cameras could shed some light.

Dinwiddy packed his crime board paraphernalia away into a drawer, set his phone square and tucked his chair tight under the desk. One of the worker bees now too, he wove through the hive—investigator's wallet tucked tight under his arm. He dropped down in the lift and made his way out into the world.

It was amazing how fast a man could find his feet, Dinwiddy mused. His lines of investigation had given him purpose and direction. Doing something for himself, at last. Nothing to block. No reason to feel anxious. He was the man for the job and the captain could count on him to do his best.

Tomorrow he'd be assigned a partner, he was sure of it: a sharp-witted officer in pristine uniform that would appreciate his thorough investigative style and horse sense. Enthusiasm running over, Dinwiddy fair bounced to his stalwart Chevy. It rattled to life, succeeded in the operation of every switch, both on and off, and pulled out into traffic with Dinwiddy joyful at the wheel.

The monorail office was across town so he'd eat his lunch on the run. He supposed the officers in Area Command were dining on something rich in vitamins and poor on flavour, to maintain those marine-fit physiques. Perhaps in time he could adjust, but away from home and out of kilter, he pined for Mama's hoecakes and redneck caviar: the hearty taste of home.

The manager over at the monorail office was used to visits from the cops. They had a special form for him to sign so the D.A. could be billed for their trouble, which was minimal. They sat Dinwiddy at a monitor, showed him how to work the system and left him to it.

He ate a nugget from his Happy Meal and found a satisfaction in its fatty smack that boosted his eagerness still further. There were four cameras on the platforms at the MGM, another on the escalator; the same at the Conference Centre plus two more on the run down to the car park. There was a heck of a lot of footage to get through and Dinwiddy wanted to get a head start on the work before reporting back to the captain tomorrow, so he settled in for the long haul and popped in another nugget.

Starting with the rush hours, he scanned the platform going out in the morning and back late afternoon. Nothing. Maybe the subject didn't leave his room that day after all. He'd scan Friday to see if he appeared.

Footage from Friday scrolled before his eyes and, even on fast forward, hours passed and Dinwiddy's back twinged. In the end he wondered if he was really seeing anything anymore and rubbed at his eyes with thoughts of Mrs Hong and the fast approaching E.T.A. He had a schedule to maintain and couldn't let her down.

He stretched out, tired of the screen and fixing to leave, as a dishevelled man lurched off the southbound 17:05 onto the MGM platform. From the escalator camera he looked downtrodden and teary and, most importantly to Dinwiddy, familiar. He caught his breath. "I found him! Darn tootin' I found him!"

He'd glanced up for only a moment, but long enough for Dinwiddy to freeze the frame and zoom in. He held the photo up next to the screen. Yes. He scanned over the timetable and tracked the train back to the Conference Centre, then pulled up the footage.

The subject appeared. He stood straight and moved at an average pace to board the train, not looking unusual. Why the marked difference when he got off?

Dinwiddy clapped his hands. "Sweet success! Excuse me—Ma'am?" he called out to the manager and when she poked her head around the door jamb, she was shrugging into her jacket.

"Do you have cameras on the trains too?"

"Yes. Yes we do."

"Could I see the southbound 16:35 on this day?" Dinwiddy asked.

"I can get it for you, but not tonight. I'm locking up in five. I have an appointment." She buttoned the jacket with a stony frown.

Feeling the exhilaration of success, Dinwiddy was reluctant to abandon his investigation, but the manager looked like she could get testy and he wanted to keep her on his side. Then there was Mrs Hong to think about. "Thank you, Ma'am. I'll be back alright," he said with a nod. "You can count on that."

SIXTY-TWO

Dinwiddy faced front and stood tall. "Yes, captain, I do believe a thorough investigation is justified." He was sure that the CIS report would be a doozie. Kabawitz waved a stubby finger in his direction. "Alright, Dinwiddy. You'd better have a partner. Greenway, you're on this. Make sure the crime log gets covered."

In the corner of Dinwiddy's eye, a man threw his hands down into his lap, earning himself a hard stare from the captain.

Greenway.

"Just get to it. If the log's too menial for you, you'd better get on with inducting our new detective."

"Sir," Greenway sighed.

Dinwiddy stretched his eyes around to take in this new mentor from LVMPD's finest. Greenway was looking right back at him: slouched in his seat with a roll of fat that hid his belt buckle. Rich irritation radiated from his eyes, and his bottom lip jutted out in a fleshy pout beneath a full, greying moustache. Dinwiddy snapped his head back around. Greenway did not look one bit like the partner he had imagined.

When the morning briefing was over, the officers filed out of the room, while Dinwiddy waited to shake the hand of his new partner. Greenway didn't seem to be an observant man and walked straight past, out into the hall.

Dinwiddy stepped out after him. "Greenway. Greenway," he called out, but the detective did not stop.

"Get your stuff, Dinwiddy. You're moving next to me."

Dinwiddy supposed it was fair for the old hand to keep their spot. After all, Dinwiddy had only been at his desk a day or two. When he finally found him, tucked into a corner, close to the vending machines, Dinwiddy didn't feel altogether surprised to find that more than one desk in his proximity was actually free. Dinwiddy chose the one closest to the window and went about re-pinning his crime map to the wall.

"Come at look at this." Greenway beckoned Dinwiddy to his side. "Don't know if you've got this down in hick Alabama, but here we use the com-pu-ter."

Dinwiddy nodded. "Why of course, Greenway."

"This is where we type in the incident number…" He tap-tap-tapped at the keyboard, "and this is where you add interview data…"

"Yes, Greenway, I am familiar with the system."

"Good. Get to it."

Dinwiddy reached for the keyboard, but Greenway slapped his hand. "Not here." He gave him an unfriendly glare and Dinwiddy turned away to scuttle back to his new and unfamiliar desk. One, two, three, four, five long paces to reach his chair. The chair wheels squeaked and the phone was on the wrong side of his monitor. Dinwiddy sat stiff and pulled the keyboard close, quietly pressing at the letters. His skin prickled with Greenway's proximity, but he'd get on with what needed doing. Greenway was not a nice man. Dinwiddy would have to focus hard to keep himself on track.

An hour or so passed in a tense silence: Dinwiddy filling in every last field he could; Greenway snacking from the vending machine and creaking in his chair. He looked over Dinwiddy's work and made no criticism.

"Goddam lazy clerks," he mumbled and punched a number out on his phone. "Detective Greenway, LVMPD. I need a status update on one male, Jeremy Brian Adler, possible John Doe." He said it with such authority that Dinwiddy was sure that the operator at the other end of the line would just spit the facts right out.

"Admitted two nights ago… Yes, I am aware of your situation… Yes, I understand you have a backlog. I'm pretty damn busy here myself, but you don't see me blaming it on the public." Greenway flicked a look to Dinwiddy, who suddenly found his reel of red cotton exceptionally interesting.

"No. Thank *you*," said Greenway tossing down the receiver. "Goddam medics think they're above us all. If we can't get anywhere over the phone, we'll have to go down there and start knocking heads together."

Dinwiddy was all for action, though slightly concerned about the physical contact.

"Come on, let's get over to the Grand. You can drive, my car's in the shop."

~

Dinwiddy slid behind the wheel and commenced switch checks: wipers; indicators; hazards; ventilation flaps set horizontal; handbrake off and on and off again.

He looked over to Greenway. "Click clack, front and back," he said and waited for Greenway to put on his belt before pulling away. They rode in silence and pulled up out front.

"I'm going to take a look at the crime scene. Check in with the manager and see if you can get me an interview room," said Greenway. Dinwiddy could see that he'd made himself boss in their relationship and he supposed that would be alright, provided Dinwiddy could carry on with his own lines of enquiry too. He watched Greenway's back disappear into the lift and made his way over to a smiling clerk in a convenient gap at the lobby desk.

"Ma'am, my name is Detective Dinwiddy of the Las Vegas Metropolitan Police Department and I need to speak with

Donald Spink, resident on the 4th floor. It's a matter of urgent police business."

"I'll check his room, officer." The clerk tapped out the number and held a handset to his ear. Dinwiddy could hear the burr of the call: over and over and over. He drummed his fingernails against his teeth.

"I'm sorry, officer, but there's no reply."

Dinwiddy flopped open the ever present file, slid a handwritten card from a pocket and handed it to the clerk. "Please have him call me on this number as soon as possible." He looked into the clerk's eyes. "It's a matter of urgent police business."

"Will do."

"I also have a note for Mr Jackson, more information required for my investigation. Would you see that he gets it please? It's a matter-"

"—of urgent police business," finished the clerk with a grin.

Dinwiddy looked at him blankly. "That's right. In fact, I see him at the end of the counter. I'll deliver it personally."

Dinwiddy made his way along the smooth counter to stand before him. "Mr Jackson."

Mr Jackson smiled and Dinwiddy passed over the envelope.

"Some more information required, if you would."

Mr Jackson shrugged his assent and Dinwiddy continued. "Actually, sir, would you be able to arrange an interview room for the department's use? We'll need to get statements from housekeeping and the lobby staff and guests in neighbouring rooms. I will also require assistance viewing in-house camera footage, as reserved."

"I'll check to see who and what we have available. If you could give me ten minutes or so?"

"Of course, Mr Jackson. Thank you kindly."

Dinwiddy was glad to have a little space to clear his head. The arrival of Greenway had settled over him in an itchy cloud that left him feeling edgy and oppressed so he decided on a breath of air outside in his ten minutes.

Twenty steps to reach the door, another thirty-three took him off the property and onto the street. By his calculations he could take another three hundred before having to think about turning around.

Arriving on The Strip, he saw the Monte Carlo: the façade of its tower blackened in waves up to the fifth floor and hoardings that ran the length of its frontage, hiding the activities behind from the pavement and prying eyes. He crossed the street for a closer look.

Burly security loomed by a makeshift entrance, staring down a hopeful news crew angling for a new lead. People came and went in teams, brushing the newsmen away. Dinwiddy walked alone.

They spotted the straggler and hustled over to meet him. The interviewer thrust a bulbous microphone to Dinwiddy's chest. "Channel 6 News. Can you give us any more on the arsonists, officer? Was it a terrorist attack? Was it a casino heist?"

Dinwiddy stepped backward blinking, trying to put some space between them.

"What are the American public to deduce from the secrecy, officer? Should we be afraid in our beds?"

"No. No!" Dinwiddy said with a vigorous shake of his head, "I'm not involved in the investigation of the Monte Carlo people. I'm on a murder case."

"A murder case!" The reporter's eyes flung wide and he slapped at his cameraman to pay attention.

Their excitement reignited Dinwiddy's own. He'd never been interviewed by a reporter before. He sure wasn't in Wetumpka anymore. He supposed they got followed round by news crews all the time here.

"What's your name? Can you tell us all about it, officer? Who's the victim?"

Dinwiddy cleared his throat and looked into the lens. He spoke low and slow. "My name is Detective Dinwiddy. I am investigating the disappearance and suspected murder of one Jeremy Brian Adler, a British man."

"Do you have any suspects, detective?"

"Well, I am still conducting my investigation," he nodded over to the reporter then back to the lens, "But there are certainly some individuals I would like to interview."

The reporter licked his lips. "Who? Who was it? Do you have any leads?"

Dinwiddy flipped open his folder and pulled out a photo. This was great: he could appeal to the public for assistance. He showed it to the camera.

"This is the victim, Jeremy Brian Adler, age forty-two. I want to find out about his movements on Friday and Saturday just gone. If anyone has any information I'd be mighty grateful to receive it at the LVMPD. Thank you."

The reporter's jaw was flapping.

"I didn't figure on getting help from the TV people. Thank y'all." He leaned in to shake the reporter's hand, who had to fumble away the microphone to oblige. He nodded to the other members of the crew and turned away to head back to the MGM.

His ears buzzed with excitement. Things sure moved fast out here. The folks back home would never believe it.

SIXTY-THREE

Adam passed gritty eyes around the room's unnatural darkness. A misshapen brown blanket, dangling from its corners, stretched unevenly across the window. Sunlight fought against its gritty fibres, but managed only to bring a dull amber glow to the squalor. As Adam's eyes became accustomed, he picked out the form of a woman he recognised as Rita, but he was shaky on the detail of who she actually was. For now she was sleeping, fully clothed, head resting on her bag, puffing out great snorts of breath that rattled at her fleshy lips.

Adam pushed himself up onto one elbow, feeling the creak of his back and stiffness in his chest.

"You alive then," said a toneless voice behind him and Adam strained his neck around to see Seb, standing over him and pulling on a joint. The sweet smoke drew at Adam's gut and he covered his mouth to quell a retch.

"You had us all shitting it last night, man. Last thing I need is a corpse on my turf." Seb shuffled from side to side.

"Thanks for your concern," said Adam, sliding himself across the grubby linoleum to lean against the wall. He bent his legs up to stop from keeling over and hugged at his thighs.

This was a new low. A night spent abusing coke had paid him back with a catastrophic downer that left him wishing he really were dead. He leant his forehead on his knees and felt the sinking dread of revelations yet to be remembered.

"Where am I?" he managed and Seb laughed.

"You had some kind of a fit down in the lobby, man, and Rita wouldn't let us leave you there." He sucked on his teeth. "Besides, a fucked up homey in your hallway's bad for business." He punched Adam on the shoulder, but lost interest when he didn't react.

Seb settled in a lawn chair in the centre of the room and tapped his joint into a beer bottle on the floor. "I suppose you feeling pretty fucked up and all," he said and Adam thought that was a fair summation.

"I have to get out of here," Adam muttered and struggled to his feet, scanning around for the exit.

Seb's place was a studio dive. A mattress squashed up into one corner had a stained quilt flopped across its naked surface at an angle, draping through an overflowing ashtray on the floor. One other lawn chair, aside from the one that Seb was currently relaxing in, and a plastic patio table and chairs over in the kitchenette was the sum total of actual furniture in the whole place. The rest of Seb's possessions seemed to be stuffed into black rubbish bags or tossed onto the floor. The air was thick with carbon dioxide, stale booze and bile. Adam needed to leave.

He headed for the only visible door, to the side of the kitchenette, pausing to lean against the counter top while his torso cramped in pain.

"You should go to the hospital, man. Last night you was proper fucked up," Seb offered.

The hospital. An ambulance, and fire trucks: pictures started playing in Adam's mind. Jerry. Jerry on the bathroom floor. Jerry on a gurney. The blood. "Oh God." Adam's hands rose to his face.

Seb got to his feet and strolled behind the counter to rattle around on the shelves beneath. "I got M," he said, producing a zip-top bag of small white tablets. "You can have some on the house, seeing as I'd like to get you out of here and all."

Adam dropped his hands away to look. "M?"

"Morphine. You in pain right? Here, take couple of these puppies. That's right, get them down. And here's a couple more for the road." Adam swallowed away the rough chalk residue and grasped the remaining pills in his sweating palm. Seb gave him a gold-toothed knowing smile and swaggered over to the door. He pulled a thick metal rod up out of its cradle and swung it back, before sliding back a dead bolt and pushing back a latch. "Can't be too careful," he said, clearing the way for Adam to leave. And leave he did.

The hallway wasn't much of an improvement on Seb's. The air stank of piss and the walls were scraped and dirty, the only sign of fresh paint in the amateur scrawls of graffiti on the walls. The solid metal doors of the lift wore an 'out of order' sign so Adam started down the stairs, leaning heavily against the wall. The memories came thick and fast: Adora's disappearing act; his anger at Jerry, at himself. How could he and Rachel be together now? His plans had come to nothing but trouble.

He stumbled down two flights, through a lobby area and finally out into the sun. His eyes smarted with the glare and he lifted his arm across his face to stop the shards of sunlight that dug into his brain. His head spun and his body felt ready to crumble.

A wide alleyway ran down the side of the block and a doorway stepped away to the side, which offered Adam a shady spot to gather himself. He slumped into its corner and threw back the other two morphine tablets. He'd just take a couple of minutes to let them kick in and then he'd get on his way.

He was kidding himself, of course. Adam's poor abused body wasn't going anywhere just yet. The only travelling he'd manage for now was in the leaps of reasoning in his mind. Jerry was out there, somewhere: a damaged witness to his madness. A witness to how out of control he had become. Adam had to find him, find him now and finish this.

SIXTY-FOUR

He was wearing a groove into the pavement when the manager showed up with her keys. She was somewhat less communicative this afternoon, but Dinwiddy had enough enthusiasm for the both of them. It took a while to fire up the systems and Dinwiddy paced the whole time. He'd left Greenway over at the MGM, waiting around for the arrival of potential witnesses and lining them up for interview later. That man had issues that Dinwiddy didn't care to guess. Momma would have licked him into shape.

"Video's up."

Dinwiddy took up his position, flicked through the carriages until he found the right one and watched the thirty-minute journey.

For a while the subject sat alone, facing away from the camera, gradually slumping down over himself. He looked kind of despondent already and Dinwiddy started to wonder if he'd made a mistake. At one stop the carriage emptied out considerably and a suited man came over. He had an arrogant swagger and a sarcastic smile.

Looked like he was talking but, Adler didn't want to listen. The new guy did some poking in his shoulder and leaned in real close, intimate. It was Adler that broke it up, but the back of his head didn't give too much away.

The new fella was still talking with a sneery look on his face. He puffed out his chest and looked up along the carriage. *Freeze frame.* Dinwiddy had seen that face before. He scrabbled into his wallet to retrieve the picture of the business associate, Donald Spink.
"There you are." He looked back to the screen.

Adler was up on his feet, the other guy laughing and pushing him around. There was a tussle and Adler got pushed to the floor. The other fellow, Spink, stood lording over him then made off ahead, leaving him sprawled there. Donald Spink, well, well. He had prime suspect written all over him.

Dinwiddy had the manager make a copy of the footage from carriage two of the 16:35 southbound and tucked the disk into a slim pocket in his folder.

He had something here that might even make Greenway smile.

SIXTY-FIVE

Spink was on the inside now, although he never imagined it would be like this. Unassuming swinging doors had taken him away for the trampled paths of the public's ebb and flow, down quiet corridors and into a windowless meeting room. Dimensions that could easily have accommodated a hundred delegates stood mostly empty, save for a single long table, three red velour conference chairs lined up along each side. Together, they squatted in the centre of the gaudy carpet, spare chairs stacked in towers against the walls.

Spink sat alone at the table, tinkering with the fake Rolex on his wrist. It might be worth a few dollars to someone, might be enough to make a stake to get him rolling. Otherwise his money was all gone. The casino had chewed him up, but still held him captive in its bowels. He looked around the otherwise empty room and wondered why they wanted him here; how long he'd have to wait.

When one of the double doors finally swished open, it was a man in shabby civilian clothes that led the way ahead of a stiff, neat uniformed police officer, who pinched a smart document wallet under his arm. Dressed in the baggy black of a fat man, the shabby one reached out his hand across the table for Spink to shake. "Detective Greenway, this is my colleague, Detective Dinwiddy." Spink shook the hand that was offered for the briefest of clinches, before it was snatched away by Greenway, who flopped down into his chair, like a soft bag of donuts.

Spink looked to Detective Dinwiddy, who busied himself unzipping his wallet, taking from it a small Dictaphone, a notepad and a pencil. He laid them straight, one beside the other, before lifting his head to meet Spink's questioning stare.

"Good afternoon, Mr Spink," he said with his southern lilt, finally addressing him.

Spink nodded, attempting a flicker of a smile. "Good afternoon, gentlemen." He leaned his forearms on the table, trying to assert some dominance, "Now, what's this all about?"

Dinwiddy clicked down a button on his Dictaphone. "We will be recording this interview for our files. It's standard police procedure, please do not be alarmed."

Spink's eyes tracked down to the recorder.

"If you should answer any of our questions with a physical gesture, please be aware that it will be described for the recording."

Spink nodded and, before Dinwiddy had a chance to describe him, added, "OK, fine."

Detective Greenway spoke from his slouch. "Please state your name for the recording."

"My name is Donald Spink."

"Also present is Detective Greenway and Detective Dinwiddy, LVMPD," he continued. "Now, Mr Spink. Can you tell me how you spent Friday and Saturday last?"

Spink looked into Greenway's frowning eyes. It was clear he wasn't going to tell him what this was about. Well, Spink was no fool—he'd keep his account basic.

"Friday was my first full day here. I got myself over to the Conference Centre bright and early. Stayed there all day."

"You're here for an event?"

"TEKCOM. I'm here to win new business for my firm."

"Going well?" Greenway fixed Spink in a stare.

"Yes. Great." Spink shuffled in his seat.

"What did you do after that?"

Spink thought about his ride back on the monorail: how he'd preened like a cat at his own cleverness; how he'd knocked Adler on his inferior arse. "I went back to my hotel; had a couple of drinks in the bar; spent some time in the casino."

"Oh? How'd you do?" Greenway flicked an interested eyebrow.

The casino had torn a strip off him. "Alright, broke even," Spink said, sitting back in his chair with a sigh and folding his arms across his chest.

The smart one scribbled on his pad and Spink let his hands fall to his lap.

"When did you call it a day?"

"I'm not sure, around midnight." That was probably true enough.

"And Saturday?"

"Saturday I was back at the show. I signed a deal off with a new client and came back early. About three."

"And after?"

"Pretty much like Friday. Look, what's this all about?" Spink shifted in his chair again and tugged at his collar. The sweet air conditioning was cloying in his throat and making him nauseous. He grimaced at Detective Greenway, who just looked back blankly. "How did you spend your evening, sir?"

Spink looked down to the floor and searched his memory for details he was prepared to share. "I came down for dinner in the buffet around six, had a drink at the bar and spent a couple of hours playing poker. I wasn't having much luck so I turned in around ten."

"Can you tell me the nature of your relationship with Jeremy Adler?"

Spink huffed out a breath and rolled his eyes. "Adler? He works for my firm as well. He's here, somewhere."

"Did you spend time with Mr Adler on Friday or Saturday?"

"No," Spink scoffed. "Why would I want to do that?"

"So you didn't see him at all?"

"No."

"Don't you think that's rather strange? Business associates here together in a foreign country, but you haven't seen him?" Greenway sat up straighter, squinting at Spink. The fat moustache on his lip hid any indication of a sneer.

"I've seen him in passing," Spink corrected himself, looking back and forth between the detectives. "I like to keep to myself, that's all." *And I hate him*, Spink thought, but declined to add. The smart one started writing again and Spink slid his eyes over to the notepad, trying to see the words.

"So on Saturday night you left the casino at ten. Where did you go?"

"Like I said, I went to bed." Spink flicked his eyes up in recall. It hadn't been his bed, not straight away. No need to tell these officers about his freebie with a prostitute though, was there? His mouth twitched a little at the corner.

"Did you hear anything unusual when you were in your room? Any kind of disturbance?"

"Slept like a baby. I'd had a couple of drinks, tends to put me out for the count. Didn't even know about the business over the road until the morning."

"You're sure?"

Spink gave them a slow nod, eyebrows raised.

"Mr Spink is nodding his head in a slow and sarcastic manner," said Dinwiddy.

"Now hang on…"

"OK. Thanks, Mr Spink. That's all we need," Greenway cut in.

Spink waved his hand in surprise. "That's it? You haven't even said what this is about."

Detective Greenway looked back for a beat in frowning silence. "No. Actually, there is one last thing. Dinwiddy, the picture."

Dinwiddy unzipped a pocket in his wallet to retrieve a black and white photo and slid it across the table to sit squarely in front of Spink. It was grainy and pixelated, the angle unnaturally high, but there was no mistaking the face of his tormentor. Spink felt the heat burn in his cheeks.

"Do you recognise this man, Mr Spink?"

Spink shuddered. He wouldn't allow Adam Fox back into his life. "I've never seen him before," he said.

SIXTY-SIX

Greenway's tremendous backside took up one third of Dinwiddy's desk and trespassed a good deal more into his personal space. He took a greedy bite from a napkin-wrapped pastry and showered crumbs into Dinwiddy's lap, talking the whole time.

"So this guy is the last known person to have contact with our victim. What have we got on him?" Dinwiddy rolled his chair back as far as it would go and surreptitiously swept the pastry from his thigh to the floor.

"So far we have managed to isolate images from the in-house cameras of the two of them in the bar, on the gaming floor and finally in the lift. They appear to be harmonious. I believe this man's name to be Adam Fox. He checked into the hotel the day after our victim and is travelling independently. He is staying in a suite on the 23rd floor. He is not registered at TEKCOM and so far I haven't been able to establish any relationship with Adler. I'm still working on general background. Credit reports show Spink to be in dire straits,

Adler to be running an average bordering low credit score, while our man Fox is very comfortable. Places of work and family outstanding."

Dinwiddy noted Greenway's nods of approval and ploughed on with the other facts he'd learned, thankful that he hadn't felt the need to open his mouth.

"The monorail footage clearly shows Donald Spink assaulting Adler on the 16:35 southbound, despite his claims of not having seen him for days. Body language during his informal interview exhibited strong indicators of deception. The account he gave was of little note, save for the absence of detail and his obvious desire to keep something from us."

"Agreed," said Greenway, through the pie.

Dinwiddy pulled himself back into the chair as much as possible. "Also, I noticed nicotine staining on the fingernails to Spink's right hand. The victim is not a smoker, but someone had been smoking in that room. Ash was present and I'd bet a dime to a dollar, it came from a cigar: I recognised that heavy fug in the air from my daddy." Dinwiddy cleared his throat and smoothed the page of his notepad. Why had he said that? He hadn't intended to share personal information with a man like Greenway.

He ploughed on. "Analysis of time logs provided by the hotel against the electronic key system and CCTV have also made for most interesting reading."

"How's that?" said Greenway, spraying out more crumbs for Dinwiddy to blink away. Why couldn't that man keep his damn pie to himself?

"Well, the penultimate unlocking of Adler's door happened at 22:42," said Dinwiddy, scratching at the back of his own hand—digging at the crawl under his skin. "In the same minute we have a snapshot of Spink timestamped in the lift. It's possible that he had time to get from the lift to that door before the clock ticked on, but as there are no cameras on the residential floors, we can't be sure. The two system clocks might also be slightly out of sync.

"Whatever the case, Spink's own bedroom door was not unlocked until 10:55. What was he doing in those thirteen minutes? Did he have to step over to his own room to fetch something? Did he leave the door ajar? All questions we need to answer.

"Adler and Fox are timestamped in the lift at 10:58 and we must assume that the final unlocking of the victim's door at eleven was carried out by them."

"We need to get this Fox character in for questioning," said Greenway.

"I concur, Greenway. Unfortunately I am currently unable to locate him and, to my knowledge, he has not returned to his hotel suite."

"I'll put out an APB. Meanwhile let's squeeze Spink under arrest. I've got plenty to be getting on with here. You go over to the Grand and pick him up."

That was fine by Dinwiddy, any chance to get out from under this shower of masticated food and spittle, he'd take. He was delighted Greenway had things to keep him busy. His desk didn't have much on it in the way of paperwork, but he supposed that family-sized pack of Cheez Doodles wasn't going to spray itself.

SIXTY-SEVEN

So this was it: Adler's last journey. He paced out the golden corridor that tapered off into the distance. Forty-two from the lift to the turn, another eighteen to the room. Dinwiddy flipped open his wallet and double checked his notes. It was a stretch, but Spink could have made it at a lick.

The crime scene tape had been removed and the key card reader now had an impenetrable black box screwed over the top, with orders not to tamper. He guessed hoteliers didn't like great stripes of blue and white interfering with their decoration. It would make the other guests nervous, guessing at what ghastly scene hid behind. With a killer on the loose, Dinwiddy thought they had a right to be nervous.

Forensics had cleaned the blood from the door and buffed off the mark on the door across the hall: the door he now knew led to Donald Spink's room. The attack on the train. A smoker in the victim's room. The disappearing associate. He chewed over his progress and digested the facts.

Dinwiddy checked his watch: Spink was likely to be back soon. He'd best get to the foyer lickety-split to relieve the manager he'd left on watch.

The lift doors slid open and Dinwiddy stepped inside to join a handful of others: Japanese tourists, waving cameras and topped off with baseball caps. They swung their lenses around to capture the scene through the glass elevator as it swept down toward the foyer. There was a view to be had all right and amidst it, to Dinwiddy's joy, was Mr Jackson, his hand on the shoulder of a bowed-up Spink, who looked like he wanted to get on his way. Dinwiddy strained to look past his lift-mates as they sank down through the lobby floor.

"Goddamit!" He stabbed at the buttons and the lift slowed to a stop. The tourists shuffled out chattering, meandering off toward the shops and the station. Left alone, Dinwiddy made further stabbings at the button then took to clapping his palms together, fingers spread into a fan. "Come on. Come on." The doors sighed closed and the lift eased back up to the foyer.

Dinwiddy flung himself out of the doors and speed walked across to the manager and his charge.

"Donald Spink," he panted.

"That's right, Detective." Mr Jackson nodded.

Spink looked up at him with a raised sardonic eyebrow. "What is this?"

"Sir, I am investigating the disappearance of one Jeremy Brian Adler."

Spink snorted. "Adler? Christ, I should have known. Look, I'm tired; I've got my own problems. Can't this wait?" He tried to sidestep, but Dinwiddy was right there, blocking his path.

"I'm afraid not, sir. This is an urgent police matter."

Spink waved a contemptuous hand at him. "I've got better things to do…"

"Sir, are you aware that it is an offence to waste police time?" Dinwiddy noted that the suspect was not a co-operative man: just what you'd expect from a ruthless killer.

"Well I hardly…"

"I need to interview you under caution as part of my investigation, so I'd appreciate you accompanying me to the Detention Centre. You do not have to say anything…"

"What? Am I being arrested?" Spink scowled in hostile derision.

"… but it may harm your defence if you do not mention…"

"Now wait a minute!" Spink took a pigeon step backward and raised his hand. Dinwiddy took it and snapped on a cuff. A grin pulled hard at the blank expression he wore.

"Resisting arrest is a misdemeanour offence, sir. I would suggest that you come along now."

Spink's jaw flapped. "This is ridiculous!"

"You will be required to take a DNA test. It is a painless procedure."

"But what for?"

"Forensic evidence at the crime scene. I need to eliminate you from my enquiries." *The hell I do*, Dinwiddy thought: *prime suspect under arrest.*

"Crime scene?" The smug expression drained from Spink's face. Dinwiddy scooped him up at the elbow and strode for the door, propelling his prisoner on scuffling tiptoe.

"Slow down, can't you?" Spink whined. "Is it far to the squad car? At least can I have a smoke, officer?" He pulled a cigar from his breast pocket and waved it.

Dinwiddy allowed himself a smile. "Anything you do or say may be given in evidence."

Outside the doors, a resting pack of newshounds were roused from their easy chatter by the squawks of panic emanating from Spink. They tossed their half-eaten burgers aside and hauled cameras and a microphones to the fore.

"Detective Dinwiddy! Detective Dinwiddy! Channel Six News. Have you found your man? Is this Adler's killer?" The reporter from the previous day hopped from side to side in front of Dinwiddy and his charge.

"Now, now, gentlemen. Let's not jump the gun. Mr Spink here's just helping us with our enquiries."

"In cuffs, Detective Dinwiddy?"

"That's right."

SIXTY-EIGHT

Rachel let the sheaf of paper flop over on itself. She wasn't seeing the numbers anymore. Evidence of treachery that had made her blood boil the day before, had fallen out of focus. She only heard his voice:

"It wasn't meant to be like this," he'd said. "I, I did it out of love. Fucked up, confused love."

She'd rolled the words around and around. What had Adam meant? He'd sounded drunk, barely coherent even. It had sounded like a confession, but he'd never really gotten around to the point and hung up. Crying? It was weird. Beyond weird.

Was he in love with her? He hadn't said it, but she'd felt such passion in his words. Why call her, if it wasn't about her? *"A fresh start."* Hadn't he said that? *"I couldn't even stitch him up properly."* He'd definitely said something along those lines. Was he talking about Jerry? But Jerry was away. Did Adam think that there was something between them? Nothing made sense.

Rachel pushed the now dog-eared credit card statement away, across the table and put her palms to her cheeks. Adam was a nice guy. He'd really helped around the place. She'd started to trust him, cried on his shoulder. In that moment when she'd fallen off the edge, consumed by the agony of motherhood and the disappointment in her spouse, she'd leaned on Adam too hard. The memory was uncomfortable now and tinged with regret. She shouldn't have done it—it was a step too far. Jerry had been driving her crazy with his weak will and deceptions, but it wasn't right to fall into someone else's arms. She and Jerry—they had to sort it out themselves.

Bloody Isabell. She was at the root of it all. Sensibly, rationally, Jerry would have to be crazy to be carrying on with her. He'd told Rachel about the nightmare of living with the woman, about all the threats she'd made when he'd wanted to move out, how she'd screwed him to the floor over money. The trouble with Jerry was that he was just too much of a pushover. Presented with the possibility of an affair with Adam, the nice helpful man, who, let's be honest here, was not at all hard on the eyes, Rachel found that she wanted to believe that Jerry didn't mean to hurt her: that he couldn't help it. She wanted to believe that it was his generous nature that allowed people to walk all over him and take advantage. She was angry with Jerry, yes, but whose fault was it really?

"Right. That bloody does it," she said, and pushed herself up to her feet.

~

The Fiat lurched onto Isabell's driveway and stopped just after knocking over a terracotta pot of fading petunias. Rachel bowled over to the front door and hammered on its glossy surface until Isabell snatched it open.

"What is this? What are you doing?" She pulled the black curls from her face, eyes skimming over the Fiat and its path of destruction. "My pot!"

"Never mind your pot, you bloody scheming bitch! What about this?" Rachel waved the offending statement in Isabell's face, catching the end of her nose with its flapping corners. Isabell slapped it away and grabbed at a page. She stared down onto it with wild eyes. "Where did you get this?"

"I've worked you out!" Rachel shrieked. "Years it's been going on for, years! Pleading poverty and innocence and bloody loneliness. Always someone else's problem. Never you!"

Isabell stood blinking, staring back at her.

"It's taken a punch in the gut, but finally I can see it. You're blackmailing him, aren't you? Manipulating him then using it against him. Admit it, go on!"

Isabell stepped out onto the porch, pulling the door shut behind her. "Jerry, he is a man like any other. He cannot help himself. I'd be a fool…"

"A fool?" Rachel cut in, "A selfish bitch is what you are."

"I am a woman, I need…"

"You don't need jack shit! You don't need to spend twelve grand on manicures and blow-dries. Jerry has a family. A child." She waved frantically at the car, where Peanut lay asleep in her seat. "A wife, Isabell. He has a wife." Rachel locked eyes with her, breaking off only when the door opened behind them.

An overweight woman, unnaturally black hair set into short even curls, huffed and puffed out onto the porch. "Ibbie, why you shouting in the street? This is no way for a good Catholic girl to behave."

Rachel snorted out a laugh. "You what?"

"Who is this person?" She looked Rachel up and down with undisguised disdain.

"I'm Rachel," said Rachel, preparing herself for a skirmish.

"That's right," cut in Isabell, "and she is just leaving." She spun the other woman around and tried to force her back into the house, but the older woman had noticed the car and wasn't about to go. "Why is Jerry's car here?"

"Because it's my car," said Rachel, folding her arms across her chest. Isabell gripped the other woman tightly around the shoulders and propelled her back into the house. "Mama, she bought it, yes. There is problem, it no work properly."

"About time your husband got rid of that piece of junk."

"Si. Go inside, Mama. I'll be in in a minute."

"Well good luck," Isabell's mother huffed and lumbered away down the hallway.

"Your husband? Your husband, Jerry?" Rachel raised a scathing eyebrow at Isabell who hurried to close the door. "Shh, can't you!"

"NO!" screeched Rachel, "I bloody can't! Are you telling me Jerry's a bigamist now too?"

"No! No!" Isabell grabbed Rachel's forearms. "Shh, please! My Mama will hear you."

"Get off me, you mad cow!" Rachel shook her loose and backed away. Isabell grabbed her again, this time by one elbow and steered her back toward the car.

"Mama cannot know who you are," she hissed. "Be quiet or you will ruin me."

Rachel's jaw flapped at the impertinence of the woman. "What the hell is the matter with you? Can't you just move on and give us all a break? What are you hiding me for?"

Isabell huffed out an exasperated sigh and looked away to the floor. A muscle jarred in her cheek and Rachel paused to examine her expression: fat spidery eyelashes, clogged with mascara, encircled eyes that flicked back and forth to the tick of a thinking clock.

"Isabell? What's going on?" Rachel demanded.

"Nothing. Don't worry yourself about it, just go."

"No, no, no, you're up to something. I can see that scheming look in your eye. Tell me, *Ibbie.*"

"You're imagining things."

"Oh, am I? I think I'll just ask *Mama* then, shall I?" Rachel pushed away from Isabell and made a break for the door, but

Isabell was fast and got in front to block her path, grabbing her wrist to hold her firm.

"No, for God's sake, no."

Now Rachel had her on the hop. Isabell was looking worried. "Out with it," she demanded.

Isabell slumped and chewed at her lip. "Oh for God's sake, they have to believe it. They have to think that we're still married or it's all over."

"What?"

"They'll cut off my allowance. You can't tell them."

"I can do whatever I like and I most certainly don't have to do anything for you," Rachel growled, "Least of all pretend you're married to my husband." She snatched her arm away.

"Please, Rachel, Please. I'm begging you."

"Why should I?" Rachel scoffed and shook her head, marching back to the car and pulling open the driver's door.

"Without their money I can never pay it back," Isabell blurted out and that gave Rachel reason to pause. She looked back to Isabell and squinted her eyes. "Keep talking."

"Don't tell them and I'll pay it all back."

"How long you talking—I'm not interested in minimum payment crap."

"I don't know, two years, maybe three."

"Eighteen months, and I want proof you can cover it."

Isabell scrunched up her face with the pain of it.

"Or we can just have a nice cosy chat with *Mama* right now…"

"Alright, alright," Isabell spat, "You win."

Rachel couldn't quite believe it: Isabell had agreed. "Right, well great. Looks like the shoe's on the other foot then doesn't it, *Ibbie*?" Rachel sneered, climbing behind the wheel, "Who's getting blackmailed now?"

Isabell scowled, but the deal was made and Rachel pulled the door closed quick to shut her out.

Her heart was thumping nineteen to the dozen as she backed out of the driveway, crunching terracotta beneath the tyres, but, by God, it felt good.

SIXTY-NINE

Beneath the flapping bedclothes, static popped fine baby hair into a shock of mouse. Lit golden by the bedside lamp, it filled her vision. A few seconds quiet, a giggle and then all wiggling arms and legs and pointy elbows. Bright shafts of sunlit joy brought hope to Rachel's bedroom.

Pushed up on podgy elbows, her baby giggled at the soft flop of cotton. Warm and safe in a maternal embrace, the love flowed between them unhindered. Rachel sighed and marvelled at the change. Everything had become so much easier. With Jerry abroad and very definitely *not* going to help, there was no longer any point in clinging to the vain hope that he was about to swan in and rescue them. She had ceased to be drowning, waiting for salvation and learned how to swim.

The heath visitor had put in their two-penn'orth of course, saying that it didn't 'follow guidelines', but to hell with them. She'd realised that actually nobody knew the answer, that it was up to her and her instincts. It was worth a try, anything was worth a try. If the milk wouldn't stay in, maybe solids would. Three months of endless screaming was quite sufficient, thank you very much. Three months of sleep deprivation and exhausted delirium. Three months of madness.

Milk still posed a problem, of course, but nothing like before. Had her digestive system turned a corner of development? Was she reacting to her mother's newfound confidence? Rachel didn't know, but it seemed that all that extra substance in her diet meant she was getting all the nutrition that she needed during the day and was only waking once at night now, for the ten o'clock feed.

She smiled and coo'ed and played. They laughed together, mother and child. The fractious Peanut had become a chubby smiling Cupid. She had become Elaina.

SEVENTY

Rachel clicked the high chair tray in place, securing Elaina in a circus-quilted fortress. A willing prisoner, she whomped the spinning bunny suckered to her tray with an open palm. Apparently it was hilarious. As long as it floated Elaina's boat, that was the main thing. "Yeah, you get him!" Rachel smiled and considered breakfast.

Cut flowers, bought in a rare moment of indulgence, stood on the windowsill. Their pinks and purples glowed jewel-like in the sleepy stretch of morning sun that reached into the kitchen. Rachel basked in its welcome while toast browned. She surveyed the room and considered the day ahead. Ever present laundry skulked in the machine, waiting to be hung, but yesterday's was folded and put away. No backlog there to weigh her down. Another day, another fresh start. She knew that she could do this now. Perfection was neither possible nor required.

She pulled a jolly cow-faced bowl from the cupboard, spooned in some baby rice and mashed in a raspberry. Elaina drummed her tray in anticipation.

Kettle filled, Rachel bopped her head in time to the thumping plumbing of the kitchen tap. "If a job's worth doing," she muttered and scanned around for the iPad to tap 'Plumbers' into the search engine. A couple of local ones came up. "Never fear! Super Mummy is here!" she said as she pulled a silly face at Elaina, who chortled and gave the spinning bunny what for.

The home phone chirruped out a couple of rings and Rachel scooped it up. An unfamiliar Southern USA drawl crackled down the line. "Good morning, Ma'am. I'm sorry to trouble you so early. My name is Detective Dinwiddy. Is this a convenient time to talk?"

"Er, sure." Rachel leant back against the table, intrigued.

"Are you Mrs Rachel Adler, wife of Jeremy Brian Adler?"

"That's right."

"I'm sorry to tell you that I am investigating his disappearance under suspicious circumstances."

Rachel made a long blink and rested harder on the scrubbed pine. A cloud moved across the sun.

"Mrs Adler? Are you there?"

"Yes. Yes, what do you mean?"

"This Sunday past your husband's hotel room was discovered in a state of bloody disarray and I do not mean that in the cussing sense, Ma'am. He has not been seen or heard from since. It is my intention to track him down. Can you tell me anything about what your husband was doing in Las Vegas?"

"TEKCOM," Rachel blurted, struggling to focus "They went out for the exhibition, Jerry and his boss. Well not exactly his boss anymore, I suppose." Her thoughts wandered.

"What do you mean by that, Ma'am?"

"They were in competition, redundancies, the best man wins sort of thing."

A pregnant pause then, "Was there animosity between them, Mrs Adler?"

"God yes, the man's a pig. I mean… You don't think…?"

"Mr Spink is currently detained for questioning. Do you know of any appointments your husband might have had? Contacts? Places to visit?"

"No." Rachel hadn't bothered to quiz Jerry on what he'd be doing on his business trip. She'd been too busy hating him. That stuck in her throat. "I'm sorry, we didn't talk about it. You should call his work."

"I'll do that. I don't like to be indelicate, Ma'am, but was everything well within the home? I mean your marriage. Were you close?"

Rachel thought about all the times she'd pushed him away, exhausted and annoyed. "I guess we've been better," she managed in a small voice.

"I see. Can you think of any reason why your husband might disappear?"

Rachel thought about their cross words and her scathing comments on his ineptitude. "No."

"Anything else that might help with my investigation?"

"I can't think. I don't know." Rachel rubbed at her brow.

Dinwiddy gave her his number in case she thought of anything. She could call anytime, day or night. He said she shouldn't worry about the time difference and that he'd be in touch, she could count on it.

Rachel returned the handset to its cradle in a fug. Why the hell would Jerry go missing? Bloody disarray?

She sank into the seat beside Elaina's high chair, then immediately jumped up again to call his mobile. It was switched off or dead. Just when she was finding her feet: she wanted to tell him about it, to tell him that everything was going to be all right.

The shock was clearing to expose a hollow in her chest and she hugged at herself in cold comfort. Now Rachel didn't know if she could ever tell him, if she would ever speak to Jerry again.

SEVENTY-ONE

Isabell sat pouting at the TV, petulant arms crossed. She hated the bloody middle cushion. Her mother luxuriated in the corner to her right, flipping channels. Her father sat upright, reading a book to her left.

Flip, flip, flip.

"It does no matter how many times you flip, you will no find *Seven Vidas*. Stop already," Isabell snapped.

Flip. One of the international news channels came on.

The camera panned across Las Vegas by night. At first the usual neon lit parade that was The Strip, but then it cut to the Monte Carlo, black smoke belching from its windows, the strobing lights of the fire department flickering in the forcground.

"The Strip in Las Vegas," said an out of shot narrator, "known for its wild night life and excess, always has a very different feel to it in the cold light of day, but especially so today after the still unexplained and potentially deadly fire that tore through the Monte Carlo Hotel and Casino on Saturday night." A microphone-clutching reporter appeared on screen, the blackened Monte Carlo by day behind her. Blonde hair shone in a bouncy blow dry. Shocking pink tipped fingers curled around the mic shaft.

"We have an extraordinary eye witness and resident of the Monte Carlo on the night of the fire with us here." The camera pulled out to include a smart-suited middle-aged man. "This is Ed Baker. Ed, can you tell us what happened?"

Ed looked tired and serious. His brow was furrowed with concern. He took a deep breath, then began. "At first I didn't realise that anything was wrong. I got up to go to the bathroom in the night and when the light went on I realised my bedroom was hazy with smoke. There were no flames and no noise to speak of then. My colleague was in the room next door so I went round and banged on her door until she answered."

"Surely there were fire alarms?" interjected the reporter.

"Initially no, but as the smoke increased then they went off. By that time Oona and I had already knocked on half the doors on the floor."

"So you saved all those people from inhaling life-threatening smoke. Staying in the building to help others?"

Ed shrugged. "Anyone would have done the same."

"I'm not so sure about that, Ed, but it doesn't end there, does it? You've set up an emergency centre, haven't you?"

"It wasn't just me. My colleague Oona and I have organised the emergency centre and it's been paid for by the company we both work for, Mango Europe. It wouldn't be possible without them. Many people are being treated in hospital still and the large number of patients means that they have been disbursed through a lot of different medical centres around Las Vegas." Ed looked into the camera lens. "Worried relatives can call the helpline any time to find out about their loved ones. Calls are free and the operators will be able to give them basic information about their relative's status and whereabouts. There is also a drop in centre in the MGM Grand across The Strip."

"Thank you, Ed." The reporter shook her golden mane with enthusiasm and turned back to face the camera. "And here's that all important number…"

Isabell watched the screen impassively. "The MGM Grand, that's where Jerry's staying," she said, scooping an emery board from the coffee table to buff at a nail.

"A wonderful heart-warming twist to a horrific tale, where real people come to the rescue of their fellow man." The reporter was making a segue. "Now this isn't the only story breaking here in Vegas. Earlier today the Channel Six News Team was on the spot to catch another story. A British man is missing, presumed murdered. Here's the report."

The image cut to a sandy-uniformed police officer who cleared his throat and looked into the camera with the demeanour of a hopeful puppy. "My name is Detective Dinwiddy," he said in a southern drawl, "I am investigating the disappearance and suspected murder of one Jeremy Brian Adler, a British man."

Three pairs of eyes widened on the sofa and snapped to the screen.

"Do you have any suspects, Detective?" barked a voice out of shot.

"Well, I am still conducting my investigation," he nodded slowly over to someone beside the camera then back to the lens, "But there are certainly some individuals I would like to interview."

Dinwiddy held a photo up and the camera zoomed in. It was Jerry's passport photo.

"This is the victim, Jeremy Brian Adler, age forty-two. I want to find out about his movements on Friday and Saturday just gone. If anyone has any information I'd be grateful to receive it at the LVMPD. Thank you."

The image flicked into a news studio, where a smart-suited anchor man sat behind a desk. "Let's hope the American public gets behind Detective Dinwiddy," he said. "It's an ongoing investigation, so we'll be sure to bring you developments as they happen, here at Channel Six. This is the number you can call if you have any information…"

Isabell stared silently at the TV and Mama jumped to her feet. "Ibbie! Did you hear that? Ibbie! Oh my God! You husband, he is missing! He is murdered!"

Papa growled out a sigh from his corner "Only Jerry…"
"Arlo!" Mama scolded, "Ibbie! Ibbie? Are you OK?"

Isabell managed a long blink and replayed the information in her head. Jerry dead. Jerry murdered. Murdered? Isabell's head swam and she lowered herself back into the now friendly cushions of the sofa.

Domitila flapped around the room squawking unintelligibly and crossing herself.

If Jerry was dead then she didn't have to pretend anymore. If Jerry was dead then she could be the grieving widow in black and not the bitch in scarlet. If Jerry was dead then she didn't have to lift a finger to persuade anybody: it was done. Her family would flock to her side to look after her. If Jerry was dead then everything would work out just how she wanted. She was going to be sick. She pushed out of the sofa and rushed to the toilet.

When the spasms abated she sat down hard on the lid and snapped the lock over to keep Mama out. Isabell's manufactured world wobbled in and out of focus. Without Jerry to spar with the pretence, which had become her reality, would be impossible. She'd acted out their marriage, long after it was finished, for the benefit of her parents, to protect them from the shame, to protect herself from being cut off by her family, at least that's what she'd told herself.

The truth of it was simpler: who wanted to be alone? No family; no children; no husband; no friends. And the weather: always raining, so grey this place. She shuddered and scratched at the thin white scars scored into her thigh. No razor blade was needed to make the final cut. No more reason required to feel the pain. It was real and unmasked, demanding to be recognised: her marriage had failed and now Jerry was gone.

Emotion pulled at her face. The phone. She dove out of the cloakroom and made for the kitchen, Mama and Papa following in her wake. She swooped up the handset and stabbed out Jerry's number to find it switched off. Her mother's arm draped around her shoulders and the dread of abandonment became undeniable reality.

A genuine tear escaped down her cheek.

"Is OK, Ibbie." Her mother squeezed her to her chest and Isabell inhaled the smell of home that lingered on her mother's clothes. Together they rocked to and fro. Comfort and protection unwound taut muscles and softened Isabell's shoulders into a droop. She leant on her mother and her mother stood firm. "I'll look after you, Ibbie," she soothed, "No worry."

SEVENTY-TWO

Adam flinched away from the jabbing in his ribs. "Hey, wake up. Wake up. What you doing there? I thought you'd blown long ago, man. What you doing out here?"

Adam traced the dark outline of a woman through bleary eyes. Rita. Rita had found him.

"Has somebody been at you? Why ain't you gone home?" She twitched her hand under her nose and crouched down to look into his face.

"I live in England." Adam sighed, pushing himself upright and stretching out his back. He had to stop waking up in bad places.

"Alright, your hotel then, dumbass. You can't lie around out here." Rita threw her shoulder bag around to her back, grabbed Adam by the hands and pulled him up. "This place ain't safe for someone like you, don't you know that?"

Adam wobbled onto his feet, made a mental appraisal of his body, and found things had improved. He could straighten up easier than the last time he'd been conscious and the onset of darkness took the strain off his eyes.

He followed Rita out onto the street, rubbing at his hair and shuffled along behind her.

"Come on, we need to get out on a busier road or we'll never find a cab," she said and bounded on ahead.

She was right, of course, what was he still doing here? He needed to get back, get back and find Jerry. Get back and sort out this mess. Rita waved and shouted at passing cars in a manner that Adam thought was more likely to scare them away, but eventually one did draw up to the curb and Rita yanked open the door before it had even rolled to a stop and pushed Adam inside.

"So, which is it? Which hotel?" she asked, twitching at her nose again.

"I'm at the MGM," Adam said and the driver looked over his shoulder from the front. "You got money?" he asked and Adam felt around his body with genuine curiosity.

"I'm good for it," he said and produced a small leather wallet for Rita to see.

"Well if that ain't nothing short of a miracle," she cooed, "Can't believe you still got that. You must of scared Seb off with that stunt of yours." She shut the door and the cab pulled away, before Adam had the chance to raise his hand in farewell. Saved by the hooker who'd sold him drugs: Adam's world kept getting more bizarre.

Acceleration pushed him into the seat's shabby upholstery, low sweeps of the cab's suspension bouncing him along unfamiliar streets, until finally they turned out onto The Strip and Adam was able to get his bearings. The MGM was just up ahead: a great blue-green monolith that stuck out of the skyline and the sight of which filled Adam, suddenly, with trepidation. He cringed at the idea of going back through its doors. He wasn't ready, couldn't face it. The cab was stuffy and small. "Pull over here. This is fine," he blurted out and throwing too much money at the driver, he launched himself out of the car.

The pavement was busy with people out for another night on the town. Adam turned his back on the offending hotel and the memories it radiated, joined their flow and washed along with the strangers, all in a hurry to be someplace else.

It reminded him of carrying Jerry through the crowd that short time ago; how the masses' obsession with themselves had rendered him invisible. Adam remembered Jerry's dead weight and felt the lightness of his currently empty arms. Then he felt the painful emptiness inside his chest and remembered Rachel.

Adam had hoped that finding love would turn his life around. Adam had hoped that Rachel would be the one to lift him out of his dire slump and deposit him back in the world of decent people. But engineering a crossroads where she could turn to him had taken him further into the world he was trying to escape. Never mind getting away from the thugs and the murderers and the dealers, he'd actually immersed himself further. How had it come to this? Hotshot lawyer with the world at his feet to drug-addled maniac in the blink of an eye. He had to pull himself together.

Still living that déjà vu moment, he took the next side road and turned into a diner that smelt good from the street. He wasn't hungry for solitude anymore, but he was desperate for food.

The hostess looked him up and down with disgust, but seated him in a small booth near the rest room, where Adam gave himself a hasty going over.
The man in the mirror looked like hell. Sunken eyes, greasy hair and a scraggy beard, to say nothing of the rumpled shirt and body odour. The fabric of his jeans was thick and crusted at the knee and it was only in the toilet cubicle that Adam found rusty smears on his skin and realised that all this time he'd been wearing Jerry's blood. He'd scrubbed at his knees until they were red and raw, but he had no choice other than to keep wearing the trousers. At least his jeans were black and hid the stains.

When he returned to the booth, his cheeseburger, fries and coffee awaited and Adam fell onto them, virtually inhaling the calories. When had he last eaten? He had no idea. Time had turned into a mush of confusion where he'd lost himself and his deeds. He sat back in the booth, slurped coffee and ran an eye around the place, now feeling more able to take it in.

Behind the counter, a waitress heaped slices of pie into dishes and a TV, that hung high on the wall, relayed news. A sandy-uniformed police officer was addressing the camera, but the sound was down so Adam couldn't tell what he was saying. The next image on the screen, however, was far easier to fathom: Adam's own passport photo. Suit and tie, tidy hair and clean shaven. A long way from the dishevelled tramp he currently resembled. Pennies started to roll. Jerry's photo flashed up next on the screen, then a short jumpy video of someone being hustled out of a hotel and into a squad car. All the while a scrolling red tape of words spelt out the information that was all Adam really needed to know: Jeremy Brian Adler, British man, missing presumed murdered. Any information to LVMPD Detective Dinwiddy, hotline number…"

Adam's coffee cup fell to the floor and smashed.

SEVENTY-THREE

The cheap motel door had to be pulled hard to click the lock shut and Adam walked away from it not knowing when or if he'd ever be back. His surprise appearance on last night's evening news had left him in no doubt that sliding his MGM room key into its lock was tantamount to slapping on his own handcuffs. And he really didn't want that, not when Jerry was missing and he appeared to be in the frame for his murder. A cheap motel was a much better option. That, and a change of clothes. He'd have to be careful—the dollars left in his wallet wouldn't last long and using his cards would give too much away.

Adam walked the length of the first floor open balcony, running his palm along the metal handrail that flaked and caught on his skin. The police didn't know where Jerry was, but at least Adam had a head start on them there. Calls made last night from the payphone in the lobby had been fruitless: deflected by steely operators at the end of their patience. He knew from experience, persuasion would be much easier in person, so today he'd be making personal calls.

He dumped a knotted carrier bag of his clothing into a bin at the base of the stairs and moved out onto the street, smoothing down his new Kmart ensemble: beige supermarket slacks, blue button-down shirt and a cap. His clothes were stiff and itchy, but they were also anonymous and that seemed like the most important thing, now that he was famous. He'd even kept the beard.

Today Adam would search for Jerry himself. Find him and convince him not to have him arrested. He had to explain and clear his conscience, had to work it out for himself, for that matter. He just hoped that Jerry was still around to convince. What if he really had killed him? Adam would have made the final appalling leap and become one of the terrible monsters he so despised and the idea of that was too much to bear. He had to know if Jerry was alive. He had to find him to see for himself.

The truth was Jerry could really be anywhere. What if he'd come round in the hospital, discharged himself and wandered out into the night? He could be walking the streets, concussed and amnesic. He could be in this very neighbourhood or miles away.

There, a shaggy mop of mouse brown, bopping along in a group: red T-shirt, walking away, on the other side of the street. A bus pulled into a stop and obscured the view. Adam squeezed his eyes shut in silent prayer: *please let it be Jerry*.

He sped up his pace, jumping up, trying to see through the grimy windows. The bus doors eased open and group of tourists poured out, making an obstacle course of people for him to negotiate. The hubbub of conversation, the growl of the engine, they melted together into the skin of the bubble that cut him off and kept him whole: the cyclone reborn. A glimpse of red: nearly there. Adam stepped around a gaggle of suitcase-wheeling girls, into a clear expanse of pavement where he could pick up speed.

That was when the police officer stepped into his path. Sharp pressed uniform and shining badge, he wore an expression of determination and inside the bubble slow motion kicked in. Adam's arms wind-milled backward to slow him down and change his course. He shifted left and steered behind the bus shelter, chancing a sideways look. The police officer continued on his trajectory, toward a destination unknown. He hadn't noticed Adam or wasn't interested.

Adam's heart beat in his ears as he searched again for the red shirt. A gap in the crowd expanded and contracted. There. Adam was on its tail, closing in. The man that wore it turned to speak to his companion and revealed a profile that did not belong to Jerry.

Then, to his left, a man with brown hair waiting to cross the street; could it be Jerry? No, not him. Another man, the right build, in a baseball cap. He turned, no not him either. Suddenly Jerry was everywhere, but nowhere and Adam was breaking out in a sweat. "Get a hold of yourself, Fox. Don't panic," he said out loud, "Jerry's not here." He took a few deep breaths. "You can find him."

Up ahead a line of taxis waited for fares and as Adam stopped at its pick-up point a yellow cab pulled from the rank and rocked to a stop beside him. Adam squeaked to the centre of its vinyl back seat and acknowledged the smiling driver with a nod. He hugged at himself and wished for a jacket. The desert hadn't turned out to be the place he'd thought it would be, not on any level.

Up front, a middle-aged Mexican sat in a haven of pink velour and tiger print. It boosted him four inches and wrapped the driver's seat in an elasticated affirmation of who was king of this casa.

The dashboard was upholstered in gold damask with a swishing fringe of scarlet. Centre stage, beneath the rear view mirror, a crowd of seashell-encrusted picture frames displayed huddles of small happy children. Together they encircled a six-inch Virgin Mary who watched over them all from a glued-down wobbly plinth.

"Where to, Mr?" The driver's forelock flapped in the breeze from an absinthe green windscreen sucker fan.

Adam's eyelids flapped while he rummaged around his brains for words. At his feet a rhinestone-encrusted tissue box nestled between the two front seats. Its construction included a deep dish where a handful of brightly wrapped toffees awaited sweet-toothed customers. This late 80's Ford Taurus was one heavily accessorised vehicle and Adam became even more convinced his life had shifted into the Twilight Zone.

"Er. Erm. The hospital," he managed at last.

The driver looked up into the rear view and caught Adam's eye. "Which one, my friend?"

"Which one?" Adam hadn't really narrowed it down.

"Si. We have thirteen medical centres within ten miles of this place." The driver turned in his seat to look directly at Adam.

"Oh. I don't actually know." He offered the driver a weak smile. "My friend got taken away in an ambulance. Where would they take him for the best?"

The driver laughed at that. "The airport, my friend! Jeez! Don't you know what it's like around here? You no heard?" He rubbed at his belly like this was the best joke he'd heard all week.

Worrying.

"Take me to the most likely one," Adam said.

"Okey dokey." The driver flicked on the meter and pulled away.

Adam cracked his window and air rushed in, pushing his hair around. He was glad of it, felt like he needed the ventilation to free up the old grey matter, to get back to himself.

Daytime Las Vegas slid by in a bright dusty blur and he worried about Jerry. What would he say to him? How could he explain his insanity? What if he'd never woken up? How bad was that head injury? There'd been a lot of blood—had he made it? The local health care sure wasn't held in high regard by his driver.

After a time the edifice of Sunset Medical Centre filled his window and the cab drew to a halt.

"Do you think you could wait? I don't want to get stuck out here."

The driver pulled at his seat belt. "I don't know... How long you think you'll be?" The taxi permit dangled in its laminated pouch from the rear view mirror. His name was Alejandro Jose Antonio Florez Ortega.

"Mr Ortega, my friend got taken away in an ambulance and I don't know where he went. Can you help me? Can you drive me around today until I find him? I'm desperate to find him." Adam clasped his hands together. Mr Ortega was a religious man with a strong love of his family. A heartfelt plea might just swing it.

The driver squinted, sizing him up. "What are we talking?"

"A rate for the day. What do you think?"

"Five hundred."

No chance. "Two hundred."

The driver flopped his hand at him. "Come on. Three fifty and I'll throw in some toffees." He waggled a pink-wrapped sweet.

Adam looked at it, bemused; he couldn't believe he was negotiating to ride around in this sideshow. Things just couldn't get any stranger. He didn't have that kind of money on him either, but if they found Jerry then it wouldn't matter if he used his card.

"All right, Mr Ortega. Three fifty." He stuck out his hand for a shake. "I'll give you the first fifty when I come out. OK?"

He was squinting again. "OK." He reached out and grasped Adam's hand, "and the name's Toni," he said.

SEVENTY-FOUR

Freshly mopped linoleum stretched from the door to the sharp white reception desk. Disembodied bleach crawled into Adam's nostrils and down his throat. He swallowed it away with a grimace. Dotted about, a couple of dozen sullen people sat bowed over clipboards or slumped, staring into fluorescent space. For a public waiting area it was eerily quiet.

Over by the desk a man shuffled foot to foot whilst talking to an unseen clerk. Adam stood a few feet behind, waiting for him to finish.

Eventually he backed away and scuttled off through double doors that swung out of sight then swallowed him up. The clerk, and source of the frightened silence, came into view. She was dressed in a smart uniform of navy and wore a badge that told Adam her name was Stephanie Gray. Her face was taut and unwelcoming.

"I'm looking for my friend, his name is Jerry Adler. Can you tell me if he's here?" Adam blurted.

"Number?" She looked at him with cold blankness.

"Number?"

"You have to take a number and wait your turn." She pointed at the foot-high red three-digit number board behind her without turning.

"Where do I…?"

She waved impatient fingers toward a round ticket dispenser on the wall by the entrance—Adam had completely missed it when he'd come in. She hitched the corners of her mouth up to reveal teeth, but nothing else about her was smiling. "You're welcome," she hissed.

Adam took a ticket: 317. He looked back at the red numbers behind the desk: 289. He sighed onto the closest vacant seat and glowered at the numbers, willing them on. Progress was slow and dehydration sucked at Adam's fervour. Coffee. He needed coffee.

The machine, lurking in a shadowy corner, consumed his coins and spewed out a plastic beaker of frothy brown. Adam winced at the first sip: it was nasty but caffeine was caffeine. Toni appeared at Adam's elbow and he showed him the number ticket.

"Good job you no sick eh?" He sucked on his teeth and eyed Adam's coffee with disdain. "Don't drink that shit."

"Just killing time."

"Killing something," he mumbled and wandered off.

Time ticked, numbers clicked and eventually Adam's turn came. He approached the desk with trepidation. The woman behind kept her head down until he cleared his throat, when she tipped her disinterested face toward his.

Adam spread his ticket on the desk before her. She didn't look at it.

"So I'm looking for someone. Jerry Adler. Can you tell me if he's here?"

"Are you a relative?"

"No, I'm a close…"

"I'm sorry, sir, but I am not authorised to give out information on patients to anyone other than next of kin." She was reaching for the button to click the number on.

"You don't have to tell me anything," Adam jumped in, "I just need to know if he's OK, alive even."

"I'm sorry, sir." No expression flicker. She did not waver from unhelpful autopilot.

Adam scrabbled around his head and found a lost lawyer. "My client is here on business with next of kin in England. I am the closest thing to family available." She eyed him suspiciously and Adam pressed on, confidence growing in the ploy. "I'm already putting together litigation against those responsible for his hospitalisation. My client is an important man."

She didn't look convinced, but he could see his persistence was getting on her nerves. She took a moment then twitched her hands over the keyboard. "I've got no-one of that name." She gave him a sour grin.

Adam frowned. "There's a good chance he didn't have ID on him and may not have been able to identify himself."

"Well he won't be on the computer then, will he?"

Adam took a deep breath. "So how can I find him?"

She reached around to the side of her desk and pulled out a wad of paper that she laid in front of him. "Fill these out. In triplicate." That grin again. "The forms cannot be processed without a current photograph. Do you have a picture?" Adam scrolled through his phone. Yes. A supposed 'before' shot taken in the gym: Jerry with his arms curled up into a sarcastic muscleman pose. Adam showed it to her.

"This is the only picture you have of your *client?*"

Adam smiled sheepishly.

She continued unabashed, "You can email it to this address." She pointed to the top of the form.

Adam plucked a pen from the pot between them and settled onto a nearby chair, not wanting to abandon his position at the front of the queue.

The form was six pages long. Name, address, not sure about his date of birth—he knew the year. His relationship to the person? Attacker? Wife thief? Lowdown scum bag life wrecker? He'd said Jerry was his client so plumped for 'Friend and Colleague'. Family? Obviously he knew about Rachel and 'Peanut' (the clerk wouldn't like that) and he cast his mind back to school days, trying to picture his parents. Bossy woman, dark hair and his dad was always working late, a banker or something. Their names escaped him utterly.

Filling it out in triplicate had seemed like a daunting task, but Adam didn't actually know many of the answers. Medical history—who knew? Insurance details—he probably didn't have any, knowing Jerry. Adam resolved to cover everything and added a note to that effect.

He sent the photo from his phone and returned his clipboard to the desk, waiting for the clerk to finish her conversation with the man now there, struggling to extract blood from her stone.

She slid the clipboard down to her lower desk level with not even a passing glance. "We'll call you in a few days if we find something."

"A few days?" Adam was incredulous. "I'll wait."

The receptionist snorted.

Adam leaned in. "Stephanie, I need to find my friend." He cranked up the winning smile. "Can I call you Stephanie?"

"No."

"I'll wait."

"It will take some time. This is a big place with a lot of departments. It'll take a day just to get through the internal mail."

Adam chewed at his lip. There had to be a way to get this done faster. "Could you email it around? Just the basics to see if he might be here? Please, Ms Gray?"

She glared at him.

"Please?"

"Oh for Pete's sake. When I get through my admin I'll send something round, OK? There's no guarantee on how long it will take for the answers to come back though. We're busy, you know, saving lives. If I were you I'd check somewhere else while I was waiting. Why don't go over to High County and pester them?"

Adam trotted back to the cab to find Toni taking forty winks in a disabled bay and slid into the back without disturbing him. In his absence the cab had taken on some extra embellishment. An inch-wide golden medallion now hung from the rear view mirror. Adam leaned across to take a better look.

"St Anthony," said Toni, shuffling upright on the velour, "Patron Saint of lost things. We could use a little divine intervention, no?"

"Oh, you just happened to have…"

"You crazy? I'm a taxi driver, I get lost all the time."

Adam gave him a raised eyebrow.

"Not aaaaalll the time. Never with you, my friend." He winked at Adam and slapped him hard on the shoulder. "So what happened?"

"I have to wait to find out. Let's go to the next place while they're checking."

Toni turned back to the wheel and twisted the ignition. Nothing happened. "Uh-oh."

"What's wrong?"

"It won't start."

"What? What the hell? Can't you fix it?" Adam couldn't believe it.

"Oh sure. I just need a fifty." Toni flopped an open palm over his shoulder.

He wasn't going to get away with anything with this guy. Adam pulled a few notes from his shrinking wallet and passed them over. Toni made a big show of turning the key and this time the engine caught.

"Well, what do you know?"

SEVENTY-FIVE

Dinwiddy liked to keep his life in order and if an undertone of bleach said home, then Sunset Medical Centre took him right back to Alabama. The woman behind the desk, however, had none of Momma's warmth. Scowling into her monitor, she hit at the keys like she was hoping to hurt them, or perhaps give anyone watching an idea of what she might do that to them. She showed no signs of paying him any attention. It wouldn't have happened in Wetumpka: you'd never leave a person standing there longer than was polite.

"Pardon me, Ma'am. May I have a minute of your time?" Dinwiddy whispered, not wanting to disturb the hush.

She took her time turning, but the sight of a uniform livened her up. "Of course, officer." It looked like she was trying to smile, but that face wasn't co-operating.

"I'm investigating a disappearance, ruling out local hospitals. Can you check your records for this man?" He flopped open the wallet, extracted a paper and placed it before her.

She looked at it, then back to Dinwiddy. "Him again. Who is this guy?"

"Excuse me, Ma'am?"

"A lawyer was here earlier looking for him, said he was his client."

"Is that right? What did you tell him?"

"He filled out forms. I said I'd contact him if anything turned up."

"May I see those forms please?" Dinwiddy's heart rate quickened: there was another player in the game.

Though thick, the form she brought contained little new information, save for the contact details of the enquirer: Adam Fox, a London lawyer. Well now, that was a turn up. The disappearing acquaintance was turning out to be more. Why would Adler need a lawyer and why was he searching the hospitals too?

Dinwiddy chewed over the facts again and this Fox discovery had changed the flavour. He'd have information pertinent to his case, most likely be in on it. This Fox was quarry now.

Dinwiddy considered the contact number. If he was involved, a call from the cops might set him running.

"Ma'am, do you have any idea where I might find Mr Fox?"

"I don't suppose he'll be at his home address, no. He's searching hospitals just like you. I sent him over to High County."

"Thank you, Ma'am. Be sure to contact me if he returns or if you do find Mr Adler." Dinwiddy tucked his papers away in their pockets and zipped up the wallet. A new hunt was on.

SEVENTY-SIX

Adam strode up to the reception desk at High County with his chin held high and an expression of confident superiority on his face.

He'd diverted off to the bathroom on arrival to get into character. Dampened hair had been combed into a neat business-like style and a breath mint bobbed on his tongue. At least when he was standing at the desk the clerk wouldn't be able to see his ill-fitting trousers. It felt like the old days, like getting ready to put on a show in court.

They had a ticket number system here, just like Sunset but Adam purposefully ignored it: Joe Public stood in line; top flight lawyers that struck fear into the hearts of lowly receptionists marched straight up to the desk.

Without waiting for her to speak, he introduced himself and slid her a BSL business card. Of course, she couldn't know that he didn't work there anymore, but the mobile was the same and it gave him authenticity.

"Good morning, Madam. I am making investigations on behalf BSL Lawyers of London. My client—," he cast his eyes down to the notepad he'd borrowed from Toni as if he needed prompting"—Jeremy Brian Adler, also of London, was hospitalised this Saturday last and has since been lost in the administration system. It is of utmost importance that he is located immediately, if additional legal action against the health care providers of Southern Nevada is to be avoided. I trust you are in a position to assist me?" He gave her the Fox smile. The clerk stared at him wide-eyed, and said nothing.

He raised his eyebrow to her in prompt.

"What is it exactly that you are asking?" she said.

"Is he here? That is the question. Tap his name into your computer and find out, then I can be on my way." He mimed typing on the raised counter with his free hand.

She didn't look sure that she wanted to do that, but tapped at the keyboard just the same.

"No, sorry, no-one of that name." She looked a little relieved.

"It is possible that my client was unable to identify himself upon arrival. Check for John Does." Adam looked down at the pad, scribbling pretend notes. Had that been too rude? It was a fine line: if he asked too politely the answer would almost certainly be 'no'. To Adam's relief she turned and obediently typed. "We don't have any unidentified patients currently. I'm a little surprised actually, after Saturday's rush."

Saturday's rush? Adam gave her the eyebrow to continue, not wanting to reveal his lack of knowledge.

"After the fire at the Monte Carlo. All those extra admissions. The paperwork's been a nightmare. Still, looks as if we're all up to date." She smiled at Adam and it had a hint of the grin from the receptionist at Sunset. He was losing her and had to work fast.

"Sunset is still checking its records," he sighed at their ineptitude. "Which other facility would you suggest was accepting ambulances on Saturday?"

She thought for a moment. "You tried Canyon Springs? I know they topped out on Saturday and diverted crews to us."

"Did they indeed? How fortuitous for you to know that." Adam cast his eyes around the reception desk, pretending to be impressed and turning up his English accent to the max. "It seems to me that you are at the hub of things here. I bet there's not a thing in this hospital that you don't know about."

"Oh, well yes, I suppose." She was obviously flattered, but confused by his change in tone. Adam pounced on her bewilderment. "Still, everyone has their limits. I don't suppose you'd know anyone at Canyon Springs…"

"Actually I'm very pally with Sue, I mean Mrs Donnehugh over at Canyon Springs. She's in my book group." She looked pleased with herself.

"Are you?" Adam looked incredulous. "But I don't suppose she'd trust you with information about patients, wouldn't tell you if my client was there."

With a huff she snatched up the phone and stabbed a single button. "Speed dial," she said with a wobble of her head.

"Sue. Jules. How are you, hun? Good. Good. Me too. Say, could you check your patient roster for me? Uhuh. Jeremy Brian Adler. Uhuh. No. OK. Any John Does admitted Saturday? Age?" She raised her eyes to Adam who told her.

"Uhuh. Uhuh. Oh. Uhuh. Yes. Got a lawyer here looking for him. A Mr Adam Fox. Yes. I expect so. OK then. Bye bye."

She laid the handset in its cradle and regarded Adam with a smug smile. "They have three John Does over there in the right age range." Adam smiled with relief, momentarily dropping the front.

Jules grinned back. "They'll be expecting you."

SEVENTY-SEVEN

Adam slid to the centre of the back seat and slammed the door. There was a thin white candle burning on the dash next to the Virgin Mary and Toni had hung a rosary over the rear view mirror. He rubbed at the cross with his thumb.

"The Holy Father himself blessed this rosary," he said in hushed tones.

"Then the Holy Father is on the team—we've got a lead! Canyon Springs has three possibles. Let's get over there."

"Canyon Springs eh?" Toni started the engine and pulled away. "That place is not so good, my friend. Terrible things in the papers."

Adam's phone buzzed in his pocket and he snatched it up. It was Stephanie Gray from Sunset. "Turns out we do have a John Doe, well at least we did. He passed away this morning."

Adam gasped and fell back in his seat. "You think—"

"That it was your weight training 'client'?" The sarcasm dripped down the phone. "No, the guy was in his eighties. The police were here by the way, looking for your 'client' too. I gave them your details. I hope that's OK. Have a nice day now." She disconnected.

Bitch. The police now knew what he was doing. It was only a matter of time before they caught up with him and he couldn't have them interfering before he'd found Jerry. He'd have to be more careful. "He's not at Sunset," Adam told Toni.

"Let's hope he is no at Canyon Springs either," Toni muttered.

"What's that?"

"Canyon Springs. My friend, that place it has the kiss of death. *Mal de ojo.*" He shuddered.

"Toni, the candle…" The candle was listing, dripping wax onto the Madonna.

"My brother's sister-in-law went there for an in-growing toenail. In and out it should have been. They butchered her. Butchered her! Infection. Then MRSA. Three weeks she was there. Three weeks! In the end we bust her out, took her home, but that's the least of it. You no want to be there if you can help it."

"Toni, the candle..."

They pulled up at lights and Tony pushed the burning candle straight. "I hear it's dirty. Surgical equipment left out in the hall for God knows what to get coughed on it." He crossed himself. "And the staff, no-one want to work there so there is no enough staff. They are all too tired or too lazy. I pray to

God I never need to go there." He rubbed at his rosary crucifix and pulled away when the lights turned green.

The candle toppled from its precarious perch into Toni's lap. He slapped at it and hopped about. "Aw no! I burned a hole in my tiger skin."

Adam rubbed at his eyes: his best friend was missing, possibly murdered by him; the police were on his tail and he was trapped in a Laurel and Hardy sketch.

"Come on, Saint Anthony." Adam pressed his palms together and prayed.

SEVENTY-EIGHT

"Oh sure, he's been here. You working on the same case?"

"That's right, Ma'am."

This fellow was wising up. No form this time, just a card slid across the desk and a smooth tongue. The receptionist had patted at her hair when he'd asked about him; twiddled it around her little finger with a faraway look in her eyes. Fox had got what he need here with considerably less trouble. He was a fast learner.

Dinwiddy flicked at the card pinched in his fingertips. "Mind if I keep this?" He wondered if the firm was real and tapped the address into the browser on his phone. It turned out that BSL was a heavy duty practice, specialising in complex fraud, terrorism, drug trafficking and money laundering, to name an unsavoury few. And now he was ahead of him again, on his way to Canyon Springs.

"Could you call them for me, ask them to keep Mr Fox busy until I get there?"

"I'm not sure…"

"Nothing dangerous, perhaps just assist him in every possible lengthy way?"

The receptionist pulled her thin lips into a pout. "I'll see what I can do."

SEVENTY-NINE

He dropped the leather briefcase by the door. No secret files were held inside. There was no mission to complete. Otto Clack was someone else's problem now. Remi shed his heavy overcoat and hung it next to her pink parka. Side by side and worlds apart, he hadn't noticed the weight of it until it was gone.

He prowled down to the kitchen. A half-full tea cup stood on the scrubbed pine table. Life had continued on without him. He wrapped his palm around the cup—it was still warm.

A sound. Remi pricked up his ears and padded back out into the hallway. A chuckle came from the living room. Nudging open the door he found her, sitting cross-legged in a nest of cushions on the floor. Soft light painted the scene with warmth and the distinctive aroma of newly washed baby infused the air like fresh baked cakes. A game of 'Peepo' was at hand.

Unseen in the doorway, he watched them with a steady gaze. He knew that he could travel the world and chase down deals and villains, but this was all that mattered: the three of them, together. Love filled his chest, and pride, and fear.

Bilbo Bunny snuck another look over the knitted hill, provoking gurgles of enchanted laughter from their child. Rachel's face was animated with happiness: a forgotten emotion that transformed her. At once he recognised the girl he used to know and realised she'd been there all along.

His mobile buzzed inconveniently in his pocket and she noticed him at last. Smiling broadly, she made motions to shuffle Peanut away to go to him.

"Don't get up." Remi tossed the silenced phone to the sofa and bounded over. He stroked back her hair and planted a soft kiss on her forehead. It felt good to touch her. "How's my baby been?"

"Oh fine, fine. We're getting along. There was a bad nappy situation yesterday, but no sign today, so fingers crossed!"

"And the little one?"

Rachel laughed and batted at his leg, "She has a nice clean nappy too."

Remi dropped into the armchair and gave himself a mental check. He never would have imagined returning home from a mission to talk to his girl about nappies and actually being happy about it. Times sure had changed.

He had no training to fall back on, nor past missions in this particular war zone. This was a whole new adventure, a road untraveled and he was going to travel it with them. It didn't matter that he had no plan to follow, that his own father had opted out and stayed at work. That was not going to happen here.

"I'm sorry that I couldn't be here before, but I am now. I really am."

Rachel lifted her hand to his face. Her eyes searched his expression for the truth. He thought for a moment that she might slap him and looked down into her deep brown eyes for reassurance. Brown? Hang on a minute, weren't Rachel's eyes green?

Something pulled at his shirt sleeve. Soft, but insistent, Bilbo Bunny grasped at his arm with felt paws. "Jerry. Jerry. Jerry. Jerry." Wool whiskers flopped up and down.

He wanted to answer, but his mouth wouldn't work. The air was thick and heavy and pushing him down. The chair drooped then swallowed him up, sucking him into its upholstery, where the world was flat and hard. Jerry didn't like it.

He could feel her pressing against him, but couldn't see her, couldn't move. Jerry fought against the bonds that held him still and with a herculean effort, opened his eyes.

EIGHTY

"Thank you, Saint Anthony! Oh thank you!"

The ceiling was formed from yellowing tiles suspended in a metal grid and it wasn't familiar. His eyes slid down onto pale green walls and an institutional doorway, all lit in a harsh unnatural light that left Jerry feeling at a loss. The weight pressing down on his chest shifted and juddered in time to the sound of throaty sobs.

"Jerry? Jerry! Can you hear me?" Adam's face reared into view, tear-streaked and blotchy. "Oh God, I was starting to think I'd never find you." He dragged the back of his hand beneath a snotty nose.

Jerry squeezed his eyes together in a long blink. "Adam?" He'd been dreaming: really being Remi, and Remi had wanted surprising things. His body still felt drugged by sleep, sunken into a groove in the mattress, and he arched up the small of his back to release it from its sweaty clasp.

"How long have I been here?" Jerry's voice rasped painfully in his throat and he rocked his head to push away the sleepy haze.

"Ages! Days!" Adam sniffed.

"Days?" Jerry rubbed at his eyes. How was that possible? He couldn't remember.

"Four, I think." Adam looked shaky and pale.

"Didn't take you long to turn into a girl."

Adam let out a laugh that turned maniacal and then reduced to sobs. He wiped the tears away on Jerry's sheet.

A doctor came into focus on Jerry's left then, sporting the obligatory white coat and dark circles. The engaging smile he wore made a fast swap with furrowed sobriety. He shooed Adam upright then shone his pen light at Jerry, first one eye and then the other.

"Uhuh. Yes. That's good." He made notes. "It's quiet remarkable. Remarkable." He paused to take a long nasal breath then fixed his eyes on Jerry's.

"First of all, we are delighted to finally know who we have here, thanks to the snivelling wreck." He looked at Jerry over the top of his horn-rimmed glasses and wafted a hand at Adam, who now stood at the foot of the bed.

"You have been missed. Just as well your CT scans look normal."

He waggled his fingers in Jerry's direction, eyes popping. "You had us all going for a while there, but it turns out you're fine. All fine." He swept his eyes to the ceiling, mouthed something Jerry didn't quite catch and continued.

"You'll need to stay in for observation for another twenty-four hours or so, but after that you're good to go, you poor bastard." He clicked his pen with a flourish, slotted the clipboard over the end of the bed and stalked out of the room.

The nurse who'd stood behind him watched the doctor leave, but made no effort to do so herself. "You can watch TV or maybe read the papers. I think you'll find it educational." She reached up to the small screen set high on the olive green wall opposite Jerry's bed and flicked it on, passing Adam the remote. "I'll find you a paper." She smiled weirdly, then left too.

The TV babbled up on the wall: a news report of some kind. Adam turned the volume down.

"What the hell happened?" Jerry rasped, reaching for a water glass.

Adam gripped at the metal bed frame. "Ah, Jerry, God, I'm sorry. It wasn't meant to, at least I didn't mean to hurt you. Definitely not hospitalise you." Adam noisily blew his nose and came round to sit beside him in the visitor's chair.

"What?" Jerry's head was throbbing. He tentatively felt around the back to a large padded dressing. The prickle of new hair growth skirted the edges. He winced. "Oh man. What are you saying? You meant to hurt me?"

"No! Well not really. I was trying to make things better, be better. I thought I was doing the right thing." Adam's voice was quiet now, his eyes cast down to the floor. He wasn't making sense.

"But I'm over it," Adam went on close to a whisper, "I was wrong, confused. I got lost it in it. I'm sorry, Jerry. So sorry."

"What are you on about?" Jerry rubbed at his temples. "Can we talk about this later? My head hurts."

"I need you to forgive me, Jerry. Please? I can't live with this hanging over me." Adam looked directly at him, his face contorted with remorse. Jerry recoiled from the emotion. "Yes, yes, shut up already would you?"

Adam grabbed Jerry's bandaged hands, making him wince with pain. "Ow! Ow! What's this?" Jerry tried to draw them away "What happened to my hands? Do you know what happened to my hands?"

Adam gave a sheepish shrug. "I may have been there."

Jerry scowled and flopped his head back to the pillow.

Up on the wall the TV report changed and Jerry gawped at the picture. "Is that…?" Adam turned to see. "Spink." Adam blipped up the volume.

'… the latest development in the mystery case that's gripped the nation. The quirky Detective Dinwiddy announced the arrest of Donald Spink last night. There is significant evidence that Spink was involved in the disappearance and possible murder of British man, Jeremy Adler.'

Jerry screwed his eyes up into a long blink and popped them open again, but Spink's face remained on the screen. "You have got to be kidding me," he rasped.

'Early findings, leaked from the forensics report, have put Spink firmly at the crime scene, confirming incidences of both fingerprints and bodily fluids.'

Jerry and Adam looked at each other open-mouthed.

"Bodily fluids," said Adam and the pair of them drew their chins back into their necks and grimaced with synchronised revulsion.

"Ew! Spink! Please tell me you didn't?" Adam groaned.

"What? Oh please!" Jerry felt sick.

Adam punched at Jerry's shoulder. "Right, like I'd believe that!"

"Argh!" Jerry tensed his shoulders in a protective flinch. "My back. What's wrong with my back?"

"Oh yeah, your back. Sorry about that."

"What?"

A uniformed police officer, now on the screen, started talking to cut Jerry off.

"I can confirm that our forensic examination of the crime scene has provided DNA evidence of Donald Spink's participation in this crime," the officer identified as Dinwiddy told the camera, "However, this was not information intended for public consumption and, as our man hunt continues with a further suspect in our sights, I would like to ask the gentlemen of the press to refrain from publicising any more discoveries."

Jerry's jaw flapped and his wide eyes turned to Adam's. "What the fuck is going on?"

EIGHTY-ONE

"Here." The nurse from earlier dropped a newspaper onto Jerry's lap. "Check out page five, you're famous!"

"The TV," Jerry spluttered, "Dinwiddy."

"Yeah, he's a peach isn't he?" She rocked back on her heels, grinning.

"Wha… I mean who…er. How?" Jerry thrashed around his brain for an explanation and found none.

"Indeed," said Adam, biting his lip.

The nurse eyed Jerry down her nose. "I can understand why you're surprised to see Dinwiddy, but *you*?" She turned her attention to Adam, "Where have you been, under a rock?"

Adam slumped and puffed out a breath. "Mostly. I may have seen him at bit."

"A bit."

"U-huh." Adam was looking down at the floor and Jerry could see he was reluctant to say more.

The nurse leaned in conspiratorially. "Do you know what actually happened?"

"Mm, yeah." Adam was really examining that lino. "We kind of had a bit of a fight," he said with a shamefaced shrug. Jerry searched around in his memory, but there was nothing in that department either. His face must have shown the blank.

"You were drunk, very drunk," said Adam, seeing Jerry's befuddled expression. The nurse sighed, "Well, you'd better get your story straight because the police are on their way." She shrugged her shoulders at them and left.

Jerry's eyes switched back to Adam, who sucked in his lips and turned back to the TV. "Yeah, they're probably following me."

"Right."

Jerry closed his eyes and tried to construct the picture. "So, we had a fight, you knocked me unconscious—"

"Well, you kind of did that to yourself." Bizarrely, Adam looked sincere.

"What?"

"Just believe me."

Jerry sighed and flopped his arm to the stiff sheet. "So, we had a fight, I beat myself over the head until I was unconscious…"

Adam shrugged.

"Then what?"

"I put you in an ambulance and here you are."

"And you have been…?"

"Drunk. Mashed. Off my face."

Jerry paused for a moment to jiggle this information with his tired brain. It wouldn't slot together so he gave up. "OK.

So let's pretend that that's all perfectly reasonable for a minute. What the hell is going on with Spink?"

They shuddered together.

"I mean how the hell did Spink get his..." Jerry rolled his hand over and over, unable to say the word "into my room. I mean, ugh."

Adam didn't speak, but he looked like he was thinking.

"And what did we fight about anyway?"

Adam tapped at his bottom lip. "Um..."

EIGHTY-TWO

Dinwiddy ran for all he was worth up three flights of stairs, time too precious to wait for the elevator. The Fox was in a hole and Dinwiddy wasn't going to let it out. He pounded down the corridor, avoiding the joins in the tiles as he ran.

He swung the double doors to Neurology wide and crashed them back against the wall. The nurses broke their huddle and straightened up to see what all the noise was. He could see that they recognised him. They'd known that he was coming and saw the determination in his eyes.

"Where is he?" Dinwiddy rushed the whisper out too loud.

"Thirteen, they're in thirteen." The nurse pointed down the corridor. The door at the end was open wide, but showing only wall.

"Unlucky for him," Dinwiddy mumbled low and hurried on.

He didn't bother to call out, figuring his presence in the doorway was all the notice he wanted to give. He gripped the frame both sides and skidded to a stop. That got the occupants' attention all right. They stared at him, one by the bed and one in it.

Dinwiddy's chest heaved and he took a moment of their surprise to wrench oxygen from the air. He held up his hand to hold them firm and they waited: expectant and bemused.

"Mr Fox? Adam Fox?" he gasped eventually.

"That's right." The man sitting by the bed spoke up. He was sharp enough to be the lawyer that cut through red tape. Dinwiddy stepped into the room, swallowing hard. The man in the bed was bandaged, but familiar. Dinwiddy scanned his face and matched it to his case file.

"Well I'll be… Now isn't that… My goodness… Are you Jeremy Brian Adler, sir?" Dinwiddy was flabbergasted by the resemblance if it wasn't.

The fellow didn't speak, but the corner of his mouth hitched up a notch and his head went to nodding.

"Well don't that just knock it catawampus." Dinwiddy put his hands on his hips and absorbed the news. His man was alive after all. How about that? For all the assumption and deduction, the murder had never taken place. Adler lay there right as rain before his very eyes.

Dinwiddy strode over to the bed, taking in the flesh and bones of the pixels he'd come to know. He scooped up Adler's hand and shook it with delight.

"Detective Dinwiddy, LVMPD. I am mighty glad to make your acquaintance, sir. I had it for sure that you was dead, but here you are, as fine as frog hair."

Adler wore a pained expression until Dinwiddy noticed the dressings on his hands and let go.

"Well perhaps not quite, but alive! You sure have made a stir!" Dinwiddy wagged his finger at him. His new friend managed only a grimace.

"Now, just how did you get into this state? Is there a charge to answer?" He flitted his eyes back and forth between the two men. Adler looked at Fox and Fox looked dolefully back.

"No, no, I don't think so," Adler said at last.

"Well." Dinwiddy scratched at his chin. "I'd sure as hell like to know what this has been about."

"My head hurts," Adler mumbled, "Can we talk about it later?"

"He just woke up," Fox interjected, "He's been unconscious for days."

Of course he had. Now that made sense. "Huh. Well I suppose. And what about you, Mr Fox?" Dinwiddy turned to look him square in the eye. "Just where do you fit in?"

Fox shook his head. "It really is a very long story." He wrung his hands but his eyes were soft, sincere and contrite. The man had seen a battle and come out the other side. Dinwiddy felt that he could trust him.

"There's not much of a murder case when you can't rely on the victim to be dead. It looks as though I've got nothing much but time and a hungry curiosity."

"There's plenty to chew on," Fox said with a nod, "You can count on that."

EIGHTY-THREE

Adam walked side by side with the now famous detective through the ward. Dinwiddy hadn't seen fit to handcuff him, even though he was under arrest and Adam was glad to be able to stretch and move his arms around.

His ribs had felt increasingly bruised since finding Jerry's room and, now that he was up and walking, a curious sensation of pins and needles was crawling down his left arm. He twitched his shoulder up to deflect a stab of pain beneath his shoulder blade and the sudden movement caught Dinwiddy's eye.

"I'm afraid there's no avoiding the process, not when the wheels of our investigation are rolling along," he said, throwing a glance over his shoulder, "Now don't get yourself all into a sweat about it."

Adam flinched at the pressure in his chest and stopped to lean his right hand against the wall.

"I'm not," he said, feeling the bead roll down his cheek. "It's just my chest." He rubbed at its centre with a bunched fist. The pain that he'd felt in Seb's apartment building returned in a wave that cut Adam down to his knees.

Dinwiddy stood over him, clearly taken aback. "Now what's this? Nurse! Nurse! Some assistance please!" he called out and the nurses who'd been quietly watching their progress ran over to help them. The one who'd been so chatty earlier laid a gentle hand on Adam's shoulder. "I thought you looked pretty grey."

"It's been a tough couple of days," Adam puffed out.

"Pains in your chest?"

Adam nodded and winced as another bolt shot down his left side.

"Heart problems in the family?"

"I don't know, I don't think so."

The nurse cupped Adam's wrist to feel for his pulse.

"Well I think they are now. Looks like you're having a heart attack."

After the week he'd had, Adam wasn't in the least bit surprised.

EIGHTY-FOUR

Jerry squeezed past the heavy door to see his old friend propped up in bed, connected to machines by wires and tubes. Jerry's emotions tussled for supremacy: relief; anger; fear. He needed a friend in this alien environment. Waking up centre stage in a police enquiry was freaking him out. Everyone he'd encountered already knew who he was, while he felt like he'd been deposited in the future with no understanding of his past. Fragments of the evening with Adam had been coming to him in stages and now he could remember their fight, but not what they'd fought about. There was just too much hoo-ha to let it go unexplained.

He stood at the foot of Adam's bed and watched the green and red lines that traced his heartbeat and breathing. They seemed steady and regular to his untrained eye. Good enough to risk waking him up. Jerry reached forward and jiggled Adam's leg. Adam rolled his head to the centre and slowly opened his eyes.

"Jerry," he said in a soft voice, "How are you?" but Jerry hadn't come for an exchange of pleasantries.

"Why did you do it?"

Adam's forehead puckered into a frown.

"I've remembered more and more. We were having fun, I'm sure of that. And I was drunk, drunker than you. And you, you were well moody in the end, you pushed me around." Jerry leant on the bed frame, feeling his adrenalin rise.

"Ah, Jerry." Adam put one hand to his face.

"I don't understand what happened, Adam."

Adam rubbed his face, trailing wires flopping at the bed clothes. "It's my fault and I don't think that you'll understand anyway."

"Why don't you try me?"

Adam sighed and gestured to the chair beside his bed. "I'll tell you, but you're not going to like it. Promise me you'll hear me out?"

Jerry walked around to the moulded plastic chair and settled himself into it, careful not to disturb the dressings on his back. "I'm all ears."

Adam swallowed deeply. "God, I don't know where to begin. You know about the job. How I spent so long working my way up. I put so much time and effort into it, Jerry. Really thought it was the right thing to do. But I wasn't." Adam turned his eyes to the ceiling and shook his head. "I didn't even see it when Gracie left me. Couldn't see how it had taken over my life. I thought I was so fucking clever: finding all the loop holes, beating the system, freeing the scum." He huffed out a laugh through his nose and then winced in his chest, finally turning to face Jerry again.

"It took a psychopath like McGinty to make me see what I had become: one of them, Jerry. I was playing for the wrong side."

"I know this. You told me this already, Adam, but I don't see…"

"She was the antidote, the opposite of them all. So much like Gracie that I thought I was dreaming to start with. Of course it was too good to be true. She'd never come back, not now."

"Gracie? When did you see her?"

"I didn't, Jerry." Adam looked him straight in the eye, "It was Rachel."

"Rachel? What do you mean? My Rachel?"

"She was so full of love. Physically so much like Gracie, it woke me up, stirred up the old feelings."

Jerry clenched his jaw. He didn't like where this was going. "You and Rachel?"

"I wanted it, Jerry, believe me I did. Felt like she had all the answers, but nothing ever happened, I swear."

Jerry leaned forward in his seat. "You're supposed to be my fucking friend."

"I know, I know it's bad. But you're no bloody saint. All that pissing about with Isabell. She cried on my shoulder, Jerry. About you."

That stung in Jerry's throat, "I wasn't doing anything with Isabell."

"You were doing enough. And not enough for her."

Jerry scowled into his face. "Don't change the subject."

"I wanted you to break up. I thought that if I gave you enough rope you'd do it yourself. I didn't think you were bothered, Jerry. You haven't been acting like someone who's bothered. She wanted to be free from the pain, from the disappointment and I was going to set her free." Adam laughed again, like he couldn't believe what he was saying. "I thought that if I got you drunk enough you'd go off with another woman and that would be that."

"You're insane."

"I know."

They lapsed into silence and Adam was the first to speak.

"It didn't work, of course, and when I could see that I got angry, frustrated. I lashed out at you, Jerry and I'm sorry. So sorry. I've been a madman."

"You can say that again."

"Yes."

Jerry shook his head and got up from his seat. "I don't know what to say."

Adam sat up in the bed, straining on his wires. "After all that time, thinking I had it all, I hadn't. I'd missed the point completely, Jerry. Turns out that success doesn't mean a high flying career or money at all. I've been working at the wrong things all this time and you, you got it without even knowing. Bloody daft Jerry and his goofy ways got to the prize before me. A family and love. That's all there is. I suppose I saw that too and I was jealous."

"You, jealous of me? Really?" Team captain, legal eagle, good-looking, minted Adam: jealous of him. Adam nodded and added a shrug.

"God, you're so fucked."

"I know." Adam snorted out an involuntary laugh.

Jerry picked at the seam of his hospital dressing gown. He appreciated the honesty, at last. "So what's wrong with you, anyway?"

"Heart attack," Adam said, tipping his head in resignation.

Jerry sucked in air through his teeth.

"It could have been worse, apparently."

"So what state are you in?"

"They gave me an angiogram and an angioplasty. They put in a stent."

"So much for Buzz Lightyear. I thought that you were Captain Fitness."

"Yeah, that and Captain Stress. Bad diet, too much booze and a bender on coke tipped me over the edge."

"Sounds like you've been having fun without me."

"No. Not fun, no."

They looked at each other and Jerry saw his old school pal, struggling with life, and the seconds ticked by as he accepted his weaknesses. People weren't always what they seemed or even what they thought they were themselves. The man who had it all turned out to be desperate and lonely, and he, the wasting fuck-up, had secured the best prize of all. Jerry had more than he'd credited and that knowledge made him stronger, but he didn't have it in his heart to bear a grudge.

Jerry crossed his arms and leaned back a little in the chair. "Doctor said when you can get out of here?"

"They said I need to stick around for a couple of days, but after that I can go home, all being well. Said I should look after my heart and take things slow."

"I'd say that's good advice, wouldn't you? For every aspect of your life."

EIGHTY-FIVE

Adam strolled out of first class and paused at the thin blue curtain holding back economy riff raff. "So long, Dinky!" he called out and snickered. Jerry jabbed him in the ribs. "Cut it out."

"He can't hear me," Adam laughed, patting his friend on the shoulder.

"You saw his face in the departure lounge: he's ready to kill me!"

"What again?"

Jerry gave him an eye roll.

"It wasn't your fault. He brought it on himself. I mean, the man has no conscience."

Jerry was giving him that look.

"What?" Hot guilt burnt at the tips of Adam's ears. "I've said I'm sorry a thousand times. Besides, you've cleared him of all blame."

"And you."

"And I thank you. Seriously, Jerry, you don't know how much it means to me—"

"Don't start that again." They tramped amiably toward the baggage hall. "Do you think he's really got a deal at Mango Worldwide?"

"Maybe, but you've still got Mango Europe, haven't you?"

"Maybe. Worldwide are a bigger division of course." Jerry chewed on a fingernail.

"Firm it up with Ed and Oona as soon as you can. You did call them, didn't you, Jerry?"

Jerry made further nibblings.

"Jerry?"

"I've been busy with my coma, remember? I'll call them first thing."

A small group of girls in their twenties stood at the adjacent baggage claim. The five of them wore matching pink T-shirts, but their subdued demeanour was at odds with the day-glo jersey. Jerry's face contorted into revelation and he wagged an accusatory finger at Adam, "You invited a hen party to my bedroom!"

"No I didn't."

"Yes. Yes you did, I remember!"

"No, definitely didn't."

Adam was finally on solid ground there, but really didn't want to get into it. Jerry wasn't convinced.

The carousel shuddered into life, diverting Jerry on its rumbling empty circuit. He drifted toward it, joining the handful of other first class passengers who gathered closer, anticipating their luggage. Adam held back to watch his friend.

With his hands in his blue jean pockets, dark blue baseball cap on his head, Jerry stood straight and tall. He was focused, positive, rejuvenated somehow. It was as if four days in a coma had charged his batteries to their fullest, restored him. The hat hid the bandage and bald spot on the back of his head and dressings to the cuts on his hands were minimal now. Their fellow passengers had no idea who he was and he blended right in.

The first bag round was an oversized Louis Vuitton. Its owner, a smart woman in her fifties, moved forward to claim it, but Jerry swept in for her, lifting it onto her trolley. He didn't linger on her thanks and served no agenda. He was self-assured, commanding. The action was courteous, suave even. Adam couldn't have imagined Jerry moving with such feline grace before. He glanced up and caught Adam watching.

"What?"

"Nothing." Adam shook his head and turned away to smile.

They gathered their bags and headed for customs side by side.

"Anything to declare, Jerry?"

"Ha. Plenty, but nothing for the customs men."

Adam raised his eyebrows at him "Meaning…"

"Meaning I've seen the light, Adam. I've been a bloody idiot. Why did you have to point out the virtues of Rachel for me to get my priorities straight? Why didn't I realise what I was doing? I've let Princess Pain-in-the-Arse distract me and focused on all the wrong stuff."

"It's easy to do." Adam was still working on his own changes.

"I took the path of least resistance, you know?" he said, "I just went the way that was the least hassle. Not the right way. I thought I wanted adventures, but when it came to it, I just wanted to go home." Jerry steered them down the green channel with a shrug.

Solid grey doors opened out into the arrivals hall. People crowded behind a hip height belt, craning to spot their loved ones. Adam ignored the people and searched for his name on a placard instead. Halfway down he found it, clutched by a bald man in a tight black suit. Adam acknowledged him with a wave. "Jerry, do you want to grab a bite to eat somewhere or just head straight for home? Jerry?"

Adam turned to find that he wasn't sauntering along behind as expected, but twenty feet away, his bags abandoned on the floor. He had Rachel in his arms. Their solid embrace formed an immovable island around which the oncoming river of passengers flowed.

As Adam watched, Jerry lifted her face to his to wipe away a tear. He planted a kiss on her lips and Adam winced, but the constriction in his chest was bearable, easier than he'd thought this inevitable moment would be. He knew the connection he'd felt before was lost: she was Jerry's wife and Jerry was his best friend. He wanted them to be happy.

"Take your case, sir?" The driver had come to Adam's side. "Thanks." Adam gave him half a smile and sunk his hands deep into his pockets to push away the emptiness. He thought to call out goodbye, but worried that the words might stick in his throat, that his voice might crack. Probably best to leave them to it, it looked like Jerry was in safe hands. He'd take the limo home alone.

EIGHTY-SIX

Rachel eased Bob's Rover to the curb outside 37 Heath Terrace and said, "Do you want me to come around to help you out?" Jerry smiled back at her; relieved that she seemed to have missed him too. "I'm fine, really." He climbed out easily enough and clunked the passenger door shut. Bob's Rover was buffed to a showroom sheen and sparkled in the winter sun. Jerry wiped away his fingerprints. Good old Bob.

"Dad's got to get off pretty sharpish, there's a match." Rachel bustled around to the boot to extract Jerry's case. He swept around to meet her there and took the handle to carry it himself. He put his other arm around her waist and paused to look up at their home.

He eyed the front door's flaking paint and dishevelled gate, not with his usual tired disdain, but with the enthusiasm of opportunity. Bob, who'd seen them arrive, opened the front door as they approached and scraped back the gate. "I'll sort that out for you next weekend if you like," he said, kissing his daughter on the cheek.

"No need, Bob. I'll do it," Jerry chirped.

"Er, hello, Jerry. How are you feeling?" said Bob, surreptitiously examining the dressing on Jerry's head.

Jerry laughed. "Head's a bit sore, but I'm OK." He strode past the bewildered Bob and into his house. "Where's Peanut?" he called from the kitchen, then doubled back to follow Rachel into the lounge.

Rachel settled onto a floor cushion beside a cheery play mat where their smiling child held Bilbo Bunny by one ear and gummed upon the other.

"I think you mean Elaina," Rachel said with a hopeful smile, "It means torch or bright light. I think in the end, she showed me the way."

Jerry looked down on the happy scene with déjà vu. Dim memories buzzed in and out of focus.

"Do you like it?" Rachel asked, uncertain suddenly, hopeful.

Jerry stopped trying to remember the memory that eluded him. How could he fail to like it? This room was filled with love and happiness and potential. He crossed it in two eager strides, settling into the armchair at her side. It felt solid and dependable. Jerry wasn't quite sure why that would be in question.

"Hello, Elaina!" he tickled at her chin. She chuckled back. "How's my little girl? How is daddy's little star, Elaina?" He threw a sideways glance to Rachel, now beaming up at him.

He scooped their gurgling child up to his lap. Elaina discarded Bilbo in favour of Jerry's soft cotton T-shirt. Pudgy fingers grasped a handful and pulled it in toward her mouth, then took one of Jerry's fingers with her whole hand and squeezed it tight. Jerry's heart swelled with love. So much had changed. "Look at you! Look at her, Rach. I can't believe how different she is."

"I know. She's amazing." Rachel scooped up Bilbo and sat him next to Jerry on the chair.

He had nothing to add.

EIGHTY-SEVEN

Their bedroom was small compared to the Vegas suite. It had none of the sleek walnut furniture, no flat screen TV nor showy decor. Rachel had decorated in muted tones of grey and dirty pastel. The furniture had all been painted, knocked and painted again. Soft furnishings were all homemade, with love. Jerry didn't know if she'd adopted the shabby style out of choice or practicality, but it suited him perfectly, just like her.

He lay content on feather pillows, Rachel nestled in beside him. Her skin was smooth and warm beneath his fingertips. She traced an imaginary line down Jerry's arm, joining the dots of his moles together. At his hand she slipped her fingers between his and squeezed, careful not to disturb the dressings on his palm. Jerry kissed her softly on the forehead and she turned her face to his.

"I love you," she said. The words he'd waited to hear.

"I love you too." With a gentle sweep he pulled her across his body, aligning her mouth with his. He kissed her again, on the lips this time and she responded. Her caress made his head spin.

Grandma Ray's clock ticked out in the hall. Jerry followed its soothing rhythm until his body found its own. In unison they remembered what it was to be together and made silent vows to never let the distance grow between them again. The clock ticked on, though time ceased to matter. Ultimately it was Elaina that brought them back into the present.

"I'll go," said Jerry, stretching out from their contented knot.

"No, I'll go. You stay here. You're supposed to be recuperating." Rachel slid out of his arms and into her robe. Beyond his view he heard her greet their child. He imagined her scooping her out of the cot. A room away, Peanut's cry changed, subdued already. *Elaina*, he corrected himself. *Elaina, Elaina*; he liked it.

A half hour later he found his girls in the kitchen. Rachel clutching a tea cup in one hand and shovelling mashed banana with the other. "You're dressed," she said, surprised.

"Yeah, I ought to go into the office for a bit."

"Jerry. No. They can live without you." Her face was serious and scolding.

"I know. They could, but there are some things I have to do." Spink's snarl at the airport was not easily forgotten. He still had to try to beat him, as ominous as that was.

Rachel looked up at him, disappointment tugging at the corners of her mouth.

"You remember why I went to Vegas? The redundancies are still looming. I don't want to leave you and I definitely don't want to see Spink, but I have to do my best to beat him. I want this job. I want a better life for us. I can't let it slide now, can I?"

Rachel shrugged. "I guess not. I was just hoping to keep you to myself for a bit longer." She put down her cup and reached out to him. Jerry took her hand and kissed it. "My lady," he said in deep voice, "I must away. Elaina, look after Mummy until I return." He ruffled her downy hair.

As he sat outside in the Fiat, the enormity of the situation seeped back into him. Despite all the drama, Jerry hadn't actually accomplished an awful lot at TEKCOM. A tentative though positive link with Ed and Oona at Mango Europe was all he'd managed and he hadn't followed that up. He routed out Ed's business card and chewed on his lip.

He might not even remember him. What if they'd just had too much to drink and got carried away on the alcoholic wave? Without them he couldn't even make up the deficit between Spink's revenue and his, let alone top whatever else Spink had pulled off on their trip. He took a deep breath and dialled the number.

"Ed Baker."

"Ed, hi. It's Jerry, Jerry Adler." His voice wobbled.

"Jerry! Bloody hell—so you are alive then!"

"Ha! Yes!" So Ed knew.

"Are you OK? Oona and I couldn't believe it when we saw you'd gone missing. All that stuff with the kooky detective on TV. We came back a couple of days ago and you were still M.I.A. then. What happened?"

"The detective, yeah, he got a bit carried away!"

"I'll say. So…?"

Ed was pressing for information and Jerry squirmed in his seat, sweating.

"It was an accident. Too many drinks and I managed to bash my head in, slipping in the bathroom."

"Ow!"

"Yeah, pretty bad actually. I was unconscious in hospital for four days with no ID on me. They didn't know who I was."

"I guess they got overloaded with the Monte Carlo. So the other guy, from work…"

"Oh. No! God no! Brrrrr." Jerry shook a twitch out through his shoulders. "Didn't see him. He must have been in my room earlier, when I was out."

"That guy sounds like a nut."

"Yeah."

"Yeah."

Jerry took a deep breath and ploughed on. "So, it was great meeting you and Oona. I was wondering if you'd like to talk shop some time? It would be so good for me to work with Mango."

Silence hung and Jerry held his breath. "Ed?"

"Are you working Jerry?"

"Yes."

"Jerry, seriously? You've just come out of a coma and you're making business appointments?"

"Well... yes, it's important to me Ed."

"I can see that, Jerry! No-one could say you're not committed!" Ed laughed down the line. "Jerry, I'd love to meet up, but take your time, OK? Bring your legal guy Adam too. I think we could do something great together."

"That would be brilliant, Ed."

"Speak to Adam, work out a date then call my secretary and get her to slot you in."

"Thanks, Ed. I'm looking forward to it."

Jerry flopped back into his seat and gulped in a breath. Thank God: he still had a chance. There was a lot of work to do though and research came first. He needed to get the cogs turning at the office and then talk dates with Adam.

Unusually, the car started first time and Jerry nodded in appreciation, wound down the window and turned up the stereo. Even the fickle Fiat was getting onside. He roared to the corner and relished the rush of fresh air that sent goosebumps up his arms. Cool oxygen tingled in his lungs: it was good to be alive.

EIGHTY-EIGHT

Spink walked the chequerboard gauntlet of carpet that ran the length of the main office. Slowly, deliberately, he strolled through their watching eyes. Whispering heads separated as he approached, and drifted apart. They didn't want to give him a reason to turn on them, but they were too weak to control their curiosity. He kept his expression placid, measured. Inside the venom boiled.

At length he reached his office and toyed with leaving the door open: he didn't want them to relax enough to start talking about him again. It was better to keep them in his line of sight so he could pick up vibrations in his web; let them know that he was listening and ready to pounce. It was a shame that he had calls to make, private matters to attend to, creditors to appease. He clicked the door closed.

Phyllis hadn't been surprised to see Mango listed on his new business pending. "Oh, another one," she'd said before turning her head away. Spink was sure she was hiding something, that she was on team Adler. Spink picked at his teeth and hoiked out some gristle from last night's dinner.

The flowers in Adler's office hadn't gone unnoticed either. Bloody little brown-noser: just cheated death, but still at work. 'Aren't I the fucking hero,' Spink sneered to himself, turning his back on the door.

Anyone would think he'd saved the world, not fallen over pissed and cracked his head open, stupid twat. Just goes to show the idiocy of the populus at large. They'd be sorry that they'd picked the wrong side when Adler was history, especially the junior staff: the ones who thought that they were oh so cool. They'd soon forget what weekends were and where they lived. If they wanted to keep their miserable little jobs, that was.

Soon enough, he'd be the victor and without Adler putting her off, he'd have sweet Gemma and her pert little breasts in his office on a regular basis. Sure, she was frightened of him, but she wouldn't say no. She could feel his power, his strength of will. She'd do what he said. Who knew where it might lead? He rubbed his thighs and savoured the potential.

Jerry couldn't beat Mango Worldwide. He was thrashing about in Spink's web and making a mess, but ultimately he was finished. Let Jerry think that he'd won, that would make crushing him all the sweeter. It was a pity there was nothing more he could do until the contract was ready, but he didn't mind time to relax. He'd just lurk out of sight and wait for his moment.

EIGHTY-NINE

"Where the hell have you been?"

Jerry sighed and leaned back in his chair.

"You no call. You just leave me in the dark. Leave me explaining to my parents." Isabell's voice went up an octave and Jerry held the phone away from his ear. "…and I don't know. I don't know nothing. Ibbie! Where is you husband? Ibbie! Is you husband run away? Ibbie! Is you husband dead? Ibbie! Ibbie! I don't know! I don't know!"

Jerry had been expecting her call. Since his return from Las Vegas, Isabell's pretence was no longer on his agenda. It had only been a matter of time before she called him on it.

"There was an accident. I got lost in the hospital system, but I'm OK now, I'm back." He tried to keep his voice even, placid. He wasn't going to fight with her.

"You could have called. You could have told me. Mama and Papa. Jerry, I needed you." Her voice tailed off.

Jerry steeled his nerve. "I'm not going to be able to come over anymore, Isabell. My priorities are with Rach and Elaina now." He braced himself for the inevitable backlash. To his surprise Isabell sighed down the line.

"Oh, Jerry." She sniffed, her voice cracking. "I don't know how to be without you."

This wasn't standard Isabell fare. Jerry kicked off his shoes and stretched socked feet into the puddle of sun on his office floor.

She went on in a whisper, "I could always think of a reason. There was always a way." Then she lapsed into silence.

Jerry spoke softly. "It's been years, Isabell. It's time to move on."

She was so quiet that Jerry strained to hear. "Is just this place, so cold and rainy and dreary. I have no-one, Jerry. You had to still be part of my life because, well, I thought there was a way back, that nothing was forever. Now I see I have lost you. You had to die for me to see you were already gone."

"I'm not dead."

"I know," she snapped, the tenderness concluded, "Is finished, that's all. My parents are going home early. Would you take us to the airport? You know, to say goodbye?"

Jerry sighed. Was she still asking him to pretend? "Isabell, I don't think so." The line crackled, but no-one spoke. Eventually Jerry broke the silence.

"Why don't you take a break? A little holiday would do you good. Go home with your parents. See how it feels. You never know, Isabell, maybe it's home that you need."

"I don't know…"

"Just think about it. I could drop you all, if you want. I've got to go, OK, but think about it. I'll talk to you later."

Jerry hung up. He didn't feel the harassed panic that usually followed a conversation with Isabell. She'd revealed a chink of humanity that put her past behaviour into perspective. She needed support and love just like everyone else. She wasn't going to get it from him. Finally, she was going to stop fighting for it.

Jerry admired the jolly bunch of yellow gerbera that stood in a cellophane pod of water on his desk, and plucked the card from its centre. It said 'Welcome back from the dead. John Locksley and the team.'

Jerry smiled. He'd take them home for Rach.

NINETY

Jerry dragged the final case from the Fiat's boot and set Domitila's bulging beauty bag on top. He couldn't imagine what she did with all this stuff. If the results were anything to go by, she was eating it.

"Let's go," he said, not bothering to lock the car. Maybe someone would do him a favour and steal it. The four of them headed for Departures, Domitila's huge and ferociously wobbling bottom leading the way. Jerry brought up the rear with Arlo, trailing luggage and averting his eyes.

"How is head?" enquired Arlo.

"Oh, not so bad," he said with a shrug.

Arlo dawdled, falling farther and farther behind the women with every short step. He cleared his throat.

"You know, Isabell is not so clever as she thinks."

"Oh?"

"She try to change the channel, hide the paper, but I got eyes." He pointed to his right one just to emphasise the fact. "I am no stupid."

Jerry suspected that he knew where this was going.

"I know you got a wife and child and I know you wife is no Isabell." He sucked in his chin and looked at Jerry with accusing eyes."

"Ah."

"You got divorce."

"Yeah." Jerry felt bad for him, hoped he wasn't too hurt. "Has she told you?"

"No, but she will. Those two: whisper, whisper. I know when there is something up." Arlo nodded and drifted into his thoughts for a moment. "You were no good for her anyway. You give in too much." He waved his hand then made a fist. "She need the passion of a Spanish man to take control. She was always too strong for you. She was the boss." He wagged his finger with a growl.

"Like mother, like daughter," Jerry replied.

Arlo narrowed his eyes, but a smile crept through. Chuckling, he slapped Jerry on the shoulder, pushing him off course. "You no wrong there! You no wrong." Both their eyes drifted to the enormous bottom rippling ahead and they lapsed back into silence.

"You know," said Arlo after a time, "I think you are OK, Jerry. This business, this injury," he waved his hand at Jerry's head, "I think it might have knocked some sense to you at last." He smiled, "I can no imagine you hanging off the wall outside Isabell's bedroom window now."

NINETY-ONE

The line for the Iberia 7912 was some twenty people deep, but Isabell didn't mind the wait. She'd already waited two years to admit her life was changing, what difference would half an hour more make now?

Mama squeezed her hand and she gazed ahead into the pool of sunlight that bathed the waiting passengers a dozen steps ahead. She wanted to run into it, shove the strangers aside and jump deliriously in its rays. Suddenly the sun was a drug she'd been denied and craved. She shuffled from foot to foot and scratched at her arm until Mama laid a hand over hers. "Is OK, Ibbie."

Isabell blew out a long breath. Yes, Mama would help her. She'd kept her suitcase small and non-committal, but no doubt about it, it would be nice to see the rest of the family: Sancho and Manola, Roberto and Alba. It had been too long.

She'd look up the widow Maria too. Now that she understood what it was to lose your husband, perhaps she could be a friendly ear and contribute something positive for a change.

How would they react to her, the cousins and the people about town? Mama had promised to handle it. She'd said she'd handle Papa too. Isabell picked at her manicure. Would she be the wounded abandoned wife or the scarlet whore that Cousin Angelina had trail-blazed? Poor Angelina, she didn't seem so bad. Why should any woman have to stay in an unhappy relationship? To save face? To be the good, repressed wife? Isabell thought not. She'd look her up too, perhaps they could be friends.

The line shuffled up and Isabell moved forward, pushing her case. "You'll be OK," said Mama, throwing her arm around her daughter and squeezing tight.

Isabell stepped into the pool of sunshine. Even in the cold confines of a London airport it made a difference. It penetrated her hair, her scalp. It soothed the knots of tension in her neck and eased their grip under its warm fingers. In that moment she knew that it would be all right. She was going home.

NINETY-TWO

When Jerry returned to the car park the Fiat was still there, but Isabell had gone. His luck had taken a different and superior course.

Cheery faces of the gerbera bouquet pressed against the car's rear window so Jerry clambered first into the back seat to rescue them from the parcel shelf. It had been the last scrap of space left in the car after all the Spaniards and their luggage. Now there was plenty of room and air and freedom. He sat them in the security of the passenger foot well, where they could jiggle a happy dance to the motion of the car.

Winding his way back toward the motorway, Jerry felt the comforting click of a piece falling into place. It looked like Isabell might be taking a turn for the reasonable. Now would be a good time to hire a decent lawyer to comb through the divorce shambles and set it straight. He put it on his mental list of important ways to spend his earnings, once he'd bagged the job.

He didn't want to start a financial war, but the balance had to be evened out and a clean break made. There wasn't any equity to be had in their old house and the bricks and mortar themselves held no appeal. Isabell had nothing that he wanted.

The small and imperfectly formed Heath Terrace was home now and for all Jerry's enthusiasm, he hadn't fooled himself into thinking he was suddenly a DIY pro.

He'd pay more attention to Bob and learn what he could, but where inexperience truly barred the way, there had already been too much hanging about. He'd admit his shortcomings and pay someone to do it: another reason to land that job.

Jerry delved into the carrier bag on his lap and pulled from it a soft toy he'd bought in the airport terminal gift shop. He'd thought Elaina would appreciate its unrealistic velvet fur as much as he enjoyed its goofy expression. Nothing said 'I love you' quite like a furry pink armadillo.

Jerry sat it on the passenger seat. "I shall call you Ami, Ami Armadillo." He grinned at his invention. "My little star will be very pleased to meet you as, no doubt, will Bilbo." He switched to a more sincere expression then, "Everybody needs a friend."

NINETY-THREE

Checking the system before the meeting, Spink had been horrified to discover that Adler was ahead. That idiot landing Mango Europe and sprinting into the lead had been a shock to say the least. It would have been a devastating blow were it not for the final ace Spink had hidden up his sleeve.

No fool, he'd timed the meeting with Worldwide to fall on the final day of their match. Just as the bets were closing, Spink would lay down his unbeatable hand and it would be too late for Adler to make a comeback. The deal with Mango Worldwide would clinch the game and finish him off for good. Spink rubbed his palms together under the table. He couldn't wait to flaunt the signed contract under his nose and watch him crumple into pathetic insignificance.

Seeing off the snapping creditors would be a great relief too. Their never-ending badgering was starting to wear him down. With nothing to give, he had delayed his last. VanDerhorn insisted on payment today and the pawn shop had already released the Mouse's jewels into general sale. He had to be quick about getting them back if he stood any chance of her forgiving his too public indiscretions. If she left, she'd take the last of her loot and his life line with her.

But there was no need to worry. Of course, his final presentation had gone like a dream. The corporate buffoons were putty in his hand.

He settled back in the ergonomic chair, just finding the top of the caster frame with his toes. The Mango Worldwide delegation of three sat across the conference table, examining his handouts with great interest. In the regulated temperature of the Mango conference suite, he'd kept his cool and slam dunked the holistic cradle to grave offering. Yes, Spink fitted right in here. His graphs and graphics had looked fabulous up there on the integrated flat screen. In this place, he couldn't help but be brilliant.

Eric Drinkwater smiled encouragingly at him across the conference table. "Thank you Donald. That has given us an excellent overview of your approach." He turned to the totty on his right. Immaculate in a crisp white blouse and tailored navy suit, she was a big step up from Gemma. Spink licked his lips and wondered how often Eric got her into his office.

Eric spoke to her directly, "Deborah, did you bring the pack from Legal?"

"It's here Eric," she said, sliding a fat brown packet across the table, "It arrived just in time this afternoon, so I'm afraid I haven't had a chance to check it."

"Ok, thanks." Drinkwater smiled, "Let's have a look."

From his place across the expanse of shiny grey, Spink was surprised to see a newspaper slide out of the envelope along with the weighty contract and additional clipped on notes.

Drinkwater's expression turned to quizzical as he read the covering letter. "Oh Donald," he said, transferring his attention to the newspaper. Spink could see a section had been highlighted. "This is most unexpected." Eric passed the notes and newspaper back to Deborah. She read it through and passed them on to her colleague on the other side. The three of them exchanged bemused glances and the final executive slid the paper across the table, into Spink's eager grasp.

The Las Vegas Review had printed Spink's arrest photo in glorious colour which was just as well because Spink could feel his own draining away. 'SEX PEST OR MURDERER?' Demanded the headline and Spink skimmed over the text. Of course he already knew the story.

"Look, I can see that this looks bad…"

Drinkwater leaned back in his chair and folded his arms.

"… but it was all a mistake, a misunderstanding. The man wasn't dead, he bashed his own stupid head in!"

Deborah raised her eyebrows at him.

"I wasn't even there." Spink tugged at his collar button.

Eric looked down at the note in his hand. "Our Legal Department is very concerned about you being associated with us. They have examined the case in detail. It says here that the forensic report puts you at the crime scene, Donald." He paused to look up "Identified your semen on the bed. What happened Donald? Did you and this man have a relationship going?"

"With Adler? Christ no."

Deborah screwed up her eyes. "So what's your explanation then?"

"God, I'm not gay. I'm a married man for Chrissake!"

"Then what, Donald?" Eric frowned.

Spink shuffled in his seat. "Come on Eric, it was Las Vegas! The party town! Everyone cuts loose. Everyone likes a pretty girl!" He flicked his eyes to Deborah and back in the hope that Eric would understand the implied meaning. "She was willing, I didn't force her!" Spink flopped back into his seat, exasperated.

Eric was squinting at him. "You didn't force her," he echoed in a small voice.

"You know, she was…" Spink gave a little wide eyed head jiggle.

Deborah was scowling. "A prostitute, is that what you mean?"

Spink raised his hands in confirmation.

"Didn't you just say that you were married?"

Spink managed a small laugh, but could see that that had been a mistake. He swallowed hard.

She shook her head. "Mr Spink, Mango prides itself on impeccable ethics. To have a man of such public iniquity run our PR would be a disaster. Even if all the charges were unfounded, as you claim, the actions that you freely admit to are entirely at odds with this company's principles." Deborah folded her hands in her lap and leant back in the chair. "I'm sorry Mr Spink, but we can't possible let you influence this company's image."

Spink ignored her and stayed focused on Eric. "We have a preliminary contract Eric," he insisted with a forced smile, but Deborah was not easily put off.

"Letters of intent are not legally binding, Mr Spink, merely a courtesy. Now I think that…"

Spink slid off the chair and onto his feet. "Eric! Are you going to allow this *woman* to railroad you out of our agreement?"

Eric shook his head. "No."

Spink flopped down into his seat, treating Deborah to a smug snarl. She turned to look at Eric with a curious expression, but he didn't take his eyes from Spink.

"I am not a man who can be railroaded. Deborah is our VP of Communications and as such has unparalleled experience and knowledge of consumer focused public relations in our sector. Having said all that, I will not be railroaded by her because I completely agree."

"Eric…" Spink heard the whine in his own voice.

Drinkwater got to his feet and the others followed suit. "This meeting is over Donald. See yourself out. I don't want to call security."

Spink watched open mouthed as his deal stalked out of the room. He couldn't believe it. The blood rolled to a boil in his chest. Eric had abandoned him, allowed that woman to call the shots. Well if he ever needed anything from him, he could forget it. Spink scraped his papers together, shoved them into his tatty briefcase and stomped out into the long corridor.

It was a windowless stretch of corporate tunnel that would lead him from the inner sanctum and spit him out into public obscurity. He seethed with every step, hackles raised, snarling derision and loathing swirling in an internal monologue.

Screw Eric and the bimbo. He didn't need them. He could always get another contract. He was Donald Spink. It was just a matter of time. Time. Three in the afternoon. VanDerhorn would not accept another delay. His membership at The Cranley was as good as cancelled. It felt colder in the corridor. Perhaps the door was open in reception. There would be no promise of money for the pawn shop today either. The Mouse was sure to scuttle back to mother. There was nothing he could do. Not enough time to find another contract before the close of play. He couldn't make up the gap in revenue to catch Adler. That whore in Vegas had blown the deal. That stupid bitch had ruined his life.

Spink rounded the corner into the foyer. The moving shapes of irrelevant people shimmered in a red mist, their chatter drowned by the hiss of adrenalin in his ears. Not quite under Spink's control, his legs walked on. The walls were looming, closing, drooping down on top of him. Throat dry, he reached the revolving glass door. Cold sweat dribbled from his armpits to soak the tight waistband of his trousers. He gripped the rail of the door with a shaking hand and spun with it out into the sharp unwelcoming air.

The wind whipped at his jacket, flapping and pestering as he stumbled across the concrete concourse toward the outer perimeter wall. Beyond its bounds, he leant hard against it and closed his eyes. Blood sank from his face and the inevitable realisation dawned: Adler had won the game and he had lost it all.

NINETY-FOUR

Jerry took his seat, studiously avoiding eye contact with Spink. He'd spent the last month making calls, honing contracts and signing up all the business that he could and now the challenge was over. He and Spink could do no more and by the end of this meeting they'd both know their fate.

Spink twitched by his side, picking at the seam of his trousers and dabbing at his forehead with a flaking tissue. He squatted in a stink of old smoke and sweat that wafted at Jerry with Spink's every move. Jerry crossed his ankles and leant back in his chair to watch the door in an effort to get his nose out of range.

When Locksley finally strode in, he gave Jerry a wink before settling into his position behind the desk, all business.

"Gentlemen," he said by way of greeting, "It's been an interesting three months and today, finally, it all comes to an end." Jerry sat forward, palms flat to his thighs.

"I've been watching you both," Locksley continued, "Not just your turnover and contracts, but also your approach and activities. I've kept my eye on your diaries and your entries on the system; I've spoken to your colleagues and monitored your use of the company's resources. It's been very interesting, very interesting indeed."

Jerry slid a look to Spink, who'd gone rather pale.

"If anything, Jerry, the number of accounts in your portfolio has gone down rather than up. Curious, isn't it?" He flicked a questioning eyebrow to Spink, who tutted and shook his head.

"Nevertheless, you have managed to increase the turnover and potential quite dramatically."

Thank God, Jerry thought: it had been touch and go.

"Several of your accounts, Jerry, longstanding small spenders, have doubled their activity, some more. You invested the time and now you're reaping the rewards: picking up jobs that were slipping through the net before. It's an approach that the more junior account handlers would benefit from understanding." Locksley's eyes crinkled into a smile and Jerry felt himself blush.

"Your portfolio, Spink, has behaved in quite a different way. The number of accounts has increased massively, yet their individual turnover is down on last year's figures." He glowered at Spink who didn't move from his assumed pose of seriousness. "Of course, our accounts system records all the changes and shows me when details like 'Account Handler' are changed."

Jerry felt his eyes widening. He hadn't wanted to be a grass, but it looked like nothing got past Locksley: Spink was so busted.

A bead of sweat rolled down his cheek and he stuttered to life. "I-I was merely protecting the company's interests," he simpered. "I wanted to make sure our best customers were getting the care they deserved."

"I really don't think so," snapped Locksley, "You skimmed the cream from the team for yourself." He pulled a flat book from his drawer. "I took the liberty of picking up your diary this morning," he said, brandishing the book. "There are no follow up meetings with switched clients. You've taken the turnover and left them to rot. You'd have to be superhuman to look after so many." Locksley held Spink squirming in his steady gaze. "I'm very disappointed, Donald."

"Spink, how could you?" said Jerry, biting back a smirk. Spink's jaw flapped, but no words came out before Locksley was talking again.

"Your use of TEKCOM was rather unconventional, Jerry, but I'm glad we got you back alive." Jerry was relieved to see a warm smile spread across Locksley's face after the ice treatment he'd just given Spink.

"But it wasn't all wasted. Mango Europe, by God! Bloody well done! Imagine what you'll achieve next year, when you're conscious the whole time!" He laughed loudly and Jerry joined in. The silence from the other visitor's chair was exceeded only by the seething.

"The figures speak for themselves," said Locksley, handing out paperwork. "I'm sorry, Donald, but it's the end of the road for you. This challenge has revealed shocking business acumen and unscrupulous cheating. I'll need you to clear your desk by the end of the day." Locksley met Spink's gaze with unwavering authority, and the latter's face contorted into a mask of fury.

"You can't…"

"Gross misconduct, Spink. That will be all, now get out." He waved toward the door. Spink dropped his heels to the floor and shoved back his chair. "You'll regret this," he growled then turned to glare at Jerry. "You're nothing, Adler, a loser!" he spat.

"Not today," said Jerry, breaking into a grin and Spink stomped growling from the room.

When Jerry looked back to Locksley, he was up on his feet.

"Well done, Jerry. I always knew you had it in you." Locksley's eyes shone with sincerity and he reached out his hand for Jerry to shake. "I'm offering you a place on the board, Jerry: Sales Director. We'll double your basic and talk about commission, but I know you won't be disappointed. What do you say?"

Jerry bit at his lip. "Actually, can I think about it?" he said, not quite able to get up out of his chair.

"Think about it?" said Locksley, still smiling, but taken aback.

"I know it seems mad, after everything that's happened, but it occurs to me that there's more important things in life than money." Jerry shook his head and let out a small laugh. "I can't believe I just said that."

Locksley cocked his head to one side. "Near death experience put things in perspective, has it?"

"I suppose."

"Well, I can understand that." Locksley sighed and took a moment to look into Jerry's eyes, before he spoke again. "I understand the ideal, believe me, but you'll still need to work. Life can't just be full of love and roses. Balance, Jerry, that's the key."

"Balance, yes."

"You can't get workshy."

"No, no. I wouldn't, sir. I just don't want to sell my soul."

"I see." Locksley turned away to pace the length of the cupboards behind his desk, hands in pockets. Jerry's eyes skipped behind him from frame to frame—snapshots of the man's success. He stopped in front of the window and looked out at the sky. "We'll make sure you max at forty hours per week. How's that? Take things slow and let you settle in. Do you still like the industry? Does it get you fired up?" He turned to watch Jerry's expression.

Jerry thought about the last few months, charging about, briefing the team and encouraging the younger members. He'd enjoyed the creativity and had never felt more at home. "Actually, yes, I really do."

"Well there's your answer. Come on, Jerry. What do you think? Are you my man for the job?"

Jerry pictured Rachel's face, she'd be so happy if he could tell her he'd got it. He remembered the improvements he'd planned for their home and arrangements to be settled with Isabell. This was the step up he'd been working for and he knew he could handle it. His friend had taught him not to get lost in the system and he wouldn't make the same mistake.

Jerry stood straighter and said in that moment what he knew was right. "Yes, Mr Locksley, I'm your man."

~

After floating downstairs, Jerry wafted into the central office, to the heart of the team who buzzed with curiosity. Thumps and crashes permeated through the closed door of Spink's office, punctuated by occasional loud swearing.

Jerry drifted into the centre of the room, drawing the gaze of the team now holding their breath, all still held in the tyranny of Spink. Their eyes tracked his progress and he looked back to them, one at a time, holding their uncertain gazes briefly before moving on.

In each face he saw hope and potential. Now that the bully had been defeated, the aftermath was obvious. With Jerry as their leader, this team, his team, could achieve great things. His smile grew.

Gemma was the first to speak. "So what happened? Did you do it?"

Jerry stopped to look at her directly, a slow nod becoming more emphatic. "Yes. Yes, I did it!" One of the juniors whooped, then another and a couple of people broke out into spontaneous applause and the rest joined in. Then they closed in around him, shaking his hand and patting him on the back. "Well done!"; "Nice one, Jerry—or should I say Mr Adler?"; "Brilliant!" They beamed and he beamed back. "When do you start?"

"Tomorrow. I start tomorrow!" The grin was uncontrollable now and he started to laugh.

That was when Spink's door yanked open. "Gemma, get in here, I need you to carry this box," he barked. The laughter cut dead and all eyes turned to the young girl caught in Spink's snare. Blood rushed to her cheeks and she took a couple of steps forward, but then stopped. Jerry felt her conflict: she was just a kid, bullied by Spink, like they'd all been. She'd found it the hardest to fend him off. The eyes of the team were on her when she clenched her jaw and turned to face him. "I'm sorry, Mr Spink," she said, polite to the last, "but I'm helping our new Sales Director move desk."

NINETY-FIVE

The tan gusseted envelope was only just big enough to take Spink's cancelled contract, the newspaper and the notes. Eric squeezed it back in, stuck Legal's return label on the front and dropped it in his out tray. He was sending it back to its creator and the shredder.

At five o'clock sharp, Audrey swept past her boss's desk to collect his mail, dropping it at Reception with a cheery wave as she went home for the weekend. Separated from its Royal Mail counterparts, the tan internal mail envelope slipped into a rough grey sack, where it squatted until eight p.m.

The internal mail boys worked the night shift, but weekends made for half a day, or night. Outbound bundles were ready to go by eleven, when vans arrived to whisk them away, direct to the other UK locations or HQ and the international mailroom.

The packet nestled in silent companionship with the others in the back of the van, bumping along the winding roads and gliding north on the M1. The journey was short, not far out of town to wind and bump again before coming to a stop. It was an unceremonious hoist and fling that changed its mode of transport from van to trolley, but off it trundled, none-the-less, under roller shutter screens and on into a lock up cage to wait out the weekend.

The early morning Monday crew were cheerful in their work. They whistled ditties to themselves, emptying sacks and separating departments. Internal mail got their very first attention, before Pat brought his heavy sacks that had to be classified at speed to make the morning round.

The pack sat flat while latecomers piled on top.

Envelope after envelope flapped and creaked into one of a hundred pigeon holes. The mail room boys tossed expert shots at Accounts and Sales and high-fived for a top shelf obscure Quality Manager, whose pitch hit home first time.

When all was done, the fat packet was zipped securely into the bag for Legal and rolled in darkness to the lift and up.

Coffee in hand, Penelope fetched her department's morning mail bag from the seventh floor collection point and took it to her desk. She divided it between the people in the team and walked it round the final leg. She saved the patient tan gusset envelope until last. It was destined for the handsome new legal advisor that had joined the team last month in a hot flush of admiration.

She touched her hair and pressed her lips together to pink them up, before knocking on his door. "Your mail, sir." She couldn't help but blush. He lifted dark eyes from the document he was studying and extended his hand to take it from her.

"Oh hello, Penelope. Thank you," said Adam Fox. Sight of the envelope triggering a smile of recognition. He knew exactly what it was.

NINETY-SIX

Adam tapped out the now familiar number for Jerry's direct line and it barely managed half a ring. "Adam?" Jerry gasped down the line, "You are not going to believe what's happening over here!"

Adam thought that he just might. "What's that?"

"Spink's clearing his office. I'm Sales Director from tomorrow. Locksley had me in first thing for the good news!" He put on his voice "*Jerry, will you join me on my board.* Holy shit, Adam! I've done it!"

Adam blew out a laugh. "Jesus, is that what he sounds like?"

"God, I'm so relieved." Jerry sniffed.

"Don't start crying, you big girl."

"I'm not. Shut up, tosser. Beer after work?"

Jerry had done it: won his new business fair and square and landed the promotion. He sounded pretty pleased with himself and Adam was relieved to hear it, happy for him, proud even.

Lobbing a spanner into Spink's works had been a gift, to make up for his misdemeanours. Jerry didn't need to know.

Adam turned to gaze out of his new office window and admired the manicured gardens of Mango HQ: burgeoning sap-filled trees, ready to explode with the glory of spring and bulbs shooting enthusiastic spears up out of the ground. He savoured the morning sunshine that warmed his skin.

A movement in the corner of his eye drew Adam's attention to the doorway, where Oona now leaned inside the frame. She wore a deep green asymmetrical dress that was one of his favourites and a watchful expression that made him feel inadequate.

"OK, well gotta go. Dog and Duck at eight? Great," he mumbled. Not waiting for a reply, he threw the handset down into its cradle, rattling it from side to side, before finally using both hands to stop it still.

"Oona! Good to see you. How are you?" He scratched at a non-existent itch on the back of his head.

Oona folded her arms across her chest and raised an eyebrow. Black shining feathers of hair swished over her flawless complexion as she tilted her head. Green eyes considered him from six feet away and Adam's mouth dried.

She pouted a tiny smile before speaking: "If you've finished pretending to work, I'll take you for an early lunch. Team debrief starts at one."

"Lunch?" Adam croaked, checking his watch, "Lunch! What else would I be doing at eleven-thirty?"

"Well, if you don't want to come..." She turned to leave.

"Did I say that?" He jumped up from his desk, yanked his jacket from the chair and knocked a pile of papers to the floor.

He dropped to his knee and fumbled around on the floor, creasing and screwing up sheets. 'Get a grip Fox,' he told himself and cringed at the chuckle that came from the doorway. God, he was pathetic—he risked a quick look to see if she thought so too.

To his great relief, she was smiling, eyes crinkling with humour and kindness that allowed him to relax a little.

"Hot, isn't it?" he mumbled, tugging at his waistband.

Today's suit, a favourite in his days at BSL, was feeling uncomfortably snug and he felt self-conscious about the squeeze of flesh that had developed around his middle. Solomon's gym hadn't seen much of him lately. At Mango HQ he'd found like-minded people, a support system, in short: a much better environment. There was no angst to burn. Still, he really ought to keep in shape, just in case there might be another reason to look his best.

Perhaps he and Jerry could go to the gym together to spur each other on, Jerry motivating him for a change. Adam grinned at the memory of propelling Jerry's unwilling body around the equipment. If he wasn't careful, it would be him with the jelly arse and bingo wings. Perhaps he'd risk confessing his spare tyre at the Dog and Duck later, for a laugh. Now that would really kill Jerry.

ACKNOWLEDGEMENTS

My very first note of thanks goes to you, the reader. Thank you so much for spending your valuable time and money on my book. I can't quite believe that this figment of my imagination has finally become a reality. I sincerely hope that you have enjoyed it and if you can spare a few more seconds please, please do leave a review on Amazon. For a new author like me reviews make all the difference to whether another reader will take a chance on the unknown. Thank you so much.

This book's been a long time in the making and there are lots of people who've helped me along the way.

My thanks go to my friends and family who've read one or other of the many drafts and given me their priceless feedback. In particular I would like to mention Alexia Winslett for all the hours she spent shuffling mountains of loose paper and the resulting insightful comment. Also, Max Halliwell for his eager consumption of the story, instalment by instalment - your support and kindness helped me to keep going. Thanks also to Sophie White for endless hours spent discussing the ins and outs of the plot. Always a pleasure - the wine helped I'm sure. Cheers!

Much time was spent on research and in this area I would like to thank Amanda Neill for her paramedic prowess – thanks for the offer of a ride in an ambulance and my DI turned dog groomer, Richard Bell, for sharing his insider knowledge. Thanks for taking the time out to help.

On the professional front I'd like to thank Doug Johnstone for his thorough assessment of the penultimate draft. Your suggestions and observations were transformative. Thanks also to Julia Gibb for her copy editing skills and John Bowen, fellow TBCer and voluntary mentor, for all your support and cover advice and TBC itself for its support and endlessly amusing exploits in the booky world.

I have been banging on about this for years now so thanks to everyone in a ten mile radius for putting up with me and I'm sorry but, you're going to have to go through it all again for the next one. Unlucky. On that note, if you would like to find out about future books please do sign up on my website for news at www.sharnhutton.com.

Printed in Poland
by Amazon Fulfillment
Poland Sp. z o.o., Wrocław